Bonds of Affection

By Kathleen Willett

Chapter 1

"We're still not married," Reb said.

"I know," Mitch answered.

"Then, why don't I feel even one bit guilty about being on a honeymoon."

"Because you deserve it!"

And a nice honeymoon it had been so far, despite the unusual circumstances leading up to it. It was February 20, and warm poolside opportunities had been few and far between, even here in Las Vegas. Thanks to Lisa, Mitch had finally remembered where she should take Reb on their honeymoon. It was where they had fallen in love, Mitch and Reb, that is. And here they were, soaking up the sun next to an outdoor pool.

"I still feel guilty leaving the way we did."

"I thought you said you didn't feel guilty?"

"I lied."

Mitch thought all this over. There they were, standing in front of the minister, exchanging vows that were as meaningful to them as any other couple on their wedding day, and whoosh, Robbie had gone into labor. Before you could say, "I now pronounce you wife and wife," the entire wedding party was headed to the hospital. Things couldn't go on. After all, Robbie was Trish's better half and Trish was Mitch's best man. The wedding guests stayed on at the party. Mitch and Reb had kept vigil at the hospital, mostly because it wasn't just any birth. Trish and Robbie's baby had been diagnosed early on with TAR. Thrombosis Absent Radii. Not even the best of specialists could guarantee that the baby would survive the birth. They tried to not think beyond that. But survive the birth he did, much to the delight of cigar-toting Grandpa Max. Rose, the newest Grandma on the block, had been more subdued. She was the practical one. There was no word yet on whether or not the baby would have retardation due to bleeding in the brain. Those tests would begin soon enough. Mitch and Reb had watched as Robbie held her practically armless baby for the first time. Both were far too overwhelmed to even attempt to go back to their own wedding celebration. But Trish wouldn't hear of them postponing their honeymoon.

1

"You go," Trish had ordered bluntly. "We're going to need you more later than right now."

Mitch understood. So, she and Reb spent the night in a quiet airport hotel room and then flew to Vegas bright and early the next morning.

"We never did get any wedding cake," Mitch said lazily.

"The way you've been hitting the buffets lately, I'm surprised you care."

"I need my strength! You're wearing me out!"

"Liar."

Mitch laughed. What Reb said about the buffets was true. And she was feeling worn out. Just not from sex. Oh sure, there had been sexual activity. It was just that they weren't kids anymore. They had never been kids. At least, not while they were together. It had to be the sun.

"I'm not lying," Mitch took hold of Reb's hand and kissed her fingers, right out in public.

"Oh, now, stop it. You're going to create a scandal."

"I hope so!" Mitch was all smiles. "You want to go swimming?"

"I'll need help."

"We'll manage."

With the assistance of the hotel aquatic staff, Reb was raised from her wheelchair and placed in the swimming pool. The fellow who did most of the lifting looked like one of those handsome guys from a beach movie. His bathing trunks, what little there was of them, were snug. They only got snugger as he manipulated Reb to the side of the pool. Mitch took over from there.

"I think you have a secret admirer," Mitch noted.

"Please! He could be my son."

Mitch almost said "grandson" and then held her tongue. She had learned a thing or two in her younger years, one being that Reb was sensitive where age was concerned. After all, she was several years senior to Mitch. Reb noticed the silence.

"What's on your fertile mind?"

Mitch scrambled for an idea. "I was wondering which buffet to attack today."

"How about that seafood one downtown?" Reb suggested.

"Sounds great," Mitch nodded approval.

2

They swam until they tired of the activity and then went upstairs to rest. Mitch took time to call Trish to get the latest on motherhood.

"Hello!" Trish answered the phone like she had pounced on it.

"Hi, Trish. It's Mitch."

"Yeah, hi. What's up?"

Mitch noted that Trish sounded frazzled at best.

"Probably my cholesterol," Mitch joked.

"Why?" Trish asked like she was a dietitian.

"Reb blames it on all the buffets."

"Oh, yeah," Trish agreed absently.

"Do you need us to come back?" Mitch asked like it was the next logical thing to do. This even got the attention of Reb, who had been listening in to Mitch's half of the conversation.

"Do what?" both Trish and Reb asked in unison.

"Would it help if we came back?"

"Right now?" Reb asked as Trish said, "No."

"Are you sure?" Mitch asked, ignoring Reb.

"I'm sure. We're doing okay."

"How is Robbie doing?" Mitch wanted specifics.

There was a pause. A telling pause.

"She's pretty good."

"Not so good?" Mitch delved.

"She's really tired and then there's the natural postpartum depression."

"Is she very depressed?"

"It seems to come and go."

"And what about you?"

"I come and go, too," Trish managed a bit of humor. "I come and go to the doctor's office, to the pharmacy, to the store…"

"That's something we could be helping out with."

"You stay in Vegas. Don't you have another week or so?"

"Something like that."

"Enjoy yourselves. We're fine, really."

They chatted for only a moment longer before Trish had to tend to an errand. Mitch reluctantly said goodbye and then puttered around the room. Reb had already changed out of her bathing suit and appeared ready for more activity.

"Let's go shopping," she suggested.

3

Mitch caved. It would at least keep her mind occupied. Together, they went shopping at a couple of world-renowned malls. Reb was in a buying mood, even for running shoes. She had recently acquired a bigger bank account from the sale of the family estate, and seemed determined to spend it on a new wardrobe.

"Running for office again?" Mitch asked, just to be sure, as she studied the footwear.

That remark got a look. When Mitch and Reb had first met, Mitch was the newest millionaire on the block while Reb was the newly-elected Governor of Colorado. It seemed like years and yet just yesterday when Reb first threw a drink on Mitch. Oh, the good old days...

"Why would I ever do that?" Reb asked.

Mitch pondered. Reb had enjoyed a somewhat meteoric rise in her political career. She went from Governor to US Senator to ex-US Senator pretty quickly. It had been about all Mitch could manage to hang on for the ride.

"Running...shoes?" Mitch indicated pointedly.

"I'm going to need them for my therapy."

"Ah," Mitch nodded. Reb had been in a wheelchair for quite some time now. She was losing bone density every moment of every day. To counteract this, she had tried on and off to keep her legs strong in simulated walking therapy sessions. Mitch worried constantly about the possibility of broken bones, but she still encouraged Reb to take whatever steps necessary. Literally and figuratively.

"You need a new pair as well," Reb pointed to Mitch's decrepit cross trainers.

"But I just have them all broken in."

"Broken down is more like it. Pick out half a dozen pairs you like and start trying them on."

"Did you happen to change your name to Diamond Jim Brady when I wasn't looking?"

"Just start trying on shoes, will you? We have a lot more shopping to do!"

The scary part was, she sounded like she *really* meant it. So, Mitch did as she was told. She started picking out shoes and trying them on. Once she began, it was fun. She and Reb hadn't

4

done any serious shopping in a long time. After shoes came slacks and blouses and sweaters (it was, after all, winter back home) and of course, lingerie. Reb was a sound believer in dressing the part. She hadn't felt an orgasm since the accident. It didn't stop her from enjoying how she looked in black lace.

"What do you think of this?" Reb held up a little next-to-nothing nightgown.

"We'd better find a suitcase store. We're going to need more luggage."

After the orgy of shopping, they hauled everything back to the hotel. Mitch decided to have all this shipped to Mary and Lisa's new house. After a brief rest, Reb was ready to go out on the town...again. She had a roll of quarters burning a hole in her pocket. So far this trip, Reb had been lucky. She was ahead about a hundred dollars in blackjack, sixty-five in roulette and a thousand on the slots. Most of which had come from one jackpot. It would be a shame to keep her from the lure of the casino. Mitch followed Reb around the slot machine area, tossing in a quarter here and there.

"They pay better if you put in the maximum number of coins."

"I figured I'd leave that to you."

"Oh, come on. I dare you to go over to that progressive slot machine and put in the maximum number of coins."

"Those are dollar machines!"

"So what? Do that and then we'll go to the buffet."

That was good enough for Mitch. She took out several dollar bills and fed them into the progressive slot machine that Reb had pointed to. These machines were lit up and the jackpot was well into the millions. As Mitch understood things, this was a multi-casino deal, so that average folks just like her in casinos all around town were doing the exact same thing. Feeding the jackpot, like a lotto. Mitch checked with Reb to make sure she was doing this correctly. How hard could it be? Insert the right amount of money, make sure all the lines were lit up for the maximum payoff and push a button. And then, whammo, wheels started to spin and whirl and then snap to a sudden halt.

"There now, can we go to dinner?" Mitch asked over the noise. It was loud all of a sudden.

"I don't think so!" Reb said.

"Why not?" Mitch asked as she took a step back from the slot machine. Without a word, Reb pushed her back toward it.

"Stay right there!" Reb commanded.

"Why?"

"Because-"

Reb didn't have time to explain any further for two very official-looking people came at her from different directions. A large crowd had now gathered and Mitch felt almost claustrophobic.

"You've won the jackpot!" Reb's voice carried over the din.

Sure enough. Mitch checked out the display on the machine. All the necessary symbols had lined up like lucky planets. Which, actually, that's what they were. Little planets glowing on the machine.

"So, what did I win? A thousand like you did?" Mitch didn't want to show Reb up.

Reb just shook her head, like it was hopeless. By this time, two security guards had also appeared and flanked Mitch. Now, things seemed really suffocating.

"Congratulations," someone in a blue suit named Mr. Baxter boomed over the din.

"Thanks," Mitch nodded.

Coins had finally stopped clunking down from the machine and it sure didn't seem like anything worth making all this fuss about.

"Would you accompany me to the casino office to make arrangements?"

"Arrangements?" Mitch sounded puzzled. It sounded like they were preparing for a funeral.

"For the payoff."

Mitch glanced down at the tray full of fake silver dollars. Well, not fake, exactly. They were tokens used for the purpose of gambling. Mitch hadn't seen a real silver dollar in ages.

"Isn't this the payoff?"

"That's just partial. Please, follow me."

By now, a security guard had scooped up the coins, placed them neatly in a tray designed specifically for the purpose of holding tokens and handed it to Mitch. It was heavier than it looked. Mitch passed it immediately to Reb. She was the recipient of all the other money Mitch had ever won. Well, almost. They still had some of those millions Mitch had won in the lottery years ago.

A small parade formed with Mitch somewhere in the middle and they went purposefully to the elevators. Mr. Baxter inserted some sort of card into a slot and they were now able to gain access to floors otherwise off limits to the public. They marched, more or less, into a swanky office area and were seated on a sofa with a glass coffee table close by. Coffee, liquor and other drinks were offered. Mitch shook her head side to side more from practice than actual thirst factor. She didn't want to take a drink until she knew what was in the works. A certain Mr. Borcelli, the occupant of this stylish office, proceeded to explain the situation to Mitch.

"In cases like this, we are required by law to calculate, withhold, and remit directly to the IRS the correct portion of your winnings."

"And, what's that going to be?"

Mr. Borcelli smiled as if to say that not everyone got it the first time around either.

"The IRS requires us to arrange for part of your winnings to be paid directly to them."

Mitch wondered if he knew that he was repeating himself.

"Well, it won't be a very large check, will it," Mitch took the tray of coins from Reb and mentally figured the tally to be not more than fifty bucks.

"I'm sure it will indeed be a large-enough check for them. They will take a good portion of your twenty-three million dollar jackpot."

Mitch pursed her lips together for an instant as if to whistle and then thought better of it. No wonder a crowd had gathered.

"Then, of course, we'll arrange for payment of the remainder to you. We'll get the paperwork started. In the meantime, the hotel would like you to be our guests for dinner."

"Gee, that's very nice of you, but we had planned on going downtown to a seafood buffet."

"We can have one of our chefs prepare a unique seafood buffet just for you and your guest, of course."

He was awfully happy for a man whose place of employment was going to soon fork over millions of dollars.

"And you are invited to be our guests for a week in one of our deluxe suites."

"We're already staying somewhere else," Mitch explained. They probably already knew that. Someone in some booth somewhere was probably already going through surveillance tapes tracking their every previous move through the casino.

"We can arrange for your luggage to be brought here."

Of course they could. They wanted those millions where they could keep an eye on them. And if Mitch wanted to gamble all of it right back into the casino coffers, they would make it as easy as possible.

"That's really nice and all, but maybe we should just stay put. We have friends who have that phone number just in case."

Mr. Borcelli was polite enough to not push the subject further. "Of course. Well, let's begin the paperwork."

This didn't take very long at all. You would've thought the casino gave away millions every day. For Mitch's share, she asked for most of it to be wired directly to her bank account. She kept only a couple thousand in cash for immediate use. They managed to escape the office in time for dinner.

"We're on our honeymoon," was all the explanation necessary. On the way out, Mitch put five coins in a machine and walked away without pulling the handle. See, she wasn't addicted to gambling after all. They changed plans, just because they could, and had a quiet dinner in an out-of-the-way franchise restaurant. Meatloaf and ketchup hit the spot for Mitch while Reb feasted on a chef's salad. It was calm and relaxing, exactly what Mitch needed for reality to set in. All twenty-three million of it. Give or take the IRS share.

"I'm certainly a lucky woman," Mitch mused over pie and coffee.

"You seem to win big money," Reb agreed.

"Who said anything about money?" Mitch looked directly at Reb and smiled.

Reb smiled back. "You want to go back, don't you?"

"To our room?"

"No, back to Denver."

How did this woman read her mind?

"I am getting a little homesick," Mitch admitted.

"I know you just want to get back so you can spoil Joshua."

Joshua was the name that Robbie and Trish had selected for their baby boy. It was a fine name indeed for a baby who would have an uphill battle of it.

"Absolutely!"

"Don't go overboard!" Reb advised.

"I won't. I promise. Is it too early to buy a pony?"

"Yes!" Reb laughed.

"How about a bicycle?"

"How about you take me back to the hotel," Reb put a fine point on it.

"Your wish is my command."

Chapter 2

What else can I get you, Honey?" Trish stood at the edge of the
bed. Robbie was preparing to rest after nursing Josh. For a little
guy, he sure was hungry. After Trish had put him in his new
crib, she had fussed happily over Robbie.
"I'm fine. Just let me get some sleep."
"Okay," Trish leaned over for a kiss. It was perfunctory at best.
She left Robbie to rest as requested and wandered into the
kitchen. Max was making sandwiches. Rose was watching the
news. It was about five past noon.
"Do we have any milk?" Max asked, his voice muffled since his
head was clear in the refrigerator.
"We had some skim just yesterday," Rose answered.
"Skim, yuck!" Max answered back.
"It's good for your heart!" Rose came back just as quickly.
"What's this other stuff?" Max was still poking around the
fridge.
"Isn't that your friends?" Rose asked suddenly.
"Huh?" Max was really puzzled now.
"There, on TV. Isn't that the Senator? Trish, take a look."
Trish turned her attention to the TV set. Sure enough, it was a
fuzzy picture of Reb and Mitch, standing next to a slot machine.
The caption below read, "Winner of 23 Million."
"It's a terrible likeness," Max was watching now as well.
"Looks like a shot from a ceiling camera."
"It's amazing they ever catch any criminals at all," Rose tutted as
she drank her coffee.
"I wonder when that happened?" Trish mused, mostly to herself.
"You just talked to them, didn't you?" Rose was curious as well.
"Yesterday."
"A lot can happen in a day."
Like, running out of 2% milk.
"I'm going to the store!" Max announced. "Anybody need
anything?"
Rose peered over her glasses. "My list is too long to dictate. I'll
go with you."
Nobody said anything, but everybody knew the truth. Rose was
going to keep an eye on Mr. Calorie. Silver, who had been

sitting quietly on a kitchen stool on the other side of the counter, got up and slipped on her coat. Silver was the on again off again bodyguard of Rose and anybody else who went with her. Silver and Rose were a mismatched set at best. While Rose was Jewish, White and diminutive, Silver was big, Black and Baptist. Still, they got along famously. So famously in fact that long after any real danger had existed for Rose, Trish still kept Silver on the payroll. And a very generous payroll it was. Now that there was the baby to think about as well, Silver had stayed close by. At last count, she had several guns, which still made Rose nervous. But she also knew that Silver couldn't very well provide adequate security by merely poking people in the eye. So, before Trish could remind them to get more eggs, the happy trio was off. The house was suddenly quiet. Trish checked in on Robbie and Josh and then decided to do some overdue chores. One thing about having a new baby in the house, a feat only accomplished by making a whole lot of promises to the pediatrician to bring Josh in for frequent office visits, was that there was suddenly a lot of baby items around as well. Which meant that the grownup's stuff needed to be relocated. The fact that there were several storage rooms downstairs was the perfect answer. Trish headed down the stairway off the kitchen with her first box load of non-essential books. With an every-four-hour feeding schedule for Josh, nobody was needing reading materials to help them fall asleep. The only thing needed to fall asleep lately was closed eyelids. She went into one of the far rooms and set the box down in the corner of the room. As she wrestled the box into place, making it square with the walls, the door to the room swung shut. That didn't bother Trish so much except that when she tried to open it, it was stuck. Very stuck. Stuck as in it wouldn't budge an inch stuck. Rather than engage in fruitless foolishness like banging her fist sore on the door or yelling herself hoarse, she went over to the box of books and selected one that she hadn't read lately. Then, she settled down to read by the light that filtered into the room through the single tiny window that was too far up to do any good. Parts of this old house were built like a fort. Even if Trish broke the window, she wouldn't be able to crawl through. Someone would come looking for her sooner or later. Wouldn't they?

11

Chapter 3

We can stay," Mitch said quietly.
"Hmmm?" Reb asked sleepily. It was late morning. They had
slept in after their eventful day and night. Which was easy to do
in their luxury hotel room. It was dark and cool.
"I said we don't have to go home right away."
"We don't?" Reb was still trying to wake up.
"We have reservations for another week. Just because we won
some money doesn't mean we have to turn tail and run."
"I don't think I've ever seen you do that under any
circumstances."
And of those, they had had their share. Mitch and Reb had met
in the spotlight years ago and hadn't managed to quite elude it
for any length of time. In fact, they seemed to gravitate toward it
more often than not. At least they were back in Denver, except
for right now, of course.
"I mean, we still have a few things left on our tourist list."
"Uh huh," Reb agreed in that voice that wanted to know more.
"And I'm not worried that I'm going to foolishly gamble away
this sudden new fortune."
"Ah," Reb intoned with the wisdom of the ages resonating across
the six or so inches that separated them. "So that's why we've
eschewed the various perks offered by the casino?"
"I think you're perky enough already," Mitch couldn't help
herself. Her forte wasn't puns, but this one she couldn't resist.
"For that, dinner is on you!"
"Is it that time again?"
"Who the hell cares. I'm starved."
They decided to make it a light meal. One could, after all, only
take so many buffets. Over a dessert of sorbet, Reb stated the
glaring obvious. "We're packing the instant we get back to the
hotel room."
"You're okay with that?" Mitch didn't have to ask, but she did
anyway.
"Last one done packing is the rotten egg."
Who needed to be legally wed when you think this much alike?
The trip home was uneventful, a rarity in modern travel. As they
were unlocking the door to home, both could hear the phone

ringing and knew full well that neither could get to it in time. They resisted the urge to stampede through the doorway. If it was so darn important, whoever it was would call back. In the meantime, Mitch checked the backlog of messages. There were thirteen. She should've gotten her first clue then and there. The first, last, and every message in-between was from Henry. Aunt BeBe's henpecked husband. Calling from the hospital. Frantically. Mitch turned the issue over to Reb, who managed to hit pay dirt on the very first call. Henry was practically hysterical, quite a change from his quiet country gentleman façade. Reb did a lot of listening and nodding, which made Mitch's stomach twist into knots that a sailor would have a hard time undoing.

"Of course, I'll come right out," Reb was nodding.

Well, at least she was still packed.

"I know what you're going to say," were the first words out of Reb's mouth the second she hung up.

"Like that's anything new," Mitch replied.

"I can manage this trip on my own."

"I don't remember saying otherwise."

Reb tried to smile, but came up short.

"It's BeBe," she managed to say before silence got the better of her.

"I figured as much," Mitch nodded, not knowing whether BeBe was alive or dead or any of a hundred other possibilities.

"I'd better get ready to go."

Mitch ruled out dead as a possibility. They always went to funerals together.

"BeBe's sick," Reb filled in one blank at least.

"I can go with you."

"I think you should stay here. There's a lot to catch up on here, isn't there?"

If there wasn't, Mitch would come up with something. Aunt BeBe wasn't exactly Mitch's favorite relative and things were definitely vice versa.

"You're sure you're not too tired?"

"I'm not ninety!" Reb snapped.

"Well, not yet," Mitch answered back mindlessly.

"What's that supposed to mean?"

Now Mitch was stuck. She didn't know what that was supposed to mean either. The words, "I'm just trying to be agreeable," came to mind and mouth simultaneously. They seemed to appease Reb, which emboldened Mitch.

"What about BeBe?"

"Oh," Reb exclaimed, forgetting that Mitch wasn't psychic. "She's in the hospital."

"Uh huh," Mitch prodded for more.

"It sounds serious."

"I see."

"I'd better go get ready."

"Of course."

As Reb took an inordinate amount of time in the bathroom, Mitch made a pot of coffee, sipped down the first half cup, and opened Reb's suitcase for her inspection.

"Do you want to take some warmer clothes?" Mitch asked when Reb emerged.

"I guess I should."

Mitch helped as best she knew how and then carried the repacked suitcase out to the van while Reb wheeled behind. It wasn't until Reb was situated in the driver's side of the van that Mitch got a goodbye kiss. As Reb pulled away, Mitch felt a deep sense of aloneness. Not only was Reb physically gone, she was also emotionally absent as well. Not exactly the best ending to their honeymoon. At times like this, there was only one thing to do. She went in the house and called Trish. Best friends could always make things better. When she called, Rose answered the phone. Always an adventure.

"Is Trish there?" Mitch asked after hearing the latest update on Josh.

"Oh, yes, we finally got her out of the basement."

Mitch knew better than to ask. Trish would make it all clear as soon as she got on the line.

"You were on TV," was Trish's opening salvo.

"And you were stuck in the basement?"

No sooner had Mitch asked than some cacophony of confusion erupted on the other end of the line.

"Come for a visit. Please?" Trish said.

"Are you sure?"

"Positive. Gotta go."

The line went dead. Oh, the joys of motherhood. Mitch smiled now at the invitation. She was always welcome at Trish's. So would be a convention, as big and sprawling as her new home and property were. Between the two of them, Mitch and Trish that is, they had a vast amount of capital, what with pure luck and an art treasure thrown in for good measure. They could well be the richest two lesbians on the planet. Well, the richest two "out" lesbians, anyway. Mitch pulled her coat closer to her body. February was no time to be going across town much less trekking to Kansas. She prayed, a rarity for her, for good traveling weather for Reb. And, as long as she figured she had God's attention, for her own sojourn across town as well.

Trish and family lived at the old Livermore Estate. That's usually all you had to say to raise most folks eyebrows. Even denizens new to Denver had heard about the place. The fact that Trish had picked it up for a song was a mystery still unexplained. She and Robbie had spent only a fractional amount of time upgrading the place and it still felt a bit like a castle sans the tapestries. When the doorbell announced the arrival of guest, Trish bounded toward the front door like they hadn't had company since the Middle Ages.

"Where's Rebecca?" Trish said when she opened the door.

"Hello to you, too," Mitch answered.

"Sorry. I just thought that the both of you were coming."

"Starved for company?"

"Something like that."

"She's on her way to Kansas," Mitch finally answered the original question as they walked toward warmer parts of the house, namely, the kitchen.

"Kansas?"

"Something's wrong with Aunt BeBe."

"Something really wrong?"

"She's not dead, that's all I know."

From anyone else, this might've sounded harsh. But Mitch's attitude toward BeBe had softened of late. Maybe it was married life, such as it was.

"Why didn't you go, too?" Trish asked in that blunt way that friends could get away with.

"I was uninvited," was Mitch's blunt answer.

Trish couldn't think of a follow-up to this that would be an easy question to answer, so she asked something simpler instead. "Do you want to see the baby?"

"I want to see the baby and then the mommy and then I want to hear about your adventure in the basement."

"Who told?"

"Rose, the fountain of information."

"It was no big deal."

"Of course it wasn't," Mitch agreed, hoping that being agreeable would keep the conversation going. It didn't.

From the kitchen, they walked to the nursery, one of the areas of the house where they had done a hefty amount of remodeling. Of course the room was blue. A really expensive shade of blue that had been mixed to Robbie's specifications. Someone had gotten really ambitious and put a decorative border right next to the ceiling. When Joshua could focus, whenever that happened in the complex developmental process of growing up, he would see clowns tumbling in a never-ending pattern. Hopefully, he wouldn't develop vertigo as a result.

Right now, it didn't matter. He was asleep. And as much as Mitch wouldn't mind holding him, it was clear that Trish wasn't about to wake him up. That saying about letting sleeping dogs lie applied more so to infants.

"I thought that he would have to stay at the hospital longer?" Mitch asked.

"He got to come home early."

"That's amazing."

"Another unexplained miracle?"

"Don't start."

As luck would have it, Mommy was asleep as well and nobody had more need of sleep than her. But she was beautiful in repose.

16

So Mitch and Trish were left to their own devices.

"Tell me about the basement deal," Mitch prompted.

"You know all there is to know," Trish avoided answering.

"This is the second time this week, right?" Mitch's eyes crinkled up in that thoughtful look that was so sexy to Rebecca but had absolutely no effect on anybody else.

"Right. The first was Max and Rose," Trish recalled the incomplete wedding they had for Mitch and Reb. Max and Rose told the tale of the mysterious woman in white. Honestly, it sounded like one of the catering crew at the time, sending Max and Rose to the basement for some wine. They had become trapped in the room that wasn't locked and now the same thing had happened to Trish.

"Except, in your case, there was no mystery woman?" Mitch asked.

"I think the door just needs adjusting."

"Let's go take a look," Mitch was up for an adventure. Trish wasn't quite as enthusiastic, but went along as Mitch trundled down the stairs. Mitch remembered the way from the last time. She and Trish were the ones who had discovered Rose and Max, the memory was indelible. And fresh. Without a care or thought, Mitch sauntered into the room. Trish held back. The reluctance did not go unnoticed.

"What?" Mitch asked.

"I'll just stay here by the doorway."

"This really has you spooked, doesn't it?"

"You haven't been trapped in here," Trish was absolutely defensive.

"You're right. I'm sorry."

The silence between them was awkward. The secret was out. For this not being much of a big deal to Trish, it was a big deal. A real big deal.

"It's a small room," Mitch made small talk. Literally.

"It sure is."

"Have you had a handyman check the door?"

"Three."

"Three?"

"I've had three repairmen look things over."

17

"And?"

"Nothing. Nothing's wrong with the door or the frame or the floor or anything else."

"Three repairmen in a week? Gee whiz, I can't even get a plumber to show up at my place."

"That's because you live in a dump."

Mitch had to think this over. Trish was one-hundred percent correct, of course. With everything that had gone on in the past many months, upgrading the ranch house had tumbled to the bottom of the list. She had made some attempt when it was clear that Reb was going to require a wheelchair and then again when Mary and Lisa were still living with them but other renovations were woefully in need.

"That came out wrong," Trish started an apology.

Mitch held up her hand. "You don't need to apologize for speaking the truth."

"I do if it comes out sounding snobbish."

"Nothing you say ever comes out snobbish. One of these days, I'm going to begin remodeling the ranch house and I may never stop."

"If I were you, I'd tear it all down and start over. Or buy a new place altogether."

"But it has a lot of sentimental value. I mean, golly, Reb and I and the FBI were holed up there together. Who wants to part with memories like that?"

Even as Mitch spoke, the absurdity was beginning to sink in. For her, the place that held the most nostalgia was the Governor's Mansion. That was the first place where Mitch and Rebecca had made love. Well, at least half of that had happened. Mitch had made love to Reb and she had fallen sound asleep. It had been, at that point in time, the single most beautiful moment in Mitch's life. From then on, Mitch and Reb had been doing nothing but making beautiful moments. But owning the original site, the Governor's Mansion was forever out of reach. The next best place had been the ranch house, a structure about two steps below anything in the realm of Green Acres Hooterville. And then, of course, there was Kansas.

"Are you okay?" Trish asked through the reverie.

"Yeah. You know, I need to get back home. See what needs to be done…"

"Waiting for a call from Reb?"

"Something like that."

"What should I do about this room?"

"If I were you, I'd take the door off the hinges."

Trish shrugged her shoulders at the simplicity of the plan. It could work.

Mitch drove across town with purpose and pulled into her driveway. The place looked as deserted as when she had left. Of course, she hadn't expected anyone to be there, but the yawning emptiness engulfed her. She buried herself in work. Laundry from the honeymoon was waiting to be washed. Mitch started a load and then set about freshening up the old place. Trish was right. Mitch should just demolish this relic and start over. She had gotten pretty good at house design after her practice in Kansas. After clearing off the wobbly kitchen table, she spread out some paper and started fiddling around with designs. She drew for a while and then rested her head on folded arms on the table. Just like she used to do in school.

Through the haze of darkness and drool, the phone buzzed irritatingly. Mitch lifted her head up and blindly groped for the handset.

"Huh?" Mitch croaked into the mouthpiece.

"She wants you."

"Huh?" Mitch repeated dimwittedly.

"I said SHE wants YOU!"

For a split second, it sounded like a reverse triple X phone call. Then, it dawned on Mitch that it was Reb's voice. It sounded so strange. Mitch was beginning to remember why. Aunt BeBe. Kansas. Oh hell.

"Okay," Mitch said.

"When can you get here?"

It sounded more like an order than a loving request. Mitch, in these circumstances, tended to become passive resistive.

"I'm doing laundry."

"Forget about the laundry. How soon can you leave?"

19

"If I leave the laundry in the washing machine, it will mildew."

"Can you fly out?" Reb talked like she wasn't listening.

"I prayed all day and all night and God still hasn't given me wings."

This remark brought the entire conversation to a standstill, which was Mitch's intention. She waited patiently for further communiqués.

Finally, Reb said quietly and steadily, "Could you please come out here?"

"I'll leave in ten minutes."

"Thank you."

With that, the phone clicked in her ear. At least she got a "please."

Mitch stuffed the laundry into the dryer, went to the bathroom, and then left everything behind for Kansas.

There was no way on God's Green Earth that this trip could be any more boring. Whoever coined the term, "God's Green Earth" had never seen Kansas. Okay, so that wasn't quite fair. Mitch wasn't trying to be fair. She was trying to get to Reb's side as soon as was humanly possible. She had chastised herself a thousand times for being such an idiot on the phone. She would remember to apologize the minute she saw Reb. Rather than fly out, Mitch had opted to drive. It was just easier in the long run. There were no reservations to be made, no needing a lift out to the airport, no needing to be picked up from the airport, no need to rent another car. The list went on and on. As did this highway between Denver and Utopia. But at least there was a highway. Aunt BeBe had moved into Utopia proper when they left the family farm. And when they used the word "proper" in Kansas, they meant it. Never before had Mitch met quite so many religious church goers as when she and Reb had lived out here. It had all started with a death in the family, and the subsequent settling of the estate. Reb had inherited the family farm and Aunt BeBe had gotten almost nothing. The event shocked the town and shattered the family. Things had become even uglier than when Mitch had first met Aunt BeBe. Without even knowing who she was, she ran into her at the hospital way back when Reb had first had the accident which had left her paralyzed from the waist down. Well, Mitch ran into Aunt BeBe's fist, to put a fine point in it. It would take years of therapy to sort this out, which, by the tone of Reb's phone call, was a luxury that Aunt BeBe could no longer count on. Not that she would've ever opted for therapy. As far as Aunt BeBe was concerned, it was the rest of the world that had a problem, not her. Which was kind of how Mitch was as well. Maybe they could mine this vein of alikeness to form a more closer bond? Maybe not? Mitch took a wild guess and assumed that everyone would be at the local hospital's waiting room. Bingo.

Reb looked tired but beautiful. Mitch had looked up the word "beautiful" once way back when to see if she could find another word that would be more descriptive of Reb's beauty. There were lots of words to choose from. There was "attractive" and "becoming" and "glamorous" along with "sexy," "resplendent," and the ever-popular "nonpareil." But when she started to use these words, Reb accused her of swallowing a thesaurus. So, she more or less just stuck to "beautiful." Which she didn't even use out loud right now. Somehow, it didn't seem appropriate.

"Hello," Mitch said.
Reb started out of her reverie. "You got here."
"I made it."
"Did you fly?"
"I drove."
"You look tired."
"Just a little. So, what's new around here and how can I help?"
"BeBe is very ill."
"What's wrong?"
"She has liver cancer."
"Oh, dear. That's not good."
"No. It isn't."
Mitch waited to hear more. Reb would give her some logical rundown of events if she just waited long enough. She thought. After a moment or two, when it was obvious that Reb was going to remain silent, Mitch asked, "What does that entail?"
"It's just not good."

21

Mitch nodded. This must be having a huge effect on Reb. It wasn't like her to be this reticent, even where bad news was concerned.

"Will there be surgery?"

"She wants to see you."

"Yes, you said that on the phone."

"I'm sorry for being so-" Reb was stuck for the right word.

"No," Mitch interrupted solemnly. "I'm the one who should be apologizing. I was an idiot."

"You were half asleep. You're always an idiot when you're half asleep."

Reb meant this to be a comfort. Mitch took it as such and put her arm around Reb.

"I hate to ask, but why does she want to see me?"

"You haven't figured it out yet?" Reb was deadly serious.

Mitch thought it over for about a millisecond. "Oh, no! Not that?" she practically despaired right on the spot.

Months ago, the strangest thing had happened to Mitch. For reasons that were never explained or for that matter proven, she was thought to have healing powers. After several incidents and much scrutiny, the whole affair sort of went away after Mitch and Reb moved from Utopia, Kansas back to Denver, Colorado. Apparently, BeBe had remembered.

"Yes, that," Reb was deeply troubled as well.

"She thinks I'm capable of healing her?"

"It was the first thing out of her mouth. Not 'hello.' Not 'thanks for coming on such short notice.' Just 'where is *she*'?"

Mitch could tell that Reb was bent out of shape. Bent *way* out of shape. We were approaching a pretzel level of irritation.

"I'm sorry about that," Mitch didn't know what else to say to appease Reb.

"There's no use for you to apologize for what my sister does."

"Well, if I don't, who will?" Mitch asked rhetorically.

"You might just as well go in and get it over with. Then, you can go home."

If Mitch felt uninvited, she didn't let it show. Reb's main objectives were to appear strong and let Mitch off the hook. Neither of which was necessary, but Mitch didn't know the right combination of words to say to reassure Reb. So, she remained silent.

"Well, what are you waiting for?" Reb asked.

"I don't exactly know," Mitch heaved herself to her feet. It felt as though a thousand-pound weight had taken up residence on her shoulders. It wasn't easy being the charlatan of the family. She walked with steady pace down the hallway and entered Aunt BeBe's room. How could this have happened in one week? When Mitch and Reb were attempting to get married just days ago, Aunt BeBe and Uncle Henry had graced the event with their presence. The fact that the ceremony had been truncated afforded little time for socialization. Still, Aunt BeBe had looked okay. Now, she didn't.

"What are you lookin' at?" was Aunt BeBe's hello for the day. She might have been ill, but she was the same old BeBe.

"Hello, yourself," Mitch said quietly. She was still sorting out the amazing transformation in her mind.

"Don't just stand there! Come over here and do whatever it is that you do so we can all get out of here. The food's lousy!"

"What's wrong with the food?" Mitch chose to work backwards through the conversation.

"What isn't wrong with it!" BeBe bounced back with her retort. "They put the dinner rolls in the microwave and by the time you get them, you'd need an extra pair of teeth to chew through them."

"Is that so?" Mitch was finding herself enlightened by this bit of homespun wisdom. "I didn't even know you owned a microwave?"

"I don't!" BeBe was huffy. "I wouldn't have one of those contraptions through the front door! Two years ago, that fool Henry got me one for Christmas and I made him take it right back to the store. Right then and there!"

"But, the stores aren't open on Christmas Day, are they?" Mitch was now caught up in the story line.

"I made him leave it outside. It wasn't snowing or anything." Mitch didn't know what that had to do with anything, and was going to ask, but about that time, Reb wheeled in.

"How are things going?"

"Aunt BeBe is telling me about the weather two Christmas's ago."

Reb nodded her head like this was normal conversation between these two. Of course they were talking about Christmas weather. Why would they talk about anything else?

"Was that the year that Henry gave you the microwave?" Reb asked.

Okay, so Mitch was the only one who hadn't heard about the microwave incident? She didn't know whether to feel relieved or left out.

"Yes, the old fool."

"And you put it on the porch."

"It had to stay in the original box or we couldn't get our money back."

"And you were damn lucky that it didn't get ruined in the elements."

So, this was what people talked about when they didn't share common ground? Mitch mused to herself. Gifts rejected on days when it didn't snow.

"Let's get this over with!" BeBe broke through Mitch's thoughts.

"I hate to let you down, BeBe," Mitch felt the overwhelming responsibility to cushion the disappointment, "but there's never been any proof that I can heal people."

"I expect you to give your best efforts for family!" BeBe called it as she saw it.

Which shocked the hell out of Mitch, frankly. Never once had Aunt BeBe ever made an effort to make Mitch feel like a part of the family. If that was changing now, that was the real miracle to be documented.

"I'll do my best," Mitch went over to the bed and perched on the edge. It was the closest that Aunt BeBe had ever allowed Mitch to be and she braced herself like she was going on a roller coaster ride. You would have thought that she expected the bed to start spinning. Mitch placed a soft hand on BeBe's forehead, like she was checking for a fever. BeBe felt cool and dry. A good sign. Then, Mitch took hold of one of BeBe's hands in both of hers. Just because she could.

"Is that it?" BeBe sounded apprehensive. "I didn't feel a thing!"

Mitch hadn't felt anything either. Which didn't surprise her. She never felt anything before or during the alleged healings. Except when she had been coming down with the Chicken Pox. She had fainted dead away that night. And it was all caught on tape. How embarrassing was that.

"I think I've lost my touch," Mitch made one last attempt to convince BeBe of the painful truth.

"We'll know soon enough!" BeBe used her free hand to ring for the nurse.

"What are you doing, BeBe?" Reb asked.

"I'm going to get those doctors in here to run some tests. They love doing that. They charge double and do twice as many tests as they need. We should be happy they play so much golf or nobody would be able to afford to be sick."

At the winding up of this diatribe, the nurse came into the room. She looked like a true angel of mercy. Maybe they assigned only saints and runners-up to Aunt BeBe.

"What can I help you with?" she asked sincerely.

"I need one of those MREs."

It sounded like a military food ration to Mitch. If that's what they were using for food, no wonder Aunt BeBe wanted out.

"I'll page your doctor," the nurse bustled back out.

Then, it dawned on Mitch that they were talking about an MRI. Mitch really didn't understand any of this and kept her mouth shut. Reb took up the conversation from there.

"Are you sure you want another test so soon?"

"Either the healing happens immediately or it doesn't!"

She had that right, Mitch thought back. Apparently, Aunt BeBe had kept careful track of events. Who hadn't, in Kansas? They had been all over the news back then.

Aunt BeBe wrestled her hand out of Mitch's gentle grasp. It appeared that she had had enough of holding hands with a lesbian for one day. Or one lifetime?

"Do you need a rest?" Mitch asked.

"Wake me up when the doctor gets off the golf course."

With that, Mitch and Reb were dismissed. They wandered out to the waiting area and sat as close together as Reb's wheel chair allowed.

"You can go home now, like I promised," Reb stated flatly.

It was like everyone in the family had gone on emotional disconnect.

Mitch knew how to handle this. "I don't even get lunch?"

Reb rustled around in her small but stylish purse. "Here's five dollars. The cafeteria is on the ground floor."

"Join me."

"I ate a late breakfast."

"Join me anyway."

This got Reb's attention. It was mostly the tone of Mitch's voice that conveyed the importance of compliance.

"Why don't I join you?" Reb said calmly. She wasn't about to be bullied, but she couldn't say "no."

They took the elevator to the lowest level and found their way to the cafeteria. It was a relic of a place, which made Mitch feel comfortable. There was nothing like an old-fashioned hospital cafeteria to get the gastric juices flowing. They bought enough food for three people for fifteen bucks. Which aroused less Epicurean suspicion than getting enough food for fifteen people for three bucks. Mitch started with her pie and got the "nutrition police look" from Reb.

"Want some?" Mitch asked.

"I'll see how hungry I am after I finish my healthy salad," Reb explained it all with one sentence. Not bad for a politician.

"This is lemon meringue pie. It helps to fight scurvy."

"And when were you diagnosed with that?"

"Maybe tomorrow, if I'm not vigilant."

That's when it happened. Reb smiled. There obviously hadn't been much occasion for that lately. It made all those long, dreary highway miles worth it. Now Mitch knew she would stay on. It was going to be sorrowful times ahead. She was needed.

"So, where are we staying?" Mitch asked.

Reb paused before answering. Then, she said, "Why don't you find us a nice place."

It wasn't a question, even though it began with the word "Why."

"Do you want a house, an apartment, or a hotel with room service?"

"You decide."

Mitch nodded agreeably. It was plain that Reb's mind was still upstairs with her sister. And that was as it should be. Leave the mundane details to the mundane.

"I'll have something lined up by tonight."

"Okay."

Reb reached over and took the rest of the pie from Mitch and forked right in. Scurvy prevention was very important in the great scheme of things. This gave Mitch the opportunity to start up on her meatloaf. It was melt-in-your-mouth delectable. If Reb reached for this, there could be trouble.

"You can stop circling the wagons. I'm full," Reb remarked.

"Really?"

"Can I have a bite?"

"I thought you said you were full?"

"You have such an orgasmic look on your face that I thought a taste would be worth the risk."

Mitch didn't say anything but pushed the plate just a little in Reb's direction. She savored a tidbit.

"For meat, that's pretty good."

"Pretty good?"

"The pie was better."

Mitch could only agree.

"We'd better get back up there," Reb began to bus the table.

"We're waiting for a doctor, right?"

"Right."

"I wouldn't get in a rush. Doctors don't often show up or run tests just because patients request it."

"Still, she might need a pep talk."

If she didn't, Florence Nightingale would, Mitch thought to herself.

"You coming?"

"I'll be right behind you."

They paraded back upstairs and after peeking in to see that BeBe was still asleep, settled into a quieter, better-appointed waiting room. Technically, it was the "bereavement room." Translated meant that this was the place where families go to pray, talk to clergy and call the mortuary. They were allowed in here because Aunt BeBe was dying. This was one of the perks of death.

Reb settled in to do nothing in particular while Mitch perused the phone book for lodging. She had decided on a plan. The last time they were in Kansas, building a home to live in, it was Reb who had felt so strongly about leaving. The thought of living in Kansas was so disturbing that Mitch had decided against renting a house or apartment. That left her with the option of a hotel with nice suites. Utopia actually had such an establishment.

"You're working on a plan?" Reb inquired.

"I'm working on a plan."

"Good. Because I'm going to need somewhere soon."

Mitch stood up. "Give me the key to the van."

"I'll be stuck here."

"Not for long."

Reb produced the key and gave it to Mitch. She got a kiss in return. Not a bad trade.

True to her word, Mitch took care of the chores and was back at the hospital just after Aunt BeBe had finished browbeating her doctor.

"He's agreed to the additional tests, but he's not happy," Reb updated.

"Have any of BeBe's doctors ever been happy?"

"Did you find a place?" Reb ignored the subject of doctors.

"You ready to go?"

"The test won't be until tomorrow."

"Let's go."

Mitch drove Reb to the hotel. They had stayed here once a long time ago.

"Promise you won't be angry?" Mitch asked as she led the way to the elevator.

"What have you done *this* time?"

"I got two suites."

Reb didn't say anything, but Mitch could hear it anyway.

"They had two adjoining suites available, so I snatched them both up. That way, we'll have a lot of room."

"Are you planning to have a spring break party?"

"That's a thought."

Their nervous banter subsided once they toured the rooms. It was roomy. One commodity they had in Kansas was room.

28

"This was a good idea," Reb conceded once she saw the layout. "How much is it going to set us back?"

"Depends on how many room service bills we rack up."

"Is meatloaf on the room service menu?"

"I forgot to check."

Mitch had put their suitcases next to the closet and now began to unpack. Reb interrupted her work.

"I want to say something to you. Come over here."

Mitch complied. Mostly because she was crazy in love with this woman.

"I just wanted to tell you that this really was a good choice and that I'm glad that you came all the way out here and I'm really glad that you stayed."

"I wouldn't want to be anywhere else."

"And if room service doesn't have lemon meringue pie, I'll cook you one myself."

"Have you ever done that before?" Mitch was curious.

"Well, no."

"Okay."

"You don't think I can, do you?"

"I'm sure that if you had a fully-stocked kitchen, you could make a lemon meringue pie the likes of which nobody had ever seen." If answers could win Nobel Peace Prizes, Mitch was a contender.

"You know there's going to be hell to pay if Aunt BeBe's tests don't turn out good."

"Everything happens for a reason."

After Mitch finished the unpacking, they ordered dinner. It was decent for expensive hotel food. Then, they settled into bed like an old married couple and watched TV. The next thing Mitch knew, it was light and she could hear voices. Maybe just one voice. It was Reb. In the other room. On the phone. What was this? Mitch stretched to an upright position and padded to the bathroom. Everything would have to wait until this chore was finished. It took a scant five minutes and then, Mitch was ready to take on the day.

"Are you up?" Reb asked as she rolled into their sleeping room.

"Barely."

"Are you hungry?"

"Didn't you already call room service?"

"I was talking to BeBe."

"How is she?"

"On pins and needles. Perhaps literally?"

"This isn't going to be good," Mitch shook her head.

"What about breakfast?"

"You want to go down to the coffee shop?"

"Sure."

They dressed in comfortable waiting-room type clothes and went downstairs. Uncharacteristically, Mitch ate little. Reb noticed.

"You really are nervous about this, aren't you?"

"It's going to be tough to take it when Aunt BeBe begins to hate me even more than she already does."

Reb was stuck for a response. There was no use denying the animosity that BeBe demonstrated toward Mitch over the years. How could it possibly get worse?

Chapter 4

Trish wasn't happy. She had paid good money to have work done and it hadn't been. She was angry at the workers and somewhat miffed at herself for not catching the glaring problem earlier. After all, she did have things on her mind. Important things.

When Robbie gave birth to Josh, it had been naturally assumed that he was going to be the big concern. And in most ways, he still was. But for a baby with a lot going against him, he was a dream to care for. For a tiny baby, he slept well. Trish had heard stories about colicky babies and such, but there was no sign of this here. The fact that he was missing the lower part of his arms didn't make that much of a difference overall. That might've seemed callous, but there were larger concerns to deal with.

He was alive. Right here and now. If bleeding started, particularly in his brain, that could change everything in a heartbeat. Literally. And if that wasn't enough to deal with, Trish sighed, there was Robbie. Something had happened to Robbie. Something Trish couldn't quite put her finger on. Rose had diagnosed it as postpartum depression. Having never given birth, nor spent much time around those who do, Trish relied on someone who had. And besides, Silver concurred. The conversation had gone something like:
Trish: "I didn't know you had children, Silver?"
Silver: "I've never even given it serious thought, Ms. Sullivan."
Trish: "So, how have you experienced postpartum depression?"
Silver: "When my baby sister was having her second baby, she had a roommate in the hospital who did nothing but cry for three days straight. The entire time they were in the hospital back in the good old days when you didn't have to pop your baby out and leave all in the same afternoon."

It hadn't been at all like that with Robbie, Trish thought as she turned this conversation over in her mind. There had been some tears. A few. That was only natural. Trish had choked back a

31

few herself trying to be brave above it all for everybody else. She had things buried so deep that they'd need to contract out a construction crew to exhume her worry and grief. But for Robbie, there had been no deluge. No river of tears. No uncontrollable sobbing. Maybe that was what had to happen to break through this gloomy aura that had settled around Robbie.

"Do you think that Robbie needs to cry more?" Trish asked Rose across the kitchen table. It was lunchtime. Just the two of them. This had happened a lot lately. Max was off to the hardware store with Silver in tow. He had to be doing something to stay busy in a house full of females. And Robbie was taking all her meals in bed. At this rate, she was going to lose all of her muscle tone.

"Why would you think that?" Rose answered the question with one of her own.

Trish had to remember what the original question was, so lightening fast had her thoughts been. "I keep thinking about what Silver said. You know, about the lady who cried for three days."

"And she might still be crying for all we know. Some people are just like that."

"Like what?"

"Some women just have a hard time adjusting to motherhood." This concept made Trish's stomach clench. Was this what was going on with Robbie? Or was it just the certain circumstances? That alone could make anyone blue for a while. Except that it hadn't happened prior to the birth. Robbie had seemed fine about motherhood back then. Hadn't she?

"You're very concerned about this, aren't you?" Rose stated the obvious in such kindly terms.

It had a soothing effect on Trish. "I hide it from everybody else, so you see things in triplicate, probably?"

"I'm honored that you trust me, but I'm not sure that's what's best for Robbie. Or for you?"

"What should I do?"

"You should not act quite so stymied. You never have before. Why start now?"

Trish worked on this advice as Rose tended to the dishes. Trish had given up long ago trying to help with this chore. It didn't matter which way Trish washed the dishes, Rose redid the task. At first, she had done it surreptitiously. Trish had caught her sneaking back into the kitchen, sometimes way late at night, to rewash dishes that had been put on the shelf hours ago. After she had been apprehended, Rose no longer masqueraded her efforts to attain kitchen perfection. So, Trish had surrendered KP duty to the expert. No use wearing the finish off the dishes.

"It's just that this is my first baby."

"Welcome to parenthood. It's not for the faint of heart."

Trish nodded.

So, now, she had two choices. She could go into Robbie's room and begin to sort through this enigma of a puzzle called parenthood or she could call up the workers who had promised to remove the pesky door on the basement room that kept sticking shut. Once this second item had crossed her mind again, she began to get peeved. Well, at least as peeved as she ever got. She had paid them without inspecting the work and as far as she was concerned, it was tantamount to stealing on their part. She pulled the phone close and dialed the number from a tablet that she kept handy for house repairs. What a shock, the phone was picked up on the second ring by an actual human being. In a prerecorded world of punch number one for this and number two for that, getting a live voice on the other end of the phone was almost disconcerting. Trish had to think what to say.

"Hello, this is Ms. Sullivan."

"Yes, how can we help today?"

"You can start by having your people come back out and actually do the work I paid them for."

"Can you be a little more specific?" the soft voice said without a trace of defensiveness. She was good at her job.

"I have a door that sticks and I want it removed."

Trish heard a faint rustle of papers. "I have a note here that shows the job complete, but I will send a crew out right now. They should be there in, oh, about a half hour? Would that fit into your schedule?"

This lady was real good. Trish's peevishness dissolved. "That would be fine."

"Expect them at about 1:30."

"Thanks."

Trish hung up and looked at Rose. "The door people are going to be here in a few minutes."

"I'll have a snack ready for them."

Rose made it sound like they were dropping bologna sandwiches left and right to rush out to the house.

"Why don't we see if they actually do some work first."

Rose didn't argue. But she did turn the oven on. Even instant cookies needed heat to blossom.

Trish took the few minutes available to check in on Josh and Robbie. Both were sleeping. Still. Again. They would probably stir awake about the time the work crew showed up, but Rose would be here to take care of things. Trish simply couldn't do what she needed without Rose on the premises. So if she wanted to wash every dish twice and bake cookies for repairmen, Trish would just have to adjust. She sat in a chair for thirty-seven minutes watching Robbie breathe. The presence of Rose at the doorway brought her back to the moment. Without a word, Trish left Robbie to rest. So much for being un-stymied.

Three gentlemen were crowded around the kitchen table when Trish walked in. Imagine a collision between the three billy goats gruff and blue-striped overalls and you had the right idea. They had all been given a plate with cookies and a cup of coffee. It was like a tea party with the teamsters. Rose was in her element. And loving it. And why not? The only other people she got to visit with were Robbie, Trish, Silver, and Max. For all she knew, Rose might be paying these guys on the sly to botch up the work they did just so they could come back for more conviviality.

"Good afternoon, gentlemen," Trish said evenly.

"Hello, Ms. Sullivan. We're back."

"Yes, you are."

"Order says you're still having trouble with the door we took down?"

"The trouble I'm having is that the door is still up."
They looked from one to the other like the asylum had lost one
of their own and they had just found her.
"The door we took off?"
"It's still there."
"It's still where we left it?"
"On the hinges, yes."
"We didn't leave it on the hinges. We left it propped up along
the wall just like we were supposed to."
"It's still on the hinges."
The leader of the work crew scanned the faces of his crew.
"Mikey?"
Mikey looked like a kid, certainly the youngest of the billy goats.
How did thirteen-year-olds get on these crews anyway, Trish
thought to herself. Having cookie crumbs around his mouth did
little to make him look mature. She was surprised that Rose
gave him coffee instead of milk.
"I, I took it off," he started out with a stammer and ended with a
jutting chin.
"Well, let's go see."
Everyone got up at once. Rose apparently thought she was part
of the carpentry union as well and took the lead as they crept
down the too-old stairway. This was next on the list of repairs,
Trish mused as she brought up the rear. They paraded to the
door in question and stood in a semicircle of awe. For all to see,
the door was still on the hinges. Mikey looked like he was going
to pass out.
"I took it off, I swear!" he was acting like a man on death row.
"I'm sure you did," his supervisor said in that tone of voice
reserved for workers who must've toiled in their sleep and
forgotten their chore list. "Go ahead and take it off again. This
time for real."
Mikey said nothing else in his defense until he set to work in
earnest. "There they are," he muttered.
"There what are?"
"Those. The marks on the hinges. See? That's where I marked
things up last time."

Everyone strained to look. Sure enough, there were scratch marks for all to see. A sure sign of poor workmanship dressed up as exculpatory evidence.

"And you're sayin' you're proud of that work there?"

"No, I'm not saying that. I'm just saying that they're there."

"Thank you, Mikey. Remind me to not have you do the next example of removing a door for the other apprentices."

The dripping sarcasm was lost on the kid. He completed the work and, holding the extra-heavy door in adequately-muscled arms, awaited further instructions.

"Where do you want it, Miss?"

"Just put it down there," Trish pointed to the wall across from the doorway.

"Just like last time," Mikey got in his two cents.

"Really?" Trish asked.

He didn't speak, but nodded. He wasn't about to point out the other scratch marks made by the door scraping the floor and wall. Apparently, the sarcasm hadn't been a complete waste of oxygen.

Everyone took a collective breath of dust mites and then trooped back upstairs.

"Of course, there's no charge," the chief explained and they headed out the back door.

"And there's no charge for the cookies," Trish said to their backs after they had long disappeared down the driveway.

Rose looked at her in that tone of eyes that said, "You're in a mood."

"I'm going to check on Robbie."

That was always good for an exit strategy.

She was awake, if not entirely with it.

"Hi, Honey," Trish went over to the bed and sat on the side.

"Hi."

"How are you feeling?"

"I don't know. Where's Josh?"

"Sleeping."

"It's time for his feeding."

"I'll get him."

Trish went down the hall to find Josh curiously awake and yet content to stir quietly in his bed. Most other infants would've been yelling their lungs out. Not him. Not the Joshie. Trish changed his not-so-used diaper and then picked him up in careful arms.

"Come on, fella. Time for lunch."

She carried him closely to Robbie's waiting arms and then watched for a moment just because this is what life was all about. When Josh and Robbie were together, everything was fine. They were fine. Josh was fine. The world was fine. Doors being off hinges was fine. Whatever was going on with Robbie had little or nothing to do with being a mother. So, what on earth was it?

Chapter 5

"I told you this wasn't going to be good," Mitch said to Rebecca.
"Do you need to be right, or do you just need to repeat yourself?"
Reb answered.
They had spent the better, or in this case worse, part of the day
waiting for test results and the tension made them snappish.
There was nothing like the effect of dread mixed with sitting on
vinyl furniture to bring out the bearcat in everyone. And the
longer they waited, the more unbearable the atmosphere became.
It was borderline noxious.
"I hope I'm wrong," Mitch offered as apology.
Reb sighed. She only had one person to take all her frustrations
out on. The old saying about going once too often to the well
was beginning to hit home.
"How do you put up with me?"
"I took a course once in college."
"You took a course?" Reb was immediately skeptical, for good
reason.
"Oh yeah. It was called, 'How to Put Up With People Who
You're Crazy in Love With.'"
"No self-respecting college would name a course something that
ended with a preposition."
"You didn't let me finish."
"Okay, so finish it."
"Y'all."
"What?"
"Y'all. Like, 'People Who You're Crazy in Love With, Y'all.'"
"Well, that certainly makes it tons more respectable."
"I thought so."
"So?" Reb was still needing answers.
"So?" Mitch was in the proverbial dark.
"So, what kind of grade did you get?"
"I flunked it. Twice."
"They let you take it twice?"
"Three times, actually. I finally passed with a D."
"You're making all of this up, aren't you?"
"Just from the beginning."
"Why?"

"Because it beats having us snap at each other about actual events."

"Somehow that makes perfect sense."

Further spinning of stories real or otherwise was interrupted mercifully by the appearance of the doctor. If he spent any time out on the golf course, it didn't show. He was as pale as a piece of loose-leaf notebook paper minus the lines.

"I'm ready to go in and talk to your sister. Do you want to be present?"

Reb studied his face for a millisecond. The news wasn't good. "Of course."

They walked into the room where BeBe was sleeping. At least she was still able to do that without undue effort. Reb went over and touched her arm. She awoke instantly. Many years on the farm had instilled in her the ability to have all of her faculties present immediately upon awakening. Mitch took about a year and a half just to remember where the coffee pot was most mornings. Notwithstanding the look in Reb's eyes, BeBe jumped right into things.

"Well, give me the news. I'm paying you by the hour!"

Apparently, the doctor was used to anger. This was the Oncology Wing, after all. He gave her the news in terms that floated in and out of Mitch's mind like words at a spelling bee. She hadn't studied up on the terminology and was hopelessly confounded. If it was good or bad news, it would need to be said in plainer English than this. Which they finally got around to. All too suddenly.

"You mean, it didn't work!" BeBe was looking at Mitch like it was all her fault.

Instead of being angry, Mitch felt rebuked. Like it somehow really was all her fault. And if that would make Aunt BeBe feel better about both life and death, then so be it.

"I guess it didn't work."

The doctor looked from one to the other. Someone had forgotten to mention the real reason why he had been expected to perform these additional tests. Might as well have four upset folks in the room. That way, nobody would feel left out.

"BeBe thinks I'm a healer." Mitch began lamely.

"I have other patients to attend to. We'll discuss this later."

And then, he was gone. With all the precision of a drill sergeant, he had turned on his heel and stalked out. This had "There'll be hell to pay" written front and backwards all over it. Great. Now everybody was mad.

"Well, you're just going to have to try again!" Aunt BeBe was back to giving orders.

Mitch had no earthly clue what to say, so she just stood there waiting for lightening to strike. Next best thing, lunch arrived. Now, Aunt BeBe had to choose between a turkey sandwich or grilled Mitch.

"Come back after lunch," was her abrupt reprieve.

Mitch broke all records getting to the hallway and now breathed like it was her first oxygen in weeks.

"You want to sit down or eat?" Reb asked.

"Both."

They made a return trip to the cafeteria and in a strange turn of events, Mitch selected all healthy food.

"Not having pie?" Reb inquired.

"Not yet. Maybe later."

Now, Reb was deeply concerned. She watched as Mitch ate a salad without dressing. After three bites, Mitch noticed.

"What?"

"You're eating salad."

"I've eaten salad before."

"Not without dressing."

"So?"

"So, you used to list ranch dressing as your favorite beverage in surveys."

"I did not? I've listed gravy as my drink of choice, though."

"Ranch dressing was a close second."

"It's okay that you're picking on me. I'd be mad, too, if you hadn't been able to heal my sister."

The change of subject achieved the desired impact. Reb became circumspect.

"I'm not blaming you."

"I know."

"Not any more than I blame you for not being able to heal me."

Well, at least they got to the heart of the matter while they were still on the salad course.

"If I could control this whatever it is, you'd be the first person I'd heal. You know that."

"I know."

"And besides, it's all just a bunch of hooey."

"I know."

"And now your sister knows as well. She has anywhere from three to six months to come to terms with that."

"There's still conventional medicine. She could live longer."

Mitch didn't answer. She didn't have much faith in medical advances where liver cancer was concerned. And by now, she couldn't hide her pragmatism from Reb.

"You don't think so?"

"I think that however long your sister has left isn't as important as how that time is spent."

Mitch kept herself busy polishing off her dry salad, giving this concept of quality versus quantity time a chance to sink in.

"What do you think should happen in the next six months?" Reb asked.

"She's not my sister," Mitch answered abstrusely.

"Give me a hint anyway."

"I don't think it matters much whether or not she got a full refund on a microwave oven."

"You were the one talking to her about it."

"Well, like I said, she's not my sister. I don't know what the two of you need to talk through so you won't feel guilty when she dies."

Things got real quiet. Again. Almost too quiet.

"I'm going to get some more salad. You want anything?" Mitch asked.

Reb shook her head no. Which sent more than one signal to Mitch. A second salad should've prompted some comment. Mitch ate while Reb picked at her food. Wherever she was mentally was right where she needed to be. Finally, she asked, "Why should I feel guilty?" It came out in a challenging tone. No surprise there.

"Because everyone feels guilty when a loved one dies."

Reb didn't argue. How could she? Mitch had a handle on virtually every universal truth known to mankind. Why should death be any different?

41

Chapter 6

Okay, now Trish was really peeved! Enough was enough. She didn't mind the fact that the repair crew must be going for some world's record when it came to cookie eating. As long as she didn't have to pay for the work, it really didn't matter. Except that they should only get away with the same old stunt once. Twice at the most. But this was just too much. And besides that, who did it? Which one of them had sneaked back in and put the damn door back on the hinges? She had gone down to check on a lost book and big as life, the door was back on the doorframe. She was startled, but not for long. Her surprise turned to irritation and she was upstairs and on the phone before Rose could get the details.

"No, I'm not going to be put on hold!" Trish enunciated clearly but was clicked over to music. She hung up, redialed, and then made herself clear without saying hello, "DON'T even think about putting me on hold again!"

It must've done the trick for she continued talking. "Yes, this is Ms. Sullivan, again. Yes, I'm having a problem, again. It's the basement door, again."

And then, she hung up and gave Rose a look that said that she'd better not even be thinking about lighting up the stove.

"What about the door?" Rose asked, wondering as she did if she had any baked goods cached away for just such an emergency.

"It's back on the hinges!"

"It is?" Rose was stunned.

"It is," Trish confirmed.

"It can't be. Why would it be back up?"

"I wouldn't know. Would you?"

It took Rose a second to figure out that she was tops or first-runner up on the suspect list.

"It wasn't me!" she said in icy tones. Folks worried about global warming could enlist the help of Rose when she got in this mood.

Trish backed off. The image of an elderly woman wrestling a heavy wooden door didn't make any sense. She just wasn't thinking clearly.

"You don't suppose Silver is putting it back on for security reasons, do you?"

"Probably not without asking first. But maybe we'd better find out before *you* jump in the middle of those nice repairmen. Again."

"We'd better hurry. They come ninety miles per hour when they think your confections are at the finish line."

It took about five seconds to locate Silver. One second to call out her name and four seconds for her to come to what she perceived as "the rescue." At least she didn't have her gun drawn. Yet.

"What's wrong?" her hand hovered over the general vicinity where her revolver was tucked away in the hidden holster. Kevin Costner couldn't do it any better.

If Rose felt like Whitney Houston, she hid it well.

"We just wanted to ask you a question," Rose was calm as ever. Silver seemed a little let down. There were days when she felt that she didn't earn her pay. But then again, Rose was still alive. And that was the primary objective.

"Okay."

"Do you know anything about the door downstairs?"

"Which door?"

"The door that sticks?" Trish took over.

"The one the guys took off?"

"Right."

"That's all I know."

"You didn't put it back on?"

"Why would I do that?"

"We thought it was some security issue."

Silver didn't say anything but she had an expression on her face that indicated that she was irked when amateurs tried to second guess her methods. Rose, who had allowed Trish to handle the interrogation, now stepped up with a plate of cookies. Where did she get these anyway? Silver didn't care. She pulled up a kitchen stool and plunked herself down.

"Got any coffee?"

Rose had a pot ready already. Just as her cup was filled, the crew showed up as well. They were all so jovial that Trish was having a hard time remembering that she was ticked off. This

43

time, they decided to check things out before having their coffee break. Just because she was on duty, Silver led the way and Trish brought up the rear. Trish was still carefully watching her step while everyone went ahead. She heard voices.

"What do you want us to do?" the foreman was asking.

"Take the door off-" Trish stopped dead in her tracks.

Even from this limited vantage point, she could see that the door was propped up against the wall, right where Mikey had left it. Except that this morning, it had been back on its hinges. It really had been. Trish looked at Rose, who rather than seemed irritated, looked back in concern.

"Are you feeling alright, Sweetie?"

"Huh?"

"You're going pale."

By now, Silver was by Trish's side. Of course she looked pale next to Silver.

"We'd better get you upstairs," Silver had a firm grip on Trish and was guiding her along like a marionette sans strings.

"Where are we going?"

"To bed."

Several inappropriate comments flew through Trish's mind but she was so addled that nothing came out of her mouth. Lucky for her. Silver would've been mortified. Silver maneuvered Trish to the guest bedroom and had her situated by the time Rose was dialing 911.

"What are you doing?"

"I'm calling for help."

"I'm fine. Don't call anybody."

"Too late. They're on the way."

"I don't need them."

"Well, I do!" Rose was emphatic. "Besides, you pay your taxes just like everybody else."

Trish resisted getting into a debate about taxes and instead talked common sense. "If they come with full sirens, it's going to wake the baby and scare Robbie."

"I'll take care of that," Silver took off with her mission well-defined. Before the paramedics were even halfway to the house, Robbie was beside Trish.

"What happened?"

Trish gave what she could muster up as a warning look to Rose and then answered, "I just got a little dizzy. Guess I don't have enough iron in my blood."

Thankfully, there was no mention of the door episode.

"And you called 911 for that?" Robbie asked.

"I scared your mom," Trish answered, fighting back any defensiveness she might be feeling.

"You certainly did!" Rose concurred.

"You do look pretty pale."

"You look beautiful."

At least there was nothing wrong with Trish's eyesight.

"You just rest until the paramedics get here."

"Yes, Ma'am." Trish was feeling better just seeing Robbie up and around. Maybe she should swoon more often? The reverie was interrupted by an onslaught of medical personnel. How all these many people fit into this small a room was astonishing. Robbie was gone. In her place, two or three medics began to check Trish for life signs. This was going to be embarrassing. She was fine, really. A couple more were talking to Rose, getting the rundown on symptoms. It was at this exact moment that Trish realized just how concerned Rose had been.

Meanwhile, they were going for the best two out of three on the blood pressure reading.

"What's the verdict?" Trish asked.

"It's a little bit high. Do you take medication?"

"For blood pressure?"

"For anything."

"No. Should I?"

"Let's give it a few minutes."

Which they did. Trish closed her eyes and tried to calm herself. It must've worked. They removed the cuff and generally stopped fussing over her. And she might've dropped clear off to sleep except that Rose prodded her.

"I'm awake."

"They think you're okay. They're leaving without you."

"That's nice."

Soon, it was just the two of them. "You weren't kidding about the door?" Rose was whispering like the FBI was listening in.

Trish opened up one eye, then the other. "No, I wasn't kidding about the door. Is that why you called 911?"

"You were dizzy."

"You thought I was hallucinating, didn't you?"

"No," Rose answered, absolutely lying through her teeth.

"Well, what do you think?" Trish wanted a diagnosis.

"I think you just saw something that nobody else saw."

Trish had to think about this one. Wasn't that the definition of a hallucination?

"What did you see?" Trish wanted to know. Just because.

"What?"

"Downstairs. What did you see?"

"I saw a door set up against the wall. What did you see?"

"Same thing. That time."

"When did you see it differently?"

"This morning. I went down there early and the door was on the hinges."

"Maybe you were sleep walking and having a dream."

"Sleep walking? I've never done that."

"Well, maybe you're starting. You have been under a great deal of strain lately."

"And you think that causes sleep walking."

"Well, it either causes sleep walking or hallucinations. Which one do you want to be having?"

Gee, what a choice! Trish didn't voice this or anything else.

"Don't say anything to Robbie," Rose admonished needlessly.

"I wasn't going to. If I'm going to go crazy, I want it to be just our little secret."

Trish meant it as a joke. Rose took it seriously.

"Okay," she nodded like she knew who really killed Kennedy, too.

Chapter 7

"For a lesbian, you sure dated a lot of boys!" This was Aunt BeBe's way of sharing. Mitch and Reb had spent a difficult hour or two going down memory lane with Aunt BeBe and it was all Mitch's fault. She was the one who had foolishly suggested that Reb and BeBe set their emotional house in order after BeBe's medical tests turned out not so good.

"Yes, I sure did," Reb answered back.

Mitch looked around for help. Where in the hell was Henry? When he called Reb to come out to Kansas, he had been frantic. Now, he had just been absent. AWOL absent. It was like he found reinforcements and then deserted the troops.

"Where is Henry?" Mitch ventured a question. It beat the heck out of listening to stories of how many boys Reb had dated. Lovers should only have to listen to so much of this.

"What's that got to do with who Rebecca dated?" BeBe looked over at her. At least they were still on speaking terms. It was still pretty venomous, but they were talking.

"Nothing, I hope," Mitch meant it as a humorous response.

"I suppose you slept with him, too?" BeBe was concentrating on Reb again.

"What do you mean, *too*?" Reb snapped just a little.

"I mean, too. As in also and in addition to. There wasn't a boy that I dated that you didn't give the eye to."

"What on earth are you talking about?" Reb was dumbfounded.

"Don't pretend you didn't. And don't even try and pretend that I didn't notice."

"Name one."

"Bernard Longmaster."

Sounded like a porn star's sobriquet to Mitch.

"Bernie? When did you date Bernie?"

"After you got all done breaking his heart!"

"I didn't break his heart!"

"You most certainly did!"

"I did not!"

"Did too."

Mitch was beginning to get a headache. Maybe it was all of those salads she had been eating lately. It was like the vitamins were overloading her brain, clearing out the toxins. Mitch had read once where toxins were like teeth. They hurt coming in and they hurt going out.

"I could not have broken Bernard Longmaster's heart because he was gay to begin with!"

Reb cleared the air on that episode.

"He was not!" BeBe reacted like it was a personal attack on her to have mended the broken heart of a gay man.

"He was so. Did you ever sleep with him?"

"I could ask you the same thing!"

Mitch began to rub her temples. Not only was she in pain, but the room was hot as well. Here it was February going into March and the heat was running full blast in the hospital. She would only find respite in the surgical ward and you couldn't go in there unless there was something to chop out. Or poke in.

"I don't sleep with gay men," Reb stated firmly

"Don't pretend you have any standards in that department!"

BeBe was now going full bore.

Mitch excused herself from the room before her head might explode. She walked down to the "dying waiting room" and stretched out on the bereavement couch. Reb was there before too long.

"You okay?"

"You're the one she's calling a slut. How are you holding up?"

"Oh, I've heard worse than this."

"You have?"

"I'm from a small town. Jealousy is a cottage industry around here. So is prying into other people's lives."

"So, tell me about Bernie."

"Bernie was a young man who liked other men. He and I ran around together. And, no, we never slept together. But I was a pretty good beard for him."

"So, you did have a reputation?"

"Don't tell me that you're so provincial that you think farm girls are virginal."

Mitch sat up. The pain came flooding back. It didn't matter. This was important.

"Maybe I was wrong. Maybe you and BeBe don't need to talk anything else over. I think it would be better in the long run for you to feel guilty after her death."

"The only way I'm going to feel guilty after her death is if I kill her myself."

It had to be the headache. For a minute there, Reb sounded like she meant it.

"You hungry yet? You must be starving after that salad. That's all you've been eating lately. What's wrong with you?"

"I'm trying to turn green from the inside."

"Well, you're succeeding. Let's go get something a little more substantial."

"Is it safe to leave BeBe?"

"Right now, it wouldn't be safe for me to be in there alone with her."

When they got on the elevator, Reb pushed the button for the garage level parking.

"What? You're not taking me for another stupendous meal and the cafeteria?"

"We've got months of this. Better find several places to eat."

"There's always *our* diner."

"Let's keep that for special occasions."

"Like, tomorrow?"

"What's so special about tomorrow?"

"It's not today. That would make any day special."

They exited the elevator and climbed into the van. Reb drove around for a few minutes, checking to see if any new and interesting restaurants had spring up during their absence. There was a spruced-up deli nestled into the corner of an L-shaped strip mall. Reb and Mitch snapped up a booth. Every other seat was empty. Business was slow.

"It's early," Reb noted.

"It's eleven-thirty," Mitch noted back.

"You're still thinking 'big city.'"

"Speaking of the big city, we should call home soon. See how things are with everybody."

"We can do that tonight."

"Is it true?" Mitch asked.

"That we can call tonight?"

"No. It is true that you stole all BeBe's boyfriends?"

Reb was just going to answer when the waitress came over.

"You decide yet?"

"I'd like the grilled chicken sandwich and coleslaw," Reb ordered first.

"And you?"

Mitch hadn't had much time to study the menu, so she ordered a hodge podge of items. "I'd like some fruit and the mashed potatoes and some kind of vegetable."

This confounded the waitress. None of this matched the nice, neat orders she usually wrote down.

"Are those side orders?" she asked.

"Yes, I'm ordering ala carte."

"But, you're eating here, right?"

"Uh, right," Mitch was sitting down. She really was.

"I'll see what I can do."

Mitch took a sip of water and noticed the steely look from Reb.

"What?"

"What happened to ordering meatloaf and pie?"

"It just doesn't sound good right now."

"And fruit and mashed potatoes does?"

"It sounds…clean."

"Clean?"

"Simple?"

"It didn't sound so simple to the waitress."

"Well, she doesn't have to eat it and I do."

"You're going to be hungry again before two."

"So you can take me to an early dinner."

"And what? Go to the International House of Tree Bark?"

Mitch knew why they were examining her current eating habits in detail. It was to avoid talking about BeBe and Reb and the teenage years.

"They have one of those here?" Mitch feigned glee.

"Drink your water."

"So, tell me about all your old boyfriends."

"We don't have that much time."

"Oh, sure we do. It's going to take them a while to figure out my order."

"You would've had to order a lot more than that."

"Really! Like, how many courses?"

"More than you could eat."

Mitch sat back in the booth. "I had no idea!"

Reb was trying to be nonchalant about the whole deal, but a hint of color rose in her cheeks.

"You had no idea that I dated?"

"I guess I figured that the only guy you ever dated was Jeff."

"My ex? You thought I only dated my ex-husband?"

"I just never gave it a lot of thought," Mitch trailed off.

Somewhere in the back of her mind, she was thinking about Lisa. Lisa was her ex. And through the years, Mitch had carried a good deal of guilt weight over the fact that she traveled in and out of their lives on a regular basis. While Mitch and Jeff had managed to enjoy each other's company the few times they had occasion, Reb and Lisa were always at odds over something. Mitch had pegged it all up to jealousy and felt this tremendous amount of culpability over this issue. To find out now that there was a manifest list of boyfriends that Mitch could've been feeling jealous about all these years was unsettling.

"What's wrong?" Reb saw the look in Mitch's eyes.

"Nothing."

Reb didn't challenge immediately. She just watched and waited. A tactic that always worked in the past. For some reason, though, it didn't work today. Mitch remained taciturn.

"You're very good for me, you know that, don't you?" Reb worked around the edges.

"Huh?"

"Not everyone would stand by and be insulted by a stultifying sister-in-law."

"I figure that we're in this together. Wasn't that one of our marriage vows? To put up with stultifying sister-in-laws?"

"And a lot of ex-boyfriends?"

Mitch went silent again.

"I'm really sorry that I dated all those guys."

"Don't be sorry on my account."

"I'm not. I'm sorry on my account! I wish I would've run into you a long time ago. Believe me."

"I do."

"Sounds like our marriage vows again."

"Yeah, the part we never got to."

"We'll need to fix that one of these days."

"Just as soon as things calm down," Mitch said.

"That might take a while."

"I'm not going anywhere."

"Good, because lunch is coming."

Reb's food looked pretty good. It was a standard meal right off the menu. Mitch's was another story. The mashed potatoes looked a bit watery because they were from an instant mix. The vegetable was cold canned green beans. But the fruit. The fruit was the most interesting offering of the three. The definition of fruit in this place was the scoopings-out of a piece of blueberry pie. It was like pie without the crust. The coup de grace was that it was all on the same plate and the shared juices were turning the edges of the potatoes a funny shade of pale blue green.

"You want anything else?" the waitress had the nerve to ask.

Reb looked at Mitch for the answer.

"No, thank you. This looks divine."

After she skirted away, Reb looked at Mitch.

"I didn't know you were so good at lying."

"You didn't?" Mitch tried to look surprised. "Why, Ms. Fairbanks, I'm an expert at lying."

"So, what have you been lying to me about all these years?" Reb followed up like the lawyer that she used to be.

"You really want to know?"

"Yes, I really want to know."

"All those years I told you that you were beautiful?" Mitch began.

"Yes?"

"I lied."

"You did?"

"You're breathtakingly beautiful."

"I don't consider that a lie as much as a clarification."

"Yeah, but try and use that excuse with the IRS and see how far it gets you."

"You think?"

52

"You start clarifying your expense report and you'll spend your lifetime making small rocks out of big rocks."

"It doesn't work that way."

"Maybe not for you lawyer types."

"Eat your lunch!"

At least Mitch didn't have to worry about Reb stealing anything off her plate. Nobody would want this meal. Homeless people would get back in line for something better. But she ate without complaint because it was simple and healthy. Except for the ton of sugar in the blueberry pie filling. And the fake butter, what little they used, in the mashed potatoes. And whatever chemicals and microbes that were lodged deep inside the processed green beans. Other than that, it was just peachy.

"Can we go to the grocery store sometime soon?" Mitch asked.

"How about right after lunch?"

"No. We need to get back to the hospital. BeBe isn't finished vilifying me yet today. How about later tonight?"

"I don't know if I'll have enough energy."

Mitch studied Reb. She did look tired. Mitch chided herself for not noticing sooner.

"I can do the shopping. Let's make a list when we get back to the hospital."

And so it was that between listening to a rehashing of proms long gone and dead silence, Mitch penned a shopping list. When Reb glanced at it, she gave Mitch her best studious look.

"Did I forget something?" Mitch asked.

"Only the fact that we don't have the refrigerator space of a medium-size restaurant."

"We have two refrigerators in the hotel room."

"Two very small refrigerators."

"Well, okay. Why don't you tell me what won't fit."

It came out sounding more like a dare than Mitch had intended, and now Reb took it as such. She began picking apart the list in detail.

"Since when do you eat apples?"

What this had to do with refrigerator space Mitch didn't know.

"I've eaten apples."

"Name one when it wasn't in a pie."

"I've had a plain apple or two in my life."

"One or two?"

"It's not like I'm going to buy a bushel and a peck."

"Okay, fine."

"Okay, what else?"

"What are you going to do with green peppers?"

"I thought I'd talk the hotel management into installing an oven in our room so I can bake apple-stuffed green peppers."

Mitch actually managed to say this with a straight face.

"You want to borrow my recipe?" Reb sounded serious as well.

"I took it when you weren't looking."

"Fine. Don't tell me what you're planning to do with the peppers. I just want to know one more thing."

"Sure."

"Are you buying plain oatmeal and vanilla soymilk with the idea of somehow combining them?"

"I thought I'd experiment with it."

Aunt BeBe had refrained from comment until now. A miracle unto itself. Now, she couldn't help herself. "Has she gone nuts?" BeBe directed the inquiry to Reb. Only the most observant would've noticed that Reb took offense at this remark. It was okay for her to give Mitch a bad time about grocery lists, but it was her territory and hers alone to do so. But before things could get ugly between sisters, Mitch blurted out, "That's what I forgot! Nuts! I want to get some walnuts! Thank you for reminding me, Aunt BeBe."

Mitch took the list back from Reb's prying eyes and added walnuts to it.

"Are you going to put them in the stuffed peppers or the oatmeal?"

"Maybe both. It all sounds so good now that you mention it."

Reb shook her head. "Why don't you go to the store and I'll see you back at the hotel."

Mitch looked from Reb to BeBe. Normally, she would've begged for an opportunity to take her leave of the ongoing family feud type discussions, but today, something was different.

"Are you sure? I could stay around a while longer?"

"You go on. I know you have a lot to buy."

It was a dismissal. A gentle one. Mitch took it as such. It wasn't every day that Reb wanted time alone with her sister, and Mitch had to respect that.

The local grocery store in Utopia was actually quite modern for small-town America. It had been refurbished and upgraded since last Mitch had shopped here and she knew she was going to be in nothing but trouble when she got home. The fresh produce aisle was particularly nice. For whatever reason, Mitch was craving fresh foods. One too many years of eating barely-warmed-up beef stew out of a can had altered her perception of eating. Reb was a positive influence as well. So, before she could calculate the actual cubic inches of refrigerator space she had, the shopping basket was half-full of green and orange and red and yellow vegetables. So, half a shopping cart had to equal two small refrigerators, didn't it? She also picked up some fresh herbs in packages, just because they smelled so good. The whole-wheat bread was fresh, and in a demonstration of sheer will power, Mitch selected it over the also-freshly-made donuts. After finding everything else on the list, and a dozen or so items besides, she went through the checkout line. If the clerk recognized her from the last time she was in town, she refrained from making any mention of it. The more anonymous Mitch was, the better she liked it. Reb was waiting back at the hotel. Whatever private time she took with BeBe couldn't have been too long.

"Where have you been?" she asked.

"At the store."

"It's been over an hour."

"So, what did you and BeBe talk about for the ten minutes that you had alone together?"

"That's a helluva way to ask a question."

Mitch knew she would be in trouble when she got home. She just had labored under the false assumption that it would be for her buying habits rather than for not being psychic.

"Okay, I'll rephrase the question," Mitch said as she went over to Reb and got close enough to actually touch her. "You and BeBe must have talked about something pretty upsetting?"

Reb looked at Mitch with eyes that held the grief of the ages. "I guess it shows."

"What happened?"

"I never knew my sister was so bitter about life."

Well, for God's sake, Mitch had known this forever. Someone like BeBe broadcast their bitterness out through every fiber of their being twenty-four hours a day, seven days a week, fifty-two weeks a year. Surely, that wasn't a surprise to Reb?

"What is she bitter about?" Mitch asked like this was news to her.

"She thinks that I was the favored child."

"And were you?"

"Absolutely not!"

"Well, did you think that BeBe was the favored child?"

"I just hadn't given it much thought."

This sounded more like an evasion than an answer. Which only said one thing to Mitch. Tread carefully. Maybe some people could joke about who mom liked best, but for too many siblings, these were the type of issues that ripped the human heart clear out of the chest. Mine fields are safer to negotiate than family favoritism issues.

Mitch went another pathway. "Why does BeBe think you were favored?"

"I didn't ask."

Mitch envisioned an abrupt ending to the conversation back at the hospital. Going back tomorrow would be dicey unless they got more of this out in the open tonight.

"Well, then, why do you *think* she feels that way?"

Reb inhaled in that way that suggested that she was going to tell Mitch to just drop everything. And then, she didn't.

"I'm sure it's difficult to have an overachiever in the family."

"You're referring to yourself?"

"Of course. Who else would I be talking about!"

"Of course," Mitch nodded diplomatically.

"But I certainly wasn't that way to annoy anybody. Especially on purpose."

"Or to be the favorite?"

"Everyone wants the love and acceptance of their parents. What's so wrong with making that a priority?"

"Absolutely nothing," Mitch agreed. Too readily for Reb not to notice.

"You think there's something wrong with that?"

"What I know is that gay youth are often overachievers."

"They are?"

"That's what I've heard."

"Well, that doesn't apply to me."

"It doesn't?"

"Of course not. I wasn't gay when I was a kid."

"You weren't?" Mitch was fully engaged now. Forget about putting away the groceries.

"Well, no. Of course not," Reb repeated herself.

"You were straight as a child?"

"Of course. Isn't everyone?"

"Well," Mitch hedged, "I haven't met everyone and asked them."

"You don't have to be a smart alec."

"I guess generalities just bring out that quality in me."

"What generalities?"

"The one about *everyone* being straight as a child."

"You're telling me that I'm wrong about that?"

Mitch knew better than to fall for that old lawyer's trap.

"It isn't about being right or wrong about the issue. It's more about considering all the possibilities."

"Like what?"

"Like you, for instance."

Reb shifted in her chair. A common reaction to either becoming the example of one of Mitch's theories or fatigue at sitting in one place for too long.

"What about me?"

"When did you first figure out that you were gay?"

"That's a silly question."

"Indulge me."

"It was when I met you."

"Really?"

"Really."

"Truly?"

"Honestly."

"And not one minute before?"

"And not a moment too soon."

"So, it's your belief that people become gay one day right out of the blue?"

"It happened to me."

"Right. But what if it happens much earlier for some people?"

"I'm sure that can happen but I don't think that people are born gay."

"Why not?" Mitch probed gently.

"Because there's no proof."

Ah, the old proof problem.

"Science hasn't proven the theory of gravity either, but you don't see folks floating by."

"You're saying that you think that some people are born gay."

"I don't rule out the possibility."

"Well, it has to be one way or the other, doesn't it?"

"Why?"

One-word questions were always the toughest to answer.

"You don't think so?" Reb evaded.

"Oh, I know what I think. I'm just trying to figure out what you think. We've been together an awfully long time not to have had this conversation."

"That's because we've been too immersed in the practicalities of life to ruminate about the theoretical."

"So, now do you think people can be born gay?"

Reb studied Mitch. "I get it now! You were born gay, weren't you?"

"It's all I've ever known."

"Then, that's good enough for me."

"Have we truly never discussed this before?" Mitch couldn't hide her amazement.

"If we did, I wasn't paying attention. I was too dazzled by your beauty to keep my mind on anything else."

Normally, it was Mitch who waxed mushy.

"I think it's about time we got you out of your chair and into bed."

"I bet you say that to all the girls."

"Just the ones I'm married to."

"Before we do *that*, you need to put away the groceries and I need to phone the kids."

By "kids," Reb was referring to Mary and Lisa. By "that," heaven knows what Reb was referring to. Mitch went right to work stuffing produce into the small fridge. Form be damned.

Reb dialed, waited, and then hung up. "It's six o'clock. What could they be doing?"

Mitch kept her first guess to herself. She didn't have a second guess. "Are we having dinner in bed?"

"Of course. Let's order room service."

"What? You don't want raw green peppers stuffed with apples and walnuts?"

"Oh, gee, maybe for breakfast. What should I order?"

"Something healthy."

"Don't I always?"

For room service, it wasn't too bad. The hotel could steam vegetables and bake potatoes like they invented the techniques.

"You're not eating your chicken," Reb pointed out the obvious.

"I guess I'm just not in the mood."

"You have to be in a mood to eat chicken?"

"I think I'm just a little tired of the taste."

"That's been happening a lot lately. What's wrong?"

"I don't think there's anything wrong. I just don't have a craving for chicken anymore."

"Or steak. Or pork chops. Or meatloaf."

"I can tell you're trying to make a point."

"You haven't had a lot of meat lately."

"You've been watching?"

"It's a little hard to miss. We do take all our meals together."

"Yes, we do."

"You're becoming what? Vegetarian?"

Mitch put her fork down and met Reb's eyes. "It's even worse than that, I'm afraid," she said with just a hint of a smile.

"What could possibly be worse than becoming a vegetarian?"

"I'm going Vegan."

Reb looked at Mitch like Vegan was a planet and the mother ship was on the lookout for landing lights. "What is that? That whatever you just said."

"Vegan. V-e-g-a-n. It's where you don't eat animals and animal products."

"Animal products?"

"Right. Like milk."

"I've never seen you drink milk."

"I haven't for a long time. I think it gives me migraines."

"Okay, what else?"

"What else?"

"What else are you giving up?"

"By extension, ice cream and cheese."

"And where exactly are you going to get your calcium?"

Mitch was ready for this question since she had already asked it of herself. "I'm going to drink calcium-fortified soy milk."

"I've heard that's good for hot flashes."

"I wouldn't know. I'm not there yet."

"I didn't see any soy milk when you put the groceries away?"

"I didn't buy any yet. I thought we should have this talk first."

"You thought you needed my permission or blessing to change your diet?"

"I just wanted to give you fair warning, I guess."

"So, you're revamping your eating habits entirely."

"Kind of."

"Well, what are you going to eat. I mean, what's left?"

"Let's see. There's green peppers and apples and walnuts."

"And what else?"

"Tofu?"

"Next time you go to the grocery store, I'm coming with."

"You've got a date," Mitch sounded happy and relieved.

"Meanwhile, hand me the phone. Maybe the kids are home."

Indeed, the kids were home. Mary must've answered, Reb chatted nonstop for ten minutes. Something she would've never done with Lisa. Then, things changed. Abruptly.

"You want to talk to Mitch?" Reb asked distantly before automatically handing the phone over. It was Lisa now.

"Hi. What's new?" Mitch asked. She could never be as clinical as Reb might have wished her to be when talking to Lisa. And after hearing all those who took whom to the prom stories, she suddenly didn't feel the need to anymore.

"Mary got a job."

"Why?" was all Mitch could think to ask.

"Somebody's got to pay the bills."

"You have bills?"

"We tried to get groceries for free but the store frowned on that."

Mitch had financially assisted Mary and Lisa when they were trying to renovate the family homestead in Kansas. After the fire and Lisa's subsequent discharge from the hospital, Mitch had found a really nice house for Mary and Lisa to live in back in Denver. They had insisted on paying back most of the money she had originally lent them. Between that and the hospital bills, it left them with a much smaller nest egg than before the fire.

"You should have told me sooner. I can fix that problem," Mitch sounded testy.

"Oh, hey, don't worry about it. Mary needs a good excuse to not have to look at me eight hours a day. Nine if she works overtime."

It was excruciatingly obvious that Mary wasn't listening in on this. At least, Mitch hoped not. But Reb still was.

"I'll either wire you more money or come in person. Which do you prefer?"

A year or so ago, Lisa wouldn't pass up the opportunity to make the most of a double entendre. Or to see Mitch in person. It was a surprise to hear her say, "Neither."

"Okay," Mitch totally ignored the answer. "I'll be there tomorrow morning. I'll call you when I get in."

With that, Mitch disconnected the call. Then, she looked at Reb. "I'll be home for dinner."

"You'd better phone in your flight reservation now."

Mitch caught a lucky break. There was a seat left in coach on the morning flight to Denver. It saved her the expense of chartering a flight, something she would have done without hesitation in order to get this done and over with. So, she would fly in, meet Lisa, go to the bank, have lunch, fly out, be back in time for plenty more of dysfunctional adventures with Aunt BeBe.

"You're okay with this?" Mitch double checked.

"It's okay if Mary works for a living."

"It's okay if Mary works if she has a job she enjoys. What is she doing anyway?"

"She mentioned something about auditing."

"Does she enjoy that?" Mitch asked. It sounded like about as much fun as gutting fish although not nearly as messy.

"It's challenging work. She approaches it like a puzzle that needs to be solved," Reb yawned as she explained.

"That's good. I guess. I'll still give them enough money to ease their burdens. They are our kids, after all."

Reb didn't comment. She must've drifted off to sleep. Which was okay. It was going to be an early morning. Mitch switched off the lights.

As flights go, this one was short. Lisa was waiting for Mitch and then walked ahead of her right to the No Parking Zone where she had left the car. It was still there, miracle of miracles. The next bill to pay would be the mother of all parking tickets, though.

"Why didn't you just park in the terminal?" Mitch asked with just a small measure of sarcasm.

"They don't allow that anymore," Lisa answered glibly.

"Where's your luggage?"

"I brought the checkbook. That's all I need."

"You're not staying overnight?"

Her question had a plaintive quality to it. It wasn't lost on Mitch. "You thought I planned to spend the night?"

"I hoped, I guess."

It was worse than she thought. "Are there clean sheets on the guest bed?"

"There are clean sheets on *every* bed."

Mitch didn't want to venture a guess on what exactly she meant by this, so she stayed in safe territory. "You always were a great housekeeper."

"Oh, gee, thanks," Lisa was only driving about fifteen miles per hour over the speed limit. Down from her usual twenty. No wonder Mary had to hold down a job. The speeding fines alone had to be a fiscal burden.

"You can slow down anytime."

"At least you didn't ask me where the fire was," Lisa remarked and then eased up on the accelerator.

"Am I the only person you can take your anger out on?" Mitch asked gently. It had only taken what, two years for this to dawn on her?

"No, but Mary's sick and tired of it and you're fresh meat."

"I've been called worse…"

Lisa abruptly turned into a parking lot.

"Where are we?" Mitch asked.

"You *are* buying me breakfast, aren't you?"

"As usual."

They went in and got a corner booth. Lisa didn't even crack open the oversized plastic menu. Apparently she had it memorized. A waitress appeared with a jug of coffee and two cups. They must have looked thirsty.

"You know what you want yet?" she asked as she clunked down the cups and filled them to the brim.

"I want the Super Duper Special Wheshall Breakfast." Lisa rattled off her choice.

Mitch found it on the menu. It took two paragraphs to describe it.

"How 'bout you, Hon?"

Mitch loved it when waitresses called her, "Hon."

"I'll have dry toast."

"White, wheat, sourdough, or rye?"

Gee, Lisa didn't have to answer any multiple-choice questions! "Wheat."

The waitress took off like she was shot out of a cannon. They apparently needed a lot of time in the kitchen to cook everything Lisa had ordered. Like, a week.

"Dry toast?" Lisa asked.

Mitch looked at her. In spite of all her scars, she was still able to arch her eyebrow like a movie star.

"God, you're beautiful," Mitch said before her brain told her to shut up.

"Flatter me all you want. You're still picking up the check."

"It's not flattery if it's true," Mitch persisted.

"Does Rebecca know you talk to other women this way?"

"She knows I tell the truth to people."

Lisa turned quiet but there was just a hint of a smile. If Mitch could have touched her face without drawing stares, she would have. But instead, she sat on her hands and asked, "What's going on at home?"

"Nothing."

"You mean that literally, don't you?"

"Yeah."

So much for the hint of a smile.

"Have you thought about therapy?"

"Sex therapy?"

"I was thinking about plain old therapy. You know, where people sit around and discuss things."

"Like, for instance, 'why don't you think I'm hot in bed anymore' types of things?"

"That would certainly get a discussion going."

"No, it wouldn't. You want to know why?" Lisa didn't wait to see if Mitch wanted to know why. She barreled on, "Because what can Mary say other than 'all those gruesome scars are a big turnoff.'"

"Did she say that?"

"She doesn't have to. It's obvious. Alright?"

Mitch didn't have an intelligent reply. She couldn't think of one appropriate thing to say. Here she was, sitting on her hands so they didn't get her into trouble and now her mouth had finally disconnected from her brain about two minutes too late and it was still before breakfast, Lisa Standard Time. Where was that dry toast anyway? Mitch reached to get a drink of coffee. Lisa reached over and put her hand on Mitch's forearm. The soft underpart that is so very, very sensitive.

"I guess I still know how to stop a conversation in its tracks."

"You do get to the point."

"I'm sorry," Lisa said as she ran just one finger up and down Mitch's arm. What hadn't gone numb started to tingle.

"There's nothing to be sorry about. Everybody needs someone in their life who they can get right to the point with. It's just that most people have Dr. Phil."

"And I have you. Instead of Mary."

"Maybe Mary just needs more time."

"And what do I do in the meantime? Learn to knit?"

"Is that something you want to do?"

"No. I just thought you could use a new sweater."

Mitch smiled. She had a drawer full of sweaters and Lisa knew it. The other thing that Lisa knew was that every time she rubbed Mitch's forearm, goosebumps ensued.

64

"How are you going to eat your toast sitting on your hands?"

"I figured you'd hand feed me."

"It wouldn't be the first time."

Mitch surrendered and took hold of Lisa's hand in both of hers. At least the goosebumps would now subside. She looked steadily into Lisa's eyes and said in an even voice, "I want with all my heart for you and Mary to work this out."

Without hesitation, Lisa replied, "So do I."

As if on cue, breakfast arrived. That was fast. Mitch's toast was on a small bread plate. Lisa's feast came on three platters. Good thing they had that corner booth after all. They needed the table space. But it was all really just for show. Everything could've fit on one plate. Especially if mom was doing the dishes.

"You got enough to eat?" Lisa asked.

"I was about to ask you the same thing."

"I'll share. What do you want?"

"I'm fine for now."

Mitch wasn't kidding. Between having a quick breakfast before she left home and forming a knot of concern in her stomach for Lisa and Mary, there wasn't much room left. Dry toast was the perfect prescription. Lisa was a fast eater and they were on the road again in twenty minutes.

"Where do you want to go next?"

"Let's get the banking over with."

Lisa actually drove the speed limit for a change. Maybe it was so Mitch could fill out the check. There were so many zeros and so little time.

"How many millions do you want?" Mitch asked, pen poised.

"You're kidding, right?"

"Within reason. Would one-million tide you over or do you think you need two?"

"I don't think we need more than a couple thousand."

"Okay. One million for starters."

People may come and people may go, but bank presidents never forget their millionaire customers. Although Mitch tried to transfer the funds in the relative anonymity of the teller's line, she soon found herself and Lisa in *his* office partaking of still more coffee. Except that his brew tasted like battery acid and was having a similar effect on Mitch's stomach. After chatting about nothing in particular for ten minutes while clerks took care of the paperwork, he was confident that most of the money was staying put. Lisa would be doing good to spend the interest. Frittering away the principal would take a bit more effort.

"Don't spend it all in one place," was his banal parting comment. Lisa smiled back. He spilled the rest of his coffee on his eight-hundred dollar suit. When they got in the car, Mitch looked over at Lisa and said, "You've still got it."

Lisa looked back. "Oh, hush."

"Where are we going next?" Mitch was the passenger after all.

"I guess it's too early for lunch."

"When was the last time you saw Trish?"

"Not since the baby came."

"Let's give her a call. See if she needs anything."

Trish needed something alright. She needed a hug from Mitch and a hug from Lisa. And then, she just needed to hold on to Mitch's arm for a moment. It was almost a cling.

"When you called, I thought it was from Kansas. What are you doing back in town?"

"Oh, I just came to take care of some paperwork. Lisa's been good enough to chauffeur me around."

"Have you had breakfast?"

"Twice," Mitch assured her.

"That explains the dry toast," Lisa remarked.

"Reb stuffed a healthy portion of oatmeal down me before my flight."

"I'm glad I wasn't around to see that," Lisa murmured as Trish still held onto Mitch for dear life.

"But, you'll have lunch with us, won't you?"

"As long as it's not in five minutes."

"It's not. Not even close. It might be a while in fact. Max and Rose are running errands. Silver, too."

"And is Robbie awake this time?"

As Mitch asked the question, she felt Trish's grip tighten on her arm. A lot like one of those blood pressure cuffs that tighten and tighten to the point where you think your fingers are going to pop.

"Let me check," Trish let go so that blood could flow back to Mitch's heart. When she was out of earshot, Lisa said, "She sure had a death grip on you, huh?"

Mitch flexed her hand. Lisa followed up, "Almost cut off the circulation entirely?"

Mitch just shook her head, a signal to drop the subject. She wandered into the kitchen, followed closely by Lisa.

"Shouldn't we wait in the foyer?"

"Why? You want to have some more coffee? Try and break a world's record or something?"

"Okay. Sure."

For it not being her idea, Lisa now happily made herself at home on one of the kitchen stools parked next to the breakfast island. Mitch poured. They waited in silence so thick they could hear each other swallow. Trish found them like there was never any doubt where they had meandered.

"Good news! Robbie's awake and ready for company."

"You go," Lisa waved them off.

"Not coming?" Trish asked.

"Only two visitors at a time."

"This isn't a hospital."

"Yeah, but they make those rules for a reason. Pour me another cup of coffee and I'll wait here."

Mitch complied, refilling Lisa's coffee cup before following Trish to the hallway. Trish wanted to talk first before going to see Robbie.

"What's up with Lisa?"

"What do you mean?"

"Why is she really staying behind?"

"She's still really edgy about her scars."

"She doesn't need to be. They are nearly invisible."

"That's easy for us to say, isn't it?"

Trish nodded like she finally understood but still wasn't finished.

"Do you always do everything Lisa tells you to do?"

"Like what?" Mitch was puzzled.

"Like serving coffee."

"Hey, if all Lisa asks me to do is refill her coffee cup, it's a good day."

Mitch considered the subject closed. Trish knew better than to continue the questioning. She led the way to Robbie's room.

Two things were immediately evident to Mitch. The first was that Robbie had made a great effort to appear cheerful and happy. The second was that it wasn't a successful effort. Not deep down anyway. Past the smile, there was no twinkle in Robbie's eyes. Mitch knew what twinkles looked like after living with Reb all these years. She went over and perched on the side of the bed.

"How are you doing, Mom?"

"I'm fine. How is the Senator?"

Robbie usually referred to Reb as the Senator. And always asked about her. Always.

"Reb's sister is very ill. So Reb is going through a lot right now."

"And I'm sure you're being a pillar of strength for her as always."

"Actually, I'm probably doing my best to distract her."

"I'm sure that's what she needs."

"And as long as I'm in town, what can I get for you that you might be needing?"

"I have everything I need right here."

Mitch looked over at Trish, who was smiling like they had both already submerged all their true fears deep into the part of the brain reserved for just such monsters.

"Do I get to see the wonderful Josh?"

"I'll go see if he's awake," Trish was more than happy to be useful.

The saints be praised, he was awake. And hungry. He was a boy, after all. Anybody ever see a boy who wasn't hungry? Mitch moved to the side of the room while Robbie and Trish arranged for feeding time. And since she was no longer being paid attention to, she moved clear out into the hall as long as she was moving. Trish found her after a few moments.

"Are you okay?"

"Oh, I'm fine. I just didn't want to get in the middle of such a private matter."

"When he gets done, I'll bring him out so you can hold him."

"I look forward to being burped upon. Meanwhile, I'm going to go back to the kitchen. See if there's any more coffee to be poured."

Mitch was all ready to file a report with Lisa, but when she got back to the kitchen, it was empty. Leave it to Lisa to break her promise to sit still. With all the coffee consumed, she was probably availing herself of the facilities. For that, she would be excused. In fact, it didn't sound like such a bad idea. Mitch found her way to the bathroom and discovered it to be unoccupied. She didn't think twice about it and took a turn. By the time she got back to the kitchen, Trish had reappeared, but she didn't have Josh with her.

"How's it going?" Mitch asked generically.

"Slowly. Sometimes, it takes a while for feeding."

"I imagine so," Mitch said even though she had no idea at all about feeding babies.

"And then, he'll probably need a change."

"Oh, sure. I get that part entirely."

"He's going to the doctor's tomorrow."

"What for?"

"Routine checkup."

"Why doesn't the doctor come here?"

"We have to get Robbie out of bed somehow."

"You know, if something like this had happened to me, I'd be tempted to spin myself into the tightest cocoon imaginable. For a long, long time."

"Except that somebody's got to interact with the real world."

"And so it's good that she has you."

"I'm just worried."

"Is she bonding with Josh?"

"Oh, yeah, that's going fine."

"So, don't worry about anything else right now. Robbie is doing what she needs to do to be the best mother she can be."

"You're right as usual."

"Of course I am. I guess Lisa and Robbie are having a nice talk."

"Lisa's not up with Robbie."

"You didn't send her up?"

"I haven't seen her since you refilled her coffee cup."

"Me neither. Where could she have gotten off to?"

"The bathroom?"

"I was there."

"The other bathroom?"

"Should we check?"

"And then, there's the other bathroom…"

"I'm not even going to ask how many bathrooms this castle has."

"Not as many as you think. It's all retrofit."

"Another term for 'there used to be an outhouse?'"

"Something like that."

"Even if she's in the bathroom, it's taking a while. I hope she's okay."

"Why wouldn't she be?"

"You didn't see what she had for breakfast."

"I'll check the house. You wait here."

Maybe it was because when they were passing out the patience DNA, Mitch was out taking a walk, but the words, "You wait here" just didn't sink in. Mitch figured that if Trish was searching the main floor and upstairs, she could handle the basement. She remembered the way from the last time she had descended into the cellar. It took about ten seconds to find the closed door and one second to open it up. And there was Lisa, sitting on the floor, knees drawn up to chin, tears streaming down her face. Mitch went over and gingerly sat next to her.

"You okay?" Mitch asked.

Lisa didn't stir at all. By now, Trish had figured things out and appeared in the doorway not looking so steady herself.

"What the hell?" Trish asked no one in particular.

"What the hell what?" Mitch replied as she kept focused on Lisa. She was staring straight ahead now and the tears had subsided.

"What happened?" Trish asked Mitch directly.

"I came down here and found Lisa like this."

"Where was this door?"

"Where it is right now. Except it was shut. I thought you were going to take it off?"

"I did. Twice. At least."

The answer didn't register with Mitch because Lisa had now turned to her and grabbed hold of her like she needed a lift out of quicksand. Mitch held her like a child and soothed her. "It's okay. I've got you. You're okay. You are, aren't you?"

Lisa finally focused her eyes on Mitch. "What happened?"

"We were hoping you could tell us?" Mitch replied calmly.

Lisa looked over at Trish, who wouldn't come in the room but instead stood wary guard by the door.

"I don't know what happened," she said like already no one was believing her. And then, she clung even more tightly to Mitch. They were going to need the proverbial crowbar to get them apart at this rate.

"You don't remember coming down here?"

"Where am I anyway?" she asked in return.

"You're in Trish's basement."

"I'm in the haunted room, aren't I?"

"The haunted room?" Mitch queried like she was in the dark about the subject even though she had secretly known about this possibility all along.

"Yeah. The room where Max and Rose got locked in at your wedding."

"And the door is back on its hinges," Trish was standing there just watching it like it was going to jump off and start dancing around.

Mitch studied Lisa's face. She was looking more normal now but her face was still wet from tears. Mitch wiped some of the moisture away with her thumbs and asked, "Are you ready to go back upstairs?"

Lisa nodded and allowed Mitch to help her up since she still hadn't quite found the strong part of her knees. Mitch could feel her shaking, but didn't broadcast the news. As they passed Trish, Mitch inquired, "You coming?"

"You bet."

They got back to the kitchen about the time that Rose, Max and Silver returned from their errands. Rose immediately realized that something was wrong and helped get Lisa to the couch.

"Do you want us to call a doctor, Honey?" she asked as she rearranged pillows and patted her hand.

"No, I'm going to be okay."

"I'll make you some soup."

"I don't want you to go to any trouble."

"It's no bother. We have that kind that you microwave."
Rose gave a motherly smile to Lisa, and then the "look" to Mitch as she went to the kitchen. Mitch gave it two beats and then adjourned to the kitchen as well. The meeting was called to order as Rose prepared to make instant chicken noodle soup. "Is your friend pregnant?" she asked with her usual candor.
"I'm sure she isn't."
"How sure?"
"Very sure."
"Well then, if she's not with child, what happened?"
"She was downstairs, in *that* room."
Rose was, if possible, even more alert now. "*The* room?"
"Right."
"But you can't get stuck in *that room* anymore."
"Why not?"
"Because we had the door taken off."
"Trish said something about that."
"Said something?"
"The door was on the hinges. I opened it up myself."
"You watch the soup. I'll be right back," Rose headed for the basement stairs.
Mitch gave watching the soup about half a second of consideration and then trailed after Rose. They regrouped in silence at the site of the door on the hinges like it was the eighth wonder of the modern world.
"I've already called 911 once about this door," Rose muttered.
"What did it do? Fall off and hit somebody?"
"It didn't have to. It doesn't need to. You've seen what it can do."
"First hand. But why did you call 911?" Mitch pressed for an answer.
"Trish nearly passed out."
"Because of the door?"
"It won't stay off its hinges."
"It won't what?"
"You heard me."
"Yes, I did."
"But then, it was off the hinges when Trish said it was on and that's when we called 911."

Mitch was going to need a scorecard, she could tell already.
"Let's go upstairs and check on that soup."
"Right. Let's go check on the soup," Rose repeated like it was a mantra.
Max had taken care of the soup already. He was a wonderful soul. Lisa was sitting up and sipping the broth politely. Trish, Max reported, was up checking on Robbie and Josh. Things were usual in the house that had a misbehaving door. And a room that could evoke tears from the strongest of people. Which is how Mitch had always characterized Lisa. She sat down next to her.
"Are you feeling better?"
"Uh huh."
Mitch wasn't totally convinced and took her hand to see if she had stopped shaking and resumed normal pulse.
"Are you a doctor now?"
"It's either me or 911."
"Then, I choose you. 911 is for real emergencies. And besides, you're cuter."
"Do you remember what happened yet?"
"It's still just a blur."
"That's okay. Just sit and relax."
It was a prescription that wasn't easy to follow. People were staring at her and who could relax with that going on. "Could we maybe head home? To my home I mean. I think I'd rest better there."
"Of course. You're okay to travel?"
"Absolutely."
They waited a few minutes for Trish to finish her parenting duties and then said their good-byes.
"Will you be able to stop by again before you leave town?" she asked.
If there was a conspiracy to keep Mitch in town overnight, it had hatched relatively quickly. "If I can."
Mitch took over the driving and actually obeyed the speed limits all the way to Lisa and Mary's house. Mary was still at work, which maybe was all for the best. Mitch got Lisa upstairs and into bed. And not the way it sounds.

"Join me, for a minute," Lisa requested as only one old lover can request from another.

"Excuse me?" Mitch wanted to clarify.

"You can stay on top of the covers. Just stay close for a minute so I can try and tell you what happened."

"Oh, okay."

Mitch arranged herself comfortably on top of the covers as instructed and waited for Lisa to debrief.

"There's something very strange going on at Trish's house. Isn't there?" Lisa made eye contact with Mitch.

"There seems to be."

"What is it?"

"I thought you were going to tell me what happened."

"I'm going to just as soon as you come clean on what you haven't told me."

"I didn't know much more than you did until today."

"Something weird happened at your wedding."

"That's putting it mildly."

"I mean about the room!"

"Right. Max and Rose got stuck in the room. You knew that happened."

"And then, what has happened since?"

Mitch crinkled up her eyes so she could think more clearly. "I remember Trish getting stuck down there. I called one day and Rose told me about it and then when I went to the house, Trish went down and we talked about taking the door off the hinges. And then, that's the last I heard until today when Rose informed me that they had taken the door off its hinges. At least twice already."

"And it keeps what? Getting back on its hinges?"

"I would've found out more, but you needed to come home."

If it sounded like a rebuke, the care in Mitch's voice softened the effect.

"You just couldn't wait to get me home and into bed. Just like old times."

"Yeah, that's it."

And then, Lisa began to cry. Again. Mitch scoured her memory for a time when Lisa had ever cried twice in one day. It was a rare occurrence. Rather than tell her that everything was going

74

to be okay and that she should hush, Mitch held her and let her
know just by actions that it was okay to keep this up as long as it
was necessary. Crying females were her specialty. When Lisa
was finished with the emotional release, she relaxed and fell
asleep. It was now time for Mitch to go downstairs and await the
other half of the household. Mary was on time.
"Hello!" she was pleased to see Mitch. Maybe she was pleased
to see anyone other than Lisa. "Where's Lisa?"
"Upstairs. In bed. Asleep."
"Really? That's not like her. Doesn't she feel well?"
Somehow, this patter didn't sound like there was any discord.
Mary wasn't the kind that could hide her feelings so perfectly.
"She had an episode today."
"Oh no. Did someone point at her scars or something?"
"No. Why?"
"It happens once in a while and it really upsets her."
"Can't blame her for that, can we."
"Not in the least. So, are you staying the night? I'm sure the
guest room is clean."
"Oh, gee, I'd better call your mom. I haven't checked in with
her yet today. And if things are going fine there, I can stick
around for another day."
"What about your airline ticket?"
"I flew one way."
"Okay. Well, I'm going to go upstairs and check on Lisa. By
the way, what did happen to her?"
"That's a good question."
"What does that mean?"
"It means that we don't know what happened to Lisa. She's not
by any stretch of the imagination pregnant, is she?"
"Pregnant? Why on earth would you ask that?"
"It was someone else's idea. Not mine. But she's acting like it."
"What do you act like when you're pregnant?"
"You cry a lot."
"But, Lisa doesn't cry a lot."
"Why don't you go up and see what you can find out. And then
I'll tell you the rest of the story."
"There's more?"

"There's more. Go on up to her. I'll be here when you get back."

Mary went upstairs as Mitch dialed Reb's cell phone number. She picked it up on the first ring.

"Hello?"

"Hi, it's me."

"Hi, Me."

"How are you and BeBe doing?"

"Are you coming home tonight?"

"Do you need me? I can still get home."

"You're not at the airport?"

"I'm at Mary's."

"Still?"

"Yeah. There was an incident at Trish's house today."

"Are you staying there?"

"Mary and Lisa have invited me to spend the night."

"And you'll come home first thing in the morning?"

"First thing."

"Very first thing?"

"I'd be there right now if there hadn't been this complication."

"What's going on?"

"I think Trish's house is really haunted."

"Okay. Now, tell me the real reason you're staying over."

"That is the real reason."

There was a pause at the other end of the line. It was the length of pause you used to get from your teacher when you told her the dog ate your homework. Finally, she spoke, "I'll see you first thing tomorrow morning."

"I'll be there."

And then, Reb hung up. She never was one for long good-byes. Mitch got about two seconds to breathe and then Mary was back and demanding answers.

"What is going on?"

"I don't suppose I could have a glass of wine or something?"

"We have pop."

"White or red?"

"Huh?"

"I'll take whatever you have."

"Sit over there and I'll get it and then I want some answers."

Mitch obeyed like the nice houseguest that she was but was beginning to think that she should've gotten a hotel room for the night. Mary was back with a glass of ice and a can of diet cola. She poured it, handed it over and then sat down to wait for all the answers.

"I don't exactly know what happened today," Mitch began simply.

"Neither does Lisa. She won't talk about it."

"That's because she really doesn't have a clue what happened."

"Why don't you just tell me what you saw."

"We were over at Trish's and I found Lisa in the room downstairs that has the door that sticks. And she was in some sort of trance and was crying."

"About what?"

"We don't know and she had no idea how she even got down to the room."

"Was she upset that she couldn't get out?"

"I'm not sure she even tried. And then Trish got real unsteady because apparently, she's had the door taken off the hinges a couple of times and it just keeps getting back on the hinges."

"You're not making any sense at all."

"I know. And I wanted to talk more to Trish, but I thought it was best to bring Lisa home as soon as possible. I figured that you would be the logical person to help her."

"Help her how?"

"I don't know. I haven't figured that part out yet. I guess I just thought that if anyone would know why Lisa was crying, it might be you?"

It all sounded so logical when Mitch said it, but the underlying nuance was dawning on Mary.

"You think that she's crying because of me?"

"I didn't say that."

"But you implied it."

"She's either crying because of you or because of the ghost that's haunting Trish's house. Which answer do you think we need to pursue?"

"You've finally gone off the deep end, haven't you?" Mary asked Mitch but it was Lisa who answered. She had come quietly down the stairs and heard the last remark.

"No, she hasn't gone off the deep end. If anyone has gone off the deep end, it's me."

Mary stood up and went to Lisa. "Why don't you come over and sit down."

"I'm cold."

"I'll bring your robe and slippers."

"Mitch can do that. Just sit with me."

Mary checked with Mitch. She would find the necessary garments in the closet. No problem there. When she returned with the items, Mary went off to make tea.

"What you need is a straight shot of brandy," Mitch suggested.

"We don't seem to have any in inventory."

"I noticed. What did you do? Join the Temperance movement?"

"It's just that I was on so much medication for a while that we got out of the habit of medicating ourselves the liquid way."

"As soon as Mary gets back with the tea, I'm going to call Trish and get the straight story on the door to that room. None of us has gone off any deep ends. I just need to find out if we're dealing with a prankster or something a little less explainable."

"You think it's a ghost."

"I don't know what to think."

"You think it's a ghost," Lisa repeated. She knew what Mitch was always thinking. Why did they even communicate through speech? Mitch just looked at Lisa.

"It would be helpful if you could remember anything that happened."

"I just remember being very sad after you took hold of me."

"You don't remember going downstairs?"

Lisa closed her eyes to think more intently. "I remember hearing a noise."

"A noise like what?"

"I don't remember."

"Did you see anything?"

"You mean like somebody running around in a white sheet?"

"Okay, so you didn't see anything. How about smell. Did you smell anything?"

"Salt water."

"Salt water?"

"That's what you smell when you cry," Lisa explained it like Mitch was *the* most dense human being on the planet.

"Oh," was all *the* most dense human being on the planet could think to say.

"Why all the questions?"

"Because I want to know what to look for when I go back over there tonight."

"You're going back tonight? Why?"

"It's the only time I have. I'm due back in Kansas tomorrow."

"Just in case anybody ever wants to know…"

"What?"

"You don't look good on a short leash."

Mitch took the comment in stride. Mitch took a lot of comments in stride lately. One more wouldn't hurt. Besides, Mary reappeared with tea so it was time to call Trish. One nice thing about friends was that you could invite yourself over, sometimes for the night.

"Can I borrow a car?" Mitch asked and then looked from Mary to Lisa.

"After what you did today, you can *have* my car," Lisa said.

You didn't need to be psychic to know that only two out of three of the people present in the room knew what Lisa meant by that. Mitch, when weighing her options of sleeping here or in a haunted house, was actually relieved to be choosing the haunted house.

"You probably still have the keys," Lisa stated.

"I do. But I'll still need a ride to the airport."

"Why don't you catch a cab from Trish's? We'll arrange to get the car later," Mary suggested.

"Are you sure it's no trouble?"

"None at all."

Mary seemed to like the idea of Lisa not having ready access to a car. Mitch knew from experience that that wouldn't last long. There would be a shiny new SUV in the driveway by tomorrow afternoon. She said her good-byes and headed back across town. Her plan was simple. She was going to spend the night in the haunted room in Trish's basement to see if she could shed any light on recent spooky events. It took five minutes of explaining and another fifteen minutes of convincing before Trish and family agreed. They spent an otherwise quiet evening together and then Mitch headed for the basement with a sleeping bag, a spare blanket and two pillows. She settled in for the night and found herself contemplating her life rather than sleeping. Here she was, one of the richest women in the state, stretched out on a hard concrete floor, waiting for a specter to appear. She closed her eyes to concentrate on any weird sounds that might be audible and the next thing she knew, Trish was at the doorway.

"What?" Mitch asked.

"I said, what do you want for breakfast?"

"What time is it?"

"Ten."

"Ten! Ten in the morning ten?"

"We let you sleep. We didn't know if you had that much."

"That's all I did."

"Did you discover anything?"

"I discovered that if somebody could invent a softer brand of concrete, they'd make a fortune."

"Reb called."

"I imagine so. Am I in big trouble?"

"I guess you'd have to define 'big' before I could answer," Trish said with a hint of a smile.

"Give me a hand up."

"No way," Trish stood her ground at the doorway.

"Why not?"

"I make it a habit to not come in this room. If I can help it."

"You're afraid of getting stuck in here again?"

"Yes."

"Come and sit next to me. If we get stuck in here, they'll come and find us. Eventually."

Trish gave this the kind of consideration that nations reserve for treaties. "Okay."

She came forward and sat on the sleeping bag next to Mitch.

"Lisa has no idea what happened to her yesterday. But she sure had a strong reaction."

"I didn't have the reaction that Lisa had."

"I think that for whatever reason, your ghost has figured out the people who can help him or her and you and Lisa must be the ones. I want you to do something for me."

"Uh oh."

"And the only reason that you have to do this is because the ghost lives in your house."

"Are you even listening to yourself?"

"I was down here all night and nothing happened and you walk in and sit down and the door shuts."

Trish looked over and groaned audibly. "Not again." She got up and tried the door. It wouldn't budge.

"So, here's what you need to do," Mitch went on like doors shut tight were just all part of her story. "You and Lisa need to research the previous owners of the house to see why there might be a haunting."

"You sat here and watched the door shut and said nothing?"

"The ghost is trying to give us a message. I think the least we can do is try to figure it out."

"What kind of message do you send with doors that shut?"

"Or maybe," Mitch intoned, "what kind of message do you send with doors that won't open?"

"You know this isn't going to be easy."

"Why?"

"Well, I never met the Livermores when I bought the house. I'm not sure any of them are still alive?"

"Who did you buy the house from? I mean, who showed up to the closing?"

"A lawyer."

"It's a place to start."

"You want me to-"

"You and Lisa."

"You want me and Lisa to go to some lawyer's office and start asking if this is a haunted house?"

"Sounds like a plan to me."

"And then what?"

"See where it leads?"

"I have things to do around here as it is. I don't need to go inventing extra work."

"I have two thoughts about that."

"Two?"

"First off, you can use Lisa for most of the work. Mary has a job. Lisa needs to do something with her free time besides sitting around the house looking at her scars in the mirror. And since she's most strongly affected by the haunting, she'll be a great resource."

"Was that all number one?"

"Yeah."

"So, what's number two?"

"It's your door. And your house. And by virtue of those two facts, your ghost. Isn't that enough incentive to do at least a little digging?"

Trish thought this over for a second. "Okay. I'll do a little investigating and I'll even include Lisa in the process. But I'm not going to do a doctoral thesis on the subject."

"I don't think it's going to take that much effort. I mean, how many skeletons could possibly be buried in one family?"

"Literally or figuratively?"

"Just go and try the door again."

"Why?"

"Just try it."

Trish got up and went over to the door. She turned the knob and it opened like there was grease on the hinges. She looked back over at Mitch. If she thought for even one second that Mitch had stayed up all night jerry-rigging the door, she kept her opinion to herself.

"I guess the ghost likes the plan?" Mitch mused.

"You think it's been listening in?"

"It probably had its ear to the keyhole all along."

"Should I check for ghost earwax marks?"

"I'd leave that until after breakfast."

"I've already eaten."

"Yeah, but I haven't."

Chapter 8

Mitch was back in Kansas before dinner time. She had missed her morning deadline and wondered if anyone would even notice. When she walked into the hospital room, Reb did zero to sixty to greet her. Mitch bent down to kiss Reb hello, and an audible groan emanated from Aunt BeBe's general direction.

"*Must* you do that in front of normal people?"

They made it a quick one. For the sake of the homophobic in the audience.

"Hello, Aunt BeBe," Mitch greeted like she hadn't even heard the admonition. "How are you feeling?"

"You haven't been gone long enough for there to be any change. Pity about that."

Mitch didn't feel like pointing out that it was maybe good news that there hadn't been a change for the worse. Those changes would come soon enough.

"Have you had dinner?" Reb asked like she needed an excuse to vacate the room. For about a week.

Mitch had snacked all day. "I'm starved," she lied.

Reb knew a lie when she heard it, but this fell into that famous category of white ones that we tell each other.

"I'll buy you dinner."

"Wonderful! Can we bring you back anything?" Mitch asked BeBe.

"Of course not!" she answered like anything that Mitch brought back for her to eat would be infested with gay cooties. Intentionally.

"Not even a nice big juicy steak?"

"No! Thank you!"

"Don't you like steak?"

"Of course I do! I'm not one of those freak acid-head vegetarians!"

"How about some chocolate cake?"

"I've had my dinner!"

"Okay, well if you change your mind, just call us on the cell phone," Reb said as she herded Mitch out of the room.

When they were safely on the elevator, Mitch asked, "Has it been this way all day?"

"It's been a day," was all that Reb would say on that subject.
"What took you so long?" was what she really wanted to talk about.
"A ghost."
"You mentioned some nonsense about that over the phone. What's the real reason?"
"That is the real reason. Trish has something very peculiar going on at her house and I think it's a haunting of some sort."
"You can't be serious about this?"
"I don't have a choice in the matter. I've seen things I can't explain, and so has Trish and so has Lisa. Well, except that Lisa hasn't actually seen anything."
"What do you mean?"
"Lisa is more along the lines of being affected by this ghost."
They arrived at their designated floor and got out of the elevator without further conversation. Until they got in the car.
"Where are you taking me for dinner?"
"How about The House of Steak?" Reb deadpanned.
"Have I been that bad?" Mitch teased back.
"You are serious about this ghost thing?"
"I'll tell you all about it over dinner."
They drove to the best effort that Utopia made toward a healthy restaurant. There was a chain restaurant on Third Street that had a decent salad bar and fresh vegetables. Although Mitch had snacked, she ate like this was the first food she'd seen since breakfast.
"You're on your third helping of broccoli and you haven't told me your ghost story yet."
"You remember Max and Rose getting stuck in the basement on our wedding day."
"Yes."
"Well, this room has a way of taking prisoners. Trish got stuck down there and Lisa got stuck down there and then Trish got stuck down there again when I was actually there with her."
"So, why don't they just take the door off the hinges?"
"They already have. Two or three times. It keeps reattaching itself somehow."
Reb didn't say anything. She didn't have to. The expression on her face said it all.

"I'm not kidding." Mitch insisted. "Call Trish if you don't believe me. She's had workers out there twice already."

"To do what?"

"They take the door off the hinges and, poof, it's back up. Trish turned so pale over it all that Rose called 911. And you know how unflappable Rose is."

"And in the meantime, how is the baby?"

"Josh is fine. Robbie is going through a case of post-partum depression that might make the Guinness Book of World Records."

"That doesn't sound good."

"So, that's why I told Trish to use Lisa for all the work in tracking down the ghost."

"You said that Lisa hadn't actually seen anything but that she was affected somehow?"

"You really do listen to everything I say, don't you?"

"You had doubts about that?"

"I wouldn't call them doubts, exactly. It's just that I say so much…"

"So, what about Lisa?" Reb was persistent.

"She went into some sort of crying trance."

"Did you have enough Kleenex?"

"I didn't have any. She wiped her nose on my shirt. Remind me to do laundry when we get back to the hotel."

"It's good to have you back."

"It's good to be back."

"So, nobody's actually seen this alleged ghost?"

"Max and Rose saw it a while back. At least, they saw a young woman in a white silk blouse. But it didn't look like your typical ghost, if that's what you mean."

"What does the typical ghost look like?"

"Well, from my freak, acid-head vegetarian point of view, I'd say it would resemble an almost transparent white floating apparition."

"You listen to everything Aunt BeBe says?"

"You had doubts about that?"

"It's just that she says so much…"

"I got back as fast as I could. I really did."

"I know you did."

"Is there anything new with Aunt BeBe? Since she wouldn't answer me, I thought I'd better check with you."

"Not really. I don't expect changes overnight."

"I guess I don't either. Cancer is an incremental killer."

Reb just nodded. Mitch didn't feel like dessert, and there were no vegan selections on the menu where they were concerned anyway, so they paid the check and went back to the hospital to tuck Aunt BeBe in for the night. Maybe Mitch was beginning to become psychic. She could sense that BeBe was checking them for some sort of doggie bag offering. Mitch remembered that Rose had stuck a bag of chocolate chip cookies in her coat pocket before she left, as if going back to Kansas was the equivalent of an Arctic expedition.

"I have some cookies for you, BeBe," Mitch said like it was no big deal.

"What kind?"

"Chocolate chip."

"They had cookies for dessert at the restaurant?" BeBe the Skeptical asked.

"No. These were made by a wonderful lady in Denver. I can leave them here for you."

"Well, maybe I'll feed them to the nurses," BeBe sniffed.

At least it wasn't a "No." They were making progress.

Reb and BeBe got tomorrow's schedule clear between them and then it was time to go.

"I bet she has chocolate on her breath in ten minutes," Mitch said as they headed down the hallway.

"My guess is five. The night shift isn't going to know that those cookies even existed."

For some reason, this made Mitch smile. At least one effort of kindness had paid off. And she had Rose to thank for it. They were all the way home and in bed before they talked about the rest of Mitch's trip.

"How did Mary look?"

"She looked great. What little I got to see of her."

"And Lisa was okay except when she's under the influence of ghosts?"

"I wonder when they're going to talk about the million?"

"You gave them a million dollars and you don't know if they've talked about it yet?"

"I'm not sure Mary knew that the money was why I was there in the first place."

"Hopefully, Lisa will know the best time to break that news."

"Lisa knows everything. Except why ghosts make her cry."

"I never knew you believed in ghosts."

"I never knew you didn't."

"You think there are ghosts?"

"How many religions believe in spirits? Or angels? Or invisible omnipotent beings?"

"A lot."

"So, why is believing in ghosts such a leap of faith?"

"I guess because ghosts are considered to be children's stories."

"Then I guess I'm just a child at heart."

"You're going to need to be to put up with BeBe's sour temper."

"Oh, that's not so bad. If I need to go in armed every day with cookies, I'll do so. Besides, all these prom stories are interesting."

"We are past the prom stories. We are never going back to the prom stories."

"You mean, I don't get to tell about my prom?"

"If you want to tell Aunt BeBe about your prom, you go right ahead."

"As soon as I make up the story, I'll tell it to her."

"You're going to make something up?"

"Of course! The truth would be too boring. And Lord knows, we don't need to be telling Aunt BeBe any boring stories. Time's too precious for that!"

"If you want to keep her entertained, try your ghost story on her."

"Good idea! I'll do that. First thing tomorrow."

Chapter 9

"You know, this wasn't my idea!" Lisa said to Mary.
It had been a tense evening. Mary had gone to work before Lisa
had a chance to explain everything about Mitch's trip to Denver.
Lisa had spent the better part of the day retrieving the car from
Trish's house and shopping for various items. Such as a wine-
rack full of drinkable vintages and groceries for the pantry. She
had been tempted to buy a new car as well, but fought the urge
and was feeling pretty good about her efforts overall. She had a
nice dinner fixed and a glass of wine ready for Mary when she
got home from work. It had looked too much like a bribe for
Mary not to notice, so she had started in on questions. That's
when Lisa dropped the bomb about the extra million or so in the
checking account.
"What do you mean, it wasn't your idea?"
"When your mom called and talked to you and you handed over
the phone, Mitch was already talking about flying out here with a
wallet full of cash to give to us."
"And you didn't think to say no?"
"I said no. But when did the word 'no' mean anything to
Mitch?"
"Maybe you didn't say it forcefully enough?"
Lisa took the phone off the cradle and handed it to Mary. "You
call and tell her no. I dare you."
And so, even before dinner, they were at a standoff. Mary
wouldn't call Mitch back to complain, but she wasn't in the
mood to let Lisa off the hook.
"You got the car back from Trish's house?"
"Trish came and got me. We needed to talk about things
anyway."
"Things?"
"We're going to some lawyer's office tomorrow to check up on
something."
"What something?"
"We are going to see if we can get a little more history on Trish's
house."
"Why would you need that?"

"If we're going to understand why the house is haunted, we're going to need to know more about the previous owners, aren't we?"

"I'm not sure I like this idea."

"Which part don't you like more? The part about hunting down a ghost? Or the part where I might find something constructive to do with my time?"

"There are plenty of ways that you can use your time constructively."

"Well, fixing a nice dinner for you isn't apparently one of them." Mary could've said about a dozen things in reply. She didn't. In fact, she didn't say anything for so long that Lisa was worried they might go the entire evening without speaking. Mary knew one thing for sure. Lisa was a woman with a need right now. The problem was that she just couldn't quite figure out what it was.

"First of all," Mary started with just a slight shake in her voice, "Fixing dinner is one of the most wonderful things you do for me. And if I haven't been as appreciative as I could be, and that's probably the case, I apologize for taking that and you for granted."

"You don't need to apologize," Lisa conceded. "I'm the one who should be apologizing."

"I have an idea. Let's stop apologizing to each other and talk about whatever it is that we need to be talking about."

"You start."

"Okay. I know that you don't want to reenter the job force anytime soon. I understand that. But before we go taking any more money from relatives, let me try and make a living for the both of us. It's not going to be easy and I'm sure I'll come home cranky from time to time, but that's just how life is sometimes. There are a lot of young kids where I work who'll stop at nothing to advance their own careers over mine. So if I seem distant or unappreciative at the end of the day, bear with me."

"I guess it's my turn."

"Only if you want it to be."

"I feel useless. And I guess I have for a long time. And then, whatever happened at Trish's house made it seem like I was the only one who had something unique happen to me. And if that's what Trish needs to solve her mystery, then I want to help. I know it sounds ridiculous, but I feel that I've been chosen for this."

"Like a conduit to the next world?"

Lisa looked over to see if Mary was teasing. She wasn't. "Something like that."

"Are you able to guarantee that it won't be dangerous?"

"It hasn't been so far. Have you ever heard of anybody being killed by the Livermore Ghost?"

"No. But I don't fancy the idea of you being locked up in a room for hours on end either."

"That's not going to happen. Trish and I are going to keep a timetable on the room so that no one is down there alone or without someone knowing about it."

"You are really going about this in a serious, logical way, aren't you?"

"Trish and I are world renowned for being serious and logical."

"Well, in the meantime, I want you to agree to one more thing."

"What's that?"

"The money you got from Mitch goes into an escrow account and we're not going to spend it. If we can't afford what we want on my salary, we'll just not spend the money."

Lisa didn't have her fingers crossed behind her back when she agreed to this, but if it was this important to Mary, the least she could do was to try and live by the bargain.

Chapter 10

"I have ten minutes." The lawyer made it known by both voice and body language that he didn't have all day.

In lawyer terms, that had to be what? Fifty dollars? A hundred? Trish got right to the point as well. "I'd like to meet with the people who I bought my house from. Can you give me an address and phone number?"

When Trish and Robbie had purchased the house, it was the lawyer who had transacted the paperwork. Trish hadn't thought much about it at the time, but now she was curious who the real seller was. She had simply assumed it was one of the Livermore's issue.

"I'm afraid that's confidential information."

"Are they the living relatives of the Livermore family?"

"That's confidential information."

So, how much had it cost so far to get nothing? Twenty-five bucks? About the cost of a good hangover.

"If you were me, how would you go about getting this information?"

"I couldn't say."

"Okay. Well, could you at least ask them to contact me?"

"I could ask. But if I were you, I wouldn't expect an answer."

"Thanks for your time. Send the bill to me."

"I will."

They were out in the hall in three minutes. Lisa, who had remained silent for fear of running the tab any higher, now said, "He's spookier than the ghost!"

"It was rather chilling, wasn't it?"

"And it doesn't make sense, either."

"What do you mean?"

"Well, I got the distinct impression that he was hiding something. And in a very sinister way. We went in there with an innocent request and came out with a lot of doubts. If he were my lawyer, I'd fire him."

"If he were my lawyer, I'd play poker with him. Win back some of my fee."

"Well, now what? This was a dead end."

"How about lunch?"

"Sure!" Lisa was never one to turn down a meal. One of these days, her arteries were going to explode or implode or do whatever arteries do when they've had too many high-fat meals. Since Trish had been good enough to drive, Lisa kept quiet about possible bistro destinations.

"What do you feel like eating?"

"Anything is fine, really."

"We might as well live it up. We don't get out very often anymore."

Trish chose a place that had a ten-page menu and seventeen varieties of cheesecake. Lisa was in seventh heaven. After narrowing down their choices, they settled on three entrees. One apiece and one to share. It was all terribly indulgent for two people who struck out their first attempt at bat.

"You know, we could go at this another way," Lisa said as she watched other people's entrees go by, wondering what they had ordered.

"How so?"

"I bet the Livermores are all over the history of Colorado. Maybe there's a book about them or at the very least, a book that mentions them."

"You mean something like, 'Old Mansions and the Old People who Own Them' kind of book?"

"Something like that."

"Can you do some checking and get together with me later in the week? Or the week after?"

"Sure. I'll start at the library tomorrow."

"That would be great. If it's convenient."

"If it isn't, I'll let you know."

"Good. I don't want this to turn into anything resembling a job."

"Heaven forbid," Lisa laughed.

They avoided the topic of haunted houses during lunch, knowing that they would be doing enough of that in the days to come. Instead, they exchanged casual information on the happenings in their respective households. Trish, having the most to report, did the most talking. A fact which dawned on her midway through a dessert of turtle cheesecake.

"You're an awfully good listener," Trish complimented.

"You're a good conversationalist," Lisa commented readily.

"I've gone on and on about motherhood. Or perhaps parenthood?"

"It was all fascinating, considering the circumstances."

"We're lucky to even have Josh," Trish reiterated the words like a mantra.

"What is the prognosis?" Lisa asked point blank, as usual.

"If he lives past the first year, a huge milestone in and of itself, then we can begin to think about prostheses."

"So, there's a lot that can be done?"

"If and when he's ready."

"You are so brave."

"And so late. I should be getting you home."

They parted ways at Lisa's house with the understanding that they would reschedule when necessary.

The next morning, Lisa was up and bustling around the house at the same time Mary was trying to get ready for work. They hadn't had this particular experience in quite a while and narrowly avoided colliding with each other as they fixed their independent breakfasts. Lisa made something substantial with ham, eggs and diced onions. Mary stuck to the Continental plan but managed to stretch things out so that she could have table time with Lisa.

"Are you going to be busy today?" Mary asked.

"I'm going to the library."

"Which one?"

"The big one downtown."

"Really? What are you looking for?"

"Any history on the Livermore Estate."

"Do you think there will be much?"

"I won't know until I look."

"How long will it take?"

"I don't know. Why?"

"I thought we could meet somewhere for lunch. Maybe?"

"That would work out."

"Okay," Mary nodded. It wasn't the enthusiastic response she had hoped for, but at least it was a yes. "Where do you want to meet?"

"How about I come by your office?"

"Sure. Come by about noon."

"Noon it is."

It would be the first time for Lisa to visit Mary's new place of employment. As the old saying goes, there's a first time for everything. After Mary left for work, Lisa took extra time applying makeup to her scars and dressing like a professional researcher. Even she had to admit that she looked pretty snazzy in navy blue pinstripes. She drove downtown cautiously, trying to behave herself where speed limits were concerned. It wasn't so much a fear of getting a ticket as it was a new-found respect for her mission. She felt important. And important people took good care of themselves.

Sometimes, cities do things right. When the new library was erected four years ago, plans were also made for adequate parking. The lot adjacent the library allowed for long-term parking at reasonable prices. It made doing long-term research all the more inviting. By the time she got to the front door, there was a mob of a crowd gathered as well, awaiting the opening of the doors. It took only a quick glance for Lisa to discern that she was the best-dressed patron by far. When the doors were unlocked, it was every man for himself. She had never seen so many people eager to get into a library, and was content to follow at a distance. It soon became clear why there was a rush. A good portion of the crowd headed directly for the restroom and it was then it dawned on Lisa that many of these people were homeless and relied on public institutions for the most basic of necessities. Those who didn't need a bathroom break headed mostly for the research area and parked themselves in front of computer terminals. Lisa wandered by a row of these and discovered that everyone was either playing computer games, checking email, or viewing scantily-clad girls. Apparently, this wasn't the group trying to find a cure for cancer. Realizing that all the computers were taken and knowing that she wouldn't know how to use one even if she did get a turn, Lisa headed for the Information Desk. She was fourth in line. There were three librarians. Lisa scanned them, wondering who would be most helpful. The first was a young man with a bow tie, acne, and an aversion to shaving. The next was the prototype of every child's

94

nightmare of a teacher. The third and final contestant looked, frankly, like a dyke. Which meant that she was probably married with five kids. To say that the line moved at a snail's pace would've been an insult to escargot everywhere. This must be the arcane fact checking society. One thing was clear, the guy in the bow tie was trying to pace things so that Lisa would end up at his station. Just when it seemed that he had timing on his side, Lisa got called to the desk of the schoolmarm.

"I'm sorry to bother you, but all the computers were taken."

"Games and porn, right?"

"It's hard to say," Lisa didn't want to give the impression that she had been gawking over anyone's shoulder.

"How can I help you?"

"I'm looking for some information about an old house in Denver."

"One house in particular?"

"The Livermore Estate."

"The Ben Livermore Estate?"

"That's the one," Lisa nodded. It sounded like she knew of the place well.

"Let's see," she tapped a few keys on the keyboard and squinted at the results. "There isn't anything specific. Would you like the general call numbers for historical mansions?"

"It would be a place to start."

The librarian wrote out a number on a slip of paper and gave Lisa directions to the correct shelves. She took the escalator to the second level and followed the signs to the Colorado history aisle. Three books sounded promising so Lisa carried them to a table to browse through them. The first two had nothing of interest, but the third was a hit. There was a chapter, albeit brief, about the Livermore Estate. She re-shelved the other books and then went back downstairs to arrange for checking out the book. She applied for a library card, something she hadn't done since she was ten. Since the advent of the computer, it was easier to get a card and books. It was also easier to track down delinquent borrowers of library books. Lisa promised that she understood the gravity of the situation to the issuer of said card and only then was she allowed out the door with her one book. It wouldn't take three weeks to glean all the information she would need from the book. In fact, her biggest concern was that it wouldn't take three minutes to read what little there was written about Ben Livermore.

Even with much foot dragging, she arrived at the building where Mary worked a good twenty minutes early. She spent a few of those minutes reading the sparse history of the Livermore Estate. Ben Livermore arrived in Denver a brash young man in the 1920s. From humble beginnings in the insurance business things were going along just fine until the Great Depression hit. And although it was hard to make a living selling insurance to people who couldn't afford food, after showing a few fellow businessmen how they could use their insurance investments to save their homes and businesses, he forged his way into the inner circles of the movers and shakers of Colorado. A wise investment here, a prudent bit of advice there and pretty soon he had amassed not only a small fortune, but also a wife. Whom he looked upon more of an asset than a romantic interest. After all, nobody trusted a life-long bachelor in business. In order to gain respectability, one had to get married in the good old days. Having children was even better for the image. The more, the better. Easy for a man to say. Mrs. Livermore gave it her best shot. The story briefly mentioned three children. No other detail. The paucity of information registered in Lisa's mind as something to chat about with whoever demonstrated interest.

At ten 'til noon, Lisa went up twenty-seven floors to the office where Mary worked. It was obvious that word had spread through the office grapevine that Mary's significant other was stopping by. Several people milled about, doing nothing but trying to look busy as they caught a glance. Lisa silently congratulated herself on dressing nicely. If you had to be on display as somebody's lesbian lover, might as well do it up right. She smiled and nodded and exchanged hellos with those brave enough to approach. And just as it was time to attempt awkward conversation with total strangers, Mary appeared from around a corner.
"Come back and see my office," she took Lisa by the hand and led her down a labyrinth hallway.

"I had to tie a string to my doorknob the first couple of days," Mary joked.

"Better than a trail of breadcrumbs," Lisa remarked.

For an office, it was tiny. Tiny. T-i-n-y.

"It is small," Mary read Lisa's mind.

"I'd say cozy."

"You'd be polite to do so. I'm the new kid. I'm lucky I'm not in the broom closet."

"I think that big offices are overrated. We should go shopping for decor."

Mary got a look on her face that communicated how expensive this would be. And didn't they just have a talk about this?

"I'm not suggesting that we go out and buy up the Van Gogh collection," Lisa took a turn at mind reading. "But we could do a little at a time."

"How little?"

"Where are you taking me to lunch?" Lisa went off topic.

"Where do you want to go?"

"Somewhere where we can be heard without hollering."

"I know just the place."

They walked three long city blocks to a fashionable eatery built by some chef with an unpronounceable name.

"This is so nice," Lisa approved with an almost reverential tone.

"We don't go out that often. I thought this would be suitable."

"Oh, it's way past suitable."

They were shown to a table for two by a waiter who had no idea who to help with their chair so he let them both fend for themselves. Which they did. The menu was fabulous.

Whatever this fusion cooking was, it took a lot of describing. And then, there were two specials recited by the waiter with stunning clarity.

"What are you having?" Mary asked Lisa.

"I have it narrowed down to fifteen things."

This made Mary smile. There were days when it seemed like the fire had never happened. Today was one of those days.

"Order them all," she replied.

"I might just do that…one day," Lisa teased back.

After they placed their orders, one entrée per, Mary inquired, "Find out anything at the library?"

"I found out that I need to know a whole lot more about computers. The library sure has changed since I was a kid. What did they do with all those card catalogues they used to have?"

"I'm sure the librarians burned them in a bonfire."

"In celebration?"

"No doubt about it. The computer has made research so much easier."

"Well, then why do people sit around playing games when they could be learning something?"

"Which brings me back to my original question, did you find what you were looking for?"

"That wasn't your original question."

"Perhaps it should've been?"

"I did actually find the Livermores in a book."

"You did? That's great!"

"But just one small chapter."

"It's better than nothing. Any mention of locked rooms as well?"

"No, nothing of the sort."

"Well, at least it's a good beginning."

"I just don't know where to go from here."

"I'm sure Trish has ideas."

When lunch arrived, they dropped the subject of the Livermores in favor of Mary's workplace.

"You made quite the impression at work."

"I did?" Lisa feigned surprise.

"Oh, yes," Mary knew from experience when exactly Lisa needed compliments. The time was now. Exactly.

"Good or bad impressions?"

"What do you think?"

"I tried to behave myself."

"And I know how hard that is for you."

"If I'd known everyone was watching, I would've put on a better show."

"I don't think they're ready for that. They are a conservative bunch."

"Are you the token lesbian?"

"I don't know yet. I show up. I work hard. That should be enough, shouldn't it?"

"Of course," Lisa agreed readily, not wanting to venture close to anything resembling a debate. Things were going so well. And besides, she didn't quite understand Mary's point.

"I mean, gee, I don't gawk when other people's significant others show up."

"That's because they're not as beautiful as me," Lisa explained it all now that she understood.

"That would be too much to hope for on their part."

When they got back to the office and it was time for the parting gesture of affection, Mary kissed Lisa the way most people kiss at the altar when they get married. It was sweet and simple, just like how you'd kiss in front of your parents and a hundred of your closest friends.

"I'll see you for dinner?" Lisa asked just for effect.

"I should be home on time."

"I'll microwave something special."

"I look forward to eating it," Mary smiled benignly.

And she wondered why people gawked.

Chapter 11

"Did I ever tell you about my prom?" Mitch asked Aunt BeBe when there was nothing else to do but talk.
"Why would I want to know anything about that?" she snapped. Mitch hadn't expected such a pointed reply, since she had spent quite a bit of time dreaming up an involved, if entirely fictional, tale of mishap. Spielberg might want to film this yarn.
"You really don't want to hear about my prom?"
"I don't want to hear about any homo dances!"
"Really? Why not?" Mitch was truly curious.
"Why would *anyone* want to hear about such a thing!"
"You think that gay people dance any differently than straight people?"
"Well, of course they do! They dance with *each other*!"
Mitch couldn't argue with that. Gay people did indeed dance with each other. Mitch and Reb had done a little bit of dancing a long time ago. The poignancy of the memory held her tongue captive.
"Where is that fool Henry," BeBe changed the subject. Thankfully.
Since Mitch and Reb had hit town, Henry had pulled off a disappearing act that would've qualified him for membership in the magician's union.
"Has he been here today?"
"Not that I know of."
"Where did you and Henry meet?" Mitch asked, more or less out of the blue.
"Why does that matter?"
"Well, I just never heard the story and I thought it would be interesting."
And now, BeBe was stuck. If she admitted it was an interesting story, she would be obliged to carry on an actual conversation. If she said it wasn't interesting, it would make her life seem somehow less important.
"I met Henry at a barn dance and believe me, there weren't any homos dancing there."

"I imagine not," Mitch pretended to agree, knowing full well that in reality, there were dancing homos everywhere. BeBe stopped there. Mitch gave it a couple of beats and then said, "And?"

"And what?"

"There must be more to the story."

"Like what?"

"Oh, I don't know. Like, what was he wearing?"

"He had on shirt and pants. What did you expect, a poodle skirt!"

Mitch envisioned Uncle Henry in a poodle skirt. It was downright scary.

"What color shirt?"

"I don't remember."

"I bet you do. You just haven't thought about it in so long. Close your eyes and think. Was it a solid color or stripes or plaid?"

BeBe didn't close her eyes. It must've been a trust issue. But she did get a faraway look in her eyes. At least she was trying to cooperate.

"It was brown."

"What about the pants?"

"They were jeans. He was poor as dirt."

"What color jeans?"

"They only made one color back then. Then the queers got hold of the fashion industry and now everyone looks ridiculous!"

Mitch couldn't argue with the fact that some people emerge from their homes looking pretty amazing, but she didn't think the blame could all be laid at the doorstep of the gay lobby.

"I bet he wore boots, right."

"Hand-me-downs. They didn't even fit. Turned his toes in."

"I guess that made it difficult to dance?"

"He was horrible at it to begin with. The boots didn't help."

"And what kind of music did they play?"

"Barn dance music, of course."

Mitch thought about asking for clarification, but knew that if she did, she would hear Aunt BeBe's opinion about how the fags had ruined the music industry as well.

"It all sounds lovely."

"It was a barn dance. There wasn't nothing lovely about it."

"Well, then, why did you go?"

"There wasn't anything better to do. Not that there's anything better to do nowadays."

Mitch waited for the usual condemnation of the entertainment industry as well. Which wasn't forthcoming. Mitch studied BeBe. She was tiring. Mitch searched her memory to see if she could recall a time when BeBe hadn't looked tired. Whenever Mitch and Reb visited, which wasn't often admittedly, BeBe looked tired of their company before they even crossed the threshold. She had always seemed tired of being Henry's wife. Had she always been weary of being Miranda's mother as well?

"How is Miranda?" Mitch asked bravely.

"Still in jail, thanks to you."

Mitch gave this serious thought, shown externally by a furrowing of her brow. Technically, Miranda was responsible for Miranda being in jail. After all, she was the one who had torched the farmhouse. But if BeBe was a pupil of the school of thought that believed that criminals weren't responsible for their own crimes, a rarity for people of conservative ilk, it was still a stretch to blame Mitch for the incarceration. After all, she hadn't even testified at the trial. If anybody was to blame, it was Rebecca. Which made it okay to take the brunt of BeBe's criticism. Any grief she could spare Reb was a blessing. Reb was, after all, still carrying the stigma of prom night.

"Have you seen her lately?"

"No. It's a long way to travel."

It had been a long way to travel to come to Denver for the wedding, but Mitch decided not to point that out.

"It must be painful for you to see her in prison," Mitch nodded.

BeBe didn't reply. Which said something in and of itself. The woman ready with a tart to the point reply to everything else on earth was now silent.

"Would you like to see her now?" Mitch asked before she had weighed all the implications of the question.

"I'm too sick to go now."

Mitch hadn't said anything about BeBe going anywhere, the question had meant to be rhetorical.

"I guess so," Mitch agreed.

"You millionaires are all alike, aren't you," BeBe sounded much too emphatic for someone who was dying. Mitch looked around and then decided that she was the particular millionaire BeBe was referring to. How many other millionaires did BeBe know? "I guess we are," Mitch answered in her best placating, if somewhat confused, tone.

"You think that just because you have money to burn that you can do anything or buy anything you want. The rules don't apply to you millionaires, do they?"

It dawned on Mitch that this sounded an awful lot like a dare. Was BeBe taunting her to try, just try, to arrange for a visit with Miranda? Mitch had fought for years to downplay her wealth. Hell, she'd lived in a trailer for who knows how long. So, she wasn't exactly accustomed to buying influence. There was no safe comment, so Mitch refrained entirely. BeBe didn't. But she did change the subject.

"What is it that you see in my sister anyway?"

Caught off guard by the sudden switch, Mitch looked puzzled on purpose, mostly to stall for time. "I'm not sure I understand your question…"

"What's not to understand! You've been stuck on her quite some time now. I just wondered why."

It came to Mitch in a flash that this was the first time that BeBe had ever framed a question that actually sounded like she really wanted to know something about Mitch and Reb that wasn't going to be used as part of an ongoing attack campaign. No wonder Mitch was stalling for time. The surprise was nothing short of jaw dropping in its effect.

"And don't try and tell me that it's the sex because we both know how *that* went."

Aunt BeBe was just full of surprises today. Hearing her articulate the word "sex" without spelling it out was like listening to your grandmother discuss procreation in front of grandpa.

"Well, I'll have to admit that seeing Rebecca in leather the first time wasn't exactly a turnoff."

"That was before the accident."

"Right," Mitch nodded and fell silent. There were some things that she didn't want to be reminded of and this was at the very top of the list.

"You should've been more careful."

"I wasn't driving."

"Doesn't matter. She was yours to take care of."

It would be so easy to pick a fight about this but Mitch realized that they both had suffered because of Reb's misfortune.

"You still haven't answered my question," BeBe reminded.

"What question is that?" Reb wheeled in, joining the conversation. And just in the nick of time, too.

"BeBe was wondering about our sex life," Mitch answered.

"Well, that should be a brief topic of conversation," Reb said airily. At least, it probably sounded airy. If you were a complete stranger, that is. To Mitch, the message was more like "Are you out of your mind? Hush!" kind of message.

"It was brief, actually," Mitch assured her with a calming smile. "We had actually started out talking about Henry and BeBe's courtship and sort of wandered off topic."

"She was asking personal questions so I expected her to answer some as well," BeBe defended herself.

If Reb wondered what sort of personal questions Mitch had been asking, it was apparent that they were going to only talk about it later.

"Why don't you go get some lunch," Reb suggested to Mitch.

"It's only ten in the morning."

"Then get yourself a late breakfast."

"I already had a bowl of flax flakes."

"Flax flakes?" BeBe asked to make sure she heard right.

"With soy milk. It was delicious."

BeBe gave her the usual "you're a weirdo" look that Mitch knew so well by now. It was almost comforting in its familiarity.

"You go on," Reb directed Mitch.

Mitch knew when she was being dismissed. She headed to the elevator and ran into Henry when the doors opened.

"Can I buy you a cup of coffee?" Mitch all but blocked his exit.

"BeBe is waiting for me."

"Reb's in with her. I'm sure they're fine for a few minutes."

Normally, Mitch wouldn't have been this insistent, but she hadn't had a chance to have more than a few words with Henry since they had arrived. Hell, they hadn't exchanged more than a couple dozen words all the time they'd known each other. Which could very well be the sole cause of his hesitation.

"And a donut as well?" Mitch upped the stakes as she stepped onto the elevator.

"The coffee shop downstairs has pretty decent cinnamon rolls," he warmed to the idea now that sweets were involved.

Apparently, the way to this man's heart was through his triglyceride level. It was a quiet time at the coffee shop, the lull between breakfast and lunch. At the urging of Mitch, Henry ordered three pastries with his coffee. Mitch stuck to the fruit plate, knowing full well that it was going to be something canned.

"You don't eat donuts after all?"

"I used to, but I'm watching my weight."

"Looks to me like you could stand to gain a few pounds."

"You think so?" Mitch was beginning to like Henry more than she had ever expected to.

"Wouldn't hurt," he added three sugars to his coffee.

"So, how are you holding up?" Mitch asked gently.

"Oh, fair to middlin most days."

Mitch didn't quite know the exact meaning of the phrase, but it didn't sound like he had hit the depths of despair. How he managed to keep going with his only child in jail and his wife on her death bed was a testament to the human spirit.

"I mostly wanted to know if there's anything else you can think of that you need or that BeBe might need?"

Henry shrugged his shoulders like he had gone over this in his mind before and come up empty. "Just you being here has been a big relief."

Mitch nodded. It wasn't exactly a glowing compliment, but anything more would've sounded forced.

"I heard about your first date with BeBe today."

"Huh?"

"BeBe was telling me about the barn dance where you first met."

"I'm surprised she remembered."

"Why?"

"She's never mentioned it in all the years we've been married."

"I did quiz her about it extensively."

"Why?"

"Because I'm quickly running out of things to talk to her about."

"I know how *that* goes," Henry sighed.

Mitch understood. She and Reb hadn't gotten to that part of their relationship. They had their quiet moments, but she knew that it was a common experience for people in less-than-optimal relationships to cease communication at a certain point. At least, intimate communication. As Mitch contemplated the silence, and the pale excuse for fruit cocktail, Henry wolfed down his cinnamon rolls like he'd decided they'd be more filling if they went down nearly whole.

"You want something else?" Mitch asked, ready to pull out more money.

"No thanks. Three's my limit."

"Good advice for us all."

"You're not eating?" he just noticed.

"I had a big breakfast," Mitch explained, inwardly cringing just thinking about the overdose of chemical additives in this glob of badly diced fruit. Henry was looking at it too.

"You want this?"

"You don't?"

Henry accepted the offering like he was the class valedictorian of the school of thought that said you had to clean your plate. And everyone else's if polite to do so. He was done in twenty seconds and they were heading back to the elevator before Mitch had dreamed up still more topics to stimulate conversation with BeBe. Reb was still there, thank God. Mitch didn't know if she could handle a yawning silence between Henry and BeBe.

"Where have you been?" BeBe asked.

Mitch knew the question wasn't meant for her, so she kept her mouth shut. Which meant that Henry was in the hot seat.

"Had chores to do," was his succinct answer.

Mitch swore she could hear cows mooing in the distance. And then Reb caught her eye. Something was up.

"I have something to say," BeBe announced.

All of a sudden, the cows got real quiet. So did everyone else.

"I want to see Miranda before I die."

Chapter 12

It took a few moments before Trish realized that she had been
listening to silence. A rare commodity around their household.
The elders were out on the town with Silver at their ready. Josh
was asleep. Robbie was in bed. Trish joined her. Gingerly.
Things just hadn't been right since Josh was born, and Trish had
racked her brain to sort it all out. It wasn't about the lack of sex
at all. That made perfect sense. Having a baby come lickety
split out of your body and all the resulting damage pushed sex to
the very end of the priority line. Trish had prepared herself for
that. What she hadn't prepared for was the total emotional
distance that existed between them now.
"How are you feeling?"
"Tired."
No change there.
"Maybe you need to take some vitamins or something?"
"I just need sleep."
Robbie and Josh seemed to have a contest going to see who
could sleep the most. Trish knew in her logical mind that this
just wasn't right. Other moms managed to get out of bed and do
things.
"Do you want to go out to lunch tomorrow?" Trish tried the date
approach.
"No."
"You want to see a movie?"
"No."
"What can I do to help?"
"You can be quiet so I can get some sleep."
The terse reply led to still more crushing silence and as soon as
Trish knew that Robbie was sound asleep, she wandered into the
guest bedroom and reclined on the spare bed.

So, when the phone rang the next day and it was Lisa calling for
Trish, Rose had to do a room-to-room search.
"What are you doing here?" Rose asked, careful to cover the
mouthpiece of the phone.
"Sleeping."
"There's a call for you."

"Thanks."

Trish took the phone from Rose, who stood her ground as if to quietly but firmly communicate her displeasure. Over what, Trish could only guess.

"Hello?"

"Hi! It's Lisa. Are you okay?"

"Yeah. I was just getting up."

"I didn't wake you, did I?"

"No," Trish figured that was technically true. It was Rose who had accomplished that.

"I did, didn't I?"

This was beginning to sound like badly-written song lyrics. "I'm awake now. What's up?"

"I just didn't know if you wanted to get together."

Trish's mind was picking up speed now, zipping through the past twenty-four hours. Her schedule was clear.

"Sure. When and where?"

"You pick. I chose last time."

"How about 10:30 at the club?"

There was a pause at the other end of the line so dramatic that Trish wondered if she had misspoken.

"*The* Club?" Lisa asked. Every once in a while, Lisa had to remind herself that she was surrounded by gazillionaires. Mitch, Reb, Robbie and Trish...

"It's a quiet place to talk."

It was more like an echo chamber if truth be told.

"Should I meet you there?"

"No. I'll come pick you up."

It would give Trish the excuse to leave the house even earlier. Like, five minutes ago.

"Okay. I'll try and be ready."

When Trish hung up, she looked at Rose who had stood her ground through the entire conversation. So much for privacy.

"So, you'll be gone for lunch."

"Right."

Trish could hear the consternation in Rose's voice, but didn't want to deal with it.

"You slept here last night?"

"I was restless and didn't want to disturb Robbie."

108

"How restless?" Rose asked with a knowing tone in her voice, like how she knew that there was a definition of restless that wasn't good where relationships were concerned.

"I have to go."

"You'll be home for dinner?"

"I'll be home right after lunch. I'll help you cook if you need it."

"I'm not the one who needs help," Rose said somberly as she exited the room.

Trish dressed like she was going to bus tables at the country club instead of eat there. She had fallen out of the habit of dressing to impress and saw no reason to begin again. After spending a minimum amount of time checking in on a sleeping Josh and a sleeping Robbie, she headed across town to pick up Lisa. It was way out of the way, but it felt helpful. There was that "help" word again. Without even knowing all the facts, it felt like Rose was blaming Trish for everything. Now she knew what it was like to be a typical son-in-law.

By the time she pulled up to Lisa's house, her mood had gone from troubled to irritated. Lisa was nowhere in sight, not even at the window keeping watch. Trish got out of her truck and walked up to the door. She heard the unmistakable sound of high heels ticking their way across a hardwood floor. The door swung open and there was Lisa, dressed to the nines. She could've given any starlet in Hollywood a run for her money and won hands down.

"Hi. Come in. I'm almost ready," Lisa held the door open.

"You look very ready to me," Trish blurted out without thinking.

"We still are going to the country club, right?" Lisa blurted back. It was then that Trish realized what a mismatched couple they would make. Lisa looked fabulous and Trish was dressed to go out and shoot whatever they might find on the menu.

"I made reservations."

"I'm overdressed, aren't I?"

"No. In fact, you look wonderful."

"Well, okay. I'll be ready to go in a minute. Or two. Come in and sit down."

Trish was able to sit for a whole thirty seconds before she stood up and began pacing. Well, not exactly pacing. More like walking back and forth a couple of times. And then a couple more times. So she was pacing. Before she seriously wore the tread down on the new carpet, Lisa reemerged looking even more beautiful. Trish kept her opinion to herself this time. At least verbally.

"I can't forget this," Lisa picked up a book from the hall table.

"Reading material?"

"Research material."

"You've been busy?"

"Not enough to complain about," Lisa smiled.

"We wouldn't want that," Trish smiled back, thinking how lucky Mary was to come home every day to a smile like that.

They chatted about traffic, the weather, and Mitch on the way to the club. It was relatively quiet this time of year. Too cold for golf and tennis. Just right for a research lunch. They were seated in a small alcove with a view of absolutely nothing. Which suited their agenda. After drinks were brought, Lisa did what she was best at, namely, being nosy.

"Are you going to tell me what's wrong, or do I have to start guessing."

"Excuse me?" Trish wasn't quite used to this.

"You heard me. What's wrong?"

"Have I complained about anything?"

"You don't strike me as the complaining type. But that's really beside the point, isn't it."

"There's a point to this?"

"My point is that it's going to be difficult to concentrate on the business at hand when you're obviously troubled by something."

"I've been paying attention so far."

"So, you don't trust me with your problems?"

"It isn't a matter of trust. It's just that we have other things to talk about besides my problems."

"Except for the problem of your sticking basement door."

"Right. So, what have you found out?"

"Oh, nothing. Yet. I just wanted to have lunch at the club," Lisa stated and then followed up with her trademark smile. Again.

The smile that Mitch had never acquired an immunity to. Trish now knew why.

"Anytime you want to have lunch at the country club, just let me know."

"But I do have an idea that I wanted to run by you," Lisa spoke like she hadn't even heard the open-ended invitation.

"Okay, what's on your mind?"

"Somebody wrote this book that had a blurb in it about the Livermores."

Trish nodded like she knew exactly what Lisa meant. It didn't work.

"The book I brought. The library book," Lisa held up exhibit one.

"Right. Books are usually written by people."

"You're making fun of me."

"No. I'm not making fun of you. I'm waiting to hear the rest of your idea."

"The person who wrote this book couldn't possibly have written down everything they knew."

"Otherwise, the book would be huge."

"You are making fun of me. However does Robbie put up with you?" Lisa went into her southern belle routine.

"Robbie is a saint."

"That's the only possible explanation."

"So, you want to track down the author of this book and see if they remember anything else about the Livermores?" Trish ventured a guess.

"And?" Lisa prompted, just for fun.

"And...and you want my help."

"In a word, yes."

"Where do we start?"

"The phone book?"

"How about the Internet?"

"What about the publisher?"

"Should we hire a detective agency?"

"Let me see what I can do before we start throwing a bunch of money around."

"Speaking of which, what do you want for lunch?" Trish was hungry.

Lisa picked up a menu and noticed right off that there were no prices on the page. "What are you having?" she asked lightly.

"Oh, the steak and lobster are pretty good. Why don't you give that a try."

Lisa calculated that those selections alone would set Trish back about fifty bucks in a normal restaurant.

"And the cheesecake is great unless you prefer the cherries jubilee."

"I might just stick to a salad."

"You're not hungry?"

"If I eat a lot now, I won't be hungry for dinner."

Trish turned this over in her mind, looking puzzled in the process.

"And that's not very fair to Mary," Lisa explained as best she could.

"I see. Maybe I should have a salad as well. I promised to cook dinner when I get home."

"Of course."

"And that's hard to do on a full stomach. At least for me."

They ordered a salad apiece and then plotted further.

"I think I'll do a cross check of the author and the phone book first," Lisa decided.

"Let me know the minute you find anything. Or nothing."

"I'll keep you posted."

When Lisa promised to keep Trish posted, she took the promise seriously. The phone rang while Rose and Trish were preparing dinner. Rose answered. It was her favorite responsibility.

"Just a moment," she said in a not-too-tart-not-too-sweet tone of voice. She handed the phone to Trish without comment, but Trish knew who it was.

"Hi. What's new?"

"I found her."

"Good for you. Who-her?"

"The author, of course."

"Oh, yeah, right," Trish recalled the plan.

"We're meeting her in the morning. At seven a.m."

"Seven in the morning?"

"That's usually when seven a.m. is. In the morning."

"Why so early?"

"It's her best time."

"Is she booked the rest of the day?"

"She's in a nursing center. The dear lady is a hundred and one. She's probably asleep the rest of the day."

"At a hundred and one, I'm surprised that she's alive the rest of the day."

"Don't talk like that. You'll jinx the deal."

"I'll pick you up at what? Six-thirty?"

"Make it six. You're buying coffee."

"I'll spring for a whole breakfast over this lead. How did you find her anyway?"

"I have my methods," Lisa said mysteriously. She was making this all too much fun. In a really sexy tone of voice as well. She could make a decent living being at the other end of a 900 number. Which seemed like a contradiction in terms now that Trish thought about it.

"You still there?" Lisa asked.

"You want to eat before or after?" Trish asked as Rose continued to eavesdrop.

"After, I guess."

"I'll see you at six then."

It was remarkably silent when Trish hung up from the call. Everyone must've taken the fifth. Finally, Rose asked, "So, you aren't going to be here for breakfast tomorrow?"

"Neither are you."

"What do you mean?"

"You're going with me."

"With you where?"

"To visit a new friend in the nursing home."

"It's always nice to visit the elderly. Let's take Max along as well."

"That leaves Silver alone with Robbie and Josh."

"She's a bodyguard. I think she can handle it."

"Why do I have to go?" Max wasn't exactly overjoyed at the plan.

"To see how the other half lives," Trish offered.

"Besides, you get breakfast," Rose sweetened the deal.

"Who's buying?"

"Who else?" Trish answered back.

"It had better be a big breakfast."

"You're on a diet," Rose admonished.

"Not every damn day!"

"Sounds like he's ready to me," Trish gave Rose an affirmative nod.

"Ready for what?" Silver asked as she joined the group.

"We're going to the nursing home tomorrow to visit a friend."

"I'll stay home and watch the baby."

"You don't like nursing homes?" Trish asked.

"I don't tempt fate."

"I appreciate you volunteering to stay home."

"It's my job."

Technically, it wasn't her job to stay home. It was her job to follow them around and keep Rose and Max safe. But keeping the baby safe was really the new priority, so it all worked out. Meanwhile, Trish wondered if she should call Lisa and warn her about the onslaught. Her main concern was whether or not Lisa was going to be dressed like a model in search of a runway. And deeper still, she fretted about the sexy charm that seemed to exude from her at any given moment. Would Rose see it and worry even more about what could possibly be going on between the two of them, which was nothing. Nothing at all. So, she didn't call. And as it turned out, there was no reason to worry. When the group showed up at six the next morning, Lisa was dressed like she was going to church in an Amish neighborhood. Except without the bonnet.

"I read somewhere that bright colors upset elderly people," Lisa whispered to Trish.

Never mind the fact that Rose and Max were in purple and red respectively.

"You look lovely," Trish whispered back.

Rose was straining to hear so they changed the subject to the topic at hand, which was the plan for the visit.

"Why don't you ask the questions," Trish advised Lisa. "There's nothing more disconcerting than trying to carry on conversations with several people at once."

"I don't have all that much to ask."

"We'll play it by ear."

The nursing home was a surprisingly long way away, situated in the southeastern suburbs of the city. It was a treeless area, except around the building proper. There, it resembled a well-planned-out forest to give the area a bucolic aura. They checked in at the front nurses' station though there was no requirement to do so and found their way through the maze of hallways that would've confused most people. A person with Alzheimer's didn't stand a chance with this set up. Maybe that was the idea?

"What's the name of the lady we're visiting?" Trish asked for the second or third time. Lisa had lost count.

"Jeanette. As in McDonald."

"Is she heir to the hamburger fortune?"

Lisa looked exasperated. "Not *that* McDonald. She isn't even a McDonald. I was using that as a memory aid."

"Why? Are you having trouble remembering her name?"

"I'm not the one who's asked at least twice already!"

"So, what's her last name?"

"Wrightwood."

"Jeanette Wrightwood. Got it."

They arrived at the room and then clustered at the doorway, looking pensively at each other. It was a silent signal they shared communicating the deep respect they shared for the privacy lost by people inhabiting institutions. When you get to the stage in life where anyone can wander into your room without announcement, there was little else left to lose in life.

"I guess we knock?" Rose offered a common-sense suggestion. Since this whole adventure was Lisa's idea, she took the initiative, rapping loudly on the open door. There was no response.

"Maybe she's asleep?" Max appeared ready to bolt.

Lisa knocked again. From inside the room, they heard a strong voice reply, "Come in already!"

They entered single file until everyone was face to face with the comfortably reposed Ms. Wrightwood. She looked from one to the other and then asked, "Well, which one of you is the plumber?"

"Plumber?" Trish asked by voice inflection.

"I called the plumber yesterday. It's about time you got here."

Trish decided it wouldn't hurt to follow this line of conversation.
"So, what seems to be the plumbing problem?"
"Since when do they let girls be plumbers."
"I'm just the secretary. He's the plumber," Trish indicated Max.
This seemed to satisfy Ms. Wrightwood.
"There's a leak in the basement."
"I'll get right on it," Max was relieved to have any excuse to
leave the room. He whispered to Trish on the way out, "I'll see
you in the waiting room."
"Can you find the way?"
"I'm not the one who keeps forgetting people's names."
Lisa took over now, impatient to start her own line of inquiry.
"Ms. Wrightwood, I'm Lisa. I wanted to talk to you about a
book you wrote."
"I've written many books, my dear. To which are you
referring?"
"This one," Lisa produced the library book she had used as
reference.
"Let me take a look at that, Dear," Ms. Wrightwood held out her
hands. After taking the book, she studied the cover for a moment
and then opened to the table of contents. She nodded slowly as if
it was all coming back to her. "I wrote this a long time ago."
"You were a young author, then?"
"I was a young author. But I knew a lot of old people."
"And they were your references?"
"I thought it was important to get what they knew on the record
while we still could. Old people have a lot to tell, you know."
Trish nodded agreement, which did not go unnoticed by the
woman.
"Is that why you're here? To get more information out of this
old lady?"
"Well, I wouldn't put it that way exactly."
"You don't need to be pulling any punches, Dearie. There
comes a time in one's life when one knows when one is an old
lady. What is it you want to know?"
"We were wondering if you could tell us anything more about
the Benjamin Livermore family history?"
"Why do you want to know more about old man Livermore?"
She asked as she scanned for the name in the index. Her

116

casualness in reference to Mr. Livermore set off a reaction in Trish which she couldn't identify offhand. It felt a bit scornful, like she had little respect for the former pillar of the community. Trish decided to take the direct approach, heeding the request to not pull any punches.

"Because I'm living in his old house."

Ms. Wrightwood met Trish's eyes with a startlingly clear look of her own.

"So it was you who bought the creaky old place."

"Some parts of it are creakier than others."

"Sounds like my body," she flashed a sense of humor.

"Did you know Mr. Livermore personally?" Lisa squeezed in a question amid the repartee.

"It depends on what you mean by *personally*," she answered. Her tone was close to snappish. Maybe the term "personally" carried a different meaning than Lisa intended.

"Did you ever meet him?" Trish followed up, hoping that the question had a more neutral nuance.

"Why do you want to know?"

Trish felt like they were covering the same ground again. Surely Ms. Wrightwood hadn't forgotten the purpose of the visit already. Then again…

"I'm living in the house that he built."

"But that doesn't answer my question, now does it?"

"Why not?"

"Because a lot of people move into houses and never need to go asking about previous owners. Unless there's a good reason."

Trish looked at Lisa. She didn't want to give the real reason why they were asking questions to avoid prejudicing the woman's viewpoint. Still, they seemed to be backed into a corner. And by a 100-year-old lady to boot. Trish decided to call her bluff.

"Well, that's all the questions we had. We'd best be on our way."

Trish gave Lisa and Rose the eye and they stood to leave. Ms. Wrightwood let them get almost out the door before she spoke.

"Of course, I didn't put all the history in my book…"

Trish stopped and turned slightly. "What did you say?"

"You know editors. Always cutting here and there."

"I guess I wouldn't know about that. I've never written a book."

117

"You pick up a book today," Ms. Wrightwood was more than happy to explain now, "and there's everything under the sun in it. Sex, violence, hate, rumor, gossip. But back when I was writing, well, things were a lot more censored. There were just some things you didn't write about."

Slowly, as the woman talked, Trish and the others gathered at her bedside again.

"So, what you wrote was a sanitized version of the real story."

"That would be an accurate statement. Now, it's your turn to come clean."

"Excuse me?"

"I've told you what you wanted to know. Now I want to know why you asked in the first place."

Trish, Lisa and Rose once again exchanged looks. Rose said quietly, "I'm going to go check on the plumber. Meet me in the *basement* when you're through."

"We won't be long," Trish assured her.

Lisa, who had been patient to this point, spoke straight to the heart of the matter. "We think the Livermore place is haunted and we want to know why."

If Trish had expected the statement to be met with skepticism, she was surprised to see a glimmer of acknowledgement in the woman's eyes. Like she had known all along that that was the reason that they were all here. Something fishy was going on at Captain Livermore's Estate and they were in the thick of it.

"So, you believe in ghosts?" the woman spoke matter-of-factly.

"We're not sure what to believe at this point," Trish answered as she watched Lisa. It was a warning to not go too far too fast.

"Well, what would haunt a house except a ghost!"

"We don't know."

"Blondie here thinks the house is haunted. Why is that?"

If Lisa was insulted by her new hair-color nickname, she kept her reaction hidden. "We have a door that sticks shut."

"So get some oil and fix it. I used to do that all the time. I'm sure you gals could figure it out."

"It's actually a little more stubborn than that. It's as if the room wants to keep you there."

"Like a prisoner?"

Trish thought this over. "It's not exactly a threatening gesture. It's just...well..."

"Spooky," Lisa finished the thought.

"If the room holds you prisoner, how do you get out?"

"Somebody figures out that you've gone missing and they come downstairs and just open the door."

"Just like that?"

"Just like that."

"And that's all you know?"

"No," Lisa answered in the negative about the time that Trish was going to say, "Yes."

"What else do we know?" Trish asked Lisa before Ms. Wrightwood could get the chance.

"You remember...at the wedding."

"No, I don't."

"What wedding?" Ms. Wrightwood asked like she was researching material for a new book.

"Mitch and Reb's wedding."

"Mitch and Reb? Which one is the man?" Ms. Wrightwood was just full of questions.

Trish looked at Lisa with one of those "We probably shouldn't have gone down this road" looks.

"You'd have to ask them," Lisa said in spite of Trish's expression.

"Are they here now?" the writer's instinct took over and the woman began looking for a pencil and paper.

"What else happened at the wedding?" Trish forged ahead with Lisa.

"Remember? Robbie's folks talked about the woman in the white shirt?"

"There were twenty women in white shirts."

"But we never saw her again."

"We never saw any of them again."

"But she lured Max and Rose down to the room. They were the first to get trapped."

"Who are Max and Rose?" Ms. Wrightwood interrupted with a question of her own.

"The plumber and his helper," Lisa pointed in the general direction of the lobby.

"Sounds to me like you have a house haunted by a female ghost," Ms. Wrightwood looked suddenly thoughtful. And then puzzled. And then confounded.

"Shouldn't there be a female ghost?" Trish asked, noting the rapid change of expression.

"I don't pretend to know the business of ghosts."

"But you might remember the business of the Livermore family."

"I don't remember any young female in the family."

"Maybe she wasn't a member of the family?" Lisa mused out loud.

"Then, why would she be haunting the house?" Trish answered, sounding a tad more exasperated than she intended. As far as she was concerned, they had appeared to have driven clear across town just to be going in circles. She envied Max and Rose's early escape.

"Maybe we should let Ms. Wrightwood get some rest," Trish sent Lisa the unmistakable message that she wanted to be out of the nursing home now. Lisa nodded reluctantly.

"We must be going."

"Will you come back?" Ms. Wrightwood was blunt.

"I'm sure we'll have more questions," Lisa assured her without answering directly. "Thank you for your help."

Trish and Lisa had to walk clear out to the car to find Max and Rose. Evidently the waiting room had not been conducive to waiting.

"What else did you find out?" Rose asked before they were even fastened in their seat belts.

"Nothing. There's no reason to have a female ghost in the house."

"Perhaps Ms. Wrightwood doesn't know everything there is to know."

"Unless she does and she's not telling us."

"Why wouldn't she tell us?"

"Maybe she wants us to come visit her again. I'm sure she's lonely."

Trish looked skeptical but knew in her heart that Lisa wasn't going to let go of this lead that easy. It was the only real lead they had anyway. It wasn't like the movies where there were dozens of blind alleys just waiting to mislead.

"Let's give her a week or two."

"I'm voting one week. When you get to be her age, you don't press your luck."

Chapter 13

Okay, so what. So what if Mitch had pulled more strings than a puppet show. She still got only half of what she had set out to accomplish. Still, this half would do. If she couldn't bring Miranda to Aunt BeBe, at least she could arrange to take Aunt BeBe to see Miranda. Even prison wardens had a soft spot where dying mothers were concerned. Of course, Mitch had done all this on the QT just in case it didn't work out. Except for Reb, who had caught on early. Damn, she was smart. Mitch was just hanging up the phone from chatting to Warden Kingsley about her sizable donation to the correction facility fund when Reb wheeled in and asked seemingly out of the blue, "So, how is the Warden?"

"She said to say 'Hi.'"

"She did not," Reb caught that fib right away.

"Well, she would've if she knew you were eavesdropping."

"What exactly are you up to?"

"You know exactly what I'm up to. You always do. I'm putting my millions to good use."

"You've been doing that since I met you."

"Gee, I have, haven't I?" Mitch got a real nostalgic look on her face. There was that wild and adventurous trip to Las Vegas. The first one. The one where they fell in love like teenagers. And then spent way too much time ignoring the inevitable.

"Earth to Mitch," Reb brought her back to reality.

"Huh?"

"Just tell me that you're ready to explain the plan to BeBe. She's been driving me up the wall."

"If she's anything like you, she already knows the plan."

"So, when are we leaving?"

"Tomorrow."

"Tomorrow! That's really soon!"

"Yeah, like hours from now."

"She's going to need clothes."

"I certainly hope so. The thought of seeing your sister naked is just too scary for words."

"I don't mean clothes," Reb said shortly. "I mean *clothes*!"

"*Clothes!*" Mitch mimicked the emphasis, hoping to stay out of trouble.

"Something nice to wear. Something presentable."

"It's just a prison."

"This is no time for logic. I'm just trying to warn you about what BeBe's reaction will be."

"There are more department stores where we are going than where we are."

Reb thought this over. For about a nanosecond."

"Good point."

"And the Warden is going to be very flexible about our visiting schedule."

"When was the last time you saw a flexible female prison warden?"

"Do porno films count?"

Mitch got a look for that remark.

"Did I mention that I'm putting everyone up in a luxury penthouse suite with around the clock medical staff okayed by BeBe's personal physician?"

"No, I don't believe so."

"And that we're going to have limousine service for the duration of the stay?"

"Anything else?"

"We'll have three personal chefs to do all of our food preparation including BeBe's special medical dietary needs?"

"I see."

"Have I forgotten anything?" Mitch asked.

"I love you."

Mitch pulled herself as close as she could to Reb. Until she could feel her heartbeat.

"I have never forgotten that you love me."

"Well, don't start now."

"Who's going to tell BeBe to start packing her suitcase?"

"I vote we have Henry tell her. He's going to get stuck with the chore anyway."

"Let's get him on the phone."

It was a good thing that the bars were still open. Henry needed a stiff belt to bump up his courage. Mitch nursed a white wine while Reb toyed with a tonic with extra lime. She swore she could feel that case of scurvy coming on that Mitch always warned about.

"I think she hoped you'd be able to bring Miranda here," Henry explained after bolting down a double whiskey.

"The prison system isn't that accommodating," Mitch explained. It took quite the donation to get as far as they had gotten already. It wasn't everybody who had a future refurbished prison library named in their honor. Filled with very expensive new books.

"We're flying there?" Henry was looking to catch the eye of the cocktail waitress as he quizzed about the details.

"We will take a chartered jet. Plenty of leg room and champagne."

"How about whiskey?"

"You asking me or the waitress?"

"Both."

By the time Henry had his second double, four by anybody else's count, he was thawing if not quite warming up to this scheme. Mitch promised to carry along a case of whiskey if need be.

"She's gonna want to go shopping for clothes, you know."

Reb gave Mitch one of her "I told you so" looks. Every time Mitch saw BeBe, she was wearing the same thing, a farmer's wife's dress. It came to her in revelation form. It was definitely time for a change.

"We've got all that arranged. We'll take her shopping when we get there."

"That won't do. She'll want something new before she even gets on the plane."

"Is this a superstition?"

"You'll need to ask her. I'm just warning you what to expect."

"So, we'll go shopping. What else?"

"When are we leaving again?"

"Just as soon as we get the shopping done."

Henry looked down at the drink before him. "That soon?"

"As soon as possible."

"Then, it's best to keep a clear head," he stood up with a resolve that Mitch hadn't seen before. "Who's driving?"

Reb the Teetotaler got behind the wheel and they were all at BeBe's bedside before the booze had a chance to wear off.

"What are the three of you up to and is that whiskey I smell on your breath, Henry?"

"Nothing wrong with your sense of smell. We're gonna see Miranda just as soon as you get something new to wear on the plane," Henry got through the speech like he'd practiced all week.

"You are drunk, aren't you."

"Why would you think that?"

"You'd have to be drunk to suggest a shopping trip."

"It was her idea," Henry shuffled the blame off onto Reb.

"You drunk, too!" BeBe asked snappishly.

"Not yet," Reb said wistfully.

"So, where are we going shopping?" Mitch prodded the conversation forward, while they still had the upper hand.

"Dudley's, of course. Where else!" BeBe answered, already perking up in spite of herself. So while Mitch hammered out the Dudley's Department Store logistics, Reb and Henry teamed up to complete the paperwork necessary for the temporary release of BeBe from the hospital. Due to the complexity of these tasks, the shopping spree was finally set for nine o'clock the following morning. This did not seem to dampen BeBe's enthusiasm at all, but it did give Mitch and Reb the excuse to leave early to rest up for the early morning excursion.

Which was exactly what Mitch had planned to do. Little did she know that Reb had other plans. Starting with a soft nuzzle just below Mitch's right ear.

"I thought we were supposed to be getting some rest," Mitch murmured.

"You don't find this restful?"

"I'm not quite sure. Try it again and I'll let you know."

Not wanting to be predictable, Reb merely stroked Mitch's neck with a fingertip. Back and forth. Very slowly. Mitch did her very best to hold still and control her breathing. It never ceased to amaze her how such a small amount of touch could elicit the response that it did.

"Is this any more restful?" Reb asked, knowing full well that it wasn't. In fact, she knew that it was creating a restlessness unlike any other.

Mitch took hold of Reb's wandering hand and after kissing it gently, held it in her own hand.

"Had enough already?" Reb asked.

"I'll never have enough of you. I'm just savoring this moment."

"Touching your neck is driving you wild, huh?"

"Yeah."

"You must be very…needy?"

"I do need something. I need to tell you something," Mitch looked into Reb's eyes.

"What?"

"I need you to know that I couldn't do this without you and that I wouldn't even want to try."

Reb thought about this, not knowing exactly what Mitch was talking about, but nodding anyway. She could be referring to sex, the shopping spree, the hospital vigil, or life in general.

"Keep talking. I'm listening."

"I mean it," Mitch said seriously.

"I know you do. Tell me more."

Mitch checked to see if Reb was being serious. She was. "I couldn't imagine living life without you by my side."

Reb now mentally narrowed down the choices to hospital vigil and life in general. Which meant that the discussion was far more weighty than she had at first guessed.

"I would feel so alone without you, too," Reb stated.

"And I know that we've had this conversation about a hundred times already," Mitch faltered to a stop.

"But?" Reb wasn't going to pretend to be psychic.

"I've been watching BeBe and Henry these past few days and I've worried about it. I'm worried about them. About Henry in particular."

"Uh huh," Reb agreed, mostly to keep Mitch talking.

"I mean, if I even think about going on without you, my stomach clenches up and I can't swallow. You know?"

"I know exactly."

"I don't see anything like that between them."

"You're right."

"Aren't you worried about that?"

"In what way?"

"What do you mean?"

"I mean, are you worried that we're going to end up like them, or are you concerned what's going to happen to Henry when BeBe dies?"

"I'm petrified about what's going to happen to Henry. I know that we're never going to be like that."

"Well, then, let's concentrate on Henry. You two get along pretty well."

"I buy whiskey. He drinks it. There's not much to it but that."

"Friendships have been born of less."

"And so have relationships. If I recall correctly, the first drink I ever bought you, you threw it on me."

"And you see what happened from there?" Reb wrestled her hand free and went back to distracting Mitch from all her worried thoughts. Which succeeded. Beautifully.

Maybe it was all just in Mitch's imagination, but she sensed a nervousness where the sales staff at Dudley's was concerned. Like maybe they had dealt with Aunt BeBe plenty of times before and didn't exactly relish the idea of trying to please her now that she was extra sick and cranky. But those fears dissolved pretty quickly when folks noticed that there was a bit of buoyancy in BeBe's attitude. While everyone else was left to speculate on the source of this uplifted spirit, Mitch didn't have to guess. She knew exactly why BeBe was joyous. She was getting all set to spend Mitch's money. That's why. So when Reb had assumed that this was going to be an in-and-out trip with one dress in a bag, Mitch knew better. Before they were within grenade-tossing range of the "career woman" section, BeBe was admiring three different shades of nylons.

"Do you think I'd look good in nude?" BeBe asked Mitch with what might've been construed as a hint of a dare.

"I wouldn't want you in anything else," Mitch replied too innocently. "But if you need to stock up for the trip, you should buy a variety."

"Well, maybe nude and beige?" BeBe pondered.

Mitch motioned to the nearest clerk. "We'll take a dozen of every shade."

"What size?"

"I'll leave that decision between the two of you," Mitch smiled. If BeBe was "Big Mama" size, Mitch didn't want to know about it. She took advantage of the moment to have a word with Henry, who had been shifting from one foot to the other since they had landed in the lingerie department. He looked like he'd rather be drinking.

"Do they have men's clothing here?" she asked.

"Why? You need something?" he asked back.

Mitch answered slowly, like she was giving thoughtful consideration to his remarks, instead of giving the appearance of stalling for time.

"I think I have enough traveling clothes for now, but if you want to buy something or get a new suit, you might want to take the time to do that now."

"Why would I need a new suit?"

"Do you have one?"

"One old one."

Mitch tried to remember the last man she knew who only owned one suit. She came up blank. But rather than ask if he was planning to wear his old suit to BeBe's funeral, a tactless question at best, Mitch queried," A new suit might be nice to wear to the prison."

"There's nobody there who I need to make a good impression to."

Mitch made visual contact with BeBe, who was holding up panties for careful inspection. She looked back at Henry. "You can help pick out panties or you can browse through suit coats. It's your choice."

"I'll be on the second floor if you need me."

As he scuttled for the escalator, Reb rolled up.

"Where's he going?"

"As far away from ladies underwear as he can get."

"That's what they all say."

"I saw you admiring those nighties over there," Mitch wanted it to be known that her powers of observation were still sharp.

"I was imagining you in them."

"If you don't behave yourself, I'm going to leave you all by yourself with your sister and her underwear selections."

"I'll behave. I promise!"

Further silliness was interrupted by the "Yoo Hooing" of BeBe. "We did come here to shop, didn't we!?"

"Your sister came here to shop," Mitch muttered under her breath as she made her way back to the underwear display.

"Did you find something you like?" Mitch sounded cheery.

"I want something like this," BeBe held up a plain white cotton pair of panties.

"Absolutely," Mitch was relieved that it was such a bland selection. "Do you want all white or a variety of colors?"

"What do you suggest?" BeBe asked like the answer would bring forth world peace.

"I think a variety is best."

"Okay."

Mitch made eye contact with the now-hovering clerk, a rarity in today's retail. "We'll take every pair of cotton underpants you have in stock."

"But…well…that's a lot of pairs of underwear."

"Okay, that's fine," Mitch nodded as she eyed an emerald green pair of frilly silky panties. She then looked at Reb, who had an "I'm behaving myself" look on her face.

"Those are nice," Mitch indicated to BeBe.

"A girl who wears something like that is just asking for trouble."

"Really?"

"Absolutely!"

"From your lips to God's ears."

"What does that mean?"

"It means that I'm getting those in a size 5."

"That's too small for you!"

"I'm not buying them for me," Mitch looked over at Reb.

"Honestly!" BeBe huffed. "Girls buying other girls underwear!"

"I'm buying underwear for you."

"That's different!"

"How?"

"Because I'm selecting sensible things."

"I personally think that cotton is a big turn-on."

BeBe chose not to dignify that with a response and went directly to the shoe department. Reb got a pained look on her face.

"Are you okay?" Mitch went to her.

"You've never been shoe shopping with my sister, have you?"

129

"Not in this lifetime."

"It might take that long," Reb grimaced.

By the time they caught up with BeBe, she was seated in a chair and the shoe clerk was dancing attendance.

"Well! Isn't that just so interesting!" the clerk intoned like she was on stage rehearsing for a play. A play about feet.

"Your left foot is one-half size larger than your right foot."

Mitch now understood the problem. No wonder shoe shopping was so frustrating. One matching pair of shoes would never fit correctly. The answer seemed pretty simple.

"Buy two pairs of the same style of shoe and wear the correct size on each foot."

"That's the stupidest thing I've ever heard!" Aunt BeBe let her feelings be known, as usual.

"Why?"

"Well, what on Earth would I do with the other two shoes?"

"Donate them to a homeless shelter?"

"And what would they do with a mismatched pair of shoes?"

"Maybe there's someone out there just like you, only opposite."

"I doubt that!" BeBe answered back, but was then immediately distracted by several pairs of shoes that the clerk had trotted out for her approval. By the look on BeBe's face, this wasn't going to take long.

"Why don't you go and check on Henry," Reb suggested to Mitch.

"You'll be okay here?"

"We'll be in 'dresses' soon. We'll be fine."

Mitch meandered upstairs and located Henry admiring himself in a mirror. He had found a cashmere coat with a hefty price tag.

"That looks pretty snazzy," Mitch admired.

"I'm not buying it," Henry explained hurriedly. "I've just never tried on something this pricey."

"We should get it. Makes you look ten years younger."

"I don't like the idea of a woman buying things for me."

"Suit yourself," Mitch punned.

She didn't want to go back downstairs so soon. Reb would fuss and ask questions. So she walked around the main circular aisle of the otherwise deserted second floor, marveling at the various styles and colors that dominated men's fashion. Hopefully, Henry would stick with the duller stuff, at least where prison visitation and funeral attendance were concerned. And please, God, if you're still listening, have him pick up some new underwear as well. It couldn't possibly hurt. Unless it was mis-sized.

Mitch must've looked pensive, for a clerk came over to her from behind a rack.

"Can I help you?"

"Sure. Where's a good place to have lunch?"

"It's only 9:30."

Mitch resisted the urge to say, "Don't remind me," and instead politely stated, "I like to plan ahead."

She listened patiently to a listing of five promising eateries, taking mental notes about location and menu before holding up her hands in mock surrender. "That gives me plenty to choose from."

"Well, we were told to be very helpful," she smiled.

"You were?"

"Are you the one with all that money?"

Mitch didn't quite know how to best answer this question, so she just nodded her head.

"What does that feel like, having all that money?"

Again, Mitch was stymied for an answer. "I don't know if it feels like anything in particular, but you find yourself paying the bill for other people's shopping sprees a lot."

"You could buy about anything you wanted, right."

"Most of the things I want, money can't buy."

"Well, your father over there doesn't seem to have that problem. He has pretty good taste in clothes."

"You want to do me a big favor?"

"That's what we're here for."

"If he heads toward the underwear section, don't discourage him."

The clerk nodded, like she understood and took off like she was on either a mission or a commission. This freed up Mitch to go back downstairs and check on Reb. She was waiting outside the dressing room for BeBe to emerge.

"How long has she been in there?"

"She just went in."

"Does that mean I can have a kiss?"

"No."

Reb was never one for public displays of affection, but even this was too abrupt not to notice.

"Are you upset with me?"

"No."

"Not even about the green underwear?"

"Especially not about the green underwear. I'm just a little on edge."

"Of course you are. This is a difficult time for you."

"I *hate* shopping with my sister."

"I don't mind it too much. She seems to be able to make up her mind about what to buy."

"And spend your money all along the way."

"Is that what's bothering you?"

"I'm not sure."

"Because if it is, just keep reminding yourself that we could probably buy every dress in this store for her and never notice anything but a blip on our financial statements."

"So far, you've been blipping around here pretty good."

"I do my best blipping around you."

Finally, Mitch got a smile from Reb.

"You're getting farther and farther away from that kiss you requested."

"I'm a patient woman. I can wait."

"Not if last night is any indication."

Mitch was mulling a response when BeBe decided to throw a fashion show starring herself. And, darn, she looked good considering the circumstances. Aunt BeBe had never appeared in front of Mitch in anything other than what Ma Kettle wore in front of Pa Kettle, and for once, she looked very stylish.

"My goodness, BeBe. You look absolutely beautiful," Mitch was gracious with praise.

Oh, the human body is a mysterious concoction. For whatever reason known only to BeBe, she began to blush. It was either the compliment from Mitch or a menopausal hot flash. It added color to her otherwise pale countenance.

132

"Is that the first one you've tried on or just the only one you like?" Reb quizzed like they were in court.

"Well, I'm not quite sure how to answer that," BeBe's voice took on the affectation of Scarlet O'Hara. If they weren't careful, they'd get a "fiddle dee dee" in the next statement.

"That one is definitely a keeper," Mitch moved things along. "Is there another one that you would like to model?"

"Do we have time?"

"Absolutely," Mitch answered enthusiastically. She could sense another long interlude alone with Reb and perhaps a nuzzle if not a kiss after all.

"There is that yellow one, you know, with the eyelets."

Mitch nodded like she knew exactly what an eyelet was. She had no earthly clue what an eyelet was. Thank goodness Aunt BeBe wasn't handing out a pop quiz about eyelets. BeBe practically flounced back into the dressing room, which would give Mitch a few more minutes with her favorite person in the whole world. Except that now Henry showed up with a shopping bag in each hand.

"You're all balanced out," Reb commented.

"I feel like a pack mule."

"Just wait until BeBe gets done. We're going to need a truck."

"Nuthin new there," Henry settled his frame into the only remaining chair. Why this brought all conversation to a halt was anyone's guess. Mitch wondered if he, by chance, knew what an eyelet was? Should she ask? Maybe it was something embarrassingly feminine. Her opportunity was lost forever when BeBe made a return appearance in something yellow. With eyelets.

"What do you think?" she fished for compliments from everyone, Henry in particular.

"Well…it's yella."

At least he wasn't colorblind. Of course, it would've killed him to say something nice.

"I like this one almost as much as the other one. But they both look lovely," Mitch remarked kindly.

"Well, I have to choose…" BeBe sounded like this was the final jeopardy answer and she had two really great questions.

"You don't have to choose. And I certainly hope you're not finished trying things on," Mitch sounded just a smidgen panicked to herself and hoped it hadn't come out sounding that way. It was still way too early for lunch.

"Well, there was that one other dress, but it was a bit too colorful, I suspect."

"Try it on, by all means. You can't tell how it looks on the hanger."

"Okay, but that's it. I've never bought more than one dress at a time let alone three."

As soon as she disappeared, Henry stood up and announced that he would be waiting in the car. When he was out of sight, Mitch looked at Reb and mused, "I hope he brought a good book."

"I wish I had," was Reb's only response.

Mitch didn't know quite how to take the remark, so she hushed up. The minutes ticked by slowly. Mitch chalked it up to the fact that BeBe was slowing down. She had been a trooper to attempt the outing at all. Whatever reservations BeBe had about dress number three being too colorful were dispelled as soon as she posed in front of the mirror. A fashion miracle had occurred right in front of them. Too bad Henry had missed the moment. His idea of a miracle was a quick getaway from the mall. Which also occurred when BeBe suddenly ran out of steam. She was dying, after all. They skipped lunch and took her back to the hospital so that she could rest up for the big trip. They were scheduled to fly out at five, which was pushing it even for a healthy person.

Nap time was quiet. Mitch and Reb spent two hours actually resting in bed. They weren't kids anymore.

"You are good to my sister."

"She's family after all."

"But it's more than that with you. I've seen how some families treat each other. And I know how she has treated you."

"That's water under the bridge, don't you think?" Mitch found comfort in platitudes.

"You can forgive her that easily?"

"I think the real question is, can you forgive her for all the slights of childhood?"

"What's that supposed to mean?" Reb sounded defensive, even though she tried to hide it behind surprise.

Mitch shifted around to make eye contact. "The two of you haven't exactly been close all these years. I don't think it all started with your high school prom. Of course, I could be wrong…"

Reb was quiet for so long that Mitch wondered if she had dozed off. And then, she stirred and looked at Mitch.

"What?" Mitch prompted.

"I'm trying to remember the last time you were wrong about anything."

"There was this time in high school trigonometry class when I got sine and cosine mixed up. Gee, was I embarrassed."

"The whole class laughed at you?"

"Oh, heck no. They didn't know the difference either."

"And you never told me?" Reb was trying to sound engaged.

"I didn't want to go off on a tangent."

"Oh, boo!" Reb laughed gently.

"So, you know something about trigonometry?"

"Not as much as you do."

"And I don't really know anything about you and your sister."

"We're two different people. That's all you need to know."

Mitch could've thought up about eighteen different responses, but she kept her mouth shut. She knew that if and when Reb decided to let her into the sacred sanctum of what it was like to have a sister, it would happen.

"We'd better get dressed," Reb stated flatly.

"We are dressed."

"I mean, for the flight."

"I'm wearing this."

Mitch hadn't bought anything new for herself during the shopping spree and she hadn't bought anything new for Reb, come to think of it, unless you counted that little next-to-nothing green lovely that was still tucked away in some shopping bag. It was just a charter flight after all. There was no one to impress but the pilot and he was only impressed by the timely payment for his services.

"You're wearing that?" Reb made it sound like Mitch resembled an unmade bed.

"I thought you liked my rumples."

"I live and breathe for your rumples. Now…what are you going to wear on the plane?"

Mitch didn't feel like fussing about fashion. If Reb wanted her to dress up a bit for the flight, it was an easy thing to do to please her. And since that was her main joy in life, she would comply without grumbling.

"I do have my old blue blazer."

"The one that makes you look like a Republican?"

"Yeah."

"Perfect!"

If the pilot had any observations about a boarding party consisting of a dying woman in a yellow dress with eyelets, a woman in a wheelchair dressed like Julia Roberts, a man who looked itchy in a suit and a woman who looked at home in a perfectly tailored suit coat, he kept them to himself. He was being paid too much to do otherwise.

"You should've had her help you pick out a suit," BeBe indicated Mitch to Henry.

"I did," Henry lied.

"What did you do, take the opposite of her advice!"

"Why don't we all buckle in for takeoff," Mitch changed subjects as she helped Reb secure her wheelchair. This kept everyone busy and quiet for thirty seconds. Thirty seconds of quiet that she knew would be followed by endless minutes of strained conversation. Any regret that Mitch was feeling was assuaged by the look in Reb's eyes. Without a word exchanged, she conveyed her appreciation with that expression that wrapped Mitch up in an emotional cocoon.

"You better get yourself buckled up!" BeBe ordered Mitch like she was now in charge of the venture. So much for warm fuzzy feelings. Reb smiled and mouthed silently, "Buckle up." When she winked, life became bearable all over again.

Once they were airborne, BeBe busied herself by reading the Bible while Henry slept. Not wanting to disturb either of them, Mitch and Reb scooted to the rear of the jet and kept each other company. Which mainly consisted of holding hands and chatting about inconsequential topics. For Mitch, it was blissful. And then, things turned thoughtful.

"Do you think you'd spend time reading the Bible if you knew you were dying?" Reb asked.

"Some people say that it's cramming for the final."

"The final?"

"The final exam."

"I'm trying to be serious," Reb was almost scowling.

"I was just telling you what other people think before I tell you what I think."

"And why are you compelled to do that?"

"I think it's so I'll end up sounding smarter than everyone else."

"That only works if you quote stupid people."

"Which is why I never repeat anything you say."

"I wondered why that was."

"But back to the original question. I don't think I'd spend time reading the Bible if I knew that I was dying soon."

"Why not?" Reb wanted details. They were 10,000 feet in the air and Mitch couldn't get away.

"Well, I guess the short answer is that I've gotten this far in life without reading it and I don't see impending death as a good-enough reason to start."

"You've never read any part of the Bible?" Reb was truly surprised.

"I've heard parts of it. You know, like in church services and stuff," Mitch felt defensive for no earthly good reason. When she noticed that Reb was just looking at her, Mitch felt compelled to embellish. "I may have followed along in a prayer book. And I'm pretty sure I've seen a verse or two browsing in the greeting card section of the supermarket..."

"You've been doing your Bible study in the greeting card section?" Reb sounded disbelieving.

"Have you been to the greeting card section lately?" Mitch answered back.

"The greeting card section?"

"Sure. Between the wedding cards and the get-well cards and the Christmas cards, you have quite the selection of religious readings."

Mitch had been careful not to mention the sympathy card selection for obvious reasons, and was more than happy to quit while she was ahead, but Reb urged her, "Go on."

"Besides those, there's whole companies that specialize in religious cards. You can send Bible verses to people for their birthday and their baby's birth and Mother's Day and Father's Day and-"

"I see your point."

"In fact, the religionization of the greeting card business has turned into quite the industry."

"Is that a word?"

"Is what a word?"

"Religionization?"

"Well, what else would you call it when you start out just trying to send a card to a friend and it looks like you're trying to convert them to Christianity?"

"Not every card is like that."

"No. Halloween cards are still exempt. Nobody would send a card that says, 'Jesus wishes you a Happy Halloween.'"

Reb looked like she was getting a headache. Maybe it was just the change in altitude.

"Are we going to be there soon?"

"We're just going across Kansas. It shouldn't be long. Top speed of this particular aircraft is about 500 miles per hour."

"Aren't we only going 200 miles?"

"Like I said, it won't be long. You didn't think I had planned to stay cooped up with your sister for an extended period of time, did you?"

Before Reb could answer, the pilot announced preparations for descent, which included instructions to buckle up. And Henry hadn't even had time for a drink after his nap. Which BeBe wasn't allowing anyway, so it really didn't matter. The limo ride was nice, too. In fact, both of them were luxurious.

"Why are we taking two cars?" BeBe asked like she was paying the fare.

"Because yours is ambulance equipped, just in case."

BeBe didn't like the answer, but instead of fussing, she got in the vehicle. Henry climbed in after and they were off the tarmac and on the highway before Mitch and Reb had even settled in for their ride.

"We're going to the hotel first, right?" Reb asked.

"Right."

"And then the prison?"

"Not until tomorrow."

"BeBe's going to be a nervous wreck by then."

"Some things just can't be helped," Mitch sighed.

It was only then that Reb realized how weary Mitch was. Between all the rushing around and making all the arrangements, Reb had simply overlooked the possibility that this would have a wearing down effect on Mitch.

"Would you do one more thing for me?" Reb asked, trying to make it sound like another in a long list of chores.

"Sure," Mitch replied like she was willing, as always.

"Would you scoot closer and put your head on my shoulder."

Mitch knew a good invitation when she heard one and accepted the embrace without hesitation. She must've dozed off for when she awoke, they were at the hotel, safe and sound.

"I would've had them drive around the block a couple of times," Reb offered by way of apology after waking her up, "but I didn't want to vex BeBe."

"I'm glad you didn't," Mitch replied kindly.

Checking into a hotel when you're a millionaire is usually a little different than for everybody else, but Mitch tried her best to not act like a prima donna about it. She filled out and signed the paperwork quickly so that they could get BeBe upstairs as soon as possible. She was currently window shopping in the hotel's vastly overpriced boutique and Henry's wallet seemed to be sewn to the inside of his pants pocket.

"Could you do me a favor?" Mitch now had a request for Reb.

"Of course."

"Tell the nice clerk in the shop that the room to charge BeBe's purchases to is…1501."

"Didn't we *just* take her shopping?"

"Yes, I believe we did. Room 1501."

Reb wheeled away and when she didn't return forthwith, Mitch knew that something had caught her eye as well. Hotel boutiques always had the *nicest* things. And at the most inflated prices imaginable. It wasn't just anywhere that you could buy fifteen dollars worth of sweater for a hundred and fifty dollars. BeBe was eyeing sweaters like she was going on an Antarctic expedition. And so was Reb. The only difference being that Mitch could enjoy imagining how Reb looked in her sweaters. And out of them as well.

"1501, you said?" Reb confirmed to Mitch.

"Room number or price?" Mitch asked, not that she cared.

Reb smiled, appreciating the humor.

"What if I said both?"

"Then I'd say I got off cheap."

"Not with me around."

"I'm betting that my pocketbook can outlast the both of you."

"You're on!"

By the time they got to their rooms, BeBe and Reb both had a whole other suitcase worth of new purchases.

"Are we dressing for dinner?" BeBe asked.

Reb gave Mitch a warning look. No naked jokes.

"Let's keep it casual," Reb suggested.

They kept it so casual that BeBe took her dinner in bed. Henry took a bottle of whiskey from the bar area into the den and settled in front of the TV. It was the size of a small movie theater. Reb and Mitch sat across from each other at a table in their suite and savored a simple meal.

"This isn't bad for vegetarian fare," Reb was still getting used to Mitch's new eating regime.

"Who ever thought you could make tofu taste like pork tenderloin."

"A miracle of modern science."

At the word "miracle," Mitch winced.

"Sorry," Reb noticed.

"It's okay."

"I guess I was wrong about BeBe being nervous. She'll be asleep right after dinner with any luck."

"The flight wore her out. Did the doctor check her?"

"Briefly. There isn't much to do for her. She didn't even need a sleeping pill."

"Neither will I."

"What time are we due at the prison?"

140

"Ten in the morning."

"That's pretty early."

"We'll have time to have a nice chat before lunch."

"You did manage to arrange a lengthy visit."

"And in a year or two, we can come back and visit the Tanner Library."

"I'll put it in my appointment book," Reb sounded like that headache was coming back.

"You ready for bed?" Mitch inquired.

Reb sighed in reply.

"What?" Mitch knew a needful sigh when she heard it.

"What?" Reb asked back like she wanted Mitch to pursue the topic.

"I asked first," Mitch stood up and went around to the back of Reb's chair. She put her hands on Reb's shoulders and began to relieve about two-hundred miles of tension.

"Oh, yes," Reb murmured after a moment. And then she whimpered. And then she sighed again.

Mitch chuckled.

"What's so funny?"

"Your relatives are going to wonder what's going on in here."

"There's nothing going on in here."

"I can change that," Mitch assured her.

Mitch let her hands travel down to the first button on Reb's blouse, but her progress was halted by Reb. She took hold of each of Mitch's hands and then leaned her head against Mitch's left arm. Things got quiet. Mitch waited. For a moment.

"You okay?" she whispered.

Reb only nodded. And then Mitch felt the trickle of a tear on her hand. She leaned even closer and said, "I love you."

Reb nodded again, still not trusting her voice.

"If you go to bed with me, you can have my whole shoulder to cry on."

"I might need it."

"It's all yours."

They readied for bed just like every other night of the week and then cuddled close together. Reb was calm by now, but still craved Mitch's embrace.

"Are you just tired or is there something bothering you?"

141

"What on earth are we going to find to talk about with Miranda tomorrow?"

Mitch had wondered when this topic was going to come up. After all, what do you say to the young woman who tried to kill you by torching your house while you slept? "You're in jail and we're not" just didn't seem appropriate.

"I figured that BeBe and Henry would carry the conversation, didn't you?"

"My concern is that they won't be able to fill ten minutes at best."

"Really?" Mitch was surprised at this statement. "I thought BeBe was pretty adept at keeping up her end of the conversation."

"That's only when you're around."

"You're teasing, right?"

"No. When you are around my sister, it's like she's been vaccinated with a phonograph needle."

"That's only because she can't torment me unless she talks to me. I was hoping she would try and make her peace with Miranda now that she's dying."

"I wouldn't count on it. They won't have much to say to each other, mark my word."

"So, what do you suggest we do?"

"Have a whole bunch of your scintillating anecdotes ready just in case."

"I could always tell them about our dating history…"

"That would be a bit too scintillating," Reb raised up on one elbow, smiling.

"I'm glad to see you happier."

"I'm glad we talked."

"I'm glad we do everything we do."

"Me, too."

Chapter 14

"I was never in prison until I met your family," Mitch muttered under her breath as they waited in the visitor's area.

"That's not true. You've been in prison before," Reb whispered back.

"I meant a maximum security prison," Mitch clarified. "The other was just a holding cell."

"Well, I'm glad we got *that* cleared up."

"What *are* you two muttering about!" BeBe snapped.

BeBe had been snappish all morning long. It was understandable, but still uncomfortable. They had been met at the door by the warden herself. It wasn't every day that you could meet a millionaire lesbian, and Warden Kingsley wasn't going to miss the opportunity. Although the limousine driver wasn't exactly thrilled by the rule requiring him to surrender the keys to the vehicle for the duration of the visit, he complied. Everyone else handed over identification, endured being searched, and then were run through a metal detector. Then they went through double security doors and finally herded to the room they now occupied.

"I was saying that I've never actually been in prison."

"Don't be stupid! None of us has ever been in prison, for heaven's sake!" BeBe snapped again.

"Actually, I was once," Henry offered this confession out of the blue. "Course, it wasn't as fancy as this one."

"Are you drunk again?" BeBe demanded to know and then added, "You were never in jail!"

"It was before you knew me," Henry had a touch of defiance in his voice, like it was important for all to know that he had a life once that wasn't just being the appendage of BeBe.

Mitch glanced at Reb to see if she should follow up on a line of inquiry, but she was too late.

"Why were you in prison?" Reb asked Henry.

"Nobody wants to know that!" BeBe answered for him.

"Did you knock over a gas station or something?" Mitch chimed in, glad for some decent conversation topic.

"I drove backwards around the courthouse."

"And for that you got thrown in jail?"

"I was twelve years old at the time."

"Twelve!" Mitch asked, barely suppressing a laugh.

"Yeah. I was in my dad's Buick and it was a late Friday night. Had a five-dollar bet on the line that I could back the car clear round the block where the courthouse was and-"

The story was sadly interrupted by the clanging of doors in the distance. Damn, Mitch thought to herself, it sounded like we were just getting to the good part, too.

For whatever social reason, everyone except Reb stood up in preparation to greet a dangerously disturbed criminal. It was either politeness in general or the adrenal system getting ready to issue the flight order. When Miranda appeared, one thing stood out immediately. There was no need to worry about running away. She looked pale and timid and just a tad teetery. One other fact stood out as well, but when Mitch looked over at Reb for guidance, she got a warning look in return. BeBe stood still for a moment and then gave Miranda a quick hug. Henry shook her hand like it was a business deal. Miranda sat down and started twisting her hair with her left hand.

"Stop twisting your hair. It'll fall out," BeBe went right to mother issues.

Miranda's hand slipped down to her lap for a moment and then she resumed twisting her hair again. If it hadn't fallen out by now, there wasn't much reason to fuss about it. That didn't stop BeBe.

"Honey, stop fiddling with your hair! And tell us about how things are...in here."

"Things are fine. Everything's fine."

"Well, it looks like the food's tolerable at least," Henry added his voice to the conversation. "You don't look thin."

Miranda didn't say anything but the fingers continued twisting the hair and she locked her gaze on Mitch.

"The food's fine."

Mitch gazed back. From what little she knew, a ravenous goat would turn its nose up at ninety-nine percent of all prison food. Miranda cast her eyes to the floor, breaking the silent conversation she was having with Mitch. Mitch glanced over at Reb. She had gone a tad pale now as well.

144

"Speaking of food, weren't we going to have lunch?" Henry asked Mitch on behalf of his stomach.

"I don't think you want to eat here," Miranda cut through the cordiality.

"Why not, Honey?" BeBe asked.

"Because you don't. I have to go back to my cell block." Miranda stood to leave and because the guard was there, no one could stop Miranda.

"I thought you arranged a longer visit!" BeBe turned her wrath on Mitch.

Being the gallant sort, Mitch accepted responsibility readily. "I thought I had. I'm sorry."

Reb was poised to come to Mitch's defense, but Mitch gave a small shake of her head. The silence on the way back to the hotel was stifling. Things hadn't turned out as planned. Not even close. They split into two camps the minute they got to the hotel and Mitch and Reb found themselves sitting across from each other at the dining area table.

"What in heaven's name are we going to do?" Mitch asked.

"About what?"

Mitch looked at Reb for a long moment. "What are we going to do about Miranda and her baby?"

"I had hoped I was mistaken."

"You weren't."

"How do you know for sure?"

"I just know."

"What are we going to do?"

"I'm going back this afternoon."

"I'll go with you."

"I think it would be better if you stay here. BeBe will get suspicious if both of us go missing. And besides, it's tough getting that wheelchair of yours past security."

"What you're really saying is that you think she'll open up to you if you're alone."

"I think it's our best shot."

Mitch left without fanfare, taking a cab in case the group noticed the missing limo. She arrived at the prison after meal time and waited again for the warden to once again thank her for her generous donation before being escorted to a small waiting room.

Miranda was brought in soon after and they sat opposite to each other.

"Do you want to tell me what happened?" Mitch asked with a concern that she didn't even herself realize she had until now.

Miranda didn't say anything at first. She just continued to twirl her hair. Mitch waited. There was nowhere else to go. Nothing else to do.

"Did you come alone?" Miranda asked, not looking up from the floor.

"Yeah," Mitch answered calmly.

Miranda crossed her arms across her chest and looked at the walls.

"What do you *think* happened?" Miranda said with bitterness in her voice. It was the first glimmer of emotion Mitch had seen from her and she took it as a positive sign.

"I don't think it's a good idea to play guessing games. Don't you think it would just be easier if you tell me what happened. Take all the time you need."

Miranda uncrossed her arms and started to twirl her hair again.

"The guards, you know," she started and then stopped. Mitch almost bit her tongue to keep from interjecting. Miranda needed to do this on her own terms. At her own speed.

"They have all the power, you know."

Mitch knew about this. She had been shackled before at the mercy of a guard and had been left without bathroom privileges. It had been a humiliating experience, as intended.

"Aunt Mitch?"

Mitch came back with a start. "What?"

"You were daydreaming," Miranda sounded annoyed.

"What did you call me?"

"Aunt Mitch. I don't know what else to call you. I guess it's not okay."

"No, it's fine, really. I've just never had anyone call me Aunt Mitch before."

"You don't like it, I can tell."

"Let's get back to you and your situation."

"*Situation*. Yeah, that's a *great* way to put it."

"Did the guard offer anything in return?"

"You make it sound like a negotiation."

"What did you tell the authorities?"

Miranda just looked at Mitch like she was the densest person on the planet.

"You did report it, didn't you?"

"Of course I didn't report it!"

"Was it consensual?"

"Do you mean did I put up a fight?"

"No. I mean, did you consent. Did you say 'yes?' Did you say 'no'?"

"Look, I laid there and I took it, okay."

"I realize that you took it. I'm asking if you wanted it to happen."

"I was afraid not to. You just don't get it, do you? The guards run things around here. They're in your face every day. And if they see something they want, like a virgin for instance, well, it's not like I could go anywhere to get away."

"You were coerced."

"That's a really polite way to put it."

"If I helped you, would you make a police report?"

"It won't do any good."

"Why not?"

"Because I'm still trapped here."

"The guard is still here?"

"Of course he is."

"Does anybody know you're pregnant?"

"Not yet."

"You'll need prenatal care, for starters."

"Whatever that is."

Mitch rubbed her temples to ease the tension she felt building. And the anger. Miranda was in a huge mess with no one to help.

"I need to go make a phone call."

"You can't tell my parents! Don't tell them anything or I'll hurt myself!"

"Honey, relax. I'm going to call Aunt Reb."

"Does she know?"

"We both have pregnant radar. She knows."

Mitch went out of the visiting room and was allowed to use the phone at the guard station. Knowing that her conversation was being monitored, she attempted to keep it simple.

147

"Reb, can you come back to see Miranda."

"Sure, but I'll need to arrange transportation."

"Go ahead and take the limo. I don't think we need to worry about BeBe noticing."

"I'm absolutely certain of that. She and Henry have commandeered the ambulatory limo and headed home."

"They left?"

"That's right. They are planning to go all two-hundred-plus miles in the limo. That's going to rack up quite a bill."

"That's fine. We've got bigger problems. How fast can you get here?"

"I'll be there."

Reb was in the lobby before Mitch had figured out the best way to explain things to her.

"What's going on?" Reb got right to it.

"Miranda was raped by one of the guards and she needs our help."

"Did she say that?"

"Not in those exact words. But it's the general scenario."

Reb was famous from her previous experience as a politician for having a great poker face. Mitch couldn't tell what she was thinking when she used this expression.

"You want me to talk to her?" Reb sounded detached.

"I want you to go in there and be her Aunt Reb," Mitch emphasized the "Aunt" part.

"Just to refresh your memory, this is the psychotic girl who tried to kill me."

"Wouldn't you be crazy if you had been raised by BeBe and Henry?" Mitch argued back with the only logical point she could think of. She hadn't expected resistance from Reb.

"I'll talk to the girl, but I'm doing it against my better judgment."

"Thank you."

They were escorted back to the holding area where Miranda had been waiting patiently. Reb settled next to Miranda and said bluntly, "Mitch said you have something to tell me."

"She told me that you already know."

"Tell me in your own words."

Miranda glanced at Mitch, who nodded, giving her moral support. "I was raped by a guard. I'm four months pregnant. Nobody knows but the three of us."

"You need to make a police report."

"I can't. It's too dangerous."

"I won't help you unless you make a report," Reb was driving a hard bargain. Maybe it was just her way of testing for the truth. Miranda looked at Mitch again.

"It's your decision," Mitch said gently.

"How are you going to protect me?"

"Mitch is good friends with the warden."

"And you think that's enough?"

"What other plans do you have in mind, Miranda?" Reb bore into her.

"Well, I thought about hanging myself in my cell, but I'm already on suicide watch."

"If you're on suicide watch, how did you get raped?"

Miranda didn't say a word, but instead locked eyes with Reb. Her expression said it all. You're a smart woman. You figure it out. Mitch felt that throbbing start up again in her temples.

"Mitch?" Reb said.

"Yes?" Mitch answered.

"Go get the warden."

Chapter 15

Trish was awakened once again by silence. It seemed to bother her more than noise. Robbie wasn't in bed next to her, and she didn't hear any rustling noise in the distance. She floundered her way out of this most comfortable bed and padded up and down the hallway. Josh was asleep and Robbie was nowhere to be found. Trish wandered around the house. No Robbie in sight. She resisted the urge to panic. After all, this could be a good thing. Robbie rejoining society after an extended bout of post-partum depression. Rose was in the kitchen, drinking coffee and reading the paper.
"Have you seen Robbie?" Trish asked.
"She's not in bed?" Rose answered with a question. Trish was used to this by now.
"She's not in bed."
"She's not around here."
"Could she be outside?"
"In this weather? I doubt it," Rose answered and then called out, "Silver!"
Silver came around the corner instantaneously. She was never far away. That's just one of those job descriptions of a bodyguard.
"What's wrong?" she could read Rose's tone of voice after all these months.
"Have you seen Robbie?"
"She's not in bed?" Silver had picked up on Rose's question-asking-answer technique.
Trish began to doubt herself. "Maybe I'll check again."
"I'll do it," Silver was now using her professional tone of voice.
"I'll help," Rose put down her coffee.
"Fine," Trish said. "I'll check around here."
She waited until the kitchen had cleared out before she poured herself a cup of coffee. No use being thirsty during the search. Trish realized after a minute of wandering that there wasn't much to search on the main floor, so she went back to the kitchen. On a whim, she set her coffee down and took the stairs to the basement. She walked to the spooky room and found Robbie sitting quietly on the floor staring into space. Her knees

were drawn up to her chest and she didn't acknowledge Trish's presence. Trish took this as a warning and walked silently over to her. She sat down beside her and after a moment touched her arm. She felt cold.

"Are you okay?" Trish asked.

"What?" Robbie asked like she was waking up from a nap.

"Are you okay?" Trish repeated.

"What are you doing here?"

"I was about to ask you the same thing."

"What?" Robbie still seemed drowsy.

"Why are you down here?"

Robbie looked around like it was just dawning on her that she wasn't upstairs in bed.

"What am I doing down here?"

"Come on. People are looking for you."

Trish stood up and helped Robbie to her feet. She was stiff from sitting so long in one place.

"Who?"

"Who what?"

"Who is looking for me?" Robbie clutched Trish's arm to the point of bruising her.

"The usual suspects. Silver and your mom. You know, the posse."

"Is that all?"

"If Max had joined in, we would've had an entire cavalry, I suppose."

"How long did it take you to find me?"

"Not long once we realized you were missing."

"So, it could've been a long time?"

"It seems to have been. You are cold and stiff."

As they started up the stairs, Silver came bounding down to help. She was always ready with a strong shoulder to lean on.

"Come on, Miss Robbie. Do you need a doctor?"

"No, I'm okay."

"We'd better get you up the stairs. Miss Rose is ready to call 911 again."

Robbie turned to Trish. "Don't let her do that. The sirens will wake Josh."

"I'll see what I can do," Trish went ahead of them and intercepted Rose reaching for the phone.

"We found her."

"How is she? Is she hurt?"

"She doesn't seem to be hurt."

Before Trish could elaborate, Silver and Robbie emerged from the stairwell and into the kitchen.

"You'd better get her to bed," Rose said.

"It's warm in here," Robbie sat on one of the kitchen stools and began to drink from Trish's abandoned coffee cup.

Rose looked at Trish, "What was she doing down there?"

"Sitting."

"Just sitting?"

"Sitting and staring into space."

"Why was she down there?"

"You'll have to ask her."

"You didn't?"

"I tried. You try."

Rose approached Robbie and touched her arm. "You're still awfully cold."

"Let's take her into the fireplace room," Silver spoke with an authoritarian manner that nobody ever argued with.

"Good idea," Rose nodded.

They bundled her into the main sitting room that housed the cavernous fireplace designed back when people actually burned entire logs during the Yule season. Trish and Robbie sat side by side on the couch facing the fire and for the first time in weeks, Robbie allowed Trish to hold her close. When Rose took a breath to ask a question, Trish shook her head. She didn't want to break whatever calm mood had descended on Robbie. Which left Rose to fidget in her chair for a moment or two before leaving them alone. Trish could feel Robbie shiver occasionally as if the cold that she felt was deep within. Holding her was so welcome a change from their recent estrangement that she secretly hoped the shivering would continue. At least for a little while.

"I should go check on Josh."

"I'm sure your mom is taking care of him."

"I don't remember feeding him this morning."

152

"You must have. He seemed fine when I checked on him. Do you remember anything about this morning?"

"Not until you came down to the basement."

"So, you don't know why you went down there?"

"No. Do you suppose I was sleepwalking?"

"I guess that's what could've happened."

Trish refrained from pointing out that Robbie had never sleep walked in all the time she had known her. There was a first time for everything. By now, the shivering had stopped.

"I'm going to check on Josh," Robbie left Trish's warm embrace. It was now Trish who felt suddenly cold. It had taken a minor disturbance to bring Robbie into Trish's arms and Trish now felt guilty that she found herself wishing for more minor disturbances. Speaking of which, off in the distance a phone was ringing. Trish chose to ignore it. Rose hadn't and now brought the handset to Trish.

"It's for you," Rose handed the phone to Trish and then sat down to monitor the call. Which meant that Lisa was on the line.

"Hello, Lisa."

"How did you know it was me?"

"I had a hunch. What's up?"

"I think we should go out and interview Mrs. Wrightwood again."

"Why?"

"Just like you, I have a hunch."

"What's your hunch?"

"I'm sure she knows more than she's telling. Besides, we may have jogged her memory a little since our last chat. I'm sure it's been a long time since she's thought about the Livermores. Maybe something else has come to her by now."

"You could be right. When do you want to go?"

At the word "go," Rose twitched. That's what you get for eavesdropping. You hear things you'd rather not.

"Is today too soon?"

"Sounds fine. I'll come get you."

"I can drive to your house."

"No. I'll pick you up in an hour."

Rose twitched again. Trish handed the phone back to her after disconnecting the call.

"You're going out with Lisa," Rose stated.

Trish heard the potential double meaning of the question and chose to push it to the back of her mind. "We're going back to the nursing home. Want to tag along?"

"Are you sure it's worth another trip?"

"She's our only lead."

"What about Robbie? What if she wanders back down to the basement?"

"Are you staying or going?" Trish asked in return.

Rose pondered the question. She was torn between caring for her daughter or chaperoning Trish and Lisa.

"I only have an hour," Trish prodded after several seconds.

"I'm staying."

"Okay then, if Robbie wanders back downstairs and she doesn't respond to you, cover her with a blanket and call me on my cell phone."

"And then what?"

"And then we'll take it from there."

Rose didn't look happy with the answer, but she didn't argue. She just tutted like she didn't approve of the outing. Trish threw on clothes that were appropriate for a day in the country, old bargain-brand non-designer jeans and a well-worn-out flannel shirt. She wanted to impress upon Rose that this field trip was nothing special and therefore not an event for which to dress up.

"You're wearing that?" Rose asked flatly.

"I'm not trying to impress anybody."

"That should do it."

Trish once again took her old truck on this adventure to further drive home the point that it wasn't a date. She hoped that Lisa wasn't dressed in a tight skirt or anything that would make it difficult to get into the cab of the truck. Otherwise, she would need to change. Since the route was familiar by now, the trip seemed to go faster than normal. Trish was ringing Lisa's doorbell in distracted fashion, still thinking about the events of the morning. Lisa answered the door after a respectable amount of time.

"Hi! You got here a lot sooner than I expected."

"I drove fast."

"What's wrong?" Lisa asked as she ushered Trish into the well-appointed living room. By now, Trish knew better than to banter with Lisa about things like this. Lisa just *knew* things.

"We found Robbie in the basement room this morning."

"Oh my God, is she okay?" Lisa asked with genuine concern.

"She seems fine now."

"Or you wouldn't be here now, obviously. Do you want some coffee? Mary made it so it's okay to drink."

"Sure, that sounds good," Trish remembered that Robbie had drunk most of her coffee. Another cup sounded great.

"Cream and sugar?"

"You said Mary made it?"

'Uh huh."

"I'll take it black. I'm watching my calories, as usual."

"I don't see why," Lisa smiled and left to fetch the coffee. She was full of questions when she returned.

"Was Robbie locked in the basement room?"

"No. The door was open. But she acted like she was in a daze. She didn't remember going downstairs and it was like she was in a trance."

"So, she was just sitting down there?"

"Yeah. All huddled up and cold. Just like you except without the tears."

"So, you got her back upstairs okay?"

"She sort of came to when I found her and Silver helped."

"You are so lucky to have Silver."

"She's great," Trish smiled.

"That's better."

"What's better?"

"You are smiling again."

"It's been a long morning," Trish sipped Mary's coffee. She should've asked for cream and sugar after all, calories be damned. She also finally realized that Lisa was indeed wearing a tight miniskirt.

"What are you thinking?" Lisa had to ask for a change.

"I brought the truck."

"I noticed."

"It's a big step up to the cab."

"And you don't think I can do it in this skirt."

155

"I know I couldn't."

"You think I should change."

"I could go back home and get the sedan."

"I'll change," Lisa rose to leave the room but said as she went out of view, "The cream and sugar are on the kitchen counter." Trish availed herself of both liberally and then wandered around, too on-edge to sit patiently, drinking her coffee as she paced.

"You're nervous," Lisa remarked as she came back more appropriately dressed for truck travel.

"I've been sitting too long. You can explain the plan to me while I drive."

"Sounds great. All I need now is a plan to explain," Lisa smiled.

"You mean that we're winging it?"

"I just have one direct question to ask our geriatric authoress."

"What's the question?"

"I want to know what she knows about female offspring of the Livermore family."

"I don't follow?"

"It's just a feeling I have."

Trish didn't argue. She had seen in person how Lisa's "feelings" worked. At times, it was downright uncanny.

"You didn't bring Rose and Max this time?"

"I think their visit to the home gave then the willies."

"Too close for comfort?"

"Maybe. Besides, Rose stayed behind to keep an eye on Robbie."

"And she feels you should've done the same thing, maybe?"

"Rose doesn't approve of our meeting like this."

"Meeting like what?"

"Meeting like we're seeing each other."

"You mean like dating!" Lisa was surprised for once.

"Well, I'm not sure that 'dating' is the right word."

"I had no idea Rose thought that we would be dating. How absurd!"

"Yeah, how absurd."

"I mean, gee whiz, Mary is stuck with me and all my disfigurement. And even if I didn't have Mary, I sure wouldn't reenter the dating scene ever again."

"Why not?"

"You have actually looked at me, right?"

"Sure, yeah."

"Well, people don't date with their eyes shut!"

"Maybe they should."

"You see, even you realize how bad I look."

Trish hadn't meant that at all and was ready to become huffy about it when Lisa said quietly, "I'm sorry."

"It's okay. I just wasn't thinking."

"It's still kind of a sore subject with me."

"It doesn't need to be. You are still a stunning-looking woman, in all the best ways."

"Even out of a tight skirt?"

"Especially out of a tight skirt."

"It's a good thing your mother-in-law isn't around to hear you talk like that!"

Trish only laughed. Silly banter had been in short supply lately in her life and she didn't realize how much she missed it until now. All too soon they were at the nursing home.

"You only have one question?" Trish checked again.

"So far," Lisa noted the curious expression on Trish's face. "It all depends on the answer I get," she explained further.

As they entered the old woman's room, a faint flicker of recognition crossed Mrs. Wrightwood's face.

"Do I know you?"

"We came to visit you a while back."

"There were more of you, weren't there?"

"You remember that?"

"I may be a little fuzzy on the details, but I've not totally gone over the edge."

"The last time we were here, we were asking about the Livermore family."

"You were the one with the ghost. I remember."

"You remember that?"

"It's not every day someone comes in to visit with a ghost story to tell. It isn't every day that you get a decent meal here either. You didn't happen to bring food with you?"

"Sorry, no," Trish replied.

"There's probably a rule against it anyway. They have rules about everything around here. Take my advice. Don't grow old. Die before your life gets ruined by rules. That's my advice."

"Have you been able to remember anything more about the Livermore family?" Lisa wanted to get off the topic of dying.

"As to why they might have a ghost in the family?"

"Right," Lisa prompted.

"No. Sorry," Mrs. Wrightwood said in the blunt way that only old people could get away with gracefully. "But I know someone who might, if she's still alive."

Trish almost asked if there was a good reason to suspect that this mystery person wouldn't still be alive. Death seemed to preoccupy the author's mind today.

"Who is this woman?"

"Sheila Lancaster."

"Who's she?"

"The only other person I can remember who would know anything about the Livermore family."

"Where can we find her?"

"So, you're done with me just like that!"

"Of course not."

"No need to lie about it. I know when people aren't coming back. It's the sense that you gain in old age when everything else is falling apart."

"After we talk to this Sheila person, we'll want to check out her recollections with you for accuracy."

Trish hoped to make it sound like she would be useful. Mrs. Wrightwood chuckled. "I wouldn't trust my memory as far as I could throw it."

"You've gotten us this far. I'm sure we would've never found this Sheila Lancaster person without you."

"You still haven't found her. And that might be the tough part."

"Why?"

"She's known to be a bit of a recluse. You know, someone who avoids people."

"How will we ever find her?" Lisa sounded exasperated to the trained ear.

"Last I heard, she was somewhere in Montana."

"Montana is an awfully big state."

"But at least there aren't that many people there."

"It could still take years. Do you have any idea what city she might be living in?"

"Recluses don't live in cities," Mrs. Wrightwood was beginning to sound tired of explaining things. Or maybe she was just plain tired.

"Maybe we should go and let you get some rest."

"But it was close to a place with a funny name."

"How was it funny? Like, strange?"

"Have you ever met a smart animal?" she smiled suddenly.

"A smart animal?"

"How about a horse that can read. Or a cow that can spell."

"A spelling cow?" Trish asked.

"No," Lisa interjected, understanding how the woman's memory cue worked. "Kalispell. Kalispell, Montana."

"She was up there somewhere close to Cowspell. I remember that much."

"Close to Cowspell, uh, Kalispell. How close?"

"I don't remember. I think I'm doing well to remember as much as I've remembered so far."

"We think so, too," Lisa gave Trish a look that conveyed that time was up.

"We need to go," Trish said abruptly to Mrs. Wrightwood.

"You did promise to come back with information."

"And if they allow food, what would you like to have?"

"Fried chicken. I'm too old to worry about my arteries."

Lisa and Trish made their way to the truck and had barely settled in their seats when Lisa asked, "Where's the nearest Triple A?"

"Why?"

"We can get maps. We're going to need a really good map of Montana."

"I thought maybe we'd start with a phone call."

"To a recluse? How many recluses do you know who have a phone?"

"So, where do we go to find this map place?"

They took three wrong turns and drove at least a mile out of their way, but they finally found the place. It only took about five minutes to select everything they needed, which included maps of Montana and Wyoming as well as a general northwest map.

"Do you ladies want the travel books as well to help you select motels?"

As Trish said "No", Lisa said "Yes."

"Are you planning on sleeping in the truck?" Lisa asked with a hint of impatience.

"I'm planning on flying."

"I'm planning on driving and either way, we'll still need a room."

"Rooms. We'll need rooms."

"So, you agree that we need the motel book!"

Trish acquiesced. No use going into further debate in front of a total stranger.

"How many do you want?"

As Lisa said "One", Trish said "Two."

"You've gone from not wanting any to wanting two?" Lisa asked.

"One for you and one for me."

"You don't think I'm capable of sharing?"

"Two books please," Trish confirmed to the clerk.

Trish made it up to Lisa by offering to buy lunch. Maybe it was just an innate skill, but the place Lisa selected, while seeming very unpretentious on the outside, was terribly proper and pricey on the inside. They were escorted to a darkly-lit romantic table for two and before Trish could object, Lisa was already seated and ordering wine by the bottle. From memory. Like she had once owned a vineyard.

"Don't you want to sit next to the window?" Trish asked.

"I can watch traffic any old day of the year. I want to concentrate on you."

Trish surrendered into a chair opposite Lisa and ordered a scotch. A double. Now that the bar tab had a healthy head start, Trish tried to catch up.

"Why do you want to concentrate on me?"

"I want to know why you think it's a good idea to fly up to Montana?"

"Have you ever driven up to Montana?"

"Well, no."

"If you had, you'd know why it's better to fly."

"I think we should drive."

"Why?"

Trish had to wait for her answer. The scotch, wine and menus appeared simultaneously. Trish didn't even look at hers, knowing by now that Lisa would have it studied and readily give recommendations.

"Aren't you eating?"

"What looks good," Trish said after taking a long draw of her scotch.

"It depends on what you're in the mood for," Lisa retorted but with a smile to warm the heart. Trish mused why Mitch had ever left that smile.

"Well?" Lisa apparently wanted an answer.

"What would Mitch have ordered?" Trish asked on foolish impulse.

"It depends."

"Depends on what?"

"On whether it was before or after sex."

"Oh," Trish said like maybe she didn't want to hear much more about this but either Lisa didn't hear the inflection or simple chose to impishly ignore it.

"If it was before sex, she knew she'd need the stamina so she ate things like pasta."

"Carbo loading?"

"Something like that, even before it was in vogue," Lisa nodded and then continued to study the menu. Trish knew she had no right to either ask for or hear the second part of the answer. Lisa set the menu down.

"Don't you want to know what she wanted after sex?"

"I guess I just figured that after sex with you, a woman would want for nothing more."

"That's about the nicest thing anyone has ever said to me."

"I find that hard to believe."

"You don't need to be embarrassed by the fact that you have a way with words."

"I'm not embarrassed."

"You don't need to convince me, but it's *your* neck that's turning red."

The waiter came to Trish's rescue and dutifully memorized everything that Lisa ordered for the both of them. To avoid more talk about sex, Trish steered the conversation back to Montana.

"I can charter a jet and rent a car."

"Fine. You do that. I'll drive up alone and meet you somewhere."

"You're very persistent."

"I'm stubborn."

"Why do you want to drive when flying would take less time?"

"I'm not interested in saving time."

"What are you interested in?"

"Quality of time and flexibility."

"And driving up there helps how?"

"I can do this on my own if you feel you can't leave Robbie and the baby. I'd understand completely."

Lisa said this quietly since she knew this could very well hit a nerve. Did Trish want to go or didn't she? That was the real question. It was high time for the real answer.

"After lunch, let's go and explain all this to Robbie and Rose and Max."

"That's the best idea yet."

Trish breathed a sigh of relief, mostly thankful that Lisa had changed out of her tight miniskirt after all. Rose would not have approved. Why this mattered at all Trish couldn't even begin to explain.

"Remind me not to wear my miniskirt when we go to Montana," Lisa said suddenly.

"What?" Trish was startled.

"Well, we are taking your truck, right?" she winked.

Lunch was lovely, luscious and uneventful. By the time they got back to Trish's mansion, she had a case of heartburn, mostly from nerves. Lisa, in character, was unfazed. She had studied the Montana maps while Trish had driven and was now ready with a game plan. Before Rose could even tut once, Lisa had her involved in the logistics of the plan.

"See how far north Kalispell is? Almost to the Canadian border."

"Why are you going up there again?" Rose asked.

Lisa had sort of glossed over the preliminaries and now turned to Trish for assistance.

"That's where we think this lady is hiding out. This Sheila Lancaster."

"Is she a criminal? This isn't like that Onabomber, is it?"

"One of what?" Lisa was confused.

"You mean the Unabomber. Ted Kaczynski," Trish explained.

"What about him?" Lisa asked

"He was hiding out up there somewhere."

"But, he's not now," Trish said.

"So, my point is that people who are hiding out do so for a reason and maybe she doesn't want to be found."

"And you think she's going to blow us up or something."

"I think you need to think about things before you go traipsing all around northern Montana."

"That's what I have Lisa for," Trish explained without smiling.

"And besides, we won't be all over northern Montana. We're concentrating in the northwestern area around Glacier National Park."

"It would still be a lot of ground to cover," Rose looked at the map again.

"Would you like to go with us? We could use all the help we can get," Lisa offered.

"I'm too old to go on any wild-goose chases."

Lisa and Trish exchanged looks. Maybe it was just a wild-goose chase, but it was *their* wild-goose chase.

"I'll get my stuff packed and pick you up in the morning," Trish said decisively

"Better make it early," Lisa directed. "It's a grueling drive."

"How early?"

"Six?"

"Sure. Come on. I'll drive you home."

"I can take a cab."

"Absolutely not. If we're going to spend the better part of a week in a car, we'd best be getting used to it."

They rode together in silence. There would be time for talk later. When Trish pulled up to the curb, she asked, "Do you need help explaining this to Mary?"

163

"I think I can handle it."

"I'm sorry."

"You're sorry?"

"I don't mean to treat you like…"

"Like a child?"

"No. Not like a child. More like a stranger."

"A stranger?"

"Someone to keep at arm's length," Trish elaborated even though she was surprised by her frankness. Lisa said nothing as she got out of the truck but before she closed the door she smiled and said, "The second answer was 'more sex.'"

"I'm sorry?" Trish looked bewildered by the statement.

"That's what Mitch always wanted after sex."

"Oh, yeah," Trish did her best not to grin.

"I just didn't want to leave the question unanswered."

"I'm sure I would've figured it out sooner or later."

"I sure you would've."

Chapter 16

The following morning at precisely 5:57, Trish pulled up in front
of Mary and Lisa's house in a rented luxury SUV.

"Where's the truck?" Lisa asked as Trish came to the door.

Trish almost said, "Where's the miniskirt?" but refrained.

"I studied the map last night. I thought we needed something
sturdy."

"Your truck is pretty sturdy…"

"Are you ready or not?"

"Come in. Have some coffee. Mary's in the kitchen."

"Oh, sure, alright," Trish wandered in the general direction of the
kitchen. Lisa disappeared upstairs.

"So, you've come to take Lisa away?" Mary barely looked up
from the paper. She was reading the business section, lots of
little bitty numbers.

"We wanted to get an early start."

"Why aren't you flying?" I figured a woman with your kind of
money wouldn't waste a lot of time driving when you could
afford to fly."

It was awfully early in the morning, but Trish distinctly
remembered that she was the one who had wanted to fly in the
first place. If Lisa had misrepresented the facts, it would be
interesting to find out. Later.

"You didn't get any coffee?" Lisa came around the corner.

"I had some before I left home."

"Don't you want a cup for the road? Mary made it."

"No," Trish said almost too quickly. "Really, I couldn't."

"Well, okay. So, my stuff is out in the hallway."

"Good. I'll take it out and meet you at the car."

"Thanks."

Trish nodded to Mary who barely acknowledged her, and then
walked to the hallway. There were three large suitcases in a row.
Trish didn't know Lisa even had this much clothing. She had
two of the suitcases stashed in the hatch back of the vehicle when
Lisa came out with the third.

"You're ready, then?" Trish noted to herself the rather quick exit of Lisa. Apparently their tender goodbye didn't take long. Sort of like her own earlier with Robbie.

"Yes."

"Hop in, then. I'll drive the first shift."

"Wow, this is really nice. You spared no expense."

"It's going to be a long drive."

Trish drove three blocks and then pulled into the parking lot of a fashionable coffee house.

"What are we doing here?" Lisa asked.

"I'm getting a cup of coffee for the road. You want one as well?" Trish asked the simple question now. She had more questions for later.

"Sure."

They dutifully stood in line for a couple of minutes. It was crowded this time of the morning. Trish ordered a simple mocha and Lisa asked for a complicated brew with a caramel flavoring. It sounded like a different language to Trish.

"You want to talk here or in the car?" Trish asked.

"In the car. Like you said, it's a long drive."

They were a good thirty minutes out of town before Lisa asked, "What was it that you wanted to talk about?"

"Mary didn't seem very happy to see me this morning. And somehow she had the impression that it was me who wanted to drive."

"She's got a lot on her mind."

"Mary's not happy that we're going on this trip. Why?"

"Nobody at your house is exactly thrilled either, are they?"

"Does she think we're going after the Unabomber as well?"

"No. She just doesn't like the idea of me going off on my own."

"But you're with me."

"I didn't mean *alone* alone. I meant without her."

"She could've come along."

"She works."

"Well, we'll be back before they even have a chance to miss us. Which way are we driving up there?"

"We're going through Wyoming."

"I figured as much. Tell me more."

"Okay," Lisa referenced a map she had refolded and ready for easy reference. "We're driving north on I-25 through Cheyenne, Casper, Sheridan and then crossing the Wyoming/Montana border we veer west onto I-90 and spend the night in Billings."

"And how long will that take?"

"Between eight and ten hours, depending on how fast you drive and eat."

"So, we will be there about four in the afternoon?"

"That's about right."

"Did you make hotel reservations?"

"No. I thought I'd talk to you first."

"Look up the nicest hotel in Billings and reserve a suite. I don't want to stay in any hotel that has a number in its name."

"A suite?" Lisa asked to make sure she heard correctly.

"Is a suite okay?"

"One suite for the two of us?"

"You want your own separate suite?"

"No. It just sounds pretty fancy. A suite!"

Trish fished her cell phone out of her breast pocket and handed it to Lisa.

"It's still warm."

"When you find the hotel you want, give them a call."

"I'll need a credit card to secure the room, won't I?"

"You don't have one?"

"I left them at home."

"I see."

"Mary figured you had enough money."

Trish pulled her wallet from the back pocket of her jeans, a slick trick while driving 75 miles an hour, and handed it over as well. It was also warm to the touch and thick with cash. Her credit cards were colors that Lisa had never seen before. She selected a particularly pretty one and then dialed the number of the most expensive hotel in Billings. In five minutes, she had secured a suite for two. Trish breathed out deeply. She always liked to have a cozy bed waiting for her at the end of a long drive.

"You want your wallet back?"

"Eventually, but not right now. You keep track of it."

Lisa held the wallet as she pondered her choices. She didn't want to stash it somewhere and forget about it so she simply put

167

it between her legs. A safe spot. And it would stay warm as well.

"You mind if I play the radio?" Lisa asked.

"Sure, go ahead. As long as it's not too annoying."

"What would constitute annoying?"

"Right-wing talk shows, degrading rap, and rock music that sounds like unoiled chain saws."

Lisa tuned in 50s classics and then settled in for a nap. She was sound asleep by the second song. Trish concentrated on her driving, hoping that she wouldn't need her wallet anytime soon. They were well into Wyoming before Lisa woke up.

"Are you feeling okay?" Trish asked as Lisa stretched.

"I'm fine. I just didn't get a lot of sleep last night."

Trish didn't want to know any details, good or bad.

"Are you hungry?"

"I could eat."

"Okay."

They pulled into the parking lot of the first café in the next town they came to.

"I hope our arteries can forgive us for this," Trish switched off the ignition.

"I suppose you want your wallet back."

"Only if you want me to pay the bill."

"Here you go," Lisa handed it over.

As expected, it was warm. Very warm. Trish poked it back in her pocket and followed Lisa into the restaurant.

They were still in time for breakfast and the two page menu, while limited, had all of Lisa's favorites.

"I didn't realize how hungry I was. This all sounds so good!"

"Order anything you want."

"I haven't had a steak in weeks."

"They have steak for breakfast?"

"It's there," Lisa pointed to the menu, "See? Steak and Eggs."

"Steak *and* eggs?" Trish raised her eyebrows.

"And there's biscuits and sausage gravy. Yum!"

"Uh huh," Trish nodded. "You better get both."

"What are you having?"

"Toast."

"Toast?" Lisa sounded surprised.

"Toast and coffee."

"So! That's how you do it?"

"Do what?"

"That's how you keep your girlish figure."

"I'm just not that hungry."

"Did you eat before you left?"

"No."

"I think I'll order toast too. It sounds good now that you mention it. Order for me. I'm going to the ladies room."

As Lisa disappeared, the waitress reappeared with order pad in hand. "Are you ready?"

"I'd like a side order of toast and my friend wants steak and eggs and biscuits and gravy and toast as well."

"How many eggs?"

"I'm not sure."

"It comes with one, two, or three."

"Let's go with three."

"How does she want them cooked?"

Trish racked her brain for a memory of how Lisa liked her eggs. "Scrambled."

"She want the hash browns too?"

"Sure, why not."

"And coffee?"

"Both of us will have coffee. Regular."

Trish had three minutes of peace and quiet before Lisa returned. She looked refreshed, even her light makeup had been retouched. Where she hid her cosmetics was anyone's guess.

"You look nice."

"You look tired."

"I didn't sleep the whole way."

"I'll drive the next shift. You can catch up on your beauty sleep. Not that you need it."

"I didn't put you on the car rental agreement."

"I don't care. If you think that you're doing all the driving in that fabulous vehicle, you have another thing coming."

"I hope you can eat three eggs," Trish changed the subject.

"I'll do my best."

169

They had their answer in fifteen minutes. Lisa was past her eggs and happily working her way through everything else on the table. Trish guarded her toast like it was the last morsel of food on the planet.

"If I eat *everything*, do I get dessert?" Lisa queried in her softest voice.

"I'm sure they have pie."

"Five kinds. I saw the display on the way in."

"Do you have a favorite?"

"Cherry."

"Let's order two pieces for the road."

Trish settled the bill, left an obscenely overgenerous tip just in case they stopped here on the return trip, gave the car keys to Lisa, and visited the restroom before hitting the road. Lisa had taken Trish's words to heart and was waiting patiently in the passenger's seat. There was no reason to squabble this early in the journey. In fact, there was no reason to talk at all. After a lengthy silence, Trish said, "You're awfully quiet."

"I didn't know if you liked it if people jabbered at you while you were driving."

"I don't like people jabbering at me, but I wouldn't consider whatever you might say to be jabber."

"That's a nice thing to say."

"Do other people tell you that you jabber?"

"Not in so many words."

"Then, how do you know?"

"Because they usually just keep doing whatever they are doing."

"Well, in case of driving, I think it's necessary to keep going, right?"

"Oh, sure. I didn't mean driving."

"What did you mean?"

"You want an example?"

"Sure."

Lisa took a minute to think. Or stall. Trish couldn't be sure.

"Okay, just out of the blue as an example…like if somebody just keeps reading the paper while you're talking. Like whatever you are saying isn't worth paying attention to."

Trish thought this over as the memory of Mary reading the paper flashed in her mind.

"So, you think that people can't read and listen at the same time?"

"I'm sure some people can. And I know some people who can't. Or choose not to."

"Well, sometimes people have a lot on their mind," Trish said in the most neutral tone she could muster. If Lisa had a complaint about life with Mary, she would need to do more than speak in parables about it.

"Everybody does," Lisa said.

"Everybody does?"

"Everybody has a lot on their mind."

"That's a wise observation, Lisa," Trish smiled.

"Let me know when you get tired. I can drive sensibly no matter what you may have heard."

"I haven't heard a thing about your driving. I'd trust you with my life."

"At the looks of the terrain we'll be travelling through, it may come to that," Lisa waved a map for emphasis.

"We'll just take it slow and easy."

"Sounds good to me."

They rode in companionable silence, each knowing that when they chose to speak, it wouldn't be considered idle jabber.

Dozens and dozens and dozens of miles rolled beneath them before Lisa remembered that they had dessert on board.

"Can you eat and drive at the same time?" Lisa popped this most interesting question.

"Uh, gee, I don't know. I've never tried before. Isn't it against the law?"

"Wouldn't you know it! I'm travelling with the only person in the world who has never eaten while they drive."

"I chewed gum once. Does that count?" Trish asked.

"What flavor?" Lisa asked like the fate of the universe hinged on the answer.

"It was bubble gum."

"Geez, what were you? Sixteen at the time?"

"I was pretty young. Young and foolish. That was me."

"You want your pie or don't you?"

"There's a rest stop up ahead. I could use a break."

"And then I can drive?"

"And then you can drive."

Mostly due to the fact that March wasn't the warmest month of the year, they ate their pie in the car. Sitting still felt good to Trish. Closing her eyes felt even better.

"Are you okay?"

"That was the best pie I've ever had."

"You haven't eaten much else. I'm glad to see you eat something."

"Are you ready to take over the driving duties?"

"Absolutely."

Trish was only aware of about five miles of road before she fell fast asleep. It was the most relaxed she had been in months. When she awoke, Lisa was still happily driving.

"Where are we?"

"We're in Montana."

"Already?"

"You had quite the nap."

"So, where are we exactly?"

"We're in the Crow Indian Reservation, a few miles away from the Little Bighorn Monument. Do you want to stop there?"

Trish thought about it for a long minute. "No," she finally said.

"Even if they have a restroom?"

Trish took the hint. "You know, we could stop for a bit. We're ahead of schedule and the hotel suite is guaranteed, right?"

"Right."

Meaning no disrespect to the memory of Lieutenant Colonel (not General as some mistakenly report) George Armstrong Custer, they only stopped long enough to avail themselves of the facilities and buy a soda apiece.

"You want me to drive the rest of the way," Trish asked like she had decided to anyway and was just making the formal announcement.

"Sure. I'll navigate you to the hotel when we hit town."

"We have an hour. There's no big rush."

"I'll be ready when you are."

"That's good to know."

The hour went by quickly. They both stayed awake and listened to music. Lisa had switched genres by now, tuning in some country and western music. "When in Rome," had been her words of defense. Trish had only shrugged.

The hotel was easy to find. Lisa had studied well. Check in went smoothly and a bellhop had their luggage out of the car and into their luxury suite. All four bags. While Trish had packed light, Lisa would have her complete selection from which to choose.

The suite was fabulous. There was just no other word to describe it. When Trish had envisioned a motel in Wyoming, she had visions of dead animal carcasses on the walls and floor. This suite could've easily existed in New York.
"You take the big bedroom," Trish told Lisa.
"You're paying the bill. You should take the big bedroom."
"You have three suitcases. You take the big bedroom."
"Okay. Fine. This time. I'll unpack a couple of things and then track down some ice."
"You're not going to go out and fetch ice. I'll call room service."
"For ice?"
"Look over the room service menu and see what else sounds good."
"Are we taking all our meals in or are we going out for dinner?"
"What would you like to do? And don't say that it's up to me just because I'm paying the bill."
"We're in cattle country and a steak sounds really good."
Trish didn't bother to quibble about the fact that Lisa had already had one steak today. "I'm sure we can find a steakhouse."
"There are at least three listed in the travel book."
"Okay. I'll order up some ice and whatever else sounds good in the way of an appetizer."
What sounded good was white wine for now and brandy for later. Room service was more than obliging and before Lisa could even think of a hot shower, she had a glass of cool wine in her hand.
"Now this is living. Wine for the shower."

173

"You're taking a shower?" Trish quizzed.

"I always do. At least, I try to when I travel. Which hasn't been lately. But I like to shower when I check in. Helps to ease the tensions of the road."

"I hope I didn't make you nervous?"

"Not a bit. I just like to use somebody else's hot water for a change."

Trish settled into a comfy chair with a glass of wine in one hand and the phone in the other. She called home and got Rose on the first ring.

"Hi, Rose. I'm calling to check in."

"Okay."

"How is everything?"

"Things are okay. So far."

"That's good. Is Robbie close to a phone?"

"She's asleep"

"But not sleep walking?"

"Not yet. We're going to keep a 24-hour vigil."

"Who's got the graveyard shift?"

"Silver volunteered."

"Have her call me if anything happens."

Trish gave Rose the hotel phone number as well just in case.

"And have her leave a message if she doesn't get through to me in person."

"Okay."

Trish disconnected the call and was halfway through the bottle of wine before Lisa emerged from the bathroom in one of those huge, thickly piled bathrobes that only the best hotels furnish. She had her blond hair combed straight back, revealing much of her burn scars that were normally hidden from view. Lisa caught Trish staring.

"Do you want to see all the damage?" she asked matter-of-factly. Trish looked away as an answer.

"I'm sorry. I didn't mean to put you on the spot," Lisa patted her arm. "It's just that I'm getting so used to it by now that I guess everyone else is as well."

"I called home," Trish changed the subject. "Do you want to call Mary?"

"Maybe after dinner. She's still at work probably. But I'd have some more wine."

"Oh, okay," Trish poured Lisa a small serving. There was little left. Lisa kept any opinion about the quickly-disappearing wine to herself but Trish didn't.

"That hot shower idea sounds good after all. Why don't you order another bottle of this stuff or whatever else you want while I get cleaned up as well."

With that, Trish headed toward her separate but equal bathroom. The water was indeed hot and very soothing. It erased all the bumps and jolts of the road that the wine had missed. She wrapped herself up in a robe that gave the impression that if you fell over, you'd bounce right back up. There was nothing skimpy or immodest about it. If they chose to buy them, as the hotel promised they could, it would take another suitcase just to pack it along.

As she wandered out to the main room, Lisa had started up the gas fireplace and upon seeing Trish, poured her a fresh glass of wine.

"We are going to be in no shape to drive to any fancy steakhouse."

"That's why they invented cabs."

"That's why they invented limos. I'm sure the hotel has one that could be at our disposal."

"Wouldn't that cost a lot?"

"It's better than getting a DUI in a strange town."

"I didn't think about it that way."

"And remind me to buy an extra suitcase tomorrow," Trish stretched out on the couch facing the fireplace.

"Why?"

"I'm buying these robes for us."

"They are nice and cozy."

"Where we're heading, it's going to be cold. They don't call it Glacier National Park for nothing."

"Do you think we're going to run into bad weather?"

"I'm positive of it. I even got chains for the tires."

"Wow, you really are prepared."

"And let's be sure we have more than coffee and pie in the car for food."

"We could stop at a grocery store tomorrow. I'll help buy some food," Lisa was getting in a picnic mood.

"Should I make a list? Crackers and cheese and cookies. What else?"

"A couple more bottles of this stuff," Trish held up her glass.

"This is good, isn't it?"

"It was a little bit more expensive than the first bottle."

"It's settled then, we'll stop by the liquor store while we're at it."

"You mean tomorrow?"

"Tonight. Tomorrow. Whenever."

"I better start another list."

"Yeah, start another list," Trish yawned. The trip had apparently taken more out of her than she realized. A hot shower, a good wine, a comfy robe, a fire, and a spacious couch all conspired against her. She was sound asleep in two minutes.

When Trish awoke, which seemed to be only a few minutes from when she had dozed off, the room was dark and there was no Lisa in sight. In fact, after a brief tour, Trish ascertained that she wasn't anywhere in the suite. Apparently she had gone out to dinner on her own, a circumstance not usually prone to irritate, except that Trish had awakened hungry. She spent a moment reading through the room service menu again and was all set to phone in an order when she heard scratching sounds at the door. She opened it to find Lisa attempting to unlock the door while wrestling with a couple of plastic sacks.

"Oh sorry, I didn't mean to wake you up."

"You didn't. What's all this?"

"It's dinner. You were sleeping so soundly that I knew you'd be hungry the minute you woke up so I just went and got something."

By now, the aroma of the something had reached Trish's nose and it smelled wonderful.

"Let me help you with all this," Trish felt that the least she could do was carry everything to the small dining table in the suite.

"I hope I remembered everything," Lisa was already fussing at herself even after doing such a thoughtful errand.

"If not, it's just like ants at a picnic."

Lisa nodded, not quite understanding the meaning behind the saying. It didn't sound like she was going to get the blame if something went wrong and that was good enough for her.

"Hey, they even included little packets of steak sauce," Trish was pleased. Her olfactory sense had already told her that steak was on the menu. This was indeed icing on the cake.

"And I didn't know what you liked on your baked potato so I had them pack a few of everything."

"Okay, now you've gone and done it."

"What?" Lisa was caught off guard by the sternness in Trish's voice.

"You've spoiled me. This cannot continue," Trish smiled.

"This doesn't constitute spoiling. Butter, margarine, and sour cream do not rise to the level of spoiling."

"Then what does?"

"Organically-grown chives."

"Fine. Have you called Mary yet?" Trish abruptly changed the subject.

"I'm about to do that. Start up on your steak. I won't be long." Lisa used the phone extension in her bedroom and, indeed, it didn't take long. Trish had barely fixed her potato when Lisa reappeared.

"Mary says hi," Lisa sat down and knifed right into her steak.

"Everything okay back home?"

"Sounded okay to me."

"Good."

They ate in contented silence and no matter what Lisa had said, Trish felt very much spoiled. After dinner, they charted tomorrow's route with Lisa pointing out the obvious on an unfolded map.

"I think we should go west on Highway 90 to Missoula and then north on 93 to Kalispell."

"How many miles is that? It looks like a lot of driving."

"It is. It's about 350 highway miles from where we are to Missoula and then about a little over a hundred miles north to Kalispell."

"We can do it in one long day of driving. Do you think that you can make room reservations?"

"I can sure try but I can't guarantee this level of luxury."

"I don't need this level of luxury. The only thing I need is a bed and a cup of coffee in the morning."

Lisa didn't mention the fact that it was Trish who insisted that they avoid motels with numbers in their names and said confidently, "I'll start calling while you do the dishes."

"Deal."

The chores took an equal amount of time. As soon as Trish had cleaned up after their take-out steak dinner, Lisa had two rooms set aside for the following night.

"So, now all we need to do is get a good night's sleep."

"Right. It's going to be a long drive."

For two people who had spent the better part of the day in each other's company, their small talk suddenly sounded awkward.

"Well, I guess we'd better go to bed," Trish said.

"Yeah," Lisa answered with the best poker face imaginable.

"Well, then, goodnight."

"Sleep well."

Trish worried that she wouldn't be able to fall asleep so soon after taking a nap. For about eight minutes. The soft knocking on her door startled her awake. It was Lisa. It was morning. Logs had slept restlessly compared to Trish.

"You want instant or room-service coffee?"

"What time is it?"

"Six," Lisa answered as she moved into the bedroom.

It took Trish a couple seconds to focus her eyes. For six in the morning, Lisa looked fabulous. Trish couldn't look away.

"What?" Lisa said.

"What time did you get up?"

"A few minutes ago. Why?"

Trish resisted the urge to comment on how good she looked.

"You want to have breakfast downstairs or on the road?"

"Downstairs is pretty expensive."

"Just tell me if you're hungry."

It dawned on Lisa that Trish wasn't moving out of her bed until they made this decision so that she could be alone. Maybe she had slept in the nude? Her shoulders were bare.

"I'm always hungry," Lisa moved a step closer. "You know me by now."

"Okay, we'll eat downstairs. Give me a couple of minutes to get dressed."

"Of course. I could go down now?"

"No, let's go down together."

"I'll be waiting for you."

Lisa turned slowly and left the room, somewhat relieved that Trish hadn't felt comfortable showing any more flesh than absolutely necessary, but at the same time curious as to what created the tension in the first place. Maybe it was just simple modesty. Some people were just naturally modest. She had never even seen Trish in a skirt, let alone a pair of shorts. And never in her boudoir attire. For obvious reasons.

Breakfast was beyond what anyone's expectations of the meal could possibly be. Healthy dishes graced the buffet table alongside terribly sinful ones. Lisa was in seventh heaven and filled three plates before Trish had even one dished up.

"Find everything you wanted?" Trish asked without sarcasm.

"I wanted a taste of everything."

"You're going to need a couple more plates to do that."

"Yeah, but I didn't want to do that on the first trip."

"Hey, you might as well get your money's worth."

"It did cost a lot, didn't it."

"Not necessarily. Not for what you get anyway."

"I can find cheaper places from now on," Lisa looked guilty.

"Why are you obsessing about this?" Trish asked bluntly.

"I don't want to spend all your money."

"Do you hear this at home from Mary or what?"

"Of course not. Why would I?" Lisa's tone bordered on defensive.

"You keep bringing up the cost of things. I'm more than happy to foot the bill for this entire adventure."

"This qualifies as an adventure to you?"

"I'm wandering around the romantic west with an intriguing woman on a mission that hasn't been very well defined. I'd say that qualifies as an adventure."

"Now that you put it that way, I guess so."

"You'd better get those two other plates of food. Don't want you to go hungry."

"No chance of that."

True to form, Lisa loaded up on dessert-type items, including chocolate-filled croissants.

"Those look yummy," Trish commented, not nearly matter-of-factly enough for her own good.

"Here, I'll share with you."

"No, that's okay."

"Oh no. I can see that croissant-come-hither look in your eyes."

"There's no such thing."

"Sure there is. Otherwise you wouldn't have the look on your face."

"Gee, I guess I can't argue with logic like that."

"Come on. Eat up. We haven't got all day."

Trish followed the eating up directive, finishing half a croissant before she was full.

"You want to hide that in your pocket? Smuggle it out?"

"I don't think so. I paid eight dollars for this shirt," Trish indicated her well-worn flannel. "Wouldn't want to get grease spots on it."

"Eight whole dollars?" Lisa raised her eyebrows. This from a woman who could spend eighty dollars on a shirt.

"You making fun of my best flannel shirt?"

"That's your best flannel shirt? Out of how many?"

"You want to know how many flannel shirts I own?"

"Not if it's going to make me jealous."

"I've never seen you in a flannel shirt."

"You've never seen me out of one either," Lisa smiled her usual teasing smile. Even if Trish had room for the other half of the croissant, it certainly would not have gone down now. About three glib replies flitted through her mind and after deeming them all unsuitable, she said simply, "Well, we'd better get on the road."

"Right."

They got that instant kind of help that rich people get getting their bags into the SUV and were on the road by eight. Maybe a little later than they had planned, but they wouldn't need to eat again for at least a week. Trish was content to drive in silence while Lisa studied travel books. There wasn't much else to do other than read and stare out of the window.

"You're awfully quiet," Trish finally broke the silence.

"I was spending my energy digesting."

"Have you figured out yet what we're going to do once we get to Kalispell?"

"Besides check into the motel?"

"Yeah, besides that."

"We go looking for this Sheila person."

"And have we figured out yet how we're going to do that?"

"We're going to check local phone books and ask people. You know, snoop around."

"There has to be thousands of people up there. Can you even imagine how lucky we're going to need to be in order to find Sheila?"

"Lucky is my middle name."

"Really?"

"No. But I can pretend for this trip, can't I?"

"I won't tell a soul."

"Hey, I have a question."

"Okay."

"Do you suppose this Sheila person is gay?"

"That's one helluva question."

"I thought so."

"What prompted that?"

"I don't know. It just sort of popped into my head."

"Like an intuition?"

"Woman's intuition?"

"Gay woman's intuition, maybe," Trish mused.

"Well, what do you think?"

"I don't have a clue. I think I'd have to meet the woman first, and maybe even then I wouldn't know. I'm not very good at that kind of thing. What's your guess?"

"How many reasons are there for people to run away and become a hermit?"

"Probably plenty. But I'm not sure that being gay is one of them."

"It might be a factor, though, couldn't it?"

"I guess, using that logic, anything could be a factor."

Lisa smiled, pleased at what she heard.

"What are you smiling about?" Trish asked.

"I'm glad you think I'm logical. You've mentioned it twice this morning already."

"Not only do I think you're logical. I think you're one of the most clever women I've ever met."

"Do you mean good clever or bad clever?"

"I'm sure I didn't mean bad clever, whatever that is. What is it anyway?"

"Bad clever would mean like I'm a schemer or something like that."

"You think that being a schemer is a bad thing intrinsically?"

"Uh, well, what do you think?"

"I think that as long as nobody gets hurt, then being a schemer isn't such a bad thing."

"It's that 'nobody gets hurt' part that's always the stickler."

"I guess I meant intentionally."

"So, it's okay if you scheme with the best of intentions and if somebody gets hurt, then as long as you didn't mean for it to happen, then it's okay?"

"Yeah, like if you set up a friend on a blind date and they end up getting hurt in the process, then it's still okay because you started with good intentions."

"Unless you set them up with a total loser on purpose."

"Right."

"But what if you set them up with a total loser on purpose and they fall madly in love and live happily ever after?"

"You buy them a toaster oven for a wedding gift."

"You're going to burn them one way or the other?"

"I'm going to pretend I didn't hear that terrible pun."

"Or you could buy them a fishing pole and be off the hook."

"Am I going to have to feed you again to keep your mouth busy?"

Lisa looked at Trish in a way that she couldn't decipher, especially going seventy miles per hour.

"What? Did I hurt your feelings?"

"No. I just didn't know that you wanted to keep my mouth busy."

"It's just that I can only take about one pun every hundred miles."

"I have all of yesterday to make up for."

"Oh no you don't. Yesterday is over. There's no such thing as pun credit."

"Well, there's always the drive home."

"You're intent on making me groan the whole way?"

"Only if you want me to."

Trish made no further reply. She had the sensation that they had gone completely off the topic of pun making and didn't want to hear anymore. At least, not while driving up some unfamiliar highway to a place she had never been before.

"You just let me know when you need a break. From driving," Lisa said quietly.

"Um hum," was Trish's only reply.

A hundred and fifty miles later, Trish needed that break. The caffeine in the coffee she had politely swilled down during breakfast was having its usual diuretic effect.

"Is there a rest area coming up soon?" she asked her navigator.

"There's a small town in a few miles. Might as well fill up the gas tank as well."

"Good idea."

It had been over two hours since they had spoken. Lisa's voice sounded good.

"I've made a decision."

"What kind of decision?"

"You can tell all the puns you want."

"Really? Why?"

"Because I miss the sound of your voice."

"You'd miss the sound of anyone's voice after two hours of highway driving."

"That's not true at all."

"This is a one-exit town, so don't miss the turnoff."

"Are you hungry?"

"Are you kidding?"

"Just asking."

"Are you hungry?"

"Let's pick up some junk food at the gas station."

"Something to keep my mouth busy?" Lisa looked over with that unreadable expression again.

"I was craving some hard candy. Something to suck on."

"I understand completely. It always relieves the tension for me."

"You? Tension?" Trish made it sound like Lisa never manifested tension in her life.

"You know, jaw tension."

"Well, we'll see what we can do to assuage that."

Trish took the one and only correct highway exit for the town that promised gas, food and lodging. She pulled up to the pump and got out to fill the tank. Lisa got out as well. "Let me do that while you use the restroom."

"Okay, but don't go candy shopping without me."

"I wouldn't dream of it," Lisa took the gas pump out of Trish's hand and proceeded to do the dirty work.

The ladies restroom looked like the gas station only employed males. Trish wagered herself a hundred silent dollars that the men's room looked better than this. Anything would've looked better than this. But it was the best they could do for now. Obviously, she didn't take any more time than absolutely necessary and went back out to give fair warning to Lisa about the conditions she would encounter. She was cleaning the windows of the SUV.

"Hey, why don't you let me finish that while you take a break."

"I'm almost done."

"The restroom is nothing to write home about."

"I'm sure I've seen worse."

"You poor dear."

"Meet you in the candy shop."

"Okay."

Trish pulled the car up to the cinder block building so that someone else could use the pump and then went in to browse the tiny, claustrophobic store. It was the usual assortment of stuff that only travelers would buy. Candy, chips, pop, beer, aspirin, postcards, key chains, fishing licenses and coffee. What was it about coffee that the minute you got rid of the morning's supply, your body craved it again. Lisa showed up at Trish's elbow.

"Well, that was a draining experience," she smiled.

"Again with the puns?"

"And we're not even in the car."

"You're the one who's missing the sound of my voice," Lisa reminded her in her usual teasing way.

"Can I help you girls?" a man appeared in the candy aisle where they were browsing.

"We're just shopping," Trish said back politely. Although it grated on her nerves that she would be called a girl by this paunchy middle-aged gentleman, she hid it well.

"I have your gas total at the counter when you're ready."

"Thank you."

"When you're ready," he repeated. The name embroidered on his shirt identified him as Bud. Guess neither one of his parents spent time cracking the one-thousand-and-one baby names book.

"We'll be ready in a few minutes."

"Good."

It became terribly obvious that Bud was ready for them to leave. Maybe he didn't like two girls to be in his store. Or maybe two lesbians. It would be just their luck to have the gas station attendant have gaydar. He gave them a little breathing room when another customer came in to pay for gas. Lisa was checking out all the different types of candy.

"Having trouble deciding?" Trish asked.

"I always do."

"Well, let's not worry about it then."

"You want to just skip it?"

"No. I want to get everything."

"You mean, one of each? There has to be fifty different types here."

"I don't mean one of each. I mean all of it."

"All of it? As in all of every kind?"

"Yeah. All of every kind. And whatever else he has in the back room."

"You've got to be kidding."

"No. Let's break the news to him when he comes over again to hover over us."

Which happened immediately. "You girls finding what you want?" he asked with a voice that sounded irritated that they couldn't take a polite hint the first time around and leave.

"Yes, we are," Trish smiled a luminous smile his way. "We want all of this."

"All of what?"

"All of the candy you have."

"Is this some sort of stick up?"

Trish had been accused of a few things in her life, but now she had the prestigious honor of being accused of being a robber as well.

"Do you take credit cards?"

"Only good ones."

"Well, you want to check this one out and see if it's good?" Trish pulled out a platinum credit card and handed it over to him. "I'm sure if it's a bad card, it will show up on some list, right?" she asked innocently. She knew full well that there were ways of checking to see if credit cards were good. They had computers, even up here in the wilds of Montana. He came back in thirty seconds.

"So, you want this candy here?" he waved his arm over the display case.

"And all the candy in the back room as well."

"Are you sure this isn't a stick up?"

"Do I look like I'm packing a gun?"

Bud still looked skeptical. "It's going to take a little time to haul everything out of the back room. And then to price it."

"Why don't you just add ten percent to the case price and sell it to me that way?"

"I'm pretty sure the boss wouldn't allow that."

"Okay, well, you know how many is in each case, right? Just run the numbers that way. It shouldn't take too long and then the boss will be happy that you made such a big sale."

"But then I won't have any candy left for anybody else."

"I don't care about anybody else."

"Are you sure you have room for it in your car?"

"Do you want the sale or don't you?"

Bud was torn between giving into this *girl* and looking good to his boss.

"Give me a few minutes."

It didn't take as long as you would think to buy out the candy store. Between Trish's fine mathematical mind and the store's

computerized register, they had a car full of candy in about
fifteen minutes. Besides, he didn't have as much in stock as he
let on during the preliminary negotiations. Trish blocked Lisa's
view of the credit card total as she signed the register slip.
Keeping a woman like Lisa in the dark was a challenge Trish felt
up to all of a sudden. They stashed a few favorites between them
in the front seat and Lisa was behind the wheel and back on the
highway before she asked, "So, how much was the total?"
"I'm not telling."
"Why not?"
"Because I want you to think that I spent a lot of money on you."
"Only because you did."
"Not as much as you think. I talked him into a bulk discount
after all."
"So, now, we have a few hundred pounds of candy in the back
and that's going to really affect our gas mileage."
"At least we won't go hungry. And *you* won't be tense."
"At least my jaw won't be," was Lisa's mumbled reply.
Trish heard it anyway and didn't comment further.

They took the turn north by early afternoon and were on the
direct route now to Kalispell. It was less than two hours total
driving by now to be at the motel Lisa had rented for the night.
"It's my turn to drive," Trish reminded.
"I don't remember agreeing to that."
"You've done your fair share. Don't you want a break? Stretch
a little? Ease out that tension? In your shoulders? You know
what I mean? That spot right about here?" Trish lightly touched
Lisa on her right shoulder, halfway between her neck and the end
of her shoulder. The body part that carries the stress of driving
nonstop among other things. Lisa shuddered.
"You're as tense as a tick," Trish made her diagnosis known.
"I guess I could use a break."
"Break, hell. You could use a massage."
"Well, we know that's not going to happen."
"At least let me drive the rest of the way. If I eat any more
candy, I'm going to go into diabetic shock. And I'm not even
diabetic."
"Okay, let me find a good place to pull over."

Which wasn't difficult since by now they were practically in the middle of nowhere. Lisa got out of the car and walked around for a minute or two, rolling her shoulders first one way and then the other. Slowly. Carefully. Around and around.

"You want a different kind of candy as long as we're stopped?"

"No, I think I'll save my appetite for dinner. Whenever that's going to be."

"We're making good time. We can eat early if you want?"

"I'm fine."

"Okay."

Trish left her to finish her shoulder rolls and climbed in behind the steering wheel. She wanted to do something besides watch Lisa stretch, so she studied the map until Lisa was ready to go.

"Don't hurry on my account. You can walk around some more if you want."

"No, I'm good to go."

Trish just nodded.

The road demanded more careful attention now that they were off the major highway. In a way Trish was glad that she was on a sugar high. It was one way to explain away her pulsing blood. Lisa dropped off to sleep, looking more angelic than anything else. They were ten miles out of Kalispell when she stirred awake.

"Why did you let me sleep so long? I could've kept you company."

"I bet your shoulders feel better."

"My everything feels better."

Trish chuckled. "I'm sure it does."

"You want to find the motel first or eat first?"

"Let's find the motel first."

Lisa the navigator took over and they were on the correct road within moments. The idea of a cabin had sounded interesting to Lisa after spending the previous night in the lap of luxury.

"I didn't know we were going to be roughing it," Trish said when they pulled up to the property.

"Don't you like it? I can probably find something else. Should I try?"

"I didn't say I didn't like it. I just wasn't quite ready for it. Does it have indoor plumbing?"

188

"You want me to go in and ask?"

"I'll go in with you. Don't worry about it. It looks pretty well kept."

"It did have three stars in the travel book."

"Out of how many?"

"Five."

"Three out of five doesn't sound too bad."

The motel's office was deserted. There was a bell on the counter, one of those that you were supposed to hit with the palm of your hand in order to have it make its annoying sound. Lisa and Trish exchanged looks. Neither wished to disturb the peace. A side door opened and a balding man shuffled up to the counter.

"Got a reservation?" he inquired as he peered at them with eyes that felt like lie detectors by his suspicious gaze.

"Yes."

"You didn't ring the bell."

"We didn't want to bother you."

"Do I look like a man who wants to be bothered?"

It sounded like a trick question to Trish. No good answer came to mind.

"What's the name?"

"Sullivan."

"You don't look Irish."

"I took after my mother. Do you have our rooms?"

"We don't have rooms. We have cabins. You want a room, you need to go somewhere else."

"She meant cabins," Lisa piped up.

"Who are you?"

"I'm the one who made the reservations."

"So you are. I recognize your voice. Fill this out," he shoved the paperwork across the counter. Trish fished out her credit card for the usual imprint.

"If we need to, can we rent the *cabins* for more than tonight?" she asked.

"Nope."

"No?"

"Filled up."

"Really? Business is that good?"

"Yup."

Trish and Lisa exchanged glances again. It didn't exactly seem to be tourist season. They wrapped up the paperwork and got a key apiece.

"Cabin one and cabin fifteen."

"They sound pretty far apart."

"All I got left."

"Thanks," Lisa picked up both keys and led the way out of the office. The air was fresh and cool outside. Trish took a couple of deep breaths.

"Don't hyperventilate on me now," Lisa remarked.

"Should we go to one or fifteen first?"

"Let's go to fifteen. The farther away we get from the office, the better I will feel."

"Okay."

"They got in the truck and drove down a rutted road to the end of the line of cabins. The entire place looked deserted.

"A hundred dollars says that cabin fourteen isn't rented out tonight."

"Maybe it's a late check in."

"Maybe they are all late check ins."

"Yeah, maybe."

"Come on. Let's see what this looks like."

Cabin fifteen consisted of two rooms: the bathroom, and then everything else. A twin bed was shoved up against the north wall. A frayed pink bath mat served as a throw rug. The tap water came in two temperatures: lukewarm and lukewarm.

"Not exactly the honeymoon suite. So much for a hot shower," Trish observed.

"Good thing we took one when we had the chance."

"You want this cabin?"

"No, you take it."

"You haven't seen the other one yet."

"I'm sure it's fine."

"Let's go look, just in case."

"You want to walk or drive?"

"I could use the exercise."

They sauntered down the lonely dirt path lined with pine trees to cabin one. It was an exact replica of fifteen except that the frayed bath mat was blue instead of pink.

"See, it's fine," Lisa commented. As far as Trish was concerned, this was about as far away from "fine" as you could get, but she kept her opinion to herself. This was what Lisa had selected out of the book and it would be rude to question her judgment.

"So, you want to grab a bite of dinner before we settle in for the night?"

"Sure. Just a bite though. I'm not all that hungry."

"Yeah. Okay."

They walked back to the car and drove to a family-type restaurant that Lisa had read about in the ubiquitous travel book. Hopefully, this would be a better experience than the cabins from purgatory.

"Table for two?" the twelve-year-old hostess asked.

"Yes please," Lisa answered.

With no small amount of flourish, they were led to the first open table. It was spotlessly clean and ready for customers. The four-page menu was clear and concise. No sous chef language here.

"It looks like home cooking," Lisa murmured.

"Maybe you're more hungry than you thought?"

"I don't want to eat too much before bed."

"Well, it's not like we're going right back and jump in the sack."

"There's not much else to do."

"I wish I had a nickel for every time I've heard that."

"So, you've dated boys?" Lisa smiled, knowing that she was prying and felt comfortable doing so.

"In another life. Long ago and far away."

"Sounds like Star Trek."

"Another time space continuum."

"Before you figured yourself out?"

"Something like that. What are you eating?"

"I'm leaning toward the meatloaf with a green salad."

"That's all? Won't you be hungry later?"

"We have all that candy if I need a snack."

"Right," Trish agreed and then fell silent.

After a moment, Lisa asked, "What's on your mind?"

"That was sort of silly of me, buying all that, wasn't it?"

"I don't know if I'd call it silly, but you do have a unique way of dealing with the world. I'm just relieved that you didn't up and buy cabins one through fifteen!"

"I could you know."

"Except that they wouldn't fit in the back seat."

"At least I could hire a manager that wasn't prejudiced against gay people."

"You think that's what's going on?"

"You think it isn't?"

"I wouldn't jump to conclusions."

"You want to make a bet about it?"

"What kind of bet?"

"I'll bet that not only doesn't the place fill up tonight but that it doesn't fill up tomorrow or the next day either."

"And what are we betting?"

"Whatever you say."

"I don't have any money with me, so I can't bet that."

"Okay. So it will have to be a good deed or something like that."

"Right. Okay. Like a neck rub or something."

"That sounds reasonable."

"Okay. You're on," Lisa reached across the table and they shook on the deal.

"I'm really looking forward to my future neck rub," Trish grinned. "In fact, I'm going to do everything in my power to get all tensed up so you'll really need to work hard to pay off your debt."

Lisa only smiled. Like she knew something that no one else knew.

Dinner was wonderfully simple. They were back at the cabins, unpacked and ready to split up for the night before the weather turned too cold. It might've been near springtime in other parts of the country, but up north, there was still a numbing cold in the air. Trish noticed Lisa shivering.

"Are you going to be okay here all by yourself?"

"I'll be fine."

"Okay. I'm only about fifty-five miles away if you need me."

Lisa laughed. "Go on. I'm fine. Thank you for a lovely evening."

"It was lovely, wasn't it."

"Goodnight."

Trish walked the dark path to her cabin, noting for the record that things still seemed pretty vacated. If people were staying here, they must've walked in. No other cars were on the road. She put on her robe and tried out the bed. It was soft and squishy. If a sign over the bed had read that Lincoln had slept here, she would've believed that it was the same mattress. Nevertheless, she dropped off to sleep in about ten minutes to the sound of a light breeze rustling through the trees. Nature's lullaby.

Since they hadn't felt the need to set a definite wakeup time, Lisa let Trish sleep for as long as she wanted. It was nice not to have hundreds of miles of road ahead of you for a change.
Meanwhile, she studied the map of northwest Montana to make an educated guess as to where a recluse might be holed up.
There were literally millions of places to hide. Lisa could have just as easily put this up on a dartboard and thrown darts at it.
Which was just where her mood was when Trish knocked softly on her door.
"Hey, good morning," Trish was bright and cheerful.
"Hiya," Lisa replied, not as bubbly as she usually was.
"What's wrong?" Trish read the mood immediately.
"Nothing."
"I can see in your eyes that it's not nothing."
"I'm just frustrated because I can't even make a decision about where to begin looking for Sheila Lancaster.
"Is that all?"
Lisa stepped back so that Trish could come in.
"I called home last night," Lisa remarked.
"Okay. And what happened?"
"I don't know."
"What do you mean?"
"I mean that it was just a strange conversation, that's all. Look, let's go have breakfast or something. Is that okay? Maybe I will think better on a full stomach."
"I worried about you last night," Trish nodded.
"You did?"
"Yeah. You didn't eat much for dinner and the candy was all the way down this long, *deserted* road…" Trish had a hint of a smile on her face like she was well on the way to winning their bet.
"Yeah, whatever."

"Hey, I'm sorry that you're having some problems here. Let's go and eat and sort it all out," Trish felt awkward that she had made light of whatever was going on between Lisa and Mary. They returned to the restaurant where they had dinner. No use trying something different after such a rewarding experience. The breakfast menu was as straight-forward as the dinner menu had been.

"What are you in the mood for today?" Trish asked.

"I don't know. I'm not very hungry."

"Well, in that case, eat something salty."

"Why?"

"It will taste good. Trust me. Order something like the corned beef hash and eggs."

"That does sound good…"

"I'm splurging and having pancakes and syrup."

"That will certainly stick to your ribs."

"Hey, no puns before noon. New rule."

"Are you going to make up a new rule every day?"

"Only if I need to."

"Well, if you get to make up a new rule every day, then so do I."

"Okay. I can live with that. I think…"

They placed their order and then studied the map to see where they might start this incredulous journey.

"We could drive up to Glacier National Park to see the sights," Trish said.

"We're not here for some sightseeing trip, though, are we," Lisa retorted immediately.

Trish began to get a sense of what had transpired between Lisa and Mary during their phone call.

"No, we're not. But Sheila might be hiding up there just as much as anywhere else."

"Don't they patrol the park systems pretty well?"

"Well, maybe she wouldn't be in the park proper. But she might be on the edge somewhere. If you have a property that abuts a national park, then it's like having the world for your backyard."

"I didn't think about it that way."

"Or we could go to Columbia Falls or White Fish to see if anyone knows anything? Do that snooping around that you talked about."

"Columbia Falls sounds pretty."

"It's all pretty up here," Trish smiled at Lisa.

Their breakfasts arrived and Lisa went straight for the salty stuff. It did taste good and she cleaned her plate before Trish ventured into personal issues.

"You want to tell me what happened between you and Mary?"

"She was just tired from work."

"That's understandable."

"We're up here on what seems to be some vacation to her and she's home working."

"I see her point."

"Yeah," Lisa sighed. Apparently that wasn't all of it.

"And what else?"

"I told her about the candy store, figuring that she would think it was funny."

"And she didn't?"

"She thought that you were trying to show off in front of me."

"Really?"

"Yeah, like trying to impress me."

"Really?" Trish repeated, amazed at the very thought of it.

"You're repeating yourself."

"Really?" Trish said for a third time and then smiled.

"What's so funny?"

"Next time you talk to Mary, tell her that if I wanted to impress you, I'd do a whole lot more than buy a few boxes of candy."

"I'm not sure that I should tell her that."

"You're really serious about this, aren't you?"

"Well, Mary certainly is."

"Mary is seriously worried that I bought a bunch of candy?"

"She thinks that it's something that she can't do for me but you can."

"Is there anything else that Mary thinks I can do for you that she can't?"

"She didn't mention anything else specifically."

"If she had, would you tell me?"

"Yes, I would."

"You didn't happen to mention our bet about the neck rub, did you?"

"That didn't come up in the conversation."

195

"Perhaps that was best. You know, there is an airport close by. We could put you on a plane and send you home today before Mary gets any more worried about you. I would charter a jet if you need it."

"I don't think she's *worried* about me?"

"What do you think she is, then?"

"I think she's jealous."

"Well, this is the first time in a long time that you've struck out on your own to do something important. Maybe she just misses you. I know that I would miss you if the circumstances were reversed."

"Did you call home last night?"

"I did."

"Things are okay?"

"Things are spooky. That's why I know that we're just not up here lollygaging around. We are actually on a mission."

"Right. And I'm staying put. I didn't come all the way up here to fly home just because Mary is the one stuck home working."

"Are things bad financially?" Trish decided that it was now or never to ask this question.

"Things aren't bad. It's just that I don't work. Yet. And so the entire burden is on Mary's shoulders."

"But you have the house free and clear. Mitch did take care of that, right?"

"Right," Lisa said, conveniently omitting the part about the recent inflow of cash from Mitch. Mary had made her put it in a special escrow account and there it would stay put to be used only for emergencies.

"You know, as long as you have Mitch and Reb and me in your life, you'll always have a soft spot to land in case things get rough."

"Mary has too much stubborn pride for that."

"She takes after her mother."

"Yes, she does."

"Why don't we go back to the cabins and check out since the place will simply fill up tonight…and drive on down the road."

"I'm not conceding our bet."

"I didn't ask you to."

"So how are we going to know who won if we don't come back."

"I don't think we need to come anywhere to know who won the bet, do you?" Trish phrased the question cryptically.

"Then I guess we'll never really know," Lisa wasn't ready to give in.

"I guess we never will."

"So, let's go then. If you're ready? I don't want to rush you. I would never want to rush you."

"I would never want you to rush me either. I'm good to go."

They drove back to their cabins and loaded up the one suitcase apiece that they had taken in. When they went to pay the bill, they had no problem ringing the bell. In fact, it felt kinda good. It was their last chance to bother the proprietor. He came out of the side door, still greeting them with a suspicious eye.

"Checkin out?"

"We don't have a choice, as you explained yesterday."

"If you don't mind me askin, where'd you get alla that candy?"

"The candy in the SUV? I bought it at a gas station down the road."

"Got a receipt?"

"Yes."

"Can I see it?"

"Why would you want to?"

"The sheriff around here likes us to report suspicious things."

"And having a car full of candy is suspicious?"

"For two grown women it is."

"For whom would this not be a suspicious circumstance?"

"A candy salesman. That's about it."

Trish knew in the deepest place in her heart that they would not be being interrogated had they not been guessed to be lesbians. She had a choice between producing the receipt and going to civil rights court. She pulled the receipt out of her wallet and showed it to the man. His eyebrows looked comical as they raised high over his eyes and he blew a soft whistle as he read the price.

"That's a whole lotta money."

"It's a whole lotta candy. You want some?"

"Depends."

"On what?"

"On how much you're charging?"

"It's on the house. What kind do you like? Chocolate? Nougat? Coconut? We've got some of everything."

"Oh, I don't know…" he was hesitant now after being so bold a moment ago.

"Do you have grandkids?"

"Yes."

"Pick something out for them."

He looked from Trish to Lisa and back again.

"Come on out and take a couple of boxes of whatever you want."

"Are you sure?"

"Sure I'm sure. Come on."

They all went out to the car and Lisa opened up the back. He didn't hesitate once he got sight of his favorites. The man was a chocolate and peanut fan. He took a few bars of two varieties and then Trish motioned to Lisa and they followed him back to the office with an armful of boxes of them.

"I really couldn't take all these," he demurred.

"It's okay. If we want more, we can always make another stop."

"You know, I did have a cancellation for tonight if you need a place again."

"Well, we were planning to drive around a little. We're looking for someone."

"Who are you lookin for?"

"A friend of a little old lady back in Denver. She's in a nursing home and we're trying to find this friend of hers so that she can see her before she goes to the great beyond," Lisa explained it like she had rehearsed it all night.

"What's the lady's name. Maybe I can help?"

"Sheila Lancaster."

The man furrowed his eyebrows together. "Sounds familiar. Let me think. Do you know anything more about this friend?"

"I suppose she's a recluse. Our concern was that she didn't want to be found. And we're running out of time."

"A female recluse up here in Montana. I've heard about someone like that. Over in Hungry Horse. The lady chases people off her property with a gun. Lancaster. Lancaster. I don't remember so good. You know how the memory goes when you get old."

Trish nodded like she understood all too well. "How big a place is Hungry Horse?"

"About a thousand people. Maybe more. Maybe less."

"Anything else we should know."

"There's a storm coming in."

"What's that got to do with Ms. Lancaster?"

"You might need a room for the night. You know these weathermen. Never get it right. My left knee tells me it's a big storm though."

"We'll think about it. We have your number."

"Thanks. And keep the storm in mind. It's spring around here. You know what that means?"

"What?"

"We get snow by the foot."

"Thanks for the warning."

Trish and Lisa left the office and climbed into the SUV.

"So, where is this Hungry Horse place?" Trish asked.

"It's a little past Columbia Falls. Not far at all. We were on the right track after all!" Lisa sounded excited. Trish looked over at her and chuckled.

"What?"

"It's just good to see you this enthused."

"It's our first big break, and all due to you!"

"Me? Why me?"

"Because you were nice to the guy. Especially when you had every reason not to be. What with the goofy cabin arrangements and the candy receipt business. You could've been a real bitch to him and no one would've blamed you but you remained calm and nice and civil and really really friendly and it really came through for us!"

Trish stayed quiet. Lisa noticed. "What are you thinking?"

"I was trying to remember the last time I saw anyone this excited about anything. It's a nice thing to see."

"You're not teasing me, are you?"

Trish looked squarely into Lisa's questioning eyes. "I'm not teasing you one little bit. I'm so very glad now that I didn't put you on a plane for home this morning."

"You're not getting rid of me that easy."

"I certainly hope not."

Lisa pulled out the map and pointed out to Trish where they were headed. It wasn't highway, but there was a road. As long as there was a road, they would be in great shape.

"What do you think about our friend's weather prediction?"

"I'm not entirely convinced that one's body parts can accurately predict weather patterns, although I had a friend once who had hemorrhoids and she claimed that her butt could tell if it was going to snow."

"You know someone who has a butt that can predict the weather?"

"It was a long time ago."

"Gives a whole new meaning to the term 'smart ass.'"

"Didn't I tell you no puns before noon!"

"Sorry, I forgot."

Lisa was an excellent guide. They were on the correct road without even one back track. It was beautiful country, no doubt about that. They were close to the Continental Divide and the scenery was exquisite. If anyone wanted to run away from it all, this would be the place to run.

"What's the plan once we get to Hungry Horse?" Trish asked.

"The same as before."

"What's that?"

"We stop at the local restaurant, have lunch, and then ask questions. There's only a thousand people there. Someone has got to know Sheila."

"We seem to be having luck with the older generation. Why don't we keep that in mind."

"It's a good idea, but if this woman runs people off with a shotgun, everybody's bound to know about it."

"Yeah, but we don't want to appear to be prying information out of young people. Especially not with a back seat full of Hershey bars."

"Why not?"

"I just don't want people to think we're some sort of child molesters."

"Oh, gee, I don't know. Being lesbians and thieves seems to be working so far…"

"Isn't that one of those Cher songs?"

"I wouldn't know. She was before my time."

200

"You want me to hum a few bars?"

"Thanks but no thanks."

"You don't think I can, do you?"

"Oh, I'm sure you can…but the turn off is just up the road and I don't want you to miss it."

"How far up the road?"

"Not more than a couple thousand miles."

Trish laughed. So much for serenading Lisa off key. They were at Hungry Horse well before noon and parked at the local café. It was small, quaint and not too crowded.

"We're still serving the breakfast menu," the waitress announced like she only told this to complete and utter strangers. Everyone else knew, of course.

"That's fine," Lisa smiled.

"I could use another breakfast as well," Trish was in an agreeable mood.

"Coffee is free with one of the specials," the woman pointed out three specials on the menu, named by someone without any sense of creativity: Specials 1, 2, and 3.

"Is that okay with you, Lisa?" Trish asked.

"They all look good, don't they?"

Trish looked up. "We'll have all three."

"All three?"

"That okay with everyone?" Trish checked Lisa's gaze.

"That's fine."

"But you only get two cups of coffee. One refill apiece," the waitress spelled out the rules even though they were printed on the menu.

"Did you want something besides coffee?" Trish asked Lisa.

"Only coffee is free, you understand," the woman interjected like she was mediating a labor union contract.

"Right," Trish nodded. "We'll pay for anything extra. You want a milkshake or something like that, Lisa?"

"That does sound good."

"A milkshake for breakfast?" the waitress asked with skepticism.

"What flavors do you have?"

"Chocolate, vanilla, strawberry."

About as original as Specials 1, 2, and 3.

"We'll have one of each of those as well," Trish ordered before cobwebs grew over the table.

"Okay, so that's one of each special, one of each milkshake and two coffees."

"Perfect," Trish nodded.

"We'll decide about dessert later," Lisa handed over her menu. The waitress departed, shaking her head. Trish didn't need to hear it to know that she was muttering to herself about people who drink milkshakes and still need dessert as well.

"You're really bad sometimes," Lisa gave Trish a look that conveyed that it was a good sort of bad that she was referring to.

"Little old me? Bad?"

"Well, maybe bad isn't the right word."

"What is the right word?"

"Maybe ornery?"

"Ornery?"

"Maybe that's not the right word either."

"Maybe it is."

"You just like to sort of put people back on their heels, what word describes that?"

"How about unpredictable?"

"That might be it."

"As long as I'm not unreliable."

"That sounds like another song that you don't need to sing for me."

"You don't want me singing love songs to you in the Hungry Horse Café?"

"I think we've already made enough of a stir, Ms. Order One of Everything on the Menu."

"I didn't do that, but I still could."

Trish looked around like she was going to beckon their waitress but Lisa took her by the hand and got her attention. Lisa always got your attention when she took your hand in hers. "Now, don't be any ornerier than you already have been!"

"Okay. Am I embarrassing you?"

"No, you're not. You would never embarrass me."

Lisa was still holding her hand and let go very slowly only after she made good and sure that Trish wasn't going to forget anytime soon that she had captured it in the first place.

"Here's your coffee, ladies," the waitress had appeared out of the nether world and clunked down two cups, sloshing liquid into both saucers simultaneously. It took real talent to do that.

"Thank you," they said simultaneously.

"Sure thing."

After one sip, it was evident that they had three cups of coffee packed into one cup.

"They drink their brew strong up here," Trish grimaced at the bitterness of the coffee.

"It's kind of tasty, isn't it."

"Yeah, like in the same way that kerosene would be tasty."

"You don't like it at all?"

"I'm spoiled. I make my own at home with one of those thousand dollar coffee makers."

"I leave the coffee making to Mary."

Trish remembered how that turned out. She grimaced involuntarily again.

"Good thing you ordered milkshakes."

"I didn't even look at what all we're getting to eat."

"I didn't either. I guess it's going to be eggs and stuff like that."

"I suppose."

All of a sudden, their conversation sounded stilted again. It was as if they felt the need to pull back from each other. Which was silly. After all, they were friends. Trish looked up to find Lisa looking directly at her.

"What? Did you say something?"

"I was thinking about when we were in Texas."

"Goodness, I haven't thought about that in a whole long time."

"Now, that was a scheme," Lisa intoned.

"Yes, it was."

It would be an impossible task to make the long story short about the Texas scheme. Suffice it to say that it was something cooked up by Mitch and Mary and Trish to test the honesty and veracity of Lisa. Back when she was a grifter, before her conversion to the honest way of life. In the course of events, one of the most memorable moments happened between Trish and Lisa when they shared a kiss. It had been unplanned and brief. Well, maybe not that brief. But not that long or intense. Unless you hadn't been kissed in ages.

203

"We've all come a long way since then," Trish said.

Lisa studied Trish's eyes. Neither one had actually mentioned the kiss and yet they both knew that that was what the other was thinking about.

"You got together with Mary and I got together with Robbie. So much has happened in both our lives."

"It sure has." Lisa's hand went unconsciously to her scars. "Do you ever hear from Judy?"

"No," Trish cut the answer very short.

Good thing breakfast showed up. They were running out of avoidance dialogue. The breakfast platters were huge. Martians could take a spin around the universe on these.

"You sure you still want those milkshakes?" the waitress asked.

"Sure. Might as well."

"Okie dokie."

Lisa picked up a fork, ready to do battle with their second breakfast of the day. She started with the pancakes that Trish pushed under her nose.

"I've had my fill," Trish explained.

"You'd never win the pancake-eating contest."

"I'll mask my disappointment as best as I can."

They ate leisurely, sharing food between them and washing it down with milkshakes. It hadn't taken more than a kind word to procure six straws so they could each sip from all the flavors.

Lisa took one sip of each and combined the flavors in her mouth.

"I feel like a teenager at a diner," Lisa confessed.

"You certainly look young enough."

"Oh, stop it. I do not."

"You do too. You look like you're about nineteen."

"I told you to hush."

"No you didn't."

"Well, I am now," Lisa was starting to blush.

"How are you two ladies doing?" Penny was checking in. They had gotten on a first-name basis by now.

"Can I ask you something?" Lisa put on her sweetest expression.

"Sure thing."

"We're looking for a woman for a friend of ours."

"Are you detectives or something?"

"No. Nothing like that. We just have a friend in a nursing home and we promised we'd find her friend before she dies."

"Which one is dying?"

"The one in the nursing home. Anyway, we had a lead that maybe this friend was living around this area."

"What's her name? Maybe I know her."

"Sheila Lancaster."

"Never heard of her."

Lisa tried to not look too disappointed. "We think she's a hermit. And we heard a rumor that she chases people off her property with a gun."

"That's pretty much standard in these parts."

"Even for a woman?"

"There's only one woman who comes to mind, but her name's not Shirley."

"Sheila."

"Not that either. It's Bertie. Crazy Bertie to some folks."

"Crazy Bertie?"

"That's other people's opinion, not necessarily mine. I figure that people should get to live their lives as they see fit, loony or not."

"Where does Bertie live?"

"You got a map?"

"Right here," Lisa pulled out a detailed map of the area, complete with topographical information.

"Let me get my glasses," Penny said. She perched the glasses on her nose and turned the map around a few times to get her bearings. She drew a line and then a circle. "Last I heard of her running someone off her property, she lived there."

Trish and Lisa gazed upon these markings like it was a treasure map. They couldn't believe their luck. Two people had apparently led them to their goal.

"Thank you, Penny," Trish put a hundred-dollar bill on the table.

"I don't have enough in the cash drawer to make change."

"Keep the change."

"If I were you, I'd get up there before the snow starts."

"Do your knees hurt? Is that how you know it's going to snow?"

"Hell no. I watched the weather forecast. It's going to be a big one."

"Thanks for the warning."

Trish and Lisa headed out to the SUV, map in hand.

"Well, at least you didn't ask her if her butt hurt," Lisa remarked.

"I try not to ask people that. You get so many weird stares. How far away is this place we're going to?"

"Just a matter of miles, but the terrain might be daunting."

"You guide me there. I'll do the driving."

"I wouldn't have it any other way."

The road was decent for a mile or two and then they began to climb in elevation. It was all going to be dirt road from here on in and the ruts were challenging. Good thing they had rented this very capable vehicle.

"You could probably drive over the lunar surface in this car."

"It has served us well."

As they ascended the mountain road, the skies became gray at first and then white with snow.

"Hope you brought your mukluks," Trish mused.

"I have a sturdy pair of snow boots. What did you think I packed in those three suitcases?"

Trish didn't want to wonder out loud about what was in Lisa's suitcases. At least not while the real possibility of driving off a cliff was ever present.

"I guess I should've gotten a pair while I was in town."

"You didn't bring your boots?"

"I packed light."

"You didn't bring boots to Montana?"

"I have a really good pair of shoes."

"Your feet are going to freeze."

"Why? We're not walking up to the cabin, are we?"

"I don't have a guarantee on what this road is going to be like. We might end up walking our way in."

"It's not like I'm asking you to carry me."

"I just hope it doesn't get much worse."

"The road?"

"And the snow."

Trish took a deep breath. She could feel the tension emanating from Lisa.

"Are you worried about anything in particular?"

"Other than the fact that we might get shot at, gee, no."

"Is that all?"

"Isn't that enough?"

"How much further?"

"We should be there anytime. We've got to be within a quarter of a mile according to the circle Penny drew for us."

"Let's keep an eye out for a cabin then."

A side road came into view with a chain across it that said, "Private Property No Trespassing This Means YOU!"

"I think we found the place," Trish pulled up to the chain. She opened her door.

"What are you doing?" Lisa asked.

"I'm going to move the chain so we can drive up the road."

"I'm not sure we should do that?"

"Look, we've come this far. We can't leave the car out here on the road. It might get damaged and I'm not paying a bunch of money to a rental agency to settle the bill. If you want to wait out here until I check things out, that's fine. But if I can get past this chain, I'm going to at least get the car in the driveway."

Trish slipped out of the car and went over to the chain to check it out. It was easy enough to unhook it and she did so. By now, Lisa had slipped behind the wheel and pulled the car onto the private road. Trish hooked the chain back up and then got into the passenger side of the SUV.

"I'm ready to ride shotgun."

"Don't even say that!" Lisa said as she crept the car forward. "We're not even sure if this is the right place or not."

"We will be in a few minutes, I'm sure."

Up ahead, a structure came into view. It was a cabin alright. A pretty big one too for being out here in the middle of nowhere. One thing was for sure. If they could see the cabin, whoever was in the cabin could see them. The snow was still falling lightly, so visibility was decent. No one was barreling out of the front door with a shotgun. Trish got out and started walking. Lisa lined up with her shoulder to shoulder. If they were going to meet their maker, they were going out together. They got to the front door without any incident. Trish knocked. Nobody answered but the knob turned in her hand.

"You're not going in, are you?"

"I'm not going to stand out here in the cold and snow."

The door opened noiselessly. You would've expected a creak, but someone had taken time and care to maintain the hinges.

"If this were my door, I'd make sure it squeaked," Trish said.

"Why?"

"So you could hear someone come in."

"I hadn't thought of that."

If they had expected the usual cabin, they were in for a pleasant surprise. Whoever lived here had a flair for decorating. The furniture looked brand new, the floors were polished and the drapes were exquisite. No tattered dish towels or sheets for these windows.

"Maybe it's just my prejudice, but I think a woman lives here."

"Why?" Lisa asked as she tentatively walked into the middle of the living area after carefully wiping her feet on the door mat.

"What kind of man would select drapes like those?"

"A gay man?"

"I suppose that might be true, but I have a feeling deep in my bones that we have found the place we've been looking for."

"Mary is never going to believe this. She thought we were wasting our time."

"Do you think it would be too forward of us to bring in our suitcases before the weather gets really bad?"

"Maybe we could stash them on the porch. Then they would be close in case we needed them but it wouldn't look like we were homesteading."

"Good thinking."

They placed their suitcases on the side of the porch that had the most protection from the elements and then went in and closed the door tight and locked it. That way at least the occupant would need to fish for a key and give them time to prepare for a confrontation. And it seemed that they had arrived none too soon as far as the weather was concerned. Snow began falling at blizzard pace and the wind picked up, making visibility drop to zero. They could hardly see the car now from the cabin window.

"You know," Lisa said thoughtfully, "Whoever isn't here isn't going to be able to get here through this storm."

"I'm getting the suitcases then. Before they get any more buried in snow."

Lisa helped and then lamented that all the candy was still in the car. Trish braved the storm to bring in a couple of boxes, just in case it was all there was for dinner.

"There's even wood for the fireplace. It's stacked in a back room. Just off the kitchen."

"Are you cold? I could start a fire," Trish bragged.

"Are you a scout or something?"

"You want to see my merit badges?"

"I guess we'd better start a fire. It's going to get even colder with the storm moving in."

Trish checked to make sure the flue was open and then laid an expert fire.

"You do know what you're doing!"

"I do this at home all the time. Speaking of home, I wonder if my cell phone works up here."

She checked for reception. There was none.

"I guess we won't be able to call home anytime soon."

"I hope they don't worry about us."

"Nobody knows where we are except Penny."

"We'll be fine. We'll just wait out the storm, eat candy bars, gather more firewood."

"I guess so. It would be foolish to try and leave."

"It would be terribly unwise."

"So, maybe there are some books or something to read."

"Check around. I'm going to stretch out on the couch and get some rest."

"I'll just sit over here in this overstuffed chair."

"Do you want the couch instead?"

"No, I wouldn't hear of it. You rest. You had a long drive."

"We'll take turns. I'll nap and then you can nap."

"Of course. Good idea. You want me to read to you?"

"Did you find something good?"

"It's an Agatha Christie mystery."

"That would be fun."

Lisa opened the book and started at the beginning. Trish was asleep by page ten. Nobody had even gotten murdered yet. Lisa knew that it would be a good idea to stay awake to guard the fire, so she located a teakettle and made a cup of instant coffee. So far, this was like the best camping trip ever. As she had searched for the coffee, she found the larder to be quite well-stocked for the wilderness. There were canned vegetables, rice, beans, spices and flavorings that indicated a discerning palate. They could survive for days and days. When Trish woke up, she would discuss menu possibilities with her. Until then, Lisa munched a candy bar, sipped her coffee and read her book. Three inches of snow were on the ground by now with no end in sight. Trish stirred awake about an hour later, and saw Lisa smiling at her.

"What?"

"You look so peaceful when you sleep."

"Did you watch the whole time?" Trish sounded a bit grumpy.

"No, not really. I got all the way up to page forty. Someone is actually dead by now."

"That always helps in a murder mystery."

"Did you happen to locate the bathroom yet? God, I hope there's a bathroom and not an outhouse."

"Right around that corner. Very nice. I tested it myself while you were sleeping."

"Thanks."

After Trish reappeared, she went over to the window.

"How much snow is there now?" Lisa asked as Trish peered out.

"Looks like about six inches."

"Wow, it really is a blizzard. Two or three inches an hour is amazing. Not unheard of, but amazing."

"Is this your first big blizzard?" Trish asked, sounding a little less grumpy now that she was awake.

Lisa stood up and walked over to the window, standing just enough behind Trish to be polite but getting a good look out the window herself. She was practically on her tiptoes.

"I've been in worse."

"Me too."

"But it's not over."

"And it doesn't look like it's going to stop anytime soon either," Trish turned to face Lisa.

"Do you want to go to bed? We said we'd take turns resting."

"Um, I'm not sleepy yet. I think the coffee and chocolate have me revved up."

"You made coffee?"

"Just instant. Want some?"

"I might as well. Whenever the owner of the cabin shows up, we'll need to pay them for what we used."

"Absolutely."

"Well, take me to your kitchen."

"I had a couple ideas for dinner as well."

"Besides candy bars?"

"I think we can make a simple soup. There are canned goods and broth. And beans and rice. Stuff like that."

"A vegetable soup with rice sounds like it might keep us warm."

"And it would only take a few minutes to put together."

"I'll help. What do you need me to do?"

"So, you know your way around a kitchen?" Lisa was teasing again.

"I know my way around every room in the house," Trish teased back.

"I bet you do. Can you run a can opener?"

"Just tell me what you want opened and leave the rest to me." Lisa passed three cans of vegetables to her and then rummaged around for a soup pot to start the soup. Someone took very good care of their cooking supplies. The pot was clean as a whistle. Luck was on their side when Lisa found an onion in the small refrigerator.

"Did you happen to see wires for electricity as we pulled up?" Lisa asked.

"No, I didn't but that's not what I was looking for. I suppose there's wiring somewhere out back. Otherwise, we wouldn't have electricity. Or maybe there's a generator somewhere?"

"This is a very modern cabin for a hermit."

"Maybe Ms. Lancaster is a wealthy hermit. Just because someone wants to get away from it all doesn't necessarily mean that they are poor and backwards as well."

Lisa paused a moment and then chuckled.

"What's so funny?"

"I finally get it."

"Get what?" Trish was now very curious.

"Why everyone might call her Bertie."

"Why?"

"Bertie, a derivation of Burt. Burt Lancaster."

"Might be a nickname?"

"Now I'm sure we're in the right place. I just hope they exaggerated the part about the shotgun."

"Well, she's not in jail, so she hasn't killed anybody yet."

"That we know about."

"That's a cheery thought."

"I'm always looking on the bright side of life."

"You do have a propensity for optimism."

"Some days more than others."

"Do you still have bad days because of the accident?" Trish assumed that this was the topic of conversation.

"Just every time I look in the mirror."

"Why?"

"Why? You can't figure out why?"

Trish looked over at Lisa. Sure, she had scars. If you had never seen them before you might take notice of them. If you were looking for them. But Trish had gotten used to how Lisa looked and somehow the familiarity blocked them from her mind. Most of the time.

"I guess I just don't think about them."

"That's because they aren't on *your* face."

"I'm sorry. I didn't mean to make light of them."

"No, I'm sorry. I know better than to snap at you of all people."

"You can snap at me any time your heart desires. If that makes it all better, then it's okay with me."

Lisa looked over at Trish. There was just a hint of sparkle in her eyes like tears were trying to form.

"Why don't you let me finish the soup and you go and rest for a while," Trish offered. "Put on that cushy white robe and just relax."

"I'd like that."

Lisa decided that as long as it was well past noon that there was no harm in changing into pajamas. It was a snowy day and they sure weren't going anywhere or entertaining company. Might as well be comfortable. Her bedtime fashion consisted of a t-shirt, flannel pajama pants and, of course, the robe that they bought in Billings. She sat on the side of the couch where she could keep an eye on Trish, just in case she looked like she needed help. At least, that was the excuse she told herself. But what she found herself really doing was watching and appreciating Trish's fluid movements as she prepared dinner. It was like a kitchen ballet. Once or twice, when Trish looked over her shoulder Lisa pretended to have her head buried in the book that she had selected earlier. Somehow, being caught looking seemed embarrassing.

"Why don't you read to me," Trish called out.

"Where did we get to in the story before you fell asleep?"

"The only thing I remember was that people were going to some country home for a vacation or something like that."

"A little like our own situation."

Trish laughed. "Let's just hope that we don't end up solving a murder mystery."

Lisa read a few more pages and then began to yawn.

"Are you sleepy?" Trish came into the room proper. She was finished for now with the cooking duties and sat down in the chair.

"I'll share the couch with you," Lisa pulled her feet up to make a spot.

"That's okay. The chair is fine for now."

"Have you figured out where we're sleeping tonight?" Lisa quizzed.

Trish looked puzzled. "Here?" she answered, indicating the general area of the cabin.

"I meant specifically."

"Specifically?"

"Well, I don't feel comfortable sleeping in the woman's bed. After all, some things just aren't done."

"Oh, I see what you mean."

"And there's only one couch and there's two of us."

"This chair will be fine for me."

"I don't think that you'll get a very good night's sleep in that thing."

"It's not like I'm going out tomorrow to run a marathon. I can manage one night of sleeping in a chair."

"I think we're going to be here more than one night."

"You do?"

"Take a look out the window."

Trish got up and went to the window by the door. The snow was piling up fast and steady. It had completely covered the car and swirled up against the front door to the point where it would take a mighty shove to open it if this kept up all night. If Trish were the kind of woman who was bothered by being stranded in a snowstorm, she hid it well. She went over and added another log to the fire. Warmth emanating from the fire felt reassuring.

"We have the entire floor as well, in case I want to stretch out."

"The floor is hard."

"I'm tough. I've roughed it before."

"You're not going to sleep on the floor. We can take turns on the couch. I can curl up in the chair just as good as you can."

"You do have an elfin quality about you."

"What does that mean?"

"It means that you are slim and small and that you could probably curl up just about anywhere for a nap."

"We do have one other problem."

"What would that be?"

"We need to keep the fire going all night, don't we?"

"Probably not all night. If we sleep in this room, it will most likely stay warm enough until we restart the fire in the morning."

"I hope so. I don't want to be cold," Lisa inadvertently shivered again.

"Are you cold now?"

"I think it's just the combination of everything."

Trish went over and sat down next to Lisa. "Tell me what that means. Tell me what's making you shiver."

Lisa shook her head in reply. "It's nothing."

"It can't be both. It can't be everything and nothing all at the same time, can it?"

"I've just never been stranded in a cabin with a beautiful woman before," Lisa meant the remark to make light of her overall worries. At least, that's what she told herself. She looked at Trish, who hadn't made any sort of glib reply.

"I've stunned you into silence?" Lisa observed.

Trish stayed quiet.

"Well, I figured that if you could call me elfin, I could call you beautiful. I didn't mean for you to take the fifth over it."

"I guess it was just unexpected."

"What? Nobody's ever told you that you were beautiful before?'

"Of course they have. Just not you."

"I do have eyes and they still work pretty well. I can tell beauty when I see it."

"You should stop before I get embarrassed."

"I could do that to you? I could actually embarrass you?"

"Yes."

"So, one friend can't tell another friend how beautiful and wonderful and generous they are without causing discomfiture?"

"Well, it's just that…well, I guess in that context it's okay…"

"What other context would it be in?"

"You know, I bet our soup is about ready. Should we eat out here or sit in the kitchen?"

"It's warmer out here, don't you think?" Lisa remarked.

Trish couldn't argue with that at all. It had suddenly become very much warmer.

"I'll bring you a bowl."

After being waited on for two days, it was fun to actually prepare and serve food by themselves in the privacy of this serene environment.

"I can't believe I'm being waited on by a multimillionaire," Lisa grinned.

"What, you don't think us multimillionaires can wait tables."

"What is it like?" she asked after settling in with her bowl and spoon.

"To be a multimillionaire?"

"No, to be a waitress. Of course, to be a multimillionaire!"

"I don't know. I haven't been one long enough to give an objective answer," Trish said as she ate her soup. It was indeed warming. Not gourmet. Not fancy. But deep-down satisfying.

"You need a few more year's experience of spending bucketloads of money to know what it feels like?"

"I just don't feel much difference in the before-and-after aspect of things."

"Except that you can buy a thousand-dollar cappuccino machine on a whim," Lisa reminded her as she ate slowly.

"That was Robbie's idea."

"And you live in a huge mansion."

"Robbie picked it out."

"Am I discerning a trend here?"

"No, not really. I spend my fair share as well."

"And you have a back seat full of candy bars to prove it."

"I guess so."

"So, how long have you had trouble with your impulse control?"

"Trouble with *my* impulse control?

"Exhibit A is in the SUV."

"You're beginning to sound like Perry Mason."

"Why did you buy all that candy? Really, truly, honestly?"

"Really, truly, honestly? I wanted to demonstrate without question my purchasing power."

"To whom?"

"To the man running the gas station."

"So, you wanted to prove something about your purchasing power to a man you had never met before and will probably never meet again."

"Something like that."

"And you spent a lot of money to do that."

"Well, I got the candy as well."

"Right."

"So, Lisa, what would you do if our positions were reversed?"

"What would I do if I had your money?"

"Right."

"I have no idea."

"So, you wouldn't buy a car full of candy?"

"I might. I might buy two or three cars full of candy."

"Just on impulse?"

"Are you saying that I have problems with my impulse control as well?"

"I think that everybody has problems from time to time with their impulses. Don't you?"

"I think that there are impulses and then there are *impulses*."

"I guess so. Do you want more soup?"

"This was great, but I've had enough for now."

"Are you feeling warmer?"

"I've been feeling warmer for quite a while. Thanks."

"The fire is helping."

"Yes, it is."

Trish gathered up the bowls and spoons and went into the kitchen to do the dishes. Thank goodness they had running water. Maybe there was a well on the property. It was probably full of all sorts of minerals that city folks weren't used to. Trish nosed around and found a stash of bottled water on a shelf in the back pantry. When she took one out for Lisa, she found her dozing on the couch. Between the fatigue of the day, the bowl of soup and the warmth of the fireplace, Lisa had finally surrendered to sleep. Trish covered her with a blanket and left her in peace.

The chair wasn't all that bad for sleeping in. Trish had known all along that Lisa would spend all night on the couch. If she had argued, Trish would've probably held her down until she stopped insisting. Fortunately, it never came to that. By the time Lisa awoke, Trish had relit the fire, boiled water for coffee and had breakfast ready. Lisa stretched and walked slowly out to the kitchen.

"You were supposed to wake me up to take turns."

"The chair was fine."

"No stiff muscles?"

"Not really."

"Good, then that means I'll be comfortable in it tonight."

"We'll see."

"No. There's no 'we'll see' about it. How's the weather?"

"It's astonishing."

"How many of inches of astonishing do we have by now?"

"Go see for yourself. You won't believe me if I tell you."

"That bad?"

"Good, bad, who's to say."

"That's very philosophical."

"Are you hungry yet?"

"Starving."

"Good. I cooked a lot."

Lisa went over and peered out the window. It was still snowing. Trish was right. It was astonishing. Lisa's best guess was that there was at least two feet of snow and it continued to fall.

"We're trapped, aren't we?"

"Only in the most literal definition of the word."

"You seem calm for the circumstances."

217

"There's no reason to be otherwise."

Lisa sat down at the breakfast table and Trish put a plate of food in front of her. She didn't dive right in, despite her assertion that she was hungry.

"Are you okay?" Trish asked as she sipped her coffee.

"Aren't you the least bit worried?"

"About the weather?"

"About everything. The snow. No reception on the cell phone. Limited food supply. Well, I take that back, limited good food supply."

"God made me buy all those candy bars for a reason, I see that now."

Lisa smiled her first smile of the morning. It brightened up the room.

"But really, if we lose power, run low on food, get much more snow, it could get pretty grim."

"I don't see it that way at all. I don't see how it could possibly get grim."

"You've heard about the Donner family, haven't you?"

"I don't think we're going to resort to eating each other, do you?"

As soon as Trish said it, she knew that every innocent slip of the tongue was never really innocent. She blushed clear up to her ears. When she finally got the courage to look at Lisa, she was unreadable.

"I guess worse things could happen," was her sole comment.

"I, uh, yeah, well, eat your breakfast. You'll need your strength."

"For what?"

"Well, I am going to need my strength. I'm going to try and get a path shoveled to the car. I found a couple of snow shovels in a utility closet."

"I can help."

"You don't have to."

"No, in fact, that sounds like a good idea. It will help to get rid of some of this nervous energy."

"It's the best thing for nervous energy. A little exercise. A little hot chocolate."

"You found hot chocolate?"

"Guilty as charged."

"Sounds wonderful."

"You want some now?"

"No, I'll wait. There's just something about delayed gratification that makes some things so much better, don't you think?"

"Absolutely," Trish nodded.

They finished up breakfast, took turns in the bathroom, got dressed and went outside to start the snow-shoveling project. Agreeing to work at a slow but steady pace, they managed to work for about two hours before they took a break. It wasn't back-breaking work as much as just repetitive, but their shoulders, arms, and backs would be sore by evening. Thoughts of that neck rub won fair and square went through Trish's mind and it brought a smile to her face. Maybe tonight would be a great opportunity to cash in.

"What are you so happy about?" Lisa asked.

"Nothing."

"Nothing makes you smile like that? I wonder what you would look like if you were truly happy about something."

"Well, maybe you'll find out one of these days."

"Maybe I will."

They rested for about a half hour before returning to their work. This time, they were only able to work for about an hour and a half, the grinding effect of the manual labor was taking its toll.

"If we eat something now, we might get enough energy to keep going through the afternoon."

"I could stand some nourishment."

Lisa heated up the leftover soup from yesterday while Trish set the table.

"At least we are earning our keep," Trish said. "Maybe by the time the storm is over, we'll have the entire driveway cleared off."

"And won't our muscles just be bulging," Lisa flexed her arm.

"Gee, for a girl, you sure are strong," Trish chuckled.

They ate lunch, fought off the urge to nap and headed outside again. An hour crept by as they cleared a path around the SUV and shoveled what had fallen since the last time they were out. The snow had let up some, but it was still falling steadily. It felt

219

like a losing battle at times, but it was the only battle they had to fight.

"You ready to call it a day?" Trish asked.

"The sky is still light."

"But my shovel isn't. I swear my arms are going to fall off at this rate."

"Sure, we can quit for today. No use hurting ourselves."

"Besides, I want my reward. I've put it off long enough."

Lisa looked puzzled for a moment and then said, "Ah, yes, the hot chocolate."

"Sounds good, doesn't it!"

"Oh, yeah, it sounds great. Should we get a different kind of candy out of the car as long as we're here."

"Sure."

Lisa handed her snow shovel to Trish and then gathered up a couple of boxes and followed Trish back to the cabin. While Trish stored the shovels, Lisa boiled water and put hot chocolate powder into two cups. When she saw that Trish was heading to the chair to sit down, she intervened, physically blocking her way.

"You take the couch. Put your feet up."

"What about you?"

"Go on. Don't argue with me."

"I wouldn't dream of arguing with you. Wrestling, maybe. But never arguing."

"Yeah, well you wouldn't win a wrestling contest with me either."

"I wasn't worried about winning."

"Just go and sit on the couch and I'll bring you your hot chocolate."

"Yes, ma'am."

For once in her life, Trish followed orders. It did feel good to sit down and better yet to stretch out. When Lisa brought out her drink, she was almost too tired to move.

"You look exhausted."

"I'm not as young as I used to be."

"Nobody is," Lisa curled up in the chair with her cup.

"Can I ask you something?"

"It depends?"

220

"On what?"

"I'll know when I hear it."

"Whether or not you want to answer?"

"Right."

"Then maybe I shouldn't ask."

"What do you want to know?"

"I want to know why you brought up the subject of Texas yesterday?"

Lisa didn't answer right away.

"I guess that's what you meant by 'it depends.'"

"It was just something that you and I had in common. We've been together in each other's company for three days. I guess it was just something else to talk about. A shared experience."

"Did you have a specific shared experience in mind about the Texas trip?"

"Did you?"

"I asked first."

Lisa didn't look up from her cup. Trish waited. There was nowhere to go. Nothing to do. Nobody coming to their rescue.

"I was a different person back then," Lisa finally said.

"In what way?"

"I took things for granted. I took people for granted. I took what I wanted and didn't look back or think about how it might affect other people."

"I see."

"So, what was your specific memory? You have to answer me honestly now that I've answered you honestly."

"After hearing your answer, my answer will seem puerile."

"I doubt that. You have to tell me anyway."

Trish sat up straighter on the couch. "Come over here."

"Why?"

"Because I won't tell you the answer until you do."

Lisa set her cup down on the table and went over to the couch. She sat down beside Trish and turned toward her. "Okay. I'm here."

Trish didn't say anything but reached out and tentatively touched Lisa's scar. "Do you have feeling here?" she asked quietly.

"There is nerve damage, but the feeling comes and goes, depending on where you, where it is touched."

"Would you tell me when you feel something?" Trish asked as she moved her fingers gently over the area.

"Why are you doing this? Are you trying to prove a point?" Lisa asked bluntly.

"No, I'm not trying to prove anything," Trish moved her hand to Lisa's chin and moved closer. "I have one burning memory of our time in Texas. I know what it is and you know what it is."

"It was a long time ago."

"I haven't forgotten it. I never have."

"I didn't know it meant that much to you."

"And it didn't mean anything to you?"

"It was a kiss. A simple kiss."

"I've been kissed simply before. That wasn't a simple kiss."

"We were all playing a role. You were pretending to be a lawyer. Remember."

"And what were you pretending, Lisa?"

"I wasn't. I was in it for the money."

"You didn't have to kiss me that day to accomplish your goal."

"I did it on a lark. Pure and simple."

"Then, if I kissed you now on a lark, then it shouldn't mean anything to either of us."

"That's right."

"A kiss between friends?"

"A simple kiss between friends."

"And it wouldn't mean a thing."

"Right."

"That's good to know because that's exactly what I'm going to do," Trish whispered and then pulled Lisa closer. At first, the moment was tentative. Lisa would move closer and then stop, Trish would do the same. It was as if they were two magnets deciding whether or not they were attracted or repelled by each other. When their lips met, it was a tender, teasing joining. Nothing very simple about it and way too familiar for friends. Trish pulled back first and breathed deeply. It had been a while since she had had any affection to speak of.

"A simple kiss," Lisa repeated.

"Between friends," Trish finished the thought.

They both knew they were lying. To themselves. To each other.

"What are we going to do?" Trish asked.

"That's easy. You're going to sleep on the couch and I'm going to sleep in the chair."

"You're going to sleep on the couch and I'm going to sleep in the chair."

"No."

"That's what you said," Trish smiled.

"Okay, let's try this. Trish is going to sleep on the couch and Lisa is going to sleep in the chair."

"That's not what I want."

"Well, this isn't about what you want. It's about what we're going to do."

"You shouldn't have to sleep in the chair just because I kissed you."

"It's okay. It's my turn. Don't worry about it."

It was a good thing that early on they had mutually decided that the bed was totally off limits.

"What do you want to do for dinner?" Lisa asked.

"We could go out," Trish kidded.

"Or we could just have a pizza delivered."

"Or I could haul my carcass out to the kitchen and rustle something up."

"I can do that. You should rest."

"You worked as hard as I did today."

"Let's both cook."

"You just want me for my can-opening skills."

"Everybody's got to be good at something."

For all the talk and planning, neither of them seem inclined to move. Like that magnetism was still working to keep them together. Either that or they were both too tired to move. Trish stood up first. It was the least she could do after causing all the trouble. She pulled Lisa to her feet and they went to the kitchen. Lisa created a lemony tuna fish vegetable stir fry in about fifteen minutes.

"This is something I cooked a lot when I was in college."

"It's good."

"It beats starving."

"You could cook for me any day of the week."

"I assumed you ate fancier food than this."

"Not necessarily. Rose has everybody on a diet. That's why it's been fun to go to lunch with you."

"Is that the only reason?"

"No. I love your company as well," Trish said.

Lisa kept her eyes on her empty plate and said nothing in return. Trish couldn't stand the silence. "What are you thinking?"

"I was thinking that you are very generous with compliments."

"I'm just being honest."

"I love your honesty."

"Why don't I do the dishes while you relax," Trish offered.

"For once, I'm not going to argue with you."

Lisa took time to stoke the fire and change into her robe before checking up on Trish. She had her hands in dishwater, busily scrubbing the one-remaining pan. Lisa embraced her from behind and leaned her head between her shoulder blades.

"I want to tell you something."

"Okay," Trish stood still.

"Mary never touches my scars."

"Does it bother you?"

"Bother me how?"

Trish pulled her hands out of the water and dried them on the towel, but Lisa wasn't going to allow her to turn around.

"That Mary doesn't touch them," Trish clarified.

"Yes."

"I didn't hurt you, did I?"

"No. I just wanted you to know that I think you are very courageous."

"I don't think it had anything to do with courage. I wasn't afraid. I was probably more bold than anything. Overstepping my bounds. Trying to prove something, I guess."

"What were you trying to prove?"

"I guess that I appreciate you. Scars and all. Does that sound patronizing?"

"It sounds lovely."

Things got quiet. Trish had covered Lisa's hands with her own and now listened for guidance.

"Are you okay back there?"

When there was no audible answer, she loosened Lisa's embrace and turned to face her. Lisa hid her face, leaning into Trish's

224

shoulder. Trish respected her need for privacy and held her snugly rather than intimately.

"I don't know what to say. I had no idea how this was for you," Trish spoke quietly.

"I shouldn't expect you to. I shouldn't expect anyone to."

"Of course you should. That's what we're supposed to do for each other. You deserve that from friends."

"And lovers?"

Trish didn't know what to say next.

"I guess I'd better let you get back to your chores," Lisa said.

"I'm almost finished. Then maybe we can talk more. Or not. Or whatever you think."

"Okay."

Lisa retreated to the living room area while Trish rinsed and dried the dishes. By the time Trish sat next to her, she was more composed, but still silently conveying that she had things to say. Trish put an arm around her and waited.

"I've put Mary through hell."

Trish's first thought was to say "I doubt that," but didn't want to force Lisa to defend her statement.

"How did you do that?" Trish asked instead.

"During my rehab. I was a bitch."

Now Trish had to argue. "I know that's not true."

"You weren't there. Believe me, I was caustic."

"You had a reason."

"That's no excuse."

"What did you do?"

"I pushed her away. Just to see if she would stick by me."

"Well, she did."

"She stays with me, that's true. But..."

"But what?"

"Do you know what it's like when the light of love leaves someone's eyes? And in its place there's only obligation?"

"Relationships go through changes. It doesn't mean that they're unsalvageable."

"I don't want...I can't handle too many more *changes*."

"Was she very unhappy that you came on this trip?"

"I slept on the couch the night before we left."

"Why didn't you say something earlier?"

"I didn't want to sound like a complainer."

"Maybe I could've helped?"

"Having you come to my defense would've only made things worse. She's already suspicious."

"Suspicious?"

"I've been so excited about this entire project that I've just talked about you once too often to Mary. I know she's jealous. And I didn't mean for it to happen. I was just so glad to have something to do that felt important and helpful."

"And you have been. And I owe you an apology for kissing you."

"Did you mean it?"

"The apology?"

"No. The kiss."

"Yes, I did."

"Then you don't need to apologize. You never need to apologize for honest emotions."

"Okay."

"It's your turn to tell me what's going on in your life that you felt the need to kiss me."

"If I knew what was going on, I would tell you."

"You said something about how things are spooky?"

"Robbie hasn't been the same since the birth."

"In what way?"

"It's a good thing we have a spare room."

"You're getting the couch treatment too."

"Except that we're not even arguing. We're not talking, not communicating."

"How is she with Josh?"

"That's the only thing that's right with her. She's a very good mother. But the minute he's asleep, it's like a switch goes off and she withdraws."

"Have you thought about therapy?"

"Everyone thinks it's either post-partum or depression over Josh's disability. Everyone tells me to be patient. I guess I'm just flunking this test."

"Seems like we're both in the same situation at home. No wonder we get along so well. We truly understand what the other is going through. We're both starved for affection."

"And companionship."

"And love."

"You don't think Mary loves you anymore?"

"I'm not easy to love. For years, I relied on my good looks to attract women. It certainly worked with Mary. And when you rely on your good looks, you don't always bother to concentrate on other aspects of your life. Once your looks are gone, you're stuck playing catch-up. I'm not doing a very good job of it either."

"Have you tried to talk to Mary about it?"

"In general terms. I'm afraid what would happen if I talked about it in specifics."

"What specifically can't you say?"

"Oh, I don't know. How about, 'Did you only fall in love with me for my good looks?' for starters. What the hell would anyone say to that? No one wants to admit that, whether it's true or not."

"I see what you mean."

"Besides, I don't need to talk to her about it. I already know the answer. I can see it in her eyes every time she looks at me."

"Do you still love her?"

"I have a great affection for her. I wouldn't hurt her now for the world but that's just not enough. Not wanting to hurt someone isn't the same as loving them."

"What are you going to do when you get back?"

"Probably the same thing I've been doing. Go through the motions. Keep Mary happy if I can. Hopefully get off the couch."

"Weird, huh? Here we're fighting to get the couch and at home you're trying to get off the couch."

"It's all a matter of perspective."

"You know, one of us could probably sleep in the bedroom. It isn't like we're going to break anything."

"We could both sleep in the bed. We are grown ups. After a day like today, we're both going to need a good night's sleep."

"After a day like today, the only thing we will be able to do is sleep," Trish smiled.

"I still owe you that neck rub. Would you like it now?"

"I'll take a rain check."

"You're too tired for a neck rub?"

"No, but I'm sure that you're too tired to give one," Trish took one of Lisa's hands in hers. "Aren't your hands tired?"

"I'm young and strong."

"I noticed when you shoveled snow today. You ran circles around me."

"Oh, you did pretty good yourself."

"For an old woman."

"Oh please. You're still a sweet young thing!"

"Yeah, right."

"Why don't you get comfortable. Change into your robe and relax."

"I guess I could. Before I get too tired to move."

Trish left the room to change. It felt good to be in something soft and warm. This must be what it's like to return to the womb. When she went out to the main room, Lisa was curled up in the chair, holding the book they had been sharing. To her credit, Lisa wasn't on purpose trying to tempt Trish any more than she already did just by being herself.

"Are you going to read to me?" Trish smiled as she sat on the couch.

"Would that make you happy?"

"It would help pass the time."

Lisa's voice was lyrical and had it not been for the exertions of the day, Trish would've enjoyed more of it. But she soon dropped off to sleep and had just a faint sense of Lisa's lips brushing her forehead before she went sound asleep. So much for sharing a bed with her.

Trish woke up first and had the main room warmed up before going in to check on Lisa. She was sleeping soundly, snuggled under a down comforter. No use waking her up. They were in no particular rush. Trish went to the front window and the view uplifted her spirits. The snow had stopped and the sun was shining brightly. Today's shoveling would be a breeze compared to yesterday. She went to the kitchen and set the kettle to boil. Suddenly, hot chocolate sounded good. So did everything else after yesterday's exercise, both in snow shoveling and virtue. Trish had a decent breakfast cooked and was about ready to serve it to Lisa in bed when she appeared in the doorway.

"Good morning," Trish chirped.

"You're in a good mood."

"It's a beautiful day. Come, sit, eat."

"I thought you'd be angry."

"Why would I be angry?"

"I didn't wake you up so you could sleep in the bed."

"That's okay. It gives me plausible deniability."

"Yeah, me too," Lisa agreed curmudgeonly.

"We haven't done anything wrong," Trish said as they started to eat.

"We kissed."

"I'll take the blame for that," Trish offered quickly. "You haven't done anything wrong."

"I kissed you back."

"I'll say you did," Trish agreed quickly, not thinking that it wasn't the best reply.

"That's exactly what I'm talking about," Lisa sounded agitated.

"It was one kiss," Trish soothed. "One little brief kiss. Friends kiss. People kiss. Heads of state kiss, especially in Europe. We haven't done anything else. We didn't follow through with...you know."

"I know already. I know what you're saying. But we've also talked a lot about personal problems."

"And you feel that's an extension of being unfaithful?"

"It's a kind of sharing that seems every bit as intimate to me as making love."

"Then I will hold your words dear in my heart."

They polished off breakfast and dressed for their daily chore. If this snow had fallen in November, it might have stayed all winter. However, a spring snowstorm had less staying power. By noon, they had broken a path clear down the driveway to discover that at some point, the road had been plowed.

"We could probably leave anytime we want," Trish observed as they walked back to the porch.

"Except that we haven't done what we came here to do."

The sound of an approaching vehicle caught their attention.

"Looks like that's about to change."

A battered jeep lumbered up the driveway and rolled to a stop behind the SUV. A woman got out and to Lisa's relief, she wasn't packing a shotgun.

"Who are you?" the woman asked. She had to be sixty if she was a day.

"I'm Trish. This is Lisa. Are you Sheila Lancaster?"

At the mention of her name, the woman stopped in her tracks.

"Why would you think that?" she questioned.

"A woman named Wrightwood told us you might be here."

"What business do you have with Mrs. Wrightwood?"

"She wrote a book about my house."

"What house is that?"

"The Livermore Estate."

"You bought that old house. You must be rolling in dough."

Trish hated to agree without qualification, but she nodded anyway.

"You poor dear woman. And you came all the way up here in a snowstorm to see me about your house?"

"We've been here a couple of days. We got here right before the storm. I'm afraid we sort of made ourselves at home."

"I got stuck in town. Help me carry in my groceries."

"Sure."

Between the three of them, they had everything in the cabin and sorted out in ten minutes.

"You didn't eat much," Sheila remarked as she mentally inventoried supplies.

"We'll pay you for what we used."

"Nonsense. Let me go to the bathroom and then you can tell me what you need to tell me."

Trish stirred up the fire while Lisa straightened things up. Their hostess reappeared and sat in the chair, leaving the couch for them. They sat close and yet far enough away to give the correct impression.

"You came all the way from Denver to find me. It must be important."

"I actually have a question."

"Okay. Shoot."

"Do you have any idea why the Livermore place might be haunted?"

"You believe in haunted houses?"

"I never did until I bought one."

"That would make a believer out of you."

230

"Mrs. Wrightwood inferred that you might know why."

"Who is haunting the house?"

"We're pretty sure it's a young female," Lisa joined in.

"What happens during the hauntings?"

"A door gets stuck shut. People get stuck in a room in the basement. She's also appeared once, we think. Maybe twice."

"This door that gets stuck. Is it always the same door? The same room?"

"Yes."

"Then that room must be very significant to your ghost. I suggest you excavate it."

"What are we going to find?"

"If I were a betting woman, I'd say that you're going to find the skeletal remains of Benjamin Livermore's lesbian daughter."

Both Trish and Lisa were stunned into silence for a moment.

"How do you know that?" Trish finally found her voice.

"I'm not certain. It's an educated guess."

"Based on what?"

"Research. Interviews. Rumors."

"I need more than that."

"You have a door that turns a room into a prison. You find the body and I'll tell you more."

"Okay. You have a deal. We'll pack up and leave you in peace."

"One more thing."

"What's that?"

"The two of you make a cute couple."

"We're not a couple."

"Maybe not yet."

"Thank you for everything. Are you sure I can't pay you for groceries."

"What are you going to do with all that candy?"

"Oh, that. You want it?"

"All of it?"

"Sure."

"I won't have to buy any for Halloween," Sheila said happily.

It took about thirty minutes to head for home. Once they were on the road, they plotted their strategy.

"We should probably stay the night in Kalispell. Get a shower, a good dinner, a bed apiece," Trish said casually.

"You want to stay in a real motel this time?"

"I've had enough of cabin living for a few days."

"I understand entirely."

"What did you think of Ms. Lancaster?"

"I don't know if I'd go digging up my basement on her sole recommendation."

"Well, at least she didn't shoot us."

"Why would she. She thinks we're a cute couple."

Chapter 17

They were back among civilization in time for early check in to a nice hotel. Lisa had decided to upgrade them to the nicest accommodations in the city. Two rooms. Two beds. Two bathrooms. It was all they could ask for.

"We'd better call home," Trish said. "I'm sure they're worried about us. Stick around for a minute while I call home and then we can get a bite to eat, okay?"

"Sure," Lisa perched on the side of the bed and thumbed through the restaurant section of the phone book. She wanted it to look like she was busy doing something else besides eavesdropping. Trish dialed the phone and waited for someone to pick up.

"Hi. It's me-" the conversation stopped abruptly.

"I know. We were stranded-" again another sudden stop. The person on the other end of the line must've been really upset. Lisa hoped it wasn't Robbie jumping all over Trish. If she needed to, Lisa was ready to come to Trish's defense.

"My cell phone wasn't work-"

Another pause. A long, upsetting pause. Lisa watched as the color drained from Trish's face. The hand that held the phone to her ear went limp. She wasn't even listening anymore. Lisa went over and picked up the phone.

"Hello?" she said tentatively, hoping someone was still there.

"Who is this?" a man asked roughly.

"It's Lisa. Is this Max?"

"Yes. Where's Trish?"

"She's here but she doesn't look good at all. What's going on?"

"It's Robbie. She's dead."

"Oh, my God. What happened?"

"She killed herself. Trish needs to get home as soon as possible."

"Okay. I'll take care of everything. "I'll call you back when I get things arranged."

Lisa hung up without another word. Her first concern was Trish, who looked like she was on the verge of passing out.

"Lie down."

"What?" Trish looked like she hadn't heard anything.

"Lie down. You'll pass out otherwise. Come on."

Lisa arranged Trish like the rag doll that she had become.

"What's the name of that charter jet service you use?"

"The card is in my wallet."

"Okay."

Lisa efficiently sifted through the contents until she found the information. She made the call and arranged for a flight within two hours. Next, she found the card for the limousine service that Trish preferred and booked a ride from the airport to the house. They would meet up right at the jet. Then, Lisa called home. Mary wasn't there. She called the work number. Mary wasn't in the office. Mary was nowhere to be found. Neither was Mitch. Lisa called Max back as promised and told him the plan.

"Just hurry. That's all I ask," he said sorrowfully.

After checking out of the hotel, Lisa managed to get Trish out to the car and to the airport.

"You fly home. I'll drive the car back."

"No. You need to fly with me."

"What about the rental?"

"I'll arrange for them to pick it up here."

"Are you sure?"

"I need you with me on the plane. No more arguments."

"Okay. No arguments."

Lisa took care of the luggage and by the time they were ready to go, Trish was steadier. They boarded the jet and Lisa immediately put a drink in Trish's hand.

"I don't think I should."

"You need something. This will do you good."

It was brandy and it burned all the way down.

"This can't be happening," Trish said.

"It is unbelievable," Lisa said as she refilled the glass. "Drink another one."

"I don't know about this?"

"I do. Come on. One more and then you can talk about it."

Trish gulped the second drink and then broke down in tears. She cried all the way home.

When Trish and Lisa pulled up to the front gate of the property, there were several news crews already gathered out front. Thankfully they had been kept at bay for now by the authorities. A line of official-looking vehicles were parked farther up the drive, making it difficult to get close to the front door. Trish had to show I.D. to get past the guard at the door and had insisted that Lisa be allowed in as well. Once at the threshold, Silver was waiting to watch over them.

"Rose and Max are in the living room."

"Where's Josh?"

"In the nursery asleep for now. He's been a mess, though."

"Of course he has been. Why are all these police here?"

"When Rose found Miss Robbie, she dialed 911. I guess that triggered a routine investigation."

"For a suicide?" Trish felt too numb to think it through.

"For any death at a private home," Silver sounded knowledgeable as she led Trish and Lisa to where Rose and Max were sitting on the couch. There was an officer sitting with them.

"You got here," Rose tried to stand up but her shaky knees failed her. Trish sat next to her and gave her a hug. "I'm sorry I wasn't here."

"I'm sorry I let it happen."

"It's not your fault."

The officer was kind enough to allow them this brief exchange before interrupting. "Who are you?" he was ready to take down the information.

"I'm Robbie's significant other."

He wrote this down without making eye contact.

"And you just arrived from where?"

"I was on a trip to Montana with my friend, Lisa."

The officer gave some sort of secret signal to one of his colleagues. Another officer joined them immediately.

"Would you take her statement in the other room," he gave the command.

Lisa was escorted away in a no-nonsense manner. Apparently this was standard procedure.

"What was the nature of your trip?"

"Why is that important?" Trish answered with a question. In her grief, she was still sharp enough to realize that her answers had damn well better match Lisa's and she wanted a moment to think what Lisa might be telling her interrogator.

"It's just a routine question."

"I was trying to find out why my house is haunted."

Her blunt answer stopped things in their tracks, at least for a second or two.

"You believe your house is haunted?" the officer managed to not roll his eyes.

"Things happen that I can't explain."

"What sort of things?"

"People get locked in a room downstairs."

"She's telling the truth," Rose piped up, sensing that Trish needed defending.

"Can anyone besides the young woman you were with verify your story?"

"Is this the last routine question?" Trish had had enough of routine questions right about now.

"That depends on your answer."

"A recluse named Sheila Lancaster can verify our visit but you'll need to go personally up to Hungry Horse, Montana to take her statement. She's tough to find and doesn't take kindly to strangers."

"But she talked to you and your friend?"

"I guess she took a liking to us."

"What did you talk about?"

"I told her about the house being haunted and she told me that if I excavated the room in the basement that I might find skeletal remains. Do you want to do that or should I hire a private contractor?"

Trish figured that she might just as well get the whole story out now while people were actually listening. The officer wrote this down word for word and then asked Trish to stay right where she was until he came back. He went to see how the interview with Lisa was proceeding. She was telling the same story. When he returned, the questioning ceased. Almost.

"Have you decided on arrangements?"

Trish looked over at Rose and Max. "You haven't called anyone yet?"

"We were waiting for you."

"Where is Robbie now?"

"In the bedroom. Do you want us to go with you?"

"No one can go," the officer interjected. "They haven't cut down the body yet."

Trish looked at Rose, who was dissolving into tears.

"Is that what happened?" Trish finally asked.

Rose could only nod.

"Do you have a preferred mortuary?" Trish asked Max.

"Feldstein. I'll make the call." He stood up and walked stiffly out of the room.

"Are we finished here?" Trish asked the officer.

"For now."

Trish sat and held Rose for a long moment until Max returned.

"I need to check on Lisa and make a few phone calls, okay?" Rose nodded and then leaned against Max. Trish got up and went to the kitchen. Lisa was making coffee.

"Did you call home?" Trish asked.

"I tried, but I can't locate Mary anywhere."

"If we find Mary, then maybe we can track down Rebecca and Mitch. They'll want to know what's happened."

"Mary told me earlier that they went to Kansas to be with Aunt BeBe."

"And Mary isn't at home or work?"

"I called both places."

"What's her work number?"

"Why?"

"I'm going to call. Maybe I can get through."

Lisa looked puzzled but she dialed the work number for Trish anyway. Trish took the phone and waited for the receptionist to answer.

"Is Mary Fairbanks there?"

"Who's calling, please?"

"It's Trish Sullivan."

"I'm afraid Ms. Fairbanks is unavailable."

"But is she there?"

"Excuse me?"

"Is she physically on the premises?"

"I'm really not-"

Trish cut her off. "Look, Mary will want to know that there's been a tragic incident. Why don't you buzz her and see if she still wants to take my phone call."

"Hold the line, please."

About two seconds later, Mary was on the phone.

"Who is this?" she asked. Apparently the secretary hadn't even conveyed that information.

"Mary? It's Trish."

"What's going on?"

"We need to begin notifying people about a death and we thought we'd start with you and then find your mom and Mitch."

"Oh, dear Lord. I'm sorry. What's happened?"

"Lisa's here. She can tell you."

Trish handed the phone over to Lisa and left the room. She had lost complete patience with Mary and didn't want to convey that to Lisa. Lisa had enough on her hands without having to deal with that right now. When Trish got back to the main room, they were taking the body out the door. It was all zipped up in a black bag. Trish had no compunction to view Robbie's remains in their current state. It was all so undignified. For the professionals, it was just another day's work. But that was the light of her life that they were hauling out of the house. She went back to the kitchen and found Lisa still talking to Mary. At least they were talking now and Lisa was getting phone numbers.

"Mary wants to know what to bring. What do we need?"

"Nothing from her."

"Honey," Lisa said into the phone. "Why don't you just come over when you can and we'll figure it out from here."

Lisa nodded a couple more times and then hung up the phone.

"She'll be here in an hour."

"Okay. Rose and Max are going to need a lot of help."

"Right. I got Rebecca's contact information. Do you want to make the call?"

"I'll do it."

"What's happened?" Lisa knew just by looking that Trish needed to say something.

"They just brought Robbie down. Hopefully the house will begin to clear out now."

"You'll need to go and make arrangements pretty soon? I can make the call for you."

"It's okay. Really."

Lisa didn't know what else to do, so she did the only thing she knew she wouldn't get the chance to do for a long time. She gave Trish a hug.

"Thanks for taking care of things," Trish said.

"I'm here for you. You know that."

Trish nodded. Then she took the phone and dialed Reb's cell phone number. Reb picked up on the first ring.

"Hi, Reb. It's Trish."

"Mary said you'd call. We are so sorry. What can we do?"

"Well, don't you have your hands full out there in Kansas?"

"Mitch is coming to Denver. We've already arranged for that. I can't leave right now."

"How is BeBe?"

"Not good, I'm afraid. Thank you for asking."

"Is Mitch there?"

"No. She's already on the way. She didn't even pack a suitcase."

"That's okay. I'm sure I can find something in the closet for her."

"Have her call me when she gets there, okay?"

"Okay."

"And call me if I can do anything else from here."

"I will."

Trish hung up the phone. Lisa had been listening but hadn't heard everything.

"Mitch is on the way."

"What was that about the closet?"

"Mitch didn't pack a suitcase."

"Well, they still sell clothes, don't they."

"Would you do me a big favor?" Trish asked.

"Sure."

"Find a caterer and arrange to have food brought in for at least a week. And anything else that sounds good. I want breakfast, lunch and dinner for seven days. Can you do that for me? Use this credit card," Trish pulled out her trusty platinum.

"I'll take care of it," Lisa nodded. "But for how many people?"

Providentially, Rose and Max appeared in the kitchen. They would know how many to plan for.

"We're going to call a caterer. How many people do you expect to drop by the house over the next week?"

"Maybe twenty-five?" Rose seemed relieved to be thinking about something practical.

"Let's plan for fifty per day. What we don't eat, we'll send out the door with visitors."

"We're already on the news," Max announced with chagrin.

Trish shook her head. It was a good thing they contacted Mary and Mitch when they did. "Mitch is coming from Kansas."

"Will the Senator be here as well?" Rose asked.

"We don't think so. Her sister is dying as well."

"Then she should stay by her bedside."

"So, seven day's worth of meals for fifty people. Is that enough to go on, Lisa?"

"I'll start making calls."

"Don't forget, we need kosher food as well."

"I'll call a Jewish caterer."

"Perfect."

"We need to schedule a time to go to the mortuary," Rose said what she came into the kitchen to say.

"I need to take a shower and get dressed in something appropriate. Who is going to take care of Josh while we're away?"

"I can," Lisa said while she scanned the phone book for caterers. "You can't do everything."

"This will only take a few minutes. Then I've got nothing better to do than watch Josh. Besides, Mary will be here as well. We'll be fine. Don't worry. Take care of what you need to take care of. You're the ones who have the difficult tasks ahead. Concentrate on that and let your friends take care of everything else, okay?"

"Okay," Trish surrendered to the logic. "Max?"

"Yes?"

"Did you say we were on TV?"

"The news is running live shots of the house."

"Have Silver come and talk to us for a minute, will you?"

"Sure."

Max returned in ten seconds with Silver.

"Silver, what do you think we need to do about security measures during the next week?"

"It wouldn't hurt to have more."

"Max says the news is out front broadcasting live feed from the front gate."

"The news might go national. We should get extra personnel in here to patrol the grounds, protect visitors, screen guests. Do you want me to hire up for a week."

"Yeah. Hire up what we need. There's going to be enough to deal with without any other distractions. But I don't want people to feel put off by the extra security."

"I can hire the best of the best. Just leave it to me."

"And then, we'll need you to go with us to the funeral home."

"I'll be ready when you are."

"You always are."

Even though the hour was late, Trish readied for the trip to the mortuary. Max had arranged an early-evening time for them to begin the planning. The funeral home had been most accommodating, considering the circumstances. Trish remembered that some Jewish people believed that interment should happen as quickly as possible, but Max and Rose seemed to be in no particular hurry. A private car was awaiting them from the mortuary when Trish got to the foyer. She had taken precious time with Josh, who seemed a little more settled now that Lisa had transitioned to the role of babysitter so quickly and lovingly. She and Josh were coo-cooing at each other as if they were a mutual fan club. Mary had shown up, and beyond the perfunctory greetings, had little else to say. But then again, neither did Trish. She was still unforgiving about Mary's childishness at not taking phone calls but put it in the back of her mind. There were more important things to think about.

The drive to the mortuary was short. Once in the actual meeting, Trish had no wisdom to offer about Robbie's last wishes. They had never talked about it. They had blithely gone through life,

241

each expecting to live forever and certainly to not have to bury each other.

"Where do you want the service?" Rose asked Trish.

"How many people do you expect will attend?" Trish asked back.

"I don't think there will be that many?" Rose's voice trailed off. They were old people after all. There just weren't that many family friends left. And there weren't many on Trish's side of the family either.

"Our room holds about one-hundred and fifty," the funeral director mentioned quietly.

"That sounds big enough to me. Unless you want to use the temple?" Trish looked at Max.

"This place will be fine. Everyone will be comfortable here. Not everybody who is coming is Jewish."

Trish nodded. He was thinking about everyone else in his grief. He would be a rock for Rose in the coming days.

"And what do you want by way of actual burial plans?" the director asked respectfully.

"What are the choices?"

"There's interment and cremation. Those are the two basic choices. Once that decision is made, the other decisions are based on that."

"What do you want, Rose?" Trish asked.

"Robbie never mentioned either one to us."

"She didn't to me either. Why don't we go with a burial?"

"Okay."

"You will need to select a casket and arrange for a burial plot."

"We have the plot already," Max mentioned to Rose. "Remember?"

"We do. I had forgotten."

Trish nodded. It made sense to have them buried together in their family plot. Robbie had never mentioned it either.

"You will also need someone to identify the body when we have prepared it for burial."

"I can do that," Max nodded.

"So can I," Trish agreed.

"Our casket room is in the back. Do you want to go through it now or do you need some private time?"

"Rose?" Trish asked, "Are you up for this?"

"I'm ready."

"Okay."

The casket room was really quite fascinating if you could forget for five minutes why you were there in the first place. There were caskets of every style and color. Blue, green, even fire-engine red. Wooden and metal with pillows and lace. And all sorts of designs from religious to nature scenes.

"Of course, each of our caskets comes with a warranty."

"A warranty?"

"Yes. They carry a twenty-year warranty."

"Who would care about that?"

"You would be surprised," the director nodded sagely.

"What was Robbie's favorite color?" Trish asked Rose.

"She liked blue."

"Should we go with blue?"

"Blue is nice."

There were two shades of blue to choose from. Light and dark. They settled on the dark blue. It seemed restful. Something that Robbie could repose in for eternity. Find the peace that had deserted her so recently in this life.

"Do you want to select the readings for the service at this time?"

"Can we take something home to look through?" Trish asked, sensing that Rose and Max had made almost enough tough decisions for one evening.

"Of course. And we can send someone out to the house if that would work out for you as well."

It was at times like this that being worth millions really paid off. People were willing to go out of their way to assist you.

"We'll let you know."

"Of course. And we will need the burial clothing as well."

"Right," Trish nodded.

They went away with all the materials they needed to make the rest of the arrangements. By the time they got home, Mitch had arrived. She looked drawn and tired. Not her usual cheery bright self. Trish took hold of her and didn't let go for about five minutes.

"My dear friend, what happened?" Mitch said when she felt that Trish was finally able to hear her question.

243

"I don't know exactly."

For the second time that day, Trish broke down sobbing. Mitch walked her over to the couch by the fireplace and cradled her until she could talk.

"Lisa said she hung herself," Mitch said in a way that took the sting out of the words.

"That's what they said. I didn't see it. I couldn't bring myself to see it. I just couldn't."

"Of course you couldn't. Was it depression?"

"I think so," Trish said between sobs.

"Was it because of Josh's medical condition?"

"I don't know. She wouldn't ever talk to me about it. People said to be patient. That it was just a normal depression that she would get over. She was fine with the baby. Where is Josh?"

"Lisa has everything under control. He's had a bath and a bottle and clean jammies and everything. He's fine. Last I heard, he was asleep."

"Where is Lisa?"

"She and Mary went out for a while. They said that they would be back soon. I've been checking in on Josh now and then."

"I need to pick out the burial clothes for Robbie."

"Do you need to do that right now?"

"I don't want to put it off."

"I can help with that. You want my help?"

"I absolutely want your help," Trish looked at Mitch. "You look tired."

"It's been a long couple of days. I'll tell you all about it later."

"How is Reb holding up?"

"She said she would try and make it for the funeral. She really wants to be here for you."

"I would understand if she didn't."

"She said to let her know."

They went into the bedroom that Trish had shared with Robbie. Nothing had been disturbed beyond recognition but nobody had tidied up either.

"Do you want me to straighten things up a bit?" Mitch asked.

"No. Just leave things as they are for a while."

"Do you know what outfit you wanted for Robbie?"

"The casket is blue," was all Trish could think to say.

"I have an idea. Let's select a couple of things and then see what Rose thinks."

"Okay."

"Did she have a favorite dress or anything?"

"Robbie never dressed up much. She was just so happy being casual. Never fancy or anything like that."

"Well, then, let's just pick out what she liked to wear in happier times."

Trish pulled three outfits from the closet and laid them on the bed. If Rose had another idea, she would respect that as well.

"You're going to need to go clothes shopping as well, I understand," Trish said to Mitch.

"I've been living out of a suitcase for so long that I hated to bring it along."

"You're even going to need pajamas."

"I'll be fine. I'll go out to the house later and pick something up."

"That's right. You really do live here, although you couldn't tell lately."

"It's been a long haul. No doubt about it."

"How is BeBe?"

"Things are not going well at all."

"She doing that badly?"

"That's only half the story."

"What else is going on?"

"I don't want to burden you with all that right now."

"It's okay. I'm worried about you. You look so exhausted. Like you're carrying the weight of the world on your shoulders."

Mitch sat down next to Trish on the bed.

"You remember Miranda?"

"Of course. Nobody's ever going to forget Miranda in this family."

"She's pregnant."

"Pregnant?"

"In jail and pregnant. The warden almost had a stroke when we told her."

"You told the warden?"

"Miranda isn't very far along. She was keeping the pregnancy a secret."

"How did you find out?"

"I looked at her."

"You went to see her?"

"We arranged to take BeBe and Henry for a last visit before BeBe dies, and we get into the room and it was a fiasco. I'm not sure BeBe and Henry still know what's going on. Miranda didn't say much of anything to them, basically cut the visit off after a few minutes and they left in a huff and Reb and I stayed behind to talk to Miranda and the warden. BeBe and Henry went clear across Kansas, back to the hospital and now it's like everyone is in denial. BeBe is dying and Henry's best friend is the bottom of a whiskey bottle and their daughter is pregnant by some prison guard."

"No wonder Reb stayed behind. Maybe you should go back to be with her?"

"No, that's okay. You need me here. Reb will come out in a day or two. She will need a break by then as well."

"You know what all that means, don't you?" Trish asked like she knew the answer.

"No. What does it mean?"

"It means Reb is probably going to get custody of the child."

"Why would you think that?"

"Well, is there any other blood relative in the family?"

"There's Henry."

"Yeah. Do you think the court is going to give custody of the child to a drunk old man instead of Reb?"

"It's Kansas. The unwritten rule in Kansas is that anything is better than giving custody of a child to a lesbian. I'm sure Henry will get custody. As soon as he figures out that Miranda is pregnant."

"How can they not know?"

"They weren't there five minutes before Miranda threw them out. She swore us to secrecy. No one is saying a word. People see what they want to see and deny all else."

"What a mess. I'm so sorry you're having to go through all that."

"Seems like we're both going through horrible times, huh?"

Mitch put her arm around Trish's shoulders and they sat together in silence until Rose came into the room.

246

"We're trying to choose clothing," Trish said.

"Is it between these three outfits?"

"Or anything else that you think might be better."

"I like the blue. It will match the coffin. We're on the news again. You better come have a look."

Rose's tone of voice told them that this wasn't going to be good. The TV was on in the corner of the room and it was another live shot of the front gate, this time with a line of protestors gathered with signs.

"What is it?" Rose asked

"It's the Citizens United for Morality group. They sure got here quick."

"The what group?" Max had to hear this again. It just didn't register the first time around with a gentle old man.

"It's a group of people who protest gay and lesbian people."

"What sort of people would do such a thing?"

"Where's Silver? She better know about this right now."

"Last I saw, she was in the kitchen on the phone."

"Okay."

Silver was still on the phone when Trish got to the kitchen. She held up an index finger like she already knew what was going on and was on top of the situation.

"Right. Enough for perimeter security, crowd control, possible blocking of traffic and disobedience," she hung up without pleasantries.

"Yes, Trish?"

"Sounds like you have everything under control."

"I'm not sure about that but hopefully we'll be ready if things get out of control."

"Is it your opinion that this is just the beginning of our problems?"

"Yes."

"Me, too."

Mitch had joined them by now. "Anything I can do to help?"

"Just make sure that Reb knows about this. She might be targeted as well."

"She's used to it, but I'll give her a heads up. They actually brought custom-made signs this time. You'd better prepare Rose and Max for some new vocabulary words."

247

"Damn it," Trish said and then started to cry. At first she resisted being comforted by Mitch. She wanted to stay strong through this but Mitch pulled her close anyway and took the brunt of her anger.

"They have no right to torture us this way."

"That's why we need to stick together. You take care of your family and we'll take care of you. Okay?"

"Okay."

"When were Lisa and Mary coming back?"

"Why?" Trish asked.

"They should be warned about the possibility of being blocked trying to get here."

"I'll call them."

"I can," Mitch offered.

"No. I will."

Trish dialed the number and Mary answered, "Hello?"

"Hi. It's Trish."

"Lisa's already on her way over."

"Oh. Okay."

"I'm staying here. I have to go into work really early tomorrow."

"Of course. We were just warning people that there's a protest going on at the front gate."

"Have Lisa call when she gets there."

"I will."

"I'm really sorry."

"I am too."

Trish hung up without saying anything else.

As news spread about Robbie's death through phone calls and television reports, people started to show up to the house in crowds. Thankfully, so did the caterer. When Lisa had called, she made it clear that they were going to need immediate help. They responded splendidly. All sorts of wonderful goodies arrived in white vans and were brought in through the side kitchen door. Wine by the case was toted in and when Lisa arrived, she and Max took over the host and bartending duties until the full catering crew arrived. The house was full of people by eight and they showed no signs of leaving anytime soon. Most of them were long-time friends of Rose and Max whom

Trish had never met. After a while, Trish had disappeared from the crowd. Mitch went looking for her. She was with Josh, rocking him to sleep.

"You two doing okay?" she asked.

"We're just keeping each other company," Trish kept rocking although it was clear that Josh was fast asleep.

Lisa appeared at the doorway now as well.

"Who wants something to eat?" she whispered.

"Nothing for me," Trish said.

"I'm not going to nag you about eating," Lisa said gently.

"Thank you."

"But I am going to nag Mitch about eating."

"Why me?"

"Because I figure that if I can get you to eat then sooner or later Trish will follow your example. Come on, you guys. You need to keep up your strength. I'll bring something to you. What do you want? If the caterers didn't bring it, I'll personally go out and get it for you myself."

"Got any candy bars?" Trish looked at Lisa.

Silence descended on the room, leaving a void for whatever was obviously going unspoken between Trish and Lisa. Mitch noticed it almost right away.

"You want a candy bar?" Mitch asked.

"No, not really," Trish answered, still looking at Lisa.

Lisa was as silent as the sphinx. Mitch decided to let it pass for now but whatever the significance of the remark, Mitch would get it out of Lisa later. Under duress if necessary.

"Why don't you sit with Trish," Mitch got up and pulled Lisa over to the chair. "I'll go and get something to eat. Set that good example."

"Thank you," Lisa sounded truly grateful.

Mitch went to the kitchen and made small talk with total strangers as she kept an eye on Rose. She was looking more washed out by the minute. Mitch pointed this out to Max and they agreed to try and get her to rest when the crowd showed signs of thinning out. By nine, that time had come. Rose was pale and shaking and they only managed to get her to bed by each taking an arm and guiding her all the way. Max kindly but gently shooed everyone out the door and they were down to the seven of them by ten.

"Why don't you turn in as well, Max?" Mitch suggested.

"I need to find beds and bedding for everyone."

"No you don't. We can manage. We know what to do. You just go and take care of Rose."

"Okay."

Mitch sat on the couch and started counting on her fingers. Max and Rose had their bed. So did Josh and Silver. Mitch assumed that Trish wouldn't want to stay in her own room but the spare bedroom was available. It had a king-size bed. And then, there was this very large, serviceable couch.

"You're deep in thought," Lisa had come into the room quietly.

"I'm figuring out the sleeping arrangements."

"What did you come up with?"

"You share the spare bed with Trish and I'll take the couch."

"Uh, no. Let's do it the other way around. I'll take the couch. You take the bed with Trish."

"I don't mind the couch."

"I insist. You take the bed."

"Do you want to tell me what's going on?" Mitch asked outright.

"What are you talking about?" Lisa sounded perplexed. A little too perplexed.

"Honey, I've known you for way too long. I know when something is on your mind."

Lisa didn't answer. She sat on the couch in a proprietary way like she was here for the night.

"What was all that about candy bars?" Mitch asked.

"It was just something that happened in Montana."

"Montana?"

"You missed that part of the story."

"What about Montana?"

Lisa filled Mitch in on almost all of the facts about the trip. Almost.

"And so you had a grocery store stock of candy bars in the car?" Mitch made sure she had heard right.

"A small store. One of those gas station stores."

"And so that's why I have to sleep in the same bed with Trish?" Mitch wasn't letting go of this. She felt there was something still unspoken. Lisa didn't reply. Mitch waited.

"Are you going to get off my couch or not?" Lisa said after a full minute had gone by.

"Look, I'm not asking questions to make you mad. You know I care. We've been together a long time, first as lovers and then as friends. Don't you know by now that I know you inside out?"

"Not everything is your business just because we once slept together a long, long, long time ago.

"Gee, when you put it that way, it makes me sound old."

"I'd like to be alone. To get some sleep."

"I understand. But can I tell you one more thing?"

"Okay."

"I watched you and Mary today. And I watched you come back over and Mary stay home. And while I'm a pretty casual observer most of the time, I still know what I saw. And then, I saw you with Trish..."

"I thought you said you only had one more thing to say?"

"I'm getting to it."

"Okay. Fine."

"So, if you think that I'm being meddlesome, you won't even want to know how Reb is going to be when she sees what I see. Wouldn't it be better if you knew you had an ally?"

"This isn't a big deal, okay! What happened in Montana wasn't a big deal."

"I believe you. How big a deal *wasn't* it?"

Lisa exhaled. She knew that Mitch was right. Reb was as connected to Mary as any good mother was to any daughter.

"It was one kiss."

"Okay. One kiss. That doesn't sound so bad. Was it one short kiss or one long kiss?"

"You missed your calling. You should've been a lawyer."

"One in the family is enough," Mitch referred to Reb. "Long or short?"

"Intense."

"Are you in love with Trish?" Mitch decided to get it all out in the open. She knew that they were getting close to the truth when Lisa's chin started to tremble.

251

"I don't know. I haven't thought about it."

"Love isn't something you have to stop and think about. You know it or you don't."

"Let's just say that I've avoided thinking about it."

"Oh, geez, Lisa," Mitch put an arm around her and pulled her close. "You've got it bad, don't you?"

Lisa simply nodded.

"And then, you came back to this."

"Yeah."

"What's happened between you and Mary?"

"Me. I happened."

"What do you mean?"

"I've changed. How can Mary love me after I've changed so much?"

"Do you know for sure that she doesn't love you?"

"I know a little about sleeping on the couch."

"I see. Okay. I'll sleep with Trish and you can have the couch."

"Thanks for understanding."

"I'll find you a pillow and a blanket."

After tucking Lisa in for the night, Mitch went to Trish's spare room. She was lying down but still awake.

"Lisa and I arm wrestled for the bed and I won," Mitch sat on the vacant side. "I hope that's okay?" she added.

"It's fine. I didn't want to be alone tonight."

Mitch laid down, still fully dressed except for her shoes.

"You never did get a change of clothes."

"Maybe tomorrow."

"You can borrow something."

"I'm fine. Don't worry about me. I've slept in my clothes before. Are you going to be able to sleep?"

"I don't know."

"Do you have something to take?"

"I don't want to be all drugged up. Josh needs me fully aware."

"Okay. Wake me up if you need anything."

Mitch kept still and breathed regularly in and out until she heard Trish drop off to sleep. Not even grief can stave off total exhaustion. At dawn, Mitch eased out of bed and checked in on Josh. He was still sleeping so she went to the kitchen and found Rose and Lisa already up and sharing a pot of coffee.

"How was the couch?" Mitch asked.

"Not too bad. How was the bed?"

"Majestic. You want to switch tonight?"

"Is everybody staying another night?" Rose asked.

"Trish said she doesn't want to be alone."

"I could sleep with her," Rose offered quickly.

Mitch looked at Lisa who kept her head down.

"But then Max would be alone."

"Well, what about Mary. She's alone too."

Rose must've had the same insights that Mitch had had about Lisa and Trish and Mary. She was glad to have had the conversation when she did with Lisa.

"And Reb's coming to town," Lisa added, more or less to alter if not completely change the subject.

"She is?" Rose's eyes got big. Reb was one of Rose's favorite people.

"I was going to try and talk her into coming early. So she could have a nice long visit with Mary."

"That would be so nice for her. I just wish that the circumstances were different," Rose began to tear up.

"Come and sit with me, Rose," Mitch took her to the couch in the living room, "while Lisa checks on Josh."

"I'll do just that," Lisa was happy to be useful.

Josh was awake, but so was Trish. Lisa and Trish converged in the nursery at the same time to take care of the baby. "What can I do to help?" Lisa asked.

"Do you want to get his bottle?"

"I'll do that. Be back in a minute."

Lisa went to the kitchen to prepare the morning feeding. She had learned this quickly yesterday and now felt like an old hand at it. She raced the bottle to the hungry infant. Trish rocked back and forth while Josh contentedly took the formula.

"He's such a sweet little guy," Lisa looked on.

"He sure is. Never crabby. Never fussy."

"He takes after you."

"He takes after Robbie, actually."

"Do you want some coffee?"

"Sure. That would be nice."

"Do you want anything in it?"

"Depends on who made it."

"I did."

"Then it will be fine."

Lisa delivered a cup and Trish took a sip. It was excellent.

"What else can I do to be helpful?"

"Just sit with me. That's all."

Lisa did as she was told. She sat and gazed at Trish, the perfect mother with the perfect child. When Trish looked up at her, she looked away. Trish watched her until she made eye contact.

"I wanted to thank you for everything you did for me yesterday."

"That's not necessary. You would've done the same thing in my place."

"Are you going home today?"

"Rose thinks I should. I think I'd better."

"I was thinking about something last night," Trish said as she took the bottle away from Josh and held him over her shoulder. He burped audibly and contentedly.

"He is so precious," Lisa smiled.

"He sure is."

"So, you were thinking last night?"

"I never had a nanny because Robbie didn't want one."

"Okay."

"And I don't want some stranger coming in the house right now."

"That's understandable."

"And as wonderful as Rose and Max are, they are getting too old for the rigors of raising a child. They are perfect as grandparents, but not as parents. Does that sound brusque?"

"Not really. It sounds like you're trying to be practical."

"Good. That's what I was hoping you would think."

"So, what are you going to do?"

"I want you to take the job."

"Take the job?"

"I want you to be Josh's nanny."

"You do?" Lisa was taken completely by surprise. "But I have absolutely no experience with kids. I've never had one myself. I took a course in babysitting when I was a teenager and I was the only one who flunked the final."

"You can take a course in babysitting?" Trish asked.

254

"They had this course that you could take and I just wasn't cut out to be a babysitter."

"I'm not asking you to be a babysitter. I want you to be a nanny."

"Isn't it the same thing?"

"Not really. I need someone who can take care of Josh both physically and emotionally. I think you're the perfect person. You've already connected with him on some level to have him be so content yesterday while we were taking care of funeral arrangement. No one else could've stepped into that role as easily as you did."

"But that was just for an afternoon."

"Here, take him now," Trish passed Josh over to Lisa. She immediately cuddled and held him. He snuggled right into her shoulder, happy to be right where he was.

"He would be fussy for anyone else. Will you take the job?"

"I'll need to talk it over with Mary."

"I understand. It would be really a big help if you could do it. Maybe at least only temporarily until I find someone else. However long that would take."

"I promise I'll think about it."

"Can you talk to Mary and see if you can do a couple more overnighters, at least until things settle down around here? I'd be happy to talk to her myself if it would help?"

"Rose isn't going to like this. She's already trying to get me to go home."

"I'll take care of that. Don't worry. Everyone will just have to get used to the fact that Josh's needs are important, too. I will pay you. I'm not asking you to do this for free. I can arrange for you to make more money than Mary ever thought of making."

"Would it always be overnight?"

"No. Just for a few days. And maybe when he has to have special medical care or surgery. Times like that when we need extra hands around the house. I would have you and a nurse and whoever else might be able to help out. Otherwise, it would be an eight-to-five job, just like any other."

"Okay. It's tempting. It really is. I'll talk to Mary when I see her and then if she has questions, I'll let you know."

"That's all I'm asking. I just need some extra support right now."

"Of course you do," Lisa reached over and held Trish's hand. The tender moment was interrupted by Rose. Naturally.

"The police are here with a court order and a jackhammer. They want to speak to Trish."

"I guess they took me seriously about excavating the basement."

"They look like they mean business," Rose wasn't leaving without Trish.

"I'll be down in a minute."

Rose stood at the doorway. Waiting.

"I need to change out of my pajamas before I talk to them."

Rose turned and left to deliver that piece of news to the waiting officers. The tension left in her wake was thick.

"She's never going to go for this nanny business."

"You just leave her to me. She's a reasonable woman. Things are just too much for her to handle right now."

"And what about you? How are you holding up?"

"I'm a mess on the inside. But I need to be strong for Josh and everyone else. You're the only one I can come apart in front of right now."

"Okay. I'll be here when you need me."

"Thanks. Now get out of here while I change before Rose comes back and fusses some more."

"I'll take Josh for a wander around."

Lisa left Trish to change and went with Josh to the living room. Sure enough, it was once again full of police officers. Rose looked shell shocked. Mitch was handing out cups of coffee. Lisa retreated to the kitchen with the baby to avoid the crowd. Mitch caught up with her.

"Is this part of the Montana story?"

"Yeah. Did I forget to tell you that part?"

"Rose said something about tearing up the basement?"

"They're looking for a skeleton."

"Well, their timing sucks."

"Hey, that's not my concern. This little guy here is my concern. I'm doing baby duty until further notice."

"You? Doing baby duty?"

"Yeah, I'm doing baby duty. You got a problem with that?"

"I never pictured you and babies in the same frame."

"You don't think I'm good with kids?"

Mitch gave Lisa a penetrating look. One of those looks that said, "What aren't you telling me?"

"I'm sure you're great with kids. You're practically one yourself still."

"I'm taking that as a compliment to my youthfulness."

"Yeah, whatever. I talked to Reb. She's flying in today. I'm going to need to get a car somewhere."

"You can borrow Trish's truck."

Mitch looked at Lisa like she had lost her mind. Lisa looked back. "Oh yeah, I forgot about the wheelchair."

"Reb would take that as a compliment as well. Now, where do I rent something?"

"Ask Max. He needs something to do. He's as nervous as a bug around woodpeckers."

"Good thinking."

Mitch asked Max to help her with this difficult task. There were only a few companies that rented out handicapped vehicles and they would have to drive across town to sign the paperwork. It would at least get him out of the house while they destroyed the basement. By now, Trish had made an appearance, dressed all in black, and was sitting across from the officer with the court order. Of course they could rip up the basement. In fact, Trish seemed relieved that they were doing so and asked how she could be of more assistance.

"Just keep everyone out of the way. As much as possible."

"What are we going to do about the caterers?" Rose asked.

"Get dust covers for the food?" Trish replied.

"Let's just keep everyone who shows up in the family room. Move all the food in there."

"Good, and tell Silver to make sure that the extra security people help themselves. I've seen some of those big guys she hired. They are going to need to eat at least three times a day."

"Right."

"Now, let's go over the materials we picked up at the funeral home and plan the service," Trish said to Rose. Rose nodded. It was time. They had put it off long enough.

By the afternoon, things had gotten completely out of control. The few quiet moments that Trish and Rose had shared in planning Robbie's service were the last that would be available for the rest of the day. Constant noise emanating from the basement that would've normally frayed people's nerves was compounded by the circumstances. Mitch and Max had been the lucky ones. They had escaped the house barely after running a gauntlet of protestors that had only quintupled in size since last night in order to arrange for Reb's arrival. The car rental took forever and they were late picking up Reb at the airport. Not very late, but Reb just wasn't the most patient person these days.

"You got here," was Reb's version of hello.

"You remember Max. Robbie's dad," Mitch reminded her.

"Of course. I'm so sorry about your loss."

"Thank you," he steeled his jaw and shook her hand.

"Max helped me get a car. He's going to follow us back to the house."

"What about your luggage?"

"I have this carry on. I figured if Mitch was going to need to go clothes shopping that I would tag along as well."

He politely took the bag and led them back to the parking area. When Mitch had Reb alone in the car, she exhaled like she had been holding her breath since about a week ago.

"What's going on?" Reb asked.

"You wouldn't believe it even if I told you," Mitch told the truth, at least as much as she was willing to tell at that point. "How are things with BeBe?"

"Don't ask."

"That bad."

"It makes coming to a funeral seem like a relief."

"Not this funeral."

"How is Trish holding up?"

"Not too bad, considering the circumstances."

"Tell me what's going on."

"Okay, well, let's start with the protest, which you probably saw on the news."

"I saw a snippet."

"Well, the snippet has grown. It's a fully-grown snippet by now and spilling all over the sidewalk and the street. The signs that they are carrying are disgusting."

"Like what?"

"You'll see when we get there. I don't even say words like that out loud."

"Okay. What else? How's Mary?"

"I haven't seen much of Mary. She's working a lot. Doesn't get much bereavement time at work so she's just going to attend the funeral."

"And Lisa?"

"Lisa has really helped with Josh. She and I stayed overnight last night to help out. I stayed with Trish in the guest room. No one is sleeping in the bedroom. That's where it happened."

"I understand."

"And this afternoon, the police are excavating the basement so the entire house is filled with the sound of jackhammers and dust."

"Why on earth is that happening?"

"They are looking for a human remains."

"A body?"

"Perhaps the remains of the ghost that's been haunting the house."

"And Trish is putting up with this?"

"It was her idea. She asked the police to do it. I guess she practically dared them."

Reb became quiet. Mitch noticed. "What are you thinking?"

"I'm thinking that this makes life with my sister seem normal by comparison."

"Where do you want to spend the night?" Mitch asked.

"Well, now that you've told me all this, let's get a hotel room."

"You don't want to stay at the old homestead?"

"As wonderful as that sounds, no!" Reb sounded firm.

"Not even to pick up a few things?"

"Since you slept in your clothes last night, I take it you haven't stopped by the house yourself."

"Not yet."

"I was just wondering if the place was still standing?"

"I don't know."

Chapter 18

They pulled up to the driveway of Trish's house. The pickets were thick by now and daring them to run over them with the car. Mitch inched forward, following Max as closely as she could without touching bumpers. Reb looked at the signs. Now she knew what Mitch meant. One little girl had a placard that read, "Dyke cunts are bad for kids"

"I can see why you didn't want to leave Trish alone last night," Reb stated.

"We're trying to keep Trish away from this as much as possible."

"That's what friends are for."

They parked in the driveway and as Mitch was getting ready to get out of the car, Reb took hold of her arm in that grip that conveyed her "I mean business" temperament.

"Is there anything else I should know before we go in?"

Mitch looked over at the love of her life. God, she hated questions like this. Reb knew Mitch as well as Mitch knew Lisa.

"I've told you as much as I can tell you."

"And the rest I need to find out on my own?"

"You always do."

"Am I going to be angry with you when I do?"

"Probably."

"How angry?"

"I love you with all of my heart. How angry you get with me is up to you, not me."

Max was watching this from the side of the car. He didn't know what the hold up was, and he was shifting from foot to foot.

"You just be sure it's a really, really, *really* nice hotel room."

"Yes, Ma'am."

The minute Reb rolled in the front door, you could just tell that Rose had prepared everyone for the imminent arrival of whom she considered to be royalty, American style. Never mind the chaos. Or the dust. Or the circumstances. Rose was there to greet Reb personally, making sure that she stayed in the living room, far away from the kitchen where things were a mess despite her best efforts. Reb sat as close as she could to Rose and comforted her in her loss.

"I was so sorry to hear about Robbie. You just let me know if you need anything and I'll have Mitch take care of it."
Mitch just nodded like she always did whenever Reb spoke. This was one case where she didn't mind being volunteered. And things were going along about as smoothly as they could until Lisa came around the corner.

"Rebecca, it's good to see you again," Lisa went over to her and held out her hand. Reb took it in her own and patted it.
"Come and sit down. Tell me how you're doing. Where's Mary?"
"I'm fine. I can't sit. I'm making sure that Josh is taking a nap. Mary is at work. She'll be by this evening. Are you staying at our house?"
"Uh, no!" Mitch piped up quickly. "We're getting a room for the night. We figured that everyone has had enough of sleeping on the couch. Around here, that is."
Reb had an expression on her face like she hadn't given the remark a first thought, let alone a second, but when she made eye contact with Lisa, they both knew that that wasn't true.
"So, if you'll excuse me, I'll go take care of things."
Lisa went back to keep tabs on Josh and when Mitch figured she wouldn't be missed, she headed there as well. Mitch found Lisa sitting in the nursery, watching over the sleeping baby.
"She knows, doesn't she?" Lisa asked quietly.
"She knows something is going on. Or not going on. She's just that way. I've lived with her long enough that she just reads me like a transparent book."
"Well, it isn't too difficult when you start making remarks about who is sleeping on the couch."
"I didn't say it was you."
"You didn't have to."
"Look, I'm sorry. It doesn't matter anyway. She's going to get the details out of Mary in ten seconds. You know that and I know that and she knows that. And then what's going to happen is anyone's guess."
"Well, I'm not going to grovel. I am taking the job that Trish has offered me. I'm going to be Josh's full-time nanny."

261

"You're going to do what?" Mitch didn't believe what she was hearing.

"She offered me the job. I'm taking it. If Mary thinks that I need to sleep on a couch, I can do that just as easily over here as I can over there."

Mitch took a deep breath. This new situation needed calm, deliberate conversation.

"Are you that angry with Mary?"

"She threw me out of the bedroom when I told her that I was going on an innocent field trip with Trish. What the hell do you think is going to happen when she finds out I'm in love with her?"

Mitch thought this over. Lisa had a point. Just because Mary didn't want to share a bed with Lisa anymore didn't mean that there wouldn't be about a thousand other women waiting in line.

"Are you ready to be a nanny?"

"There's one thing you need to understand," Lisa was ready to defend her decision.

"I'm listening."

"I know what it's like to not be whole anymore. Alright! I know what it's like to have people stare at you. To have them think that just because you look a little different than they do that that makes you less of a whole person in their eyes."

"Keep going," Mitch prompted.

"And so what do you think this precious baby is going to go through in his life? Huh? How many times are people going to stare at him and think he's somehow less of a person just because he wasn't lucky enough to come out with the complete inventory of body parts. Huh? How do you think he's going to cope with that?"

"I can't imagine how it's going to be."

"That's right. You probably can't. But I have a small idea of what it's going to be like for him and that's what makes me ready to be his nanny."

"And you're going to be the best damn nanny he could ever have."

"So, I have your blessing?"

"It isn't my blessing that you need, but you have my complete support."

Trish wandered into the room. She had been resting when she heard the voices.

"What's going on?"

"I've decided to accept your offer," Lisa looked at Trish.

"That's great news."

"Reb's here in case you want to say hi," Mitch said blandly.

"Why don't you go tell her that I'll be there in a minute."

"Yeah, sure," Mitch knew when she was being given five dollars to go to the movies. She left them alone, even closing the door.

"I heard what you said to Mitch," Trish said to Lisa.

"Were we too loud?"

"No. But I just wanted you to know that I heard what you said. Everything."

"Do you still want me around?"

"Of course I do. I just want you to know that you are about the most whole person I have ever met in my life. I had no idea that you had ever felt any differently and if I knew you had, I would've said something about it a long time ago."

"I have learned one thing through all of this."

"What's that?"

"That you shouldn't spend too much time looking in the mirror to determine your self worth."

"Everyone could learn from you," Trish took Lisa in her arms and pulled her into a platonic embrace. There was a knock at the door. They parted quickly. You never knew who was going to come barging in next. It was Rose. Again.

"The police need to see you. They don't look so happy."

Trish gave Lisa a look that let her know that the only people who could possible pull her away at this time was the police. The unhappy-looking police. Trish followed Rose into the kitchen.

"We would like you to provide us with more information if you could," the officer in charge explained as he indicated that Trish should sit down for this.

"Of course. What do you need?"

"Could you tell us who led you to believe that there was a body in your basement?"

"Why? Didn't you find anything?"

"If you could answer my question first, please."

"I'm not answering your question until you answer my question."

"It would be best if we had the information first."

"Why?"

"Because we would need to do a follow up investigation."

This was sounding more serious by the minute, but Trish couldn't discern if the follow up investigation was because they found a body or because they didn't find a body. Either way, somebody was going to be in trouble and she sure hoped it wasn't going to be her.

"Other than the first person I named yesterday, there's only one other person who we had contact with and she's a little old lady in a nursing home. Are you going to go and question her?"

"Have you ever had contact with anyone else about your concerns about the house being haunted?"

Trish racked her brain. "We tried to talk to the family member who sold us the house, but we couldn't get to them. We tried to go through their lawyer, but he shut us down."

The officer nodded his head. He took notes. "What was the lawyer's name?"

"I'd have to go and look it up. We spent about fifteen seconds in his office. It cost a bunch. I'm sure his name is on the cancelled check. How soon do you need the information?"

The officer's cell phone rang. He nodded. Nodded again. Hung up.

"There's going to be a few more people showing up at your house in a few minutes."

"Who else is showing up?" Trish wondered just how many more official people the house could hold.

"It's a crime scene unit."

"You found a body?"

"We found human remains."

"Do you need everyone out of the house?"

"As many as you can get to leave. It would help."

"Okay. I'll do my best."

"I'm really sorry to put you through this at this time."

"It can't be helped. Could you do me a favor?"

"If I can?"

"Go out and find a person named Mitch. Bring her here."

264

"Sure."

In about ten seconds, Mitch was by Trish's side. "What do you need?"

"I need your help to clear the house."

"What? Is there a bomb threat or something?"

"No, nothing like that. We just need the place as empty as possible. There's going to be an investigation going on in the basement."

"So, we're going to need some hotel rooms pronto."

"Right."

"Consider it done. I'll have things set before you get packed. Don't even pack. I'll have someone do that for you."

"Don't worry about me. Just get a bed for everyone."

Mitch got the phone book and the phone and started making calls. She was smart enough to make reservations at a hotel that was close to the mortuary. No use running back and forth across town if they didn't need to. Then, she went to the nursery to inform Lisa that the move was on so she could get Josh's stuff packed and ready. Silver was the most perfect help that anyone could imagine. She coordinated security and transportation without even being asked. Rose rearranged the catering itinerary begrudgingly, adding a bonus as well. The move happened without incident, except that a couple of the protestors managed to follow them to the new location. Information traveled fast and soon the spectacle relocated to the hotel's front entrance.

After viewing the hotel suite, Mitch hoped that she was closer to being out of the doghouse as far as Reb was concerned. Of course, Reb didn't know the whole story yet, but maybe Mitch had accrued at least a little credit.

"Who's going to phone Mary to tell her we've moved?" Reb looked at Mitch.

"I suppose you can since Lisa has her hands full."

"I just didn't know if anyone else was going to think to do it."

"Why don't you make the call?"

"Why don't I."

Mitch stretched out on a bed that had to require custom-made sheets. You probably needed a permit to build something this big. Reb was dialing Mary's work number and from the gist of the conversation, it was apparent that Mary already knew about the change of venue.

"So, somebody already called her?" Mitch asked when Reb hung up.

"Lisa called her already."

"Imagine that."

"Okay. Are you now going to tell me what's going on?"

"Lisa is going to be Josh's nanny," Mitch figured she's start with the easy part.

"Josh's nanny! I wouldn't put Lisa in charge of a cocker spaniel."

Mitch didn't say anything. She didn't have to. Suddenly, the tables had turned and now it was Reb who was in the doghouse. Maybe being with her sister was having a cumulatively corrosive effect on her.

"I didn't mean it literally," Reb sensed the quiet disapproval that had descended between them.

"Do you think that Mary is too good for Lisa?" Mitch asked point blank.

"I'm sorry. I didn't mean it about the cocker spaniel."

"I'm not worried about an apology. I'm curious. Do you feel that Lisa isn't good enough for your daughter?"

"That's not what I'm saying."

"What are you saying?"

"Do you really want to know?"

"I'm waiting."

"I just don't know if they're right for each other."

"So, it wouldn't break your heart if they broke up."

Reb waited until Mitch made eye contact. "I'm glad we had this chat. I'm going to take a shower."

Mitch got two entire minutes all to herself before there was a knock at the door. It was Lisa.

"What's up?"

"Mary just called. She's on the way over. She said that her mom called her, too. I think she thinks there's a problem. What am I going to do?"

"Tell her about the nanny job. I already broke the news to Reb."

"Yeah, but it's like she gets two phone calls and it seems like her mom figures that she and I aren't speaking or something."

"I know. Here's what you do. Worry about what you're going to say to Mary about the job and leave Reb to me. You make the best, most honest choice for you and Mary and let everything else fall into place."

"It sounds easy when you say it."

"Just focus on the present situation. Who's watching Josh right now?"

"Trish is. She wanted some quiet time with him."

"Is your suite big enough?"

"I think it covers three counties."

"Good. You might need the breathing room before this is over. Mary's going to be here soon, right?"

"Yeah. Where is she sleeping?"

Mitch got a funny look on her face. "You're asking me?"

"I'm sorry. I'm just rattled."

"I got a suite for Rose, Max and Silver. One for me and Reb. One for you, Trish and Josh. Mary can either stay with you or stay at home. I didn't think it was a good idea to get Mary her own separate sleeping quarters, do you?"

"Right. It's only for a night or two. Right?"

"I hope so. Things should begin to get back to normal after the funeral and the police investigation."

"I'm going back to my room. Let me know when Mary gets here."

"Okay."

Lisa went back to her room and let herself in quietly. Josh was asleep by now and Trish was resting on one of the three beds in the suite.

"Need anything?" Lisa peeked into the bedroom.

"I'm not used to being alone."

"You want me to keep you company?"

"Do you feel comfortable doing that?"

"Oh, sure. For once we can just sit here and not have everyone come in and out. Just like Montana, except without all the snow."

Trish smiled. "I'm still stiff and sore from all that shoveling."

"You want something to eat or drink?"

"You said you weren't going to nag me about that."

"I was just going to get something for myself and I'd share it with you if you wanted to."

"That's a nice thing to do. I'd like that very much."

Lisa went to the main living room and scouted out the room service menu. She scanned the selections and made the call. Food would be arriving shortly. Lisa went back to the bedroom to report.

"What did you order?"

"A variety of sandwiches. About twenty-five of each."

"You didn't, did you?"

"I thought about it. I'm starving and Mitch is paying the bill. On second thought, I should've ordered steak and lobster," Lisa smiled impishly.

"You're beginning to sound like me and candy bars."

"You're having a bad influence on me—where food is concerned."

"Yeah. Right," Trish knew better.

A few more minutes went by before there was a knock on the door.

"That was quick! I'll take care of it. You just keep resting," Lisa jumped up and left the room to answer the door. It wasn't food. It was Mary.

"Hi! You got here."

"I got here."

"Have you seen your mom yet?"

"Yes. I stopped there first."

"Oh good. They look tired, don't they?"

"So do you. Why is everyone here instead of at the house? Mom said you'd tell me all about it."

"Sure. Come in and sit down. I ordered up some food. Can you stay and eat?"

"I took the rest of the day off. I won't get paid, but I thought that it was important to see everyone."

"Of course. Your mom doesn't get to town much anymore. I wanted to talk to you about something as well."

They settled across from each other at the table like they were mediating a deal.

"Trish offered me a job."

"A job?" Mary looked skeptical, to put it kindly.

"Yes, a job. She wants me to consider being a nanny for Josh."
Mary didn't say a word. She was totally shut down emotionally.
"Well, what do you think?" Lisa asked.
"Is it a live-in position?"
Lisa didn't care much for the tinge of sarcasm laced through the
question. She hadn't done anything to deserve it, other than to
try and have an independent life beyond being an extension of
Mary. She kept her cool and answered smoothly, "Oh, no.
Strictly eight-to-five. Overnight once in a while in a pinch."
"Is tonight one of those nights?"
"You can stay overnight as well. We made sure you had a place
here, if you wanted."
"So, you've already decided to take the job."
"It's something I'd really be good at," Lisa let it show how
excited she was by the offer, feeling that her emotions would be
safe with Mary.
"How do you know? You've never worked with children before.
You have *no idea* if you'd be good at it."
"Well, I have faith in her," Trish had come into the room more or
less to make her opinion known. "I think she's a natural with
kids. She certainly has a way with Josh."
Lisa had to concentrate very hard to keep her pleasure at the
praise from showing on her face. It would only make Mary dig
her heels in deeper.
"It seems that I'm outnumbered," Mary remarked, "Two against
one."
"Three if you count Josh," Trish redid the math for Mary.
"So, what are you going to make? Minimum wage?"
"We haven't actually discussed that yet," Lisa said.
"Then how do you know you want the job?"
Lisa looked over at Trish for support.
"Let's discuss that right now," Trish offered.
"Minimum wage sounds fair to start," Lisa was agreeable. "At
least as a starting place. Through a probationary period?"
"I was thinking more along the lines of fifty dollars an hour.
Double for overtime. Triple for holidays, weekends and
overnight. Plus four weeks paid vacation. Paid holidays. I think
that sounds fair. For starters. Don't you?" Trish demonstrated
her seriousness where hiring Lisa was concerned. Lisa was too

269

busy doing the math in her head to answer immediately. Before taxes, it was damn close to one-hundred thousand dollars per year. It was more than Mary was currently making and a whole helluva lot more than Lisa had ever thought she could be earning in an honest lifetime.

"You want the job?" Trish was looking at Lisa like Mary wasn't even in the room.

Lisa looked at Mary. She had nothing to offer as a response. Trish had demonstrated confidence in Lisa and was willing to compensate her in ways that Mary couldn't.

"Yes, I'll take the job."

"Good. We'll get the paperwork over with when we get back to the house. Consider yourself on the payroll as of yesterday."

Lisa didn't say anything and neither did Mary. There was a knock on the door. It was room service. Everything looked delicious, but Mary begged off. "I'm not as hungry as I thought I was. I really need to get back to work."

She left without even a hug or kiss. It was beginning to be a pattern.

"I guess she's really upset," Trish said to Lisa after the door closed.

"She gets this way. I've seen it before. This is exactly how she was when we left for Montana."

"If you were home, you'd be sleeping on the couch?"

"Yeah. Well, I'm hungry. Are we going to eat or aren't we?"

"Sure. You talked me into it."

They each took a sandwich. Lisa was glad to see that Trish was finally going to eat again and when she didn't mention it, Trish did. "I'm eating, okay."

"I'm so glad to see that."

"I'm glad that you're here for me."

"That's what I'm good at."

When Mary left Lisa's room, she walked blindly down the hallway of the hotel. She didn't hear Mitch calling after her until she was in the elevator and Mitch jumped through the elevator doors at the last minute.

"Didn't you hear me calling you?"

"No. I'm thinking about work. Sorry."

Mary pushed the button for the lobby.

270

"Where are you going?"

"Back to work."

"I thought you were going to hang out? Visit with your mom some more."

"I don't feel like it."

"What's going on?"

The elevator doors opened and people got in. Mitch looked at Mary and said quietly, "You want to get a drink in the bar?" Nobody said it, but one matronly looking woman stared at them in disgust like it was a lesbian pickup scene.

"Sure. Why the hell not."

Mitch looked around. The woman was still staring at her. "You want to join us?"

Thankfully the elevator doors opened before the woman gave it any serious thought.

"Should I tell my mother that you're inviting other women to have a drink with you?" Mary said when they had secured a table in the hotel lounge.

"Are you talking about you or that total babe in the elevator?"

Under any other circumstances, Mary would've laughed, but she wasn't in a laughing mood. They ordered drinks. Wine for Mitch and a double scotch for Mary.

"You want to tell me what's going on?" Mitch asked Mary after the cocktail waitress floated away.

"I think you know already."

"Tell me anyway."

"Lisa took a job with Trish without even telling me."

"You mean that Lisa is actually going to work for a living?"

Mitch tried to sound surprised that Lisa wasn't content anymore to mooch off people. Mary wasn't convinced.

"You still love Lisa, don't you?"

"Do we have to go over that again?"

"No. We don't."

Their drinks arrived and Mary downed hers in one gulp and signaled for another. Mitch didn't make any remarks. It might be easier to talk if Mary was slightly drunk anyway.

"Which means that Lisa and Trish are going to be spending even more time together."

"And you're upset about that?"

271

"It's going to disrupt our life."

"How?"

"Well, you know."

"No, I don't."

Mary's second drink appeared and she took at least twenty seconds drinking this one.

"I don't know when I'll see her. Dinner is going to be a guessing game. Who's going to take care of the things around the house?"

It all sounded so superficial to Mitch. "Can I try to put things in perspective for you?"

Mary felt a lecture coming on, but Mitch was buying the drinks. A third one showed up for Mary.

"Okay."

"Trish has just had her lover commit suicide. The funeral is tomorrow. Hope you can make it. Meanwhile, she has a disabled child who barely survived birth, might not live past six months and if he lives, he will probably be retarded and crippled for the rest of his life, and as we speak, the police are ripping up her basement, finding the body of who knows who buried under the concrete floor. And you're worried about who is going to cook *your* dinner?"

"You know that it's more than that. You know that," Mary was finally going to be honest about her fears about Lisa's affections being usurped by Trish.

"I only know one thing, Mary. I know that if you love someone, you fight for them. You don't sit around and worry about dinner and schedules and who's going to do the chores. You worry about how the people in your life feel about themselves. If having schedules being disrupted was the breaking point of relationships, believe me, your mother and I wouldn't be together today."

Silence fell between them. It was interrupted by Mitch's cell phone. It was Reb.

"Where are you?"

"I'm in the bar with Mary."

"Having drinks without me?"

"Something like that."

"I'm coming down."

Before Mitch could give any admonitions, the phone went dead.

272

"Your mother is on the way."

"Great," Mary said, not exactly thrilled about it.

"Don't worry. She's on your side."

"What do you mean?"

Mitch knew that she was going to say too much and frankly didn't care anymore.

"She always thought that Lisa wasn't good enough for you anyway."

"It wasn't her place to judge."

"Well, when did that ever stop your mother."

"It sounds to me like the two of you have been in Kansas way too long."

"Are you ready for another drink?"

"I think six is my limit."

"Your mother's on the way down."

"Maybe one more round."

Reb was at the table before the fourth drink appeared.

"How many have you had? It looks like your eyes are swimming around in your head."

"That's what it feels like."

"Did you talk to Lisa already?" Reb was in full interrogation mode.

"Yes."

"What happened?"

"There was a bidding war and I lost."

"What are you talking about? What is she talking about?" Reb turned to Mitch when it was obvious that Mary wasn't going to be making much sense.

"Lisa took the job, I guess?"

"She's actually going to be contributing to the household bank account?" Reb made it sound like an earth-shattering event.

"Yeah, that's it. That's exactly what she's going to be doing. She's going to be doing an even better job of it than I am too. So there."

Mary was beginning to feel the full effects of three double scotches on an empty stomach.

"How did you get her this drunk this fast?" Reb turned to Mitch.

"It's an inborn talent. Either you have it or you don't."

Reb didn't appreciate the sarcasm but frankly, Mitch didn't appreciate the blame.

"Fine. Let's just get her back upstairs and get some food down her before she gets alcohol poisoning or something."

"Easier said than done."

"Find someone to help."

Mitch knew who to call after a split second of thought. Silver was more than happy to come to their rescue. She was in the bar in two minutes and had Mary up on her feet and walking to the service elevator without any problem.

"It's more private to go up this way. All the security people use this elevator."

"You brought the security people to the hotel?" Mitch asked.

"Of course. You need security here just as much as at home."

"I didn't even see them?"

"You will tomorrow. Everyone gets a bodyguard for the funeral."

"Everyone?"

"The immediate family."

They got Mary back to their suite and in bed. She seemed fine. Drunk but fine. Until she laid down and then the booze started to swill its way through her bloodstream in a major way. She was in the bathroom throwing up in five minutes.

"Better now than later," Mitch said as she held her steady.

"I'm so embarrassed."

"Don't worry. Everyone does this once in a while. Your mom is ordering food and coffee."

"I'm not hungry."

"You will be."

After about fifteen minutes, Mitch was right. Mary ate something and felt better. Not good. Not great. But better.

"Hey, you know what?" Mitch said to Reb like she had just had a brainstorm.

"What?"

"We haven't gone by the house yet. Remember we had planned to do that."

"We've been busy."

"Well, now might be a good time to go. We do need clothes. Right?"

274

"Why don't you go and pick some things up. I'll stay here with Mary."

"Oh, I'm sure that Mary can take care of herself. She's over the worst of it, aren't you, Mary?" Mitch had this innocent expression on her face, but Mary knew what she was up to. If Mary had wanted to try and have a quiet, uninterrupted conversation with Lisa, they could use the suite for an hour. Or two.

"You know, I'm a hundred percent better. Almost back to normal. You guys better go and get your errands done. You're running out of time."

Reb looked at Mary and then at Mitch. There was no use arguing. "We'll be back in an hour."

Mitch said nothing but held up two fingers as she left the room with Reb.

Mary took a deep breath. She dialed Lisa and Trish's room. Lisa answered.

"Hello?" Lisa answered.

"Hi. It's me."

"Are you okay?"

"I'm down in your mom's room. She and Mitch are on an errand. Do you want to talk? Do you have time?"

"Of course I have time. I'll be down in a few minutes."

"Thanks."

Lisa barely knocked on the door before Mary opened it.

"Are you sure you're okay? You look a little green around the gills," Lisa said as Mary came into the room.

"I'm better. I went to the lounge with Mitch and had about eight shots of scotch."

"Eight shots. And you're still standing? You usually go under the table after two!"

"Can we please skip over the gory details for now?"

"Sure."

"I just wanted to say that I've been thinking about things and I've been wrapped up in my own little world a lot lately and that's no excuse."

Lisa listened to this without judgment. She had put two and two together and figured out what had happened to most of the eight shots of scotch, but it was also apparent that some of what still remained was floating around in Mary's brain, killing cells here and there at random.

"I'm not sure I follow."

"I've tried so hard to be the man of the family that I forgot how to be the woman of the family as well."

"I didn't know you had such a traditional outlook about our relationship."

"I didn't either until you began to not need me."

"In order for you to feel needed, I need to sit around the house all day and wait for you to come home? Is that what you're telling me?"

"It sounds ridiculous now that I hear it out loud."

"Is that what you wanted to tell me?"

"No. At least not all. It's just that ever since the accident, I've felt that I was supposed to take care of you. That it was my reason for existence. I felt that if I took good enough care of you, that nothing bad would ever happen to you ever again. I felt so guilty about what happened. I wasn't there for you. For days and weeks and months I've ripped myself up on the inside for not being able to do more for you. And it's left me with this skewed vision of what I thought you really needed and what I thought I really needed and what I thought we both needed..."

"You never said a word about this."

"I didn't want to burden you with my turmoil. You were going through enough already."

"And that's why you can't even bring yourself to touch my scars."

"Every time I see them, I hate myself. It has nothing to do with you."

"I never blamed you."

"I blamed myself enough for the both of us. I don't expect you to understand."

"Good. Because I never will understand. But I will accept how you feel and work it out with you. In a healthy way."

"Okay. I do want you to take the job with Trish. Can you forget that I ever doubted you?"

"Sure. I doubted myself for a while until I knew I could do it."

"Okay. And whatever it takes to make it happen, I'll take care of it. I'll learn to cook. Or clean house. Or whatever."

"There's one thing you need to do right now."

"What's that?"

Lisa didn't say anything but instead took Mary's hand and pulled it slowly toward her scars. Mary didn't pull away. She didn't even close her eyes when she began to cry.

"What are we doing here?" Reb asked Mitch. "We are due back at the hotel right this minute."

They had already gone by the house and picked up a few items of clothing. It hadn't taken long and when Mitch checked her watch, they still had an hour to kill before interrupting Lisa and Mary. So Mitch had pulled up to a park nearby.

"Oh, I thought we'd neck for a while."

"Have you lost your mind?"

"It's beginning to feel like it."

"You're serious, aren't you?"

"I don't think I'm losing my mind as much as it just seems like I'm losing my grip."

"What do you mean?"

"I feel so disconnected. You and I sit in Kansas and take abuse from a dying woman while our family and friends here at home are coming apart at the seams. I only have so much reserve left and it seems to be leaking out all over the place. I'm losing my patience with people. I'm not there for them when they need me. I'm just running on empty and I know that if I'm feeling this way then I know that you are too. After all, it's your sister who's dying."

Mitch lapsed into silence. It was true. They were both becoming frayed by the weight of it all. All of a sudden, keeping to a schedule seemed to be the last thing on Mitch's list of priorities. Reb sat quietly for a moment. Sometimes it just seemed to be the best option.

"What are you thinking?" Mitch finally asked.

"I'm thinking that I couldn't love you any more right this minute if I tried."

"That's the only thing that keeps me going."

"And I need you to try and keep it together because I can't guarantee that I can for very much longer."

"You don't need to be brave in front of me all the time. You can stay stoic for BeBe all you want. You can even be tough and brave in front of Henry and Miranda. But if you need to fall apart when you're with me, I can handle it. What I can't take is when you withdraw from me. I can't even begin to describe the void it leaves in me."

"I'm trying not to cause you pain."

"I'd rather feel pain than nothing at all."

"Okay. Just don't leave me when this is all over."

"Leave you? *Leave you*? Honey, you couldn't chase me away with a double-barreled shotgun."

Reb couldn't help herself. She started to laugh. And then she started to cry. And then it was hard to tell which she was doing as Mitch comforted her. Mitch said a silent prayer that whatever Lisa and Mary were doing, that they would be all finished in about twenty minutes.

Now that Mary had touched Lisa, she didn't want to stop. They had made love and were snuggled up together side by side. More like front to front actually.

"I really hate to bring this up," Mary said after Lisa stopped kissing her.

"What."

"Something Mitch said to me downstairs in the bar. Maybe I was drunk and misunderstood…"

"What did she say?"

"Something about Trish's basement getting torn up by the police? I must've been drunk. That made no sense whatsoever."

"That is actually happening. That's why we're all here. They thought it would be easier to do the investigation without all the crowd there."

"What investigation?"

"That's what we found out up in Montana. I didn't have the chance to tell you all about it. We talked to a lady who was a real recluse and she told us that if we dug up the basement room floor where the door sticks shut, that we would find a body."

"And on her word alone that's what the police did?"

"It seems so. And they found a body. So there's a full-blown investigation underway, which I'm sure they need to do but if they would just listen to Trish, they would know who the body belongs to."

"Who is it?"

"Benjamin Livermore had a lesbian daughter. That's who it is."

"How do you know that?"

"That's what the lady in Montana told us."

"How did she know?"

"We don't know. She said that if we found the body, that she would tell us the rest of the story. I'm sure that the police are up there now questioning her. I hope she didn't shoot at them. She has that kind of reputation, you know."

"Your trip to Montana was a lot more adventurous than I realized."

"Yup, it was."

Lisa didn't elaborate. Instead she kissed Mary one more time and said, "We'd better get dressed before the adults come back."

"I want to be with you tonight. I don't mind staying in the suite with Trish and Josh if you think that would work out. I know you have your new duties to attend to."

"I'm sure it will be fine. Really. I want you there."

"I want to be there," Mary said and then her hand traveled down Lisa's body to the place that made Lisa breathe deeply. In and out.

"Do you want to go or come?" Mary asked succinctly.

"Do you even have to ask?" Lisa whispered back.

Chapter 19

Mitch took the long way back to the hotel. Reb had regained her composure and was enjoying the ride.

"Do you want to stop in the lounge for a drink?"

"We could. And we could call the room to see if the kids want to join us."

"I don't know if Mary wants to see the inside of a bar anytime soon."

"But at least they would know that we are back."

"That's probably a good idea. Give them time to get dressed."

"For dinner?"

"Yeah. For dinner," Mitch tried not to roll her eyes.

Reb ordered a rare white wine. It wasn't a rare wine. It was just that Reb drank so rarely anymore that any wine would've been rare for her. Mitch ordered a cup of coffee. Black. No sugar.

"You're having coffee?"

"Somebody has to stay sober," she smiled.

Reb dialed the room number on her cell phone and waited for someone to pick up. It was Mary in three rings.

"We're down in the bar. Right. That bar."

"Tell her that they're low on scotch," Mitch said.

Reb ignored Mitch and continued talking.

"Right. So, are you two coming?"

A pause.

"Down to the bar? What did you think I meant?"

"Okay. Fine."

Reb disconnected the call.

"They said they would be down in a few minutes."

Mitch only nodded. Anything else would've just gotten her into trouble. Meanwhile, Reb was making dinner plans. "Do you want to eat here?"

"I think we might as well. This is where the security is. We've already gone for one long drive today. I could stand a nice, quiet hotel dinner."

"Me, too. Here's the kids."

Lisa and Mary came into the bar. The noonday sun glowed dimly compared to these two women. What a difference a half a bottle of scotch makes. More or less.

"Do you two want to join us for dinner?"

"I should check with Trish," Lisa said. "She may want to have me watch Josh."

"Well, okay," Reb said.

Mary agreed, "Call her and find out. If you need to be up there, I will keep you company."

Before anyone could make the call, Reb's cell phone rang. "Maybe that's her now?"

"She doesn't have this number."

Reb checked the caller I.D. It was long distance. Kansas.

"I have to take this," Reb grew instantly serious.

A series of "yes's" and "uh huhs" followed. Reb snapped the phone shut. "I have to go."

"Back to the room?" Mitch asked.

"Back to Kansas."

"I'll go with you," Mitch said.

"No. You stay here. You stay for the funeral."

"I have an idea," Mary said, "if it's okay with Lisa?"

Lisa looked agreeable to whatever Mary was going to say next. Having terrific, reconciliatory sex helped in that regard.

"I'll go with you."

"You don't need to."

"But I want to. She's my Aunt BeBe. If things aren't going well, I should make the effort to see her now. While I still can."

Mitch didn't say it, but the word "effort" seemed very applicable after what they had been through the last couple of weeks.

"If it's okay with you?" Mary turned to face Lisa.

"Of course. You should go. I want you to do what you think is best."

"Okay. Let's get you packed up, mom."

Mary and Reb were out of the bar before the drinks came. When they did, Mitch gave the wine to Lisa and she took custody of the coffee.

"You are such a mind reader," Lisa said as she took the glass.

"I remember that you liked wine."

"That's not what I'm talking about."

"You're confusing mind reading with paying attention."

"I didn't tell Mary about the kiss."

"I know."

"Do you think I should?"

"No. What happened in Montana stays in Montana. In every sense of the word and deed."

"I should go back up and stay with Josh. I've been gone a long time."

"Okay. Call me if you need me. I'm going to go to bed early tonight."

"Me, too."

"Except that you've already been once."

"It was more than once, but who's counting," Lisa said as she drank down the wine and left Mitch to herself.

"Kids," was all Mitch could think to say.

Mitch hated funerals. It all started when she buried her parents. It hadn't changed since. But to bury a friend who had found life too tragic to go on was excruciating. She got through it. Everyone else did as well. They were allowed to go back to the house after the graveside prayers and mourners mingled briefly before leaving them in peace. Even the protestors had given up now that the TV cameras were gone. They were once again down to seven people. Everyone but Silver, Mitch and Lisa were resting or asleep.

"Mary called and told me about BeBe," Lisa said.

"I'll go back first thing in the morning."

"Will that be soon enough?"

"It doesn't matter. There's nothing I can do now."

"Mary sounded like it was brutal."

"I'll send her home the minute I get there."

Mitch kept her word. The minute she got to the hospital in Kansas, she practically pushed Mary to the elevator doors.

"Lisa needs you."

The deathwatch of BeBe lasted two more days. The only time that Reb left her bedside was to use the bathroom. Mitch was in and out: doing chores, running errands, keeping morale up as much as possible. Mitch had taken a break to walk down the long hallway to a makeshift solarium that had been retrofitted on the west side of the building. When she turned and saw Reb approaching in her wheelchair, she knew the inevitable had happened. Reb wasn't crying. That would come soon enough.

"BeBe wanted me to give you a message after she was gone."

"Okay."

"She wanted me to tell you that she loved you."

"Well, in a way, I guess that I loved her, too," Mitch smiled.

Red took Mitch's hand. "I don't think you understand."

"Understand what?"

"She *really* loved you."

Epilogue:

One month after Robbie's funeral, Trish arranged for the proper burial of the remains of the female skeleton found in her basement. All the other Livermores got a decent burial. Trish figured it was only fitting that she should as well. The investigation is still ongoing.